THE BABYLON FILE

THE DEFINITIVE UNAUTHORISED GUIDE TO J. MICHAEL STRACZYNSKI'S TV SERIES *BABYLON 5*

Andy Lane

Virgin

*Sometimes the only way to get pertinent information is
to ask impertinent questions.*

– J. Michael Straczynski, posting on GEnie,
4 January 1993

First published in Great Britain in 1997 by
Virgin Publishing Ltd
332 Ladbroke Grove
London W10 5AH

Reprinted 1997 (five times)

ISBN 0 7535 0049 3

Typeset by Galleon Typesetting, Ipswich
Printed and bound in Great Britain by
Mackays of Chatham PLC

CONTENTS

DEDICATIONS

To Helen (finally) for sitting through all the episodes yet again and then asking for more

To Mike Zecca and Lee Whiteside, and to the mysterious person in HM Customs and Excise who keeps opening the care packages they send me

To Jim Mortimore and Craig Hinton, for keeping my ego in check

ACKNOWLEDGEMENTS

J. Michael Straczynski, for being considerably more helpful and friendly than I had any right to expect (until the hammer came down)

John Vornholt, Jeanne Cavelos and Kevin J. Anderson, for responding so promptly and so courteously

Rebecca Levene and Simon Winstone, for writing the proposal, putting my name on it and fighting off competitors (and all because the lady loves *Babylon 5*)

Anthony Brown, Jane Killick and Paul Simpson for suggestions, discussions, cups of coffee, pints of Guinness and general friendliness

Dave Bassom, for kicking a football across No Man's Land

Liz Holliday, Kristen Jones, Richard Salter, Nathan Scott, Dave Sumner, Gene Munroe and Lee Whiteside, for giving the manuscript a thorough going over

Phil Hyland and Wayne Mason for advice on American military ranks

Introduction

This book is lots of things (including big), but primarily it's unauthorised, it's eclectic and it's personal.

What do I mean by that?

It's unauthorised because neither Warner Brothers generally nor J. Michael Straczynski in particular have given their approval for it to be written. Although this has restricted my access to the set, the actors and the production staff, it does mean that I can be as honest and as scathing as I wish. Most of the time, it hasn't been necessary (this *is* the best SF TV show in the world, after all) but I think that I should be allowed to complain about the number of times a character says 'It's all going to hell!', or 'Set course for Babylon 5!'.

It's eclectic because it's more than just an episode guide: it's a compendium of facts, quotes and speculations. Around the bare bones of the episode plot and the credits I've hung all those little interesting titbits I read, heard or discovered about the episodes, giving them a perspective and a background. These titbits aren't the whole story, of course – some material has been left out because it didn't get caught in my personal filter, some because I could have been sued for printing it and some, no doubt, because I just didn't know it. As it is, there's enough here to fill a large book. *This* large book.

It's personal because I've resisted adopting an anonymous third-person style. In here are the things about the series that fascinate *me*. The series itself resists cursory analysis – as one of the episodes points out, truth is a three-edged sword. There's my truth, your truth and the real truth. I could just pretend what's in this book is the real truth, but it's not. You deserve to know that it's *my* truth.

The book itself may be three things, but I'm also expecting people to respond to it in one of three ways.

Response 1 – 'Why publish this book *now*? Why do we have to pay good money for something that covers only the first three seasons when you're bound to publish an updated version after the series has finished?'

Well, weigh the book in your hands. Flick through it. Count

the pages. There's something approaching 130,000 words in here, and that's just covering 74 episodes, 6 novels and an 11-issue comic. At that rate, a book covering the entire series in this depth would top 200,000 words, and it's just not economically viable to publish something of that length at a reasonable price. If there is a subsequent edition of this book after the end of the series (and I really hope there is), it'll have to be slimmed down considerably or increased in price.

Response 2 – 'Isn't all this information available for free on the Internet?'

Yes, buried in amongst a lot of stuff you don't want to know, and some of what is there is wrong or misleading. The Internet (and I include GEnie and CompuServe in that) is an incredible storehouse of information, but picking out the diamonds from the gravel is frequently difficult. Besides, not everyone has the option of logging on to them when they want to, and it's not the kind of resource one can flick through in front of the TV set when it suddenly occurs to you that the man playing Psi Cop Harriman Gray looks terribly familiar. Books are reader-friendly things, and they'll beat the World-Wide Web hands down as reference works for some time to come. And they don't suddenly lock up or crash out into DOS.

Response 3 – 'Oh, I never knew *that* . . .'

Thank heavens. I'm hoping that once every few pages, everyone who reads this book will learn something they didn't already know. There's a lot of stuff here that *I* didn't know before I started researching the book, or stuff that I'd heard about but never had confirmed. If I hadn't been paid to write this book, I would have had to write it anyway, just to collect all this stuff together before I forgot it.

So, here it is. Enjoy it. Keep it beside your television. Use it. And, when it gets all dog-eared and the cover falls off, buy another copy. You won't regret it. And, if you find any mistakes (and there are bound to be mistakes), please send a list of them to me, care of Virgin, or e-mail them to me at goldfinch@easynet.co.uk. That way, if there is a second edition of this book, it'll be even more definitive than this one.

Sources

A book like this takes a lot of research, and (for safety's sake) it's best that the research doesn't all come from one place. Some reference works are notoriously error-filled, and cross-checking is vital to catch all those spelling mistakes and misattributions. Just so you know I haven't made all this up, these are the primary sources I've used:

- *the episodes* – it was a struggle, but I watched all 71 of them again (I'm being ironic – actually I ended up liking the series even more than I did before I started). I found that by watching them out of order this time, hopping back and forth over the three-and-a-bit seasons almost at random, I was able to follow trails and make connections that I'd never made before. In a deliberately ironic touch, I watched the pilot episode last.

- *the comics and the books* – it's a shame these aren't better than they are – and both were initially planned to be a lot more ambitious than they eventually turned out. However, they are considered as canon by the show's creator, and the comics at least provide information that never came out in the show, so I have to include them.

- *personal interviews* – I talked with J. Michael Straczynski twice before this book was formally commissioned, and he was perfectly charming and forthcoming on both occasions.

- *convention appearances* – I've had the pleasure of sitting in the audience while various members of the *Babylon 5* cast and crew have revealed their thoughts and feelings about selected episodes. Some of the facts and the quotations in this book have been transcribed directly from the tapes I made at the time.

- *the Internet, GEnie or CompuServe* – everything you ever wanted to know about *Babylon 5* is on there somewhere – the show has been endlessly discussed there since before the pilot was even transmitted, and J. Michael Straczynski has a significant on-line presence. I could have compiled this entire book from Internet, GEnie or CompuServe sources without actually writing a word of my own, but that would have been immoral. The only things I have taken away from them have been those things said directly by Straczynski himself: all other material (facts, speculations, episode guides, cast lists, blooper lists and so on) I have scrupulously avoided.

- *magazine articles* – numerous genre magazines have covered *Babylon 5* over the years, and the articles have been a useful source of facts and anecdotes. The April 1994 edition of *Cinefantastique* is a treasure trove of information concerning the background to the series, and I am also indebted to David Richardson and Joe Nazzaro for their tenacious coverage of the series in *Starburst*, *TV Zone* and *Cult Times*.

- *other books* – I've used Dave Bassom's two *Babylon 5* books – *Creating Babylon 5* and *The A to Z of Babylon 5* primarily as a means of checking my spelling and the episode cast lists. Dave himself is a charming bloke, and we've got on very well in our various discussions.

- *discussions* - I've lost count of the time I've spent on the phone, in bars and in hotel lounges discussing the story arc, and speculating on where the various characters are going. A lot of those conversations have ended up in here, in one form or another. Thanks to everyone who took part.

THE
BACKGROUND

Approaching Babylon

By J. Michael Straczynski

[Note: This article has been reprinted from the Summer 1995 issue of *Foundation* – the journal of the Science Fiction Foundation – with the permission of J. Michael Straczynski]

It's all that damned Bradbury's fault.

Context first.

You must understand that I do not have a home town. I have a place of birth, and a place where I reside at present, but no place that could reasonably be called a home town. As I grew up, my family and I were forever on the move, going from one apartment or house to another across town, to another town, to another county, to another state, and back and forth between states on either side of the North American continent. We sometimes stayed in one place as little as six months. Never more than a year or two.

When you're nine or twelve or thirteen years old, and every year brings different schools, different faces, different street addresses and phone numbers and alibis, you learn to compensate. I have a knack for remembering phone numbers. At 40 I can still recall the phone numbers of several of the women I dated in college. And their parents' home numbers. Take me into any unfamiliar city, drive me clear across town, and I will be able to find my way back, on foot, without asking for directions.

The other thing you do when everything around you is unfamiliar is to seek out anything that is familiar. You hold it like a drowning man clutching a wooden plank, because it's all you have. For me, there were two such: television, and the local library.

Television is where as a child I discovered Rod Serling, and Paddy Chayefsky, and Charles Beaumont, and Richard Matheson, and Harlan Ellison . . . also Cecil the Seasick Sea Serpent, *Planet Patrol*, *Colonel Bleep* and *The Crawling Eye*.

I am nothing if not eclectic.

The local library was my refuge from a sea of unfamiliar faces. No matter where I went, with few exceptions, the books in the library were always the same. Even the covers were the same. I sometimes allowed myself the illusion that the books followed me from one town to another. They were my constant companions, my only consistent friends. By age 9 or 10 I'd worked my way through the children's library with frightening speed, and began making unescorted expeditions to the adult section. That's where I discovered Ray Bradbury. *The Martian Chronicles*. Separate stories, self-contained, but which taken together formed a whole that was greater than the sum of its parts. Usher II. Delicate silver sails moving silently across the Martian desert at night. The million year picnic. *Mars*.

I was entranced. Hopelessly lost. I dragged every other Bradbury book down from the shelves. *R is for Rocket*. *The Golden Apples of the Sun*. *Dandelion Wine*. All of it. As soon as I'd swallowed those books, I returned for seconds on Isaac Asimov, and Arthur C. Clarke, and Robert Heinlein, and Eric Frank Russell, and . . .

And that was when I collided with E.E. 'Doc' Smith, and had my brains bashed against the wall by the *Lensman* books. Mars? Here was the whole damned *galaxy* spread out before me. I had never known such sagas existed. I reeled from one volume to the next, blowing through them as quickly as I could, eager to find out what would happen in the next instalment, what strange and amazing place I would be propelled to next.

In retrospect, it was probably foolish of me to plunge right into *Lord of the Rings* immediately afterward, but plunge I did, and my soul was forever lost to sagas.

Looking back at the young version of myself, crouched over Eric Frank Russell's *Men, Martians and Machines* or some other book, it seems very clear that the element most emblematic of science fiction at its very best . . . is the sense of wonder. Ancient monuments that towered thousands of feet above you, mysterious secrets revealed at terrible price; great fleets of starships riding fire, passing overhead en route to distant suns; aliens whose thoughts are as akin to our own as the spider.

The sense of wonder.

So why was there so little of it in television science fiction?

It is 1983, and I am interviewing the producers of the television series *V* for the *Los Angeles Herald Examiner*. Not the creator of the original miniseries, which dared to touch wonder, but those brought on to produce the series proper. Or improper, in this case. In the course of the interview, one of the producers said, 'As long as we have aliens, ray guns, and space ships, we're *guaranteed the Sci-Fi audience automatically*. What we have to do is broaden out to the mainstream viewers.'

Their disregard for the science fiction community was undisguised and unmitigated. Plug in the hardware and the snazzy effects, and we'll come uncritically a'running. This was the case with most of the sf television series producers I'd had the chance to speak with. Invariably, they knew nothing of the genre, its history, or its accomplishments. Where networks routinely sought out mystery writers for its mystery shows, and writers experienced in police stories for its cop shows, when it came time for an sf series to hit the airwaves, they sought out soap opera writers, or sitcom writers; in the case of the *War of the Worlds* series, they brought in producers from *The Love Boat*.

When you told them, as I did on a radio show I used to host in Los Angeles, that certain plot elements in their shows made absolutely no sense whatsoever ('Everyone on Earth simply forgot that we'd been invaded by Martians?!'), the reply was a shrug and, 'It's Sci-Fi. There are no rules. You can do whatever you want. Either you buy into it or you don't.' They failed to understand that for sf to work, there must be rules, there must be consistency and logic. To them, sf meant that nothing had to make sense. Sf meant writing for juveniles, computer nerks and other cases of arrested development . . . so put in the whiz-kid who saves the day, or the funny pet that talks, or the cute robot that falls down a lot and goes 'bida-bida-bida'.

They didn't treat it the same as any other genre in terms of logic, and characterisation, and research. Producers and writers of murder-mystery TV series take great pride in the lengths they go through to research some new method of killing someone, the afternoon they spent driving around with the LAPD, or sitting in with the coroner during an autopsy. But sf? *Sci-Fi?* Doesn't matter. Just make it all up.

And in the end, nine times out of ten they'd refuse to call it science fiction (or the irredeemable *sci-fi*) because they didn't want to alienate the mainstream audience.

It. Made. Me. Nuts.

Thankfully that has begun to change a little, for the better, with people like George R. R. Martin and Melinda Snodgrass and other sf writers getting into television. Even so, the problem persists. Viz: *Space Rangers. Space Precinct*.

It's enough to make any self-respecting science fiction fan pick up a copy of Clute and Nicholls's *Encyclopedia of Science Fiction* and beat himself to death with it. (Which, at that book's weight, should only take one or two thumps at most.)

Where was the sense of wonder?

Why weren't writers who truly understood science fiction being allowed to create quality sf for television?

And most important . . . why had no one ever done a full-blown saga – something on the order of the *Lensman* books, or *Lord of the Rings*, or the *Foundation* books – for television? The British had done it, with *The Prisoner*, with *Blake's 7* and *Tripods* and some elements of *Dr Who*. Why not us?

Answer: simply because no one had ever done it.
Someone had to try it.
Might as well be me as anyone else.

One other element of context. I began writing regularly for television round about 1984, first in the field of animation, subsequently in live-action series for syndication and networks. Some of it was sf, some wasn't. *The Twilight Zone*, *Jake and the Fatman*, *Captain Power*, *Murder She Wrote*, *Shelley Duvall's Nightmare Classics*, others . . . alternately as story editor or writer/producer . . . but regardless of venue, I was astonished to learn that as much as one-third of any TV series budget is wasted due to poor planning and short script deadlines. Scripts come in a few days before you're supposed to shoot, so construction crews and wardrobe people have to work all night on sets and costumes (heavy overtime), there are delays as actors wait for revised pages to land on the stage, actors go overtime or are brought in on forced-calls . . . the cumulative effect is daunting and expensive.

When you add to that mix complex special effects, prosthetics, elaborate sets and alien costumes, science fiction shows quickly become the worst offenders. Virtually every science fiction series ever produced has run over-budget to varying degrees. *V* almost single-handedly brought down the entire Warner Bros. television division. Which is precisely why there is so little of it. The costs can't be contained. It's like a runaway train blowing money out through the smokestack.

Why couldn't a television series, even sf, be produced responsibly? Planned and executed efficiently? Does it have to be that way?

The answer, I felt sure, was no, it doesn't. I was determined to prove the point. And I would do it, not with a small series, but with what I grew up loving, and reading . . . a *saga*, a huge story that would take five years to tell, and would feature state of the art effects as well as a huge cast of characters who would change and grow as empires rose and fell around them.

I could not have been perceived as more insane if I had announced plans to sprout bat wings and fly under my own power from London to Budapest.

Though it probably would have been easier than the five years consumed in trying to get *Babylon 5* produced.

The sense of wonder.

Every day it becomes more apparent that the American culture is slowly dying. Not the American corporations, not the economy, or the institutions per se . . . the *culture*. The myths that form the underpinnings of our society. Every generation is like the street beggar in the Aladdin stories, calling out 'New lamps for old.' For centuries we have regularly traded in our old myths for new ones, reinvented and reinterpreted them. We listen for the voice that is ancient in us, and recast our core myths in more contemporary clothing, to better understand them and ourselves. Providing these myths is the responsibility and the obligation of the storyteller. But what new myths have been provided lately in American culture? Freddie Kruger? O.J. Simpson? Are Michael Jackson and Lisa Marie Presley *really* married and doing things to each other that no sane human being really wants to imagine *either* of them doing to *anyone*? The myth-maker points to the past but speaks in the voice of future history; it is the collective voice of our ancestors, speaking through us, giving us a sense of continuity and destiny; it makes connections between those who have preceded us and those who will follow us. If those myths are absent, we are cut adrift in a sea of pointless entertainments intended primarily to divert us from our own lives.

It is not the task or responsibility of television to teach your children, or babysit them, or take the place of conversation, or reinforce societal mores, or make you feel good about your neighbourhood or your job or your prejudices or your sexual orientation or your odds for hair restoration.

When television took centre stage in the world of collective and mass storytelling, it took on the responsibilities of providing new myths, fictions that point the way toward tomorrow, that remind us that there *will be* a tomorrow, a better one or a poorer one depending on what we do *right now*, and that we can't ever afford to lose sight of that. In short . . . to rekindle in the hearts of millions a sense of wonder, about the world, the future, and our place in that future.

The same sense of wonder that I had as I raced through the pages of *Grey Lensman* and *Foundation* and *Childhood's End* and *Dune* and *Stranger in a Strange Land*.

That, I knew, would have to be the third goal for my series. If I could somehow imbue it with that sense of wonder, then the effort in making it would be worthwhile.

Provided I made it a saga.

And made it with respect for the genre.

And made it for a reasonable budget, produced responsibly.

The *thud* you just heard was the entire Hollywood community collapsing with laughter. For five years, every network, every studio, every television executive said it couldn't be done. Oh, sure, you might get a pilot movie, maybe, but a series? Not likely. And even if for some berserk reason you actually got a season on the air, it wouldn't go past that. Ninety-eight percent of *all* American science fiction series have been cancelled before reaching their third season.

But we *got* our pilot, rocky as it was. We *got* our first season. We *got* our second season. All three came in under budget, to the considerable astonishment of Warner Bros., PTEN and most of the Hollywood community. (Other producers, and Vice Presidents of Business Affairs have lately begun taking tours of the *Babylon 5* facilities to try and figure out how the hell we're doing what we're doing.) And at 4.15 p.m., April 8, 1995, we were officially renewed for our third season. And it is, on every conceivable level . . . a wonder.

When first approached about writing this article, I expressed a genuine concern that I wouldn't have anything to say that could be of the slightest interest to readers of an academically-oriented review of this nature. Not to put too fine a point on it . . . I ain't that smart. Whenever someone asks how I would evaluate my work in light of current theories on deconstructionism and metafiction, I get confused and fall down.

'Do you welcome or deplore the way in which film or TV sf has come to dominate over literary sf, and the way in which fantasy has come to swamp sf proper?'

I welcome it in the sense that it provides me with a venue of unparalleled proportion. It enables me to tell the *Babylon 5* story more or less simultaneously to hundreds of millions of people in the United States, England, Ireland, Japan, Germany, Canada, France, Australia, Singapore, Israel, Thailand, Jordan, and a half dozen other countries at last count. A writer writes to be read. Or performed. The bigger the venue, the larger the crowd, the more that intent is satisfied. Whether the result is quality or not (*Baywatch* remains the #1 rated syndicated series in the world) is a separate question. But for the *intent of the writer*, the more the merrier. If a novel sells 100,000 copies, the publisher is deliriously happy. A million-seller causes downright cardiac infarction.

We're talking here potentially *hundreds of millions of people*. I would be a fool not to welcome that opportunity.

There are many sf, fantasy and horror writers who blame TV and film for destroying the print marketplace. 'Nobody reads sf any more,' they complain. Leaving aside for now the reality that literacy is declining, that schools too often fail in the task of inculcating a love of language and storytelling, that parents rarely read to their children any more, that our culture has become so obsessed with the importance of what you have as opposed to what you know that kids who have no idea who Emily Dickinson was are killing each other over high-priced basketball shoes and Chicago Bulls jackets . . . leaving all that aside for the moment . . .

At its root, I think the allegation is predicated upon a false premise and a distorted perception. How can film sf dominate literary sf when in any given year only a handful of noteworthy sf films debut, sometimes only one or two, as opposed to hundreds, even thousands of sf book titles that are published in the same year? We're talking here a vast numerical supremacy of *product*. A given film may have a larger single audience for its product, due to media hype, and the fact that we are transitioning to a visual-media-based society, but the number of genre films are still hideously outnumbered by the number of genre books published each year. (As it should be.)

The same applies to television. Each season, you get maybe one or two new sf series, sometimes a bit more. In all but a very few cases, they're gone within a few months. In over forty years of television, there have been only a handful of even nominally science fiction series that have gone three seasons or beyond. Prevailing Hollywood wisdom is that sf doesn't work on television. So how then does it dominate the field? It can dominate the discussion, yes, but dominate the field?

If the field has been weakened, it is because it has come to be dominated not from without, but from *within* by a snowstorm of mediocre, nearly identical, carefully packaged and painstakingly inoffensive books . . . the usual fuzzy-footed, Unicorn-festooned, sword-wielding Princess-reclaiming-her-throne decologies gobbed up onto the market-place for a fast buck by barely literate authors without the vaguest understanding of who and what has gone before them. Cookie-cutter sf novels and worn-out fantasy clichés that pollute the field, diminish audience expectations, and degrade the taste and selectivity of the readership.

In short . . . in large measure, *print has become television*. The same principles of acquisition apply: look for the block-buster, throw away the midlist, don't make the stories too complex, create a franchise we can milk for a few years, canvass the distributors, bring in the focus groups and for god's sake don't offend anyone.

Quality work in literary sf continues to sneak past the roadblocks and the snipers – in *Pulphouse* and *F&SF* and *Interzone* and *Tomorrow* and from the major book publishers – but it is often lost in the overcrowded spinner-racks as publicity money is drained away for the latest hoped-for blockbuster. As publishing moved from a family business to a major corporate arm of an even larger mega-corporation, the bottom-line business practices of Hollywood studios have become the business practices of New York publishers.

So to those SFWA members who quashed an attempt to resurrect the Dramatic Nebula because, as one correspondent wrote me during that heated debate, 'I work for pennies while you TV hacks get paid big bucks for turning out crap that screws up the genre for the rest of us,' it ain't the fault of television or film writers. The field has been weakened from within. Literary sf of the 1990s must again find its voice, the new paradigm that changes the field today as much as James Blish and the New Wave sf movement revolutionised the 1970s. (And I'm sorry, but cyberpunk isn't it.)

The sf community is rightfully concerned about the state of sf and fantasy publishing; but it can only be corrected when publishers stop choking the marketplace with assembly-line novels and sharecropper shared-world anthologies and high concept quickie anthologies ('Nails! That's it! We'll do an anthology called *Nails: Pointed Stories* and invite a bunch of sf writers to write about nails! We can do the nails of the cross, Madonna's nails, railroad nails, hey, maybe we can get some cross promotion going with Nine Inch Nails . . . who cares if the good sf writers won't go near it, we'll get the rest to do it, it doesn't matter because we can sell the concept, hell, maybe we can even get a follow-up anthology, *Spikes*, and we can do vampire stuff . . .').

The problem can only be corrected when publishers start giving more than lip service to such talents as James Morrow and Michael Bishop and Connie Willis and Jonathan Carroll and Kris Rusch and Barry Malzberg and Kate Wilhelm and the new, bright voices who are pointing the way to the future for the genre and for the culture.

And stop blaming Hollywood writers for your problems.

And clean up your room. It's a mess in here.

With all of that said . . . there can be no doubt that TV sf still lags behind print sf by about twenty to twenty-five years. And I pointedly do not exclude *Babylon 5* from that criticism. I've tried to bring it a bit more up to date, make it more relevant to the world of the 1990s – one of our characters has a drinking problem, another has a drug problem, in an episode from the second season there is the pretty clear intimation of a bisexual incident between two major characters, people talk about religion and politics, they have sex, they go to the bathroom, they have periods – but there is still a *long* way to go to bring TV sf up to the standards of literary sf.

Though by the time TV sf catches up to '90s literary sf, literary sf will already be in the 2010s.

Sisyphus had it easy.

* * *

16

'What is your, and Harlan's, input into the series?'

I always find this an interesting question, because it seems that very few people really have any concrete idea what an executive producer does. (Fair enough, I barely know myself.)

My input on the *Babylon 5* series is total and exhaustive. I have direct approval over casting, set design, construction, costume design, sound effects, prosthetics, computer graphics, directors, music and every other aspect of production. Along with producer John Copeland, I edit every episode after the director's cut to insure that the story is presented as I envisioned it. I sit with the composer and indicate where music is required, and sometimes what specific kind of music I have in mind. I write the majority of the scripts – twelve the first season, fifteen the second – and rewrite all the others to varying degrees. All but a handful of freelance scripts have been based on stories I've developed and assigned to outside writers. I work extensively with the directors prior to shooting to make sure we both understand the script and what it requires, and am on-set as much as my schedule allows to keep an eye on shooting.

Not all executive producers work this way. Some are far less hands-on. But this is my child.

The trick is to do this in such a way that you are not over-bearing and omnipresent. I have something over 200 craftspeople who work with me . . . actors, directors, other producers, art directors, wardrobe designers, makeup experts and others, all of whom profit from not being micro-managed. My job is to point to a spot on the horizon, and say, 'That's where we're going. I don't care what road you take, so long as we arrive at the same place at the same time.' When you have such a talented and dedicated group of people as have been accumulated on *Babylon 5*, the approvals noted above usually amount to nodding my head and saying 'yup' a lot.

To give a better idea of what I do . . . in the middle of any given season, I'm doing all of the following *at the same time*: writing episode 1; getting the script for episode 2 to the director and discussing it; prepping episode 3 for production; shooting episode 4; getting the director's cut on episode 5;

making the producer's cut on episode 6; spotting (selecting in- and out-cues for music and sound effects) for episode 7; approving final computer graphics/special effects for episode 8; mixing (inserting the final music and effects) episode 9; and delivering episode 10. You go from a meeting on any one of these to a meeting on any of the others, and you have to constantly keep it all straight in your head.

That's what I do for a living.

Did I mention I once had hair?

Harlan's input is whatever Harlan chooses. He has described himself as a mad dog nipping at my heels. I have described him as my own personal Jiminy Cricket, perched upon my shoulder and pointing out the pitfalls and chuckholes whose locations he has learned through decades in the industry. The definition we both tend to agree on is *free-floating agent of chaos*.

Consequently, his input varies. Sometimes it's a matter of looking for some ideas on costumes, and talking to Harlan about fabrics and textures and colours. Ditto for set ideas. Sometimes it's sitting down with me and a freelance writer to help figure out where the freelancer went astray. Sometimes it's suggesting characters, such as the Ombuds, created by Harlan Ellison. ('Listen, Joe, you know what you need on this show? Wapner. Judge Wapner. [From *The People's Court*.] It ain't always gonna be about saving the universe every day. Somebody's gonna sue somebody else because their dog crapped in some alien's air valve.')

Like the other masters of sf named before, the work of Harlan Ellison was a tremendous inspiration to me, and having him with me on the show is a constant compass pointing ever toward quality and challenging ideas. He's helped with the series narration (the idea of including the station's mass, 'the name of the place' and other items), recommended prop makers, suggested writers for the novels, sketched out brief scenes to humanise the characters that can be dropped into scripts where needed as leavening ... he comes to the studio when he wants, and has carte blanche to stick his nose into any aspect of production he so desires. When you have someone as eclectic and peripatetic as Harlan, your main task is just to get out of the way and let him play where he wishes. On occasion, he has been called upon to do battle with the latest media reporter who can't seem to structure his article in any other way than, 'How would you compare *Babylon 5* with *Star Trek*?'

Bottom line . . . Harlan does whatever Harlan wants.

So what else is new?

'How far have your ideas about the 5-season development of the series changed in the course of actual production?'

Very little, surprising as that answer may be.

Anyone who's ever written a novel starts with an outline of varying exactitude, but in general you know where you're starting, where the major elements are along the way, the brass rings you have to grab en route to concluding the story, and where you want to end up. Like many writers, I don't outline every detail to death; I leave room within that structure to be surprised, to allow characters to grow or change or take command of certain aspects of their portrayal. There is a point at which the character comes to life and starts arguing with you; this is no less true in television than in fiction. You have to remain open.

So in that sense, there has been some movement in terms of the characters, and who they are. It was Mira Furlan's background, coming from war-torn former Yugoslavia, that gave me some of the inner turmoil and other personality traits that ended up in Delenn. I found that some characters, like Vir, were coming to the forefront more quickly and forcefully than I'd imagined.

The change in commanding officers was not *predicted* in the outline, but came out of the outline. Or, more specifically, the writing based on that outline. Any novelist knows that you learn things partway into the writing of a novel that you can learn no other way. Sinclair's connections were all to the Minbari, and his character was fading fast in the stories I had planned for year two, eclipsed by the shadow-war. I needed to move him out, rather than risk turning him into a problem-solver and sounding board for exposition, while everyone else – Londo, G'Kar, Morden and others – was coming into the limelight. I needed someone upon whom I could pin a major part of the shadow storyline by way of a personal connection without straining credulity.

So I pulled the equivalent of a castle move in chess, and moved the character of Sinclair off to one side, and brought in Sheridan. The direction of the series changes not in the slightest; it simply makes it somewhat more efficient for me to get where I need to go.

The problem, really, is a certain element of Trek-think that naturally creeps into anyone; we're used to the captain of the ship being the captain of the ship for the duration. (Well, anyone who's never seen *Blake's 7*, which did without Blake for most of its run.) But the deeper I got into *Babylon 5*, the clearer it became that this is not really the story of one character; it's a metaphor on several levels for where I feel the American and, to a lesser extent, European societies have been going over the last several decades; it is a multi-character tapestry where anyone can live, die, or be broken on the wheel. There's a war on. *Anything can happen, at any time, to any character*.

That is, I think, part of the appeal of the story. Done properly, over its projected five-year run, *Babylon 5* will range all over the place, from Earth to Mars to Z'ha'dum to Minbar to Narn to Centauri Prime and the Vorlon homeworld, among other places; some characters will die, some will survive, but none will come through unchanged; empires will rise and others will be thrown down. To really communicate the theme of the show, it can't be tied to any one single character.

And the theme of *Babylon 5*, which emerges more fully the deeper you get into the arc, was spelled out plainly, in dialogue, in the pilot movie. In one scene, in the Zen garden, I laid out my cards plainly for all the world to see: Delenn called it 'The power of one mind to change the universe.' The strength of the individual, which for so long has been denigrated and assaulted by bureaucracy and government and others who profit from convincing us that we are powerless. Every aspect of the show points to that. Londo makes one small decision, and starts down a dark path that eventually leads to interstellar war and the death of billions of people. At one point along that path, this season, when Londo calls down the shadows to assault a Narn base, Vir says, 'You don't have to do this.'

'I have no choice,' Londo replies. Which is not true. He does have a choice. He has made it. But it's easier for him to live with what he has done by maintaining the illusion that there was no alternative. Cognitive Dissonance Is Our Friend.

Wars and revolutions are made up of individual decisions and private revelations. It was seeing a number of Prussian soldiers having dinner in a local café that led a group of French citizens to mistakenly believe that the government had called them in to help subdue the populace; enraged by this, violence broke out . . . and the French revolution came to its bloody climax.

The driver atop the carriage transporting Archduke Ferdinand was given specific instructions on where to turn in the parade. They had reportedly received intimations that an assassin might be out there somewhere, so they had taken great pains to secure the parade route. But at a pivotal intersection, the driver accidentally went *this* way when he should have gone *that* way . . . and an assassin's bullet started the chain of events that led to World War I and, by extension, World War II.

At its core, *Babylon 5* is about responsibility, and choices. It is about our obligation to society, to each other, and to the future. It reminds us that actions have consequences, and that we must choose wisely if we wish to avoid extermination. Will we decide to lead, or to be led by others?

That core has never changed, nor will it for as long as I continue to produce this series.

'Have there been disappointments as well as successes?'

Constantly. But few of them have made it onto the screen. The denouement/revelatory scene in 'The Long Dark' was nowhere near what I'd hoped for, from a production and effects standpoint. I wouldn't mind if every known copy of 'Grail' and 'Infection' mysteriously vanished and the negatives fell off the end of a pier somewhere.

More than anything else, I'd give my eye-teeth to re-edit the pilot movie. I was new to editing at the time, and out of a lack of confidence deferred too much to the director. As a result, the pilot was too slow, and most of the really good character scenes ended up on the cutting room floor. Those two factors ended up turning as many people off, as on. (Now I edit every episode with producer John Copeland to within an inch of its life, frame by frame, tightening it until it screams. We're always long on our first cuts, because I think it's better to have more story than time, than more time than story. We pack it full to bursting, and never let the pace or the story lose its intensity.)

There isn't a script I've written, or revised, that I wouldn't like to revisit for five minutes to tighten it a little. But that's the case with everything I write or produce. Someone once said, 'Art is never completed, only abandoned.' I hate the process of abandonment because I always think it could be just a *bit* better.

I wish we could've had more publicity, and less of the *Star Trek* monolith dogging us every step of the way. In the nearly thirty years since the original *Trek*, *Babylon 5* is the first American TV series to portray Earth in its far future, as a spacefaring civilisation, with a complete and consistent cosmology of other races, governments, alliances, technologies, past wars and diplomatic relations. Consequently, we were hammered on the one side by people who thought we were just like *Star Trek* and didn't want to watch one more clone; and on the other side by those who tuned in expecting *Star Trek*, found something different, and tuned out. One letter I received stated, 'I try to like the show, but it keeps breaking my sense of reality every time somebody uses one of those hand-links, when it's been established that in the future chest-communicator pins will be the accepted technology.'

It can make you crazy.

I'm sometimes disappointed that the themes of the episodes often get overlooked in the analysis of clues and treatises on the believability of computer-generated special effects. The thematic structure of *Babylon 5* is a hodge-podge of philosophical positions, Biblical allusions, Jungian archetypes, hero-myth, Greek tragedy, socio-political extrapolation, comparative religions, literary metaphor, historical parallels to both World Wars, Vietnam, the Kennedy murders and ancient Babylon . . . it traffics in notions of faith, self-sacrifice, predestination vs. free will, the price we put on our souls and the extent to which we are willing to sacrifice all that we are to keep all that we have.

(One of the things that is unique about *Babylon 5* is its use of literary devices not normally utilised in television storytelling, such as foreshadowing. Many American television stories use backwards-continuity, so that when you refer to something that happened in a prior episode it makes sense, but to the best of my knowledge few if any of them will drop a line in episode 14, not making a big deal out of it, only to have that become a major issue in subsequent episodes aired weeks, months or even years later. Someone on the *Babylon 5* set once commented that we are attempting 'holographic storytelling', in which each episode stands alone, like panes of glass with seemingly random lines etched upon them . . . but if you put each of them one behind the other, and look through them, the lines connect and form a picture that you could not see before. The more episodes you watch, the more this overlay becomes apparent.)

In any event . . . the disappointments in this show, for me, are few and far between. In television, you're lucky if the end product is 50–60% of what you even saw in your head when you were writing it. In *Babylon 5* the result is closer to 95–100% of what I had in mind. Sometimes it's even better than what I had originally conceived, thanks to the brilliant crew and cast we've assembled. And that's unspeakably rare.

'What do you think *Babylon 5*'s achievements have been?'

The easy, flip answer is: there have been plenty of them. We were the first sf series to use computer graphics on a regular basis to create ships and the textures of a space environment. We've pioneered a new form of television storytelling. We've raised the bar in terms of what people should expect from a science fiction series. We've made the point that you don't need to lumber an sf series with cute kids and even cuter robots, you don't need to make the show camp, don't need to treat the audience like children, and you don't need to avoid real science. If anything, real science – rotation to create gravity, the correct movement of ships in zero-gravity/non-atmospheric environments – adds to the look of the show.

The non-flip, and more fundamentally honest answer is a little difficult:

How successful is an uncompleted novel?

It's perhaps interesting as a curiosity, as an intellectual exercise into what might have been, but at its core, it is unsuccessful. Whatever we may have done technically falls entirely by the wayside if we don't complete the story. All of the other elements feed into that goal. You can have the best-equipped race car on the planet, but if it doesn't cross the finish line, it's just something pretty to look at.

We have completed two years of our journey into the *Babylon 5* story, and the third year has been approved. Two years beyond still remain, and there is nothing certain in television. If we are allowed to complete our story, then I think we will have accomplished something that will be discussed, analysed and remembered long after I have gone to dust. If not . . . then we will have failed. More specifically, I will have failed. Granted no producer can predict changes in attitude at any studio, or the vicissitudes of network finances; all that is beyond my control, and irrelevant to my *feelings* on the subject. Because the pieces are all there . . . the fine performers, the talented crew, the breathtaking effects . . . so the only reason for failure is if the writing is not the equal to the talents who breathe life into it on-camera.

That thought keeps me awake a lot.

Some concluding thoughts. This article is intended as a 'profession piece'. I'll have to leave it to others to judge how well it has succeeded in that regard. With luck it will help bridge the gap between print sf and media sf writers, by pointing out that we have essentially the same fears, insecurities, schedules; that we both strive to find new ways to explore the wealth of our human heritage and the possibilities of our future. Our roots are sunk deep into the same earth, the earth of Bradbury and Heinlein and Clarke and Verne and Wells. The margins in which we type our stories may vary, but they are stories nonetheless.

I once sat on a panel at an sf convention in Memphis beside Larry Niven. At the time he didn't know who I was or what I did for a living. Before we'd concluded our introductions to the audience, he launched into a proclamation that anybody who'd prostitute himself sufficiently to work in television was a hack and couldn't properly be considered a science fiction writer. In the course of the next twenty minutes, punctuated by raised voices and the invocation of agendas, prejudices and canned critiques of the state of TV sf, the one thought that kept coming to me was, 'This is really, totally, monumentally stupid.'

Too many print sf writers propagate mythologies about how TV sf writers work, what they're paid, how the industry operates. They dismiss scripts as something other than writing, and when you try to show them a script, refuse to look at it because 'I don't know how to read one of those things.'

Print sf writers, more than anyone else, should understand the penalty for deliberate ignorance of changing technologies.

Too many media sf writers shy away from real science, feel inadequate around print sf writers, don't know the history of the genre and put down writers who spend two years writing a book that nets them a five-grand advance, as though money were the surest indicator of quality. They consider most print sf writers too provincial to understand how to work for a television series, or how to properly adapt their own work to film.

Media sf writers, more than anyone else, should understand the sin of pride, and its tendency to goeth before a fall.

Television is a powerful medium, the mightiest conceivable, and like any great weapon it needs to be controlled, bent toward enlightening and ennobling and uplifting its audience, not by congressional fiat or the influence of pressure groups from either side of the political spectrum, but by people who understand the medium, and the craft of storytelling. You cannot hope to influence something until you understand it.

Hiding one's head in the sand is worse than stupid; it's suicidal. Which is one reason I tend to frequent the computer nets. Internet, GEnie, CompuServe, Bix, others . . . they provide a valuable opportunity that should be utilised regularly by television producers. They put you in contact with people in Wisconsin and Idaho and Birmingham and Suffolk, people who might never otherwise have the chance to tell a Maker Of Television what they *really* think of the end product. In just the last year, one Internet discussion group has generated over 100,000 messages, critiques, flames and critical analyses. It is, to say the least, a sobering experience.

In addition, by the time the *Babylon 5* storyline has run its course, the compilation of messages currently being archived, indexed, cross-linked and hypertext'd will form a document thousands of pages in length, chronicling the birth, development and production of a TV series. A document that can be used by students, media analysts, and ordinary people to better understand why things are done the way they are done. It will help to de-mystify the process of making television, which may ultimately be one of our more significant accomplishments.

As I write this, I am a few weeks short of turning 41. I have been fighting to bring about the *Babylon 5* series since 1987. Eight years. If we should be fortunate enough for this story to run its full measure, the tale will be finished in 1998. That's eleven years of my life dedicated to the singular task of bringing a classically structured science fiction saga to the television screen. One story told across 110 episodes, roughly 5,500 manuscript pages, equivalent to five novels, each weighing in at 100,000 words, give or take.

It is, without question, the single biggest undertaking of my creative life. Whether it will succeed or not, I don't know. Nor do I know if anyone else will be foolish enough to pick up this particular ball after I've finished playing with it, to create another multi-year, interstellar saga. The only thing that keeps me going is the hope that it may someday infect others yet to come with the same elusive sense of wonder that was my home, my friend, and my comfort when I first discovered science fiction. It is payment on a debt, however poor and ephemeral and wholly inadequate in its execution, owed to Heinlein, and Clarke, and Asimov, and Tolkien, and Matheson, and Lovecraft, and Russell, and Smith.

And Bradbury.

'I've always wanted to see a Martian,' said Michael. 'Where are they, Dad? You promised.'

'There they are,' said Dad, and he shifted Michael on his shoulder and pointed straight down.

The Martians were there. Timothy began to shiver.

The Martians were there – in the canal – reflected in the water. Timothy and Michael and Robert and Mom and Dad.

The Martians stared back up at them for a long, long silent time from the rippling water . . .

Between the Essence and the Descent

Carl Jung and *Babylon 5*

When any critic discusses the semiotic, mythical or psychological underpinnings to a particular text, there is a good chance they are reading far too much into it. Critics bring to the table their own bag of tools: their beliefs, prejudices, analytical techniques, personality quirks and past history – the totality, in fact, of what makes them a critic. When one of them talks, for instance, about a robot character in the British SF TV series *Red Dwarf* displaying, 'an effective response to binarism, symbolising what Haraway calls "an infidel heteroglossia" against which other characters' more rigid gender identities may be read,' what they probably mean is, 'I've got a degree in Gender Studies and I'm going to use it.' The longer the critique is, the more you learn about the critic and the less you learn about the criticised.

Identifying traces of Jung in the subtextual story of *Babylon 5* is, therefore, an inherently risky pastime. The author leaves himself or herself open to an instant rebuttal along the lines of: '*You* may see all that stuff in there, but *I* don't. What makes you think you're right?' In this particular case, there is little doubt that at least some of these traces are real. J. Michael Straczynski – the creator of the programme and the writer of most of the episodes – has admitted in public that he has been influenced by Jung. 'There has always been a certain element of Jungian archetypes in the show,' he has written, 'both in the Shadows and elsewhere.' Given that he has degrees in psychology and sociology, with minors in literature and philosophy, one has to assume the man knows a Jungian archetype when he sees one. Straczynski has also written: 'An analysis of some of the stuff in Jungian terms is not entirely unproductive. It really is a hodge-podge of bits and pieces, a Frankenstein monster assembled from elements of myth, and archetype, and history that I've been kind of subconsciously assembling over a long, long time. Certainly the issue touches strongly on the whole question of who we are, how we define ourselves, our place in the universe (as we perceive it, and as we are *able* to perceive it, stuck as we are in the metaphorical fishbowl) . . . So it's an ongoing process to redefine the myths, and in so doing redefine the way we perceive ourselves. Or something like that.'

If Jung's theories are to be discussed, some biographical detail about the man is in order. Like Freud, with whom he shares the honour of being the father of modern psychoanalytic thought, Jung's background and his life heavily influenced his theories, often in ways that were probably unrecognised by the man himself.

Carl Gustav Jung was born in Switzerland in 1875. His father was a religious man, a pastor in the Swiss Reformed Church, and a classical scholar as well. Eight of young Carl's uncles and one grandfather were clergymen, so it is not surprising that religion – its role in society and its roots in myth – played a central part in his later writings. He trained as a doctor and, having originally decided to specialise in surgery, he changed his mind after reading a book on the relatively new field of psychology. After he qualified, the Burghölzli mental hospital in Zürich took him on as an assistant in 1900. He married in 1903, and, given his continued fascination with myth and the past, it is almost too ironic to be true that his wife Emma later became a respected Arthurian scholar who wrote in depth about the Grail myth. Jung became a senior doctor at the Burghölzli mental hospital in 1905 and a lecturer at the University of Zürich, but he resigned his post in 1909 at the beginning of a period of mental turmoil ostensibly to pursue his private practice. In the period between then and his death in 1961 he had built his theories piece by piece, paper by paper, book by book, until he was undeniably the grand old man of psychology. He left behind a legacy difficult to ignore, but also difficult to fully understand, given his eclectic knowledge of widely differing disciplines and his difficult writing style. He is remembered as being not so much concerned with the mechanics of how minds work, although he did make major contributions to psychiatry, but more with *why* they work. His interests lay in the cultural, mythic and historical roots of consciousness rather than in the minutiae of how it functioned on a day-to-day basis. As the psychologist and author Ledford Bischoff has written, 'Jung's theory is different from others in that it is shadowy, metaphysical, of a nature almost impossible to test in a laboratory situation, and appears to reverse the current trend for statistical treatment of psychological data.'

Given that Jung's collected writings run to some eighteen volumes, any attempt to summarise his theories in a few thousand words will produce something for which the word 'superficial' seems too kind a description. It has been said of Jung's work that the only people qualified to talk about it are those who have read and reread it for years in the original German. However, even a quick examination of the topographical terrain of his theories, hypotheses and statements can identify a few mountain peaks towering above the surrounding countryside. The first of these is Jung's controversial assertion that human consciousness is made up of a number of different personalities, all cohabiting within the same mind. 'I hold that our personal unconscious . . . consists of an indefinite, because unknown, number of complexes or fragmentary personalities,' he wrote. He firmly believed that these complexes had a willpower and an ego of their own – that they were not just aspects of the one dominant personality, but that they could almost be counted as separate people. This conviction was rooted in his childhood, when he became convinced that his mother was actually two separate people – one a conventional Swiss rector's wife and one an unconventional woman who would often do something to contradict what the first one had said or done. From the age of twelve, Jung came to believe that he himself was made up of two separate characters – one an uncertain, shy schoolboy and one a confident and respected old man to whom he eventually gave the name Philemon. Philemon was, he believed, capable of insights and ideas that Jung himself was not capable of having, and he continued to 'talk' with him until late in his life.

It is possible to see within *Babylon 5* explicit examples of

Jung's conviction that we are all made up of separate personalities. The obvious instance is the licensed telepath Talia Winters. As revealed in episode 219 ('Divided Loyalties') and in issue 8 of the *Babylon 5* comic ('Silent Enemies'), Psi Corps had implanted a second personality within her mind. (See 'Key to Episode Guide Entries' on p. 47 for an explanation of the numbering system for individual episodes.) This secondary personality is radically different from the primary one: it dislikes Susan Ivanova, whereas the primary personality was attracted to her, and it is fanatically loyal to Psi Corps, whereas the primary personality was having a crisis of conscience. Effectively, they are two different people with contradictory views sharing the same body – much like Jung originally felt his mother to be.

A more subtle example of Jung's theory of multiple personalities would be Captain Sheridan: a man who, at the end of season three, is sharing his mind with an older, wiser person who can offer him advice he wouldn't have thought of by himself ('Jump! Jump now!'). Superficially, Kosh is a separate entity within Sheridan, but on a deeper level he is a voice of experience and wisdom that is a distinct part of Sheridan's mind. 'I have *always* been here,' Kosh has said, and perhaps he has. Perhaps, in some sense, he *is* Sheridan, just as Jung felt that the older, wiser figure named Philemon was a part of him.

While Kosh was inside Sheridan, offering him insights, the mysterious alien known as Lorien was outside, doing the same. Kosh and Lorien share essentially the same Jungian function, that of the wise adviser who is part of our own mind. Jung called this part of his mind Philemon and, bearing this in mind, it is interesting to note that Lorien and Philemon are fairly similar names.

Another of Jung's theories was that humanity shared a common set of ideas and beliefs, which he called the 'collective unconscious'. This emerged from his work on patients with schizophrenia (a condition then known as dementia praecox) while at Burghölzli mental hospital. Schizophrenics, he believed, were people whose personalities had shattered rather than being split naturally into discrete personalities. He started developing his theory of the collective unconscious after observing that their fantasies and delusions often mirrored elements of myth and legend. Perhaps, Jung theorised, everyone had access to a shared set of archaic residues and collective inherited images, and perhaps schizophrenia laid bare this process. The substrate of the mind, he asserted, tended to throw up similar images – which he termed 'archetypes' – regardless of race or creed, images which were incorporated into stories, myths, legends, religions and dreams. Some of these archetypes were simple images, but others were more complicated representations of idealised human beings – the Hero, the Villain, the Wise Old Man, the Old Crone – and could be found in whatever creative storytelling activity human beings indulged in over the millennia. However, Jung himself cautioned his readers against believing that archetypes were thrown, fully formed, out of the mind. They were, he argued, more like flexible moulds which could be filled with the experiences and beliefs of the individual. What went into the mould was characteristic of the individual person, but what came out would have a basic similarity from person to person. A Greek Hero would be different from a Scandinavian Hero, but both would be Heroes.

The *Babylon 5* equivalent of the collective unconscious comes in a number of forms. Firstly we have the classic archetypal figure of Kosh – an angelic form recognised by all the races who view him (as in episode 222 – 'The Fall of Night'). The image of a glowing winged figure already occurs in many human religions and myths; the point J. Michael Straczynski is trying to make in *Babylon 5* is that this collective unconscious can extend to alien species as well. Effectively, the Vorlons have been manipulating the collective unconscious of the younger galactic races in order to ensure that they were properly in awe of the Vorlons. Justin tells us as much in episode 322 ('Z'ha'dum').

Kosh also represents the archetype of the wise old adviser – the figure who frequently turns up in myth, legend and story to instruct the young hero (and whom Jung identified as part of everyone's mind). The archetype has been given many names over the years – as many names as the archetypal hero, in fact. Ulysses' counsellor, the original Mentor, gave his name to describe them all: Chiron the Centaur guided the Greek heroes Achilles and Jason, while Merlin was mentor to Arthur. More recently, Gandalf guided Frodo, and Obi Wan Kenobi fulfilled the same function for Luke Skywalker. J. Michael Straczynski willingly acknowledges the connection. 'Certainly,' he has written, 'when Kosh says "I have always been here," he is speaking in the voice of wisdom that is ancient in us. The older wiser figure whose face changes depending on your perspective, environment and training. It speaks to the root of the archetype, with the perception or name of that archetype being the perceptual encounter suit. Which also yanks us back to Campbell's *Hero With a Thousand Faces*. The theory here is that it isn't just the hero whose face changes (literally in the case of Kosh), but also the others in that archetypal hierarchy. As the wiser archetype has been with us for ages, so too has the hero . . . and once Sheridan begins the progression towards becoming that hero, then he too can be described in those terms . . . "you have always been here." The key is to step back and see the role, not the person. The person is always expendable . . . the job is not.'

In a more subtle way, the collective unconscious comes into play with the entire history of the first Great War. Many races have some form of legendary recollections of it: the Narns have the Book of G'Quan, the Markab have more or less the same set of stories (as we discover in episode 205 – 'The Long Dark') and even the Centauri still talk of that time, as their Emperor mentions in episode 401 ('The Hour of the Wolf'). Even the sight of the Shadow ships engenders an instinctive reaction of disgust and revulsion, as various pilots and characters have reported (but especially in episode 222 – 'The Fall of Night'). Effectively, the first Great War has passed into the collective unconscious of the entire galaxy.

Like Freud before him, Jung believed that the mind (or the 'psyche' as he called it) was divided into two primary parts: the conscious mind – those desires, memories and drives which were obvious to the person in question – and the unconscious mind – those which were hidden. *Un*like Freud, Jung believed that the unconscious mind was a vital part of the well-adjusted psyche. The psyche had its conscious and unconscious parts in balance. If the conscious mind went too far in one direction, or became fixated on one particular thing, then the unconscious mind compensated by pushing in the opposite direction. Creative tension keeps the psyche healthy. Dreams, fantasies and even neurotic disturbances are all attempts of the unconscious to balance the psyche. Jung was preoccupied for most of his life with this central tenet of his theories. After many years of study and thought, he became convinced that everything in the world, and perhaps the universe itself, comes about through opposition and conflict. There will always be opposites. Opposites lead to conflict. Conflict leads to progress and growth.

This, of course, is the position Justin outlines in episode 322 of *Babylon 5* ('Z'ha'dum'). The Shadows, he claims, believe that only through conflict do races become stronger. They feel it is their duty to pit races against one another to ensure that the survivors are more powerful, and every so often they will 'kick over all the anthills' to force the lesser races to evolve and develop. Conflict leads to growth and progress. Peace leads to stagnation. It's a point of view, and one difficult to refute with anything apart from emotive language.

Jung wrote often of the persona – the mask we all wear to deal with others, the face we present to the outside world. He also defined the soul-image, which is to the persona what the unconscious mind is to the conscious mind. In Jung's theories, the soul-image is always represented by a figure of the opposite sex to that of the persona – a man will have a female soul-image whilst a woman will have a male soul-image. These images he named the animus (for the male soul-image) and the anima (for the female soul-image). The anima is personified as not only being erotically seductive, but also as possessing age-old wisdom. The animus was less well defined, probably because Jung was a man, but can be characterised perhaps as a mysterious Stranger. In typical confusing style, Jung defines the animus and anima in different ways at different times. Primarily they appear in his writings in the terms described above, as the soul-images of the persona, but he also refers to them as archetypes in their own right – the animus being the archetypal man to women and the anima being the archetypal woman to men.

If we were looking for an embodiment of the anima in *Babylon 5*, we need look no further than Delenn. She is female, she is certainly erotic in Sheridan's eyes and, as we discover at various points during the second and third seasons, she possesses a fair amount of age-old wisdom, both in terms of Minbari prophecy and also in terms of what she knows about the Vorlons and the first Great War. Given the Minbari feelings about souls, the fact that she herself is an embodiment of a soul-image is curiously satisfying. Delenn also talks during episode 321 ('Shadow Dancing') about the Minbari custom that, when two people become close, the female spends three nights watching over the male to see what he looks like when all his masks are down and his true face is revealed. At the end of this episode, when Delenn actually does watch over the sleeping Sheridan, what is *actually* happening is that Sheridan's anima is looking beneath his persona to see what his Self is really like. And you thought this was just an ordinary TV series.

It is, of course, possible to go too far with this kind of analysis, as was pointed out at the beginning of this essay. For instance, Jung's term for a woman who identifies too much with her animus is *sol niger* which, translated from the Latin, means 'Black Sun'. The flagship of the Minbari fleet during the Earth–Minbari war (a time at which, Delenn admits, the entire Minbari race went temporarily mad) was the *Black Star*. Coincidence? I think it probably is.

Jung believed that no human is as virtuous as they would like to appear, either to others or indeed to themselves. He characterised these selfish, greedy, evil desires all humans have as the 'shadow' side of the personality. In archetypal terms, the shadow is dark-skinned and devilish, inferior and uncivilised. Like the animus and anima, the shadow is at the same time an archetype and also a part of the mental make-up of every person. If the Self is the entirety of a person's psyche, then it is made up of the ego (the individual's sense of purpose and identity) and the shadow (the uncivilised impulses that cannot be let out in public). The shadow is the counterpart to Freud's 'id' but, unlike Freud, Jung thought that the shadow was a necessary balance to the ego. Too much ego and the psyche becomes dangerously arrogant: too little and the basic animal desires take over.

Jung's description of the shadow is the source of the Shadows (originally the Shadowmen) in *Babylon 5*, although not the only source. 'How Jungian are the Shadows?' J. Michael Straczynski has written, 'To varying extents, yes, certainly. But there are also some elements of Joseph Campbell, the Old Testament, and Freud.' The Shadows in *Babylon 5* are certainly related to Jung's shadow, in that they represent the baser desires of power, glory and conflict for the sake of conflict. If, as Delenn says in episode 304 ('Passing Through Gethsemane') and Jeremiah says in episode 319 ('Grey 17 is Missing'), life is the universe splitting itself into small pieces in an attempt to understand itself, then the Shadows are the universe's shadow and the Vorlons are its ego. Both are necessary for a healthy universe. 'Certainly, the Shadows and Vorlons translate into very clear psychoanalytic terms,' as J. Michael Straczynski freely admits: 'id and superego, desires vs. rules, with humans (ego) caught in the middle and trying to balance the two into something resembling a life. This is probably the most blatantly obvious reference in the show, given Jung's definition of the shadow as unbridled want, unbridled need, and the conflict arising from that . . . Check back with Babylonian creation myth, in which it was stated that the universe was created through the conflict between order and chaos. So if you now take the notion of order and chaos, apply those to Jungian terms as superego and id, then you have the fundamental workings of a conscious mind . . . hence, in turn, the Minbari belief that the universe is conscious, aware, and we who live in the middle (ego) balance it out and are the vehicle through which the universe observes itself, as the ego is the self-reflective part of the mind.'

The last chapter of Jung's book *Symbols of Transference*

concerns the sacrifice of the archetypal hero figure. It was this chapter that caused him to argue with his mentor Freud, because Freud's contention was that most human behaviour could eventually be reduced to the satisfaction of sexual desire. Jung disagreed with this, and also with Adler, who substituted the love of power for the love of sex. Jung's theory was that sometimes a person needed something more than 'honour, power, wealth, fame and the love of women', as Freud put it, and aimed for a spiritual goal beyond this world. This is precisely what Captain Sheridan does in episode 322 of *Babylon 5* ('Z'ha'dum') – he sacrifices himself (or tries to) to save the future. He could have had power, he could have had fame and he certainly could have had Delenn, but he had a higher goal than this, and his own sacrifice was the price. This, incidentally, is what Sebastian was talking about in episode 221 ('Comes the Inquisitor') – the willingness to die alone and unloved for the sake of something greater than one's own self.

Jung often tried to relate his patients' neuroses to what he called 'the spirit of the age', implying that their problems were caused more by something going wrong in the world around them than by something going wrong inside them. Indeed, he himself had what amounted to a schizophrenic episode in late 1913 and early 1914, when he was plagued with visions of the world being destroyed. When World War One started, Jung felt (paradoxically) relieved. His visions, he decided, had not been hallucinations presaging madness but had, in fact, been premonitions of the war. One can see hints here not only of Londo's dream in episode 209 ('The Coming of Shadows') of Shadow ships in the sky of Centauri Prime – a dream which comes true in episode 401 ('The Hour of the Wolf') – but also of the mad bomber Carlsen in episode 302 ('Convictions'), who tells Sheridan, 'it's nothing personal, Captain, it's just the times,' as he threatens to blow up the station. As Jung said, 'About a third of my cases are not suffering from any clinically definable neurosis, but from the senselessness and aimlessness of their lives. I should not object if this were called the general neurosis of our age.'

Unlike anything else ever made for American television,

Babylon 5 is a multi-layered experience that demands repeated viewing and deep analysis if one is to get the most from it. Although it can be enjoyed on a purely superficial level as a rollicking adventure yarn with some nifty special effects and a cast of attractive heroes and evil villains, there are deeper levels in which the main elements and characters of the show cast historical and mythical shadows and deeper levels still in which the overall story arc is essentially a massive replication of Jung's theories of the mind. As Straczynski has said, 'One of the things really lacking in American culture, I think, is a sense of *myth*. So the story of *Babylon 5* has a very mythic kind of structure. I think that's important. Which is why a lot of the elements I draw on aren't traditional television devices . . . literature, poetry, religion, hard SF, metafiction, Jungian symbology . . . There are an awful lot of ingredients in this particular pie, culled from the less likely aisles in the supermarket.'

The fact that *Babylon 5* is, beneath the flash and glitter of a drama series, a hidden explication of Jungian psychoanalytic theory should not be taken to mean that J. Michael Straczynski is himself a Jungian acolyte. 'None of this should be taken as an endorsement of Jung, by the way,' he has said, 'only that the language and tools he used have some utility in crafting some elements of the story. At root, I do not necessarily agree with or endorse his views . . . but when someone hands you a hammer, and it does the job you need done for the story, you take it. I see it primarily as a descriptive tool.'

The last word should go, as is only right, to Carl Gustav Jung. Towards the end of his life a writer asked him to comment on an analysis of his work that the writer had prepared. Jung read it through carefully, then said, 'I don't believe a word of it, but I can't disagree with anything you have said.'

Choices, Consequences and Responsibility

Meaning and Subtexts in *Babylon 5*

If you want to know what a particular text is about – that text being perhaps a book, or a film, or an episode of a TV series – then the writer is usually the last person one should ask. Texts accrete meanings like rocks accrete barnacles, and those meanings are frequently at odds with what the writer intended. *Babylon 5* is one of the few exceptions to this rule. Its sole creator – J. Michael Straczynski – maintains an almost complete involvement in the progress of the series. He is currently writing every episode – his scripts contain very detailed sets of instructions for the directors to follow and he sits in on the editing sessions. As co-Executive Producer, he influences almost every choice or decision during pre-production, filming and post-production (short of those forced upon him by the exigencies of circumstance, such as Michael O'Hare leaving the series). If there *is* a meaning to the series, then it's his meaning and nobody else's. Given the depth and breadth of Straczynski's admitted influences, and also given the fact that he had been planning this series for some seven years before the pilot episode was transmitted, one can also be assured that whatever subtexts are buried beneath the surface of the story arc have been put there deliberately.

'The show is fundamentally about three things,' Straczynski has said: 'choices, consequences and responsibility for those consequences and choices.' If we take this statement at face value, we can examine the choices made by the characters first, then see how they lead on to their consequences and, ultimately, responsibility.

There are two types of choice made in the show: those where the character doesn't fully realise the implications of the path they have chosen, and those where they know exactly what the consequences will be. Londo Mollari made his choice – to side with Mr Morden and his 'associates' and thus revitalise the fortunes of his race – without any thought to what it would ultimately mean. He failed to understand the consequences of what he was doing.

'If you look at Londo as a character for a moment,' Straczynski says, 'there's someone who made certain choices in his life, and look where he has come to because of those choices.' If someone could have explained to Londo that his simple acceptance of Morden's help would lead inexorably to the devastation of his world (as seen in episode 316 – 'War Without End' Part One) then it's likely he would have refused it. Londo was only acting out of what he considered to be the best of motives: he could see his race sliding down into depravity and isolationism, eclipsed by the younger races, and he wanted to do something to help them. He made a pact with the Devil without realising who he was talking to. Once he began to see further down that road, however, once he saw how many Narn and how many Centauri had to die to satisfy his wishes and just how mad Emperor Cartagia actually was, once he saw the full implications of his decision, he took responsibility for what he has done. He could have just gone along with what was happening; he could have tried to escape and take sanctuary somewhere else. But he didn't. By the beginning of season four, Londo has decided to reverse at least some of what he has done by killing Cartagia and throwing the Shadows off Centauri Prime. The personal consequences of that choice are likely to be tragic – Londo has, after all, seen how he will die – but he makes it regardless. He has finally accepted responsibility for the consequences of his actions.

G'Kar, imprisoned in his cell on Centauri Prime at the beginning of season four (episode 402 – 'Whatever Happened to Mr Garibaldi?'), also makes a choice. Londo Mollari offers him a deal, and he accepts. He knows what the consequences will be – Londo spells it out in almost brutal detail – but G'Kar accepts them. Having taken responsibility for saving his race he also accepts the personal consequences of that responsibility. And, for a few tragic episodes, we see him walk that road in full knowledge of his destination.

Most of the major characters go through the choice-consequence-responsibility cycle at some stage in the series. Some know what their choices will entail: others do not. Delenn chooses to become human in response to an ancient prophecy (as seen in episodes 122 – 'Chrysalis' and 202 – 'Revelations'), but the consequences of her choice mean that she becomes estranged from her own race. Something she thought would bring humans and Minbari closer together ends up wrenching them further apart, and she has to take responsibility for what she has done by shattering the Grey Council and leading the Worker and Religious castes in a war against the Shadows (in episode 310 – 'Severed Dreams'). Similarly, Sinclair chooses to be transformed into a Minbari and travel back in time to become the great religious leader Valen (in episode 317 – 'War Without End' Part Two). Sinclair already knew what the consequences of his actions would be – all he had to do was accept the responsibility with his eyes wide open.

Michael Garibaldi is a man who has already made his choice – to always do the right thing – and he has to live with the consequences every day of his life. That single choice led to the murder of his friend Frank Kemmer, the gradual disintegration of his career and his descent into alcoholism. Had he known what the consequences of his choice would be, would he have still made it or would he have accepted the bribes and the corruption? Stephen Franklin has been walking away from responsibility all his life: he is happy to make choices but hates living with the consequences. It all comes home when he is bleeding to death in the Downbelow region of Babylon 5, and hallucinates a conversation with himself (in episode 321 – 'Shadow Dancing'). 'Take responsibility for your actions, for crying out loud,' he tells himself. 'You go in and fight for what matters, you don't just walk away because it's easier.'

Captain Sheridan, by contrast, is the only fully integrated character in the entire series. He doesn't seem to agonise about the choices he has to make, or worry about the consequences. When Sheridan makes a choice, he immediately accepts responsibility for whatever happens. He doesn't try to shirk his duty, or run away. He does his duty. That's why he is the archetypal Hero.

Choices, consequences and responsibility are the core of the show, but Straczynski is willing to admit that there is more to it than those three, stark words. 'And it's about changing your life,' he adds. 'Everyone in the show changes, to varying degrees. We're taught as a culture that you can't change your life: you've got to settle for what is. You can't change the government, you can't fight City Hall – which is, of course, a lie. You *can* fight City Hall. You *can* change your life. The planet's being changed all the time. The rules are being changed. The question is: who's doing it, you or somebody else? That's the operative question. Lee Harvey Oswald – three bullets – changed the world.'

Characters in *Babylon 5* change in a variety of ways. Delenn and Sinclair change physically, of course – Minbari to human and human to Minbari – while G'Kar and Sheridan both change spiritually: they are each taught to let go of their own mundane concerns and place themselves on a higher, more selfless plane. Londo not only changes the face of the universe by allying himself with the Shadows but he also changes as a person, following an arc from resigned acceptance of the end of the Centauri Republic through an arrogant belief that he could reverse their fortunes to a humble realisation that he has to halt what he has set in motion. Franklin and Garibaldi both manage to change their addictive behaviour patterns, Garibaldi by giving up alcohol and Franklin by admitting he has an addiction to stims. Even the more minor characters go through a definite personality change: Lennier arrives on Babylon 5 as a nervous innocent but, by the beginning of season four, has altered into a calm, stable and wise individual, while Vir starts off as a bumbling fool and becomes possibly the most empathic, caring person on the station.

The importance of improvisation over planning is another theme that can be discerned beneath the surface of the show. The Minbari, for instance, have been planning their response to the prophesied resurgence of the Shadows for a thousand years and yet, when the time comes to put their plans into motion, they fumble the chance. The Military caste have grave doubts about the actual truth of the prophecy, and the rest of the Grey Council are content to stand back and let the prophecy attend to itself, without realising that they themselves are part of the prophecy and must act. It is only Delenn's impulsive act in breaking the Grey Council apart that allows the prophecy to come true. Had the Minbari been left to tend the thousand-year plan, Babylon 5 would have fallen either to Earth or to the Shadows (and that may have ended up as the same thing). 'One of the problems the Minbari have,' Straczynski has said, 'is that they are not very good at improvisation. They need someone like Sheridan, who can respond to changing situations. The Minbari caste structure – Warrior, Religious and Worker – helped prevent the civil wars that they had and stabilised the culture, but over the last thousand years has ossified that structure. It's gotten too rigid, and now must begin the process of re-examining itself and pulling itself apart a little bit. Certainly in "Severed Dreams" you see her [Delenn] break the Grey Council, which is the first step toward unravelling that tight structure. So that's a very definite deliberate difference.'

The contrast between the human ability to improvise and the Minbari desire to stick to plans is highlighted by the use of the *White Star* during season three. In episode 301 ('Matters of Honor'), Delenn tells Sheridan the *White Star* is not powerful enough to destroy a Shadow ship. Had he believed her, the *White Star* would have been destroyed, but Sheridan improvises a solution by entering hyperspace while inside a jumpgate, setting off a huge energy release that destroys the Shadow ship. This is neatly reversed in episode 308 ('Messages From Earth') when it is Delenn who improvises a plan to escape the Earthforce vessel *Agamemnon* by opening a jumpgate inside the atmosphere of Jupiter. Had she not learnt how to improvise, she and Sheridan would have either died or been taken captive by President Clark's forces.

The Vorlons are, perhaps, the masters of long-term planning, but they also display the remarkable ability to cast aside those plans when the opportunity for improvisation presents itself. They have been fighting the Shadows for millions of years and, like a chess grandmaster too familiar with his opponent's strategy, they respond almost by rote to the moves the Shadows make. The plan was written a long time ago, but both sides play it out until Sheridan makes his sacrifice. 'He has opened an unexpected door,' the new Vorlon Ambassador to Babylon 5 tells Delenn. 'We do now what must be done now. His purpose has been fulfilled.' In other words, the plan has changed thanks to a sudden improvisation on the part of one of the pieces on the board. The Vorlons are quick enough to take advantage of the distraction, but their response is terrifyingly excessive.

Babylon 5 displays a great deal more intelligence than most other original television shows, and has depths to it that are rarely displayed outside the novel. The individual episodes do not only permit analysis and interpretation: some of them positively demand it. Getting a show with this amount of complexity on to American television is no small feat, and J. Michael Straczynski would be the first to admit how difficult a task it was. 'When they asked me at PTEN, "What's the show about?" I tried to sell it to them – "Well, it's about choices, responsibility, consequences."

' "Where are the bikinis?"

'What do you say at that point?'

THE
EPISODES

Key to Episode Guide Entries

A note about spellings: although alien character names are usually referenced in the beginning or end credits, alien planets, ship names, customs, ceremonies and objects are frequently mentioned only in dialogue. I've done my best to render these names as accurately as possible, given the particular idiosyncrasies of the language in question (such as the Narn fondness for apostrophes).

Transmission Number: This tells you which season and where in the season the episode was transmitted: 312, for instance, is the twelfth episode of the third season; 208 is the eighth episode of the second season. This is the order in which, for continuity purposes, we assume that the events happened. Any mentions of episode numbers in this book refer to the transmission number.

Production Number: This operates in the same way as the transmission number, but tells you in what order the episodes were made, rather than transmitted. This may seem like a needless distinction to you, but 'Chrysalis', for instance, was the 12th episode made in season 1 but the 22nd episode transmitted. In the case of 'Chrysalis' the decision to film it out of order was made for logistical reasons. In other cases episodes had to be swapped at the last minute for other reasons – such as effects not being ready in time. Sometimes episodes actually make more sense if you watch them in the order in which they were made. Sometimes they don't.

Written by: The series' creator and producer – J. Michael Straczynski – has a policy of putting only one name as writer on the credits, no matter how many people contributed to the episode. So, for instance, if Mark Scott Zicree writes an episode which is then rewritten by Straczynski, Larry DiTillio and Harlan Ellison, only Mark Zicree's name appears as writer. Where possible, I've tried to indicate where particular scenes were written by someone else (usually Straczynski). Straczynski has said on numerous occasions that he rewrites episodes only where necessary, not just to put his imprint on them.

Directed by: This should be unambiguous, or would be if some of the directors didn't keep on changing their names on the credits. I'm assuming, for simplicity's sake, that John Flinn and John C. Flinn III are the same person, as are Mike Laurence Vejar and Michael Vejar, and David Eagle and David J. Eagle.

Cast: I haven't listed all the names appearing in the opening or closing credits, but only those people playing characters who had a major impact on the events of the story, or had a lot of lines, or sometimes just one or two good lines. Please don't treat this as a comprehensive list of characters – it really isn't.

Date: Sometimes the actual day and date are mentioned during the course of the episode. I've recorded them here because I'm sad that way. Note that some episodes take place over a couple of days or a couple of weeks, and I haven't made any attempt to track this unless it is explicitly mentioned in the episode itself.

Plot: A brief overall review of the story will be followed by a breakdown into three sections: the 'A' plot, the 'B' plot and the 'C' plot. It's a semi-standard template for action/ adventure series like *Babylon 5* to have three plots working together. Cutting between them stops the viewer from getting bored and provides a richer, multi-layered texture to the proceedings.

The 'A' Plot: This is the main action plot, where external events usually threaten the main characters. It's the plot set up by the last few moments of the teaser before the main titles.

The 'B' Plot: Where the 'A' plot is about action, external threat and danger, the 'B' plot is about people, internal threat and emotions. Frequently it covers the same point as the 'A' plot, but in a different way, and more often than not it's the plot that starts the teaser off.

The 'C' Plot: This is usually the comic relief.

The Arc: This section attempts to tease out all of the material in the individual episodes which is part of the greater, over-arching five-year story. This includes primarily the Shadow War, but also the secrets concerning the Minbari prophecy and the Minbari souls as well as things to do with Psi Corps.

Observations: Things you may not have known about the episodes, or which you may have known but forgotten, or which you knew and remembered but hadn't thought about in that way before. This is the anecdotal bit of the episode guide, and the bit I actually find most interesting. But that's just me – you may prefer the **'Date'** section.

Koshisms: Kosh may come up with some seemingly nonsen-sical lines, but there's a widely held belief that everything he says is important. Judge for yourself.

Ivanova's Life Lessons: Ivanova has an attitude. Frequently the funniest things in the episode are her dry little asides.

Dialogue to Rewind For: Those things that either raise a titter or make you think.

Dialogue to Fast Forward Past: J. Michael Straczynski is a hugely talented writer, but every so often he forgets that he's writing the best SF TV series ever, and starts coming up with clunky, on-the-nose dialogue better suited to *Murder, She Wrote*.

Ships That Pass In The Night: J. Michael Straczynski has occasionally said that the names of the various spaceships in the series sometimes reflect something that is going on in the plot. Sometimes, of course, a cigar is just a cigar.

Other Worlds: *Star Trek* and its various children have a horrendous characteristic of throwing alien planet names around as if they were confetti, usually attached to the names of animals, drinks or food. *Babylon 5* initially copied them (Carnellian bed sheets, Antarean flarn) but thankfully soon stopped. The only planets mentioned now are usually those which have some connection to the plot.

Culture Shock: We've found out much about the various races inhabiting or passing through Babylon 5 during the course of the series – including humanity itself – and this section lists some of their more colourful habits, beliefs and distinguishing physical characteristics.

Station Keeping: Where *was* Grey 17 before it went missing? What *are* the airlocks on the station made out of? Who *is* Major Atumbe? These and many more questions about the operation of Babylon 5 itself are answered in this section.

Literary, Historical and Mythological References: Every so often J. Michael Straczynski (and almost never any of the other writers) will throw in what appears to be a reference to the 'outside' world. This encompasses not only SF novels (of which Straczynski has a wide knowledge) but also literature as a whole, including romantic poetry of the nineteenth century. I've tried to pick up all the references I've noticed. No doubt many have escaped me; no doubt also I've spotted a few that are just coincidences. No writer likes to be accused of plagiarism, and so I'll point out now that the references are just glancing nods of acknowledgement towards books and poems that have influenced or affected Straczynski personally: the plots and themes of *Babylon 5* are Straczynski's and his alone. *Babylon 5* is not *Lord of the Rings*, nor is it *Dune*. It isn't even the Bible.

I've Seen That Face Before: Despite the vast percentage of actors in Los Angeles who are 'resting' at any one time, the same faces keep cropping up in similar TV series. Partly this is due to type-casting (for which, read 'lazy casting agents'), but in the case of *Babylon 5* there are other reasons. Firstly, the specific demands of the make-up, especially for the legions of background aliens, mean that it is more cost-effective for a series to reuse an actor whose head has already been cast for a mask than to find a new actor who will have to go through the whole process from scratch. Secondly, J. Michael Straczynski has a fondness for using British actors in the series, because he believes their training in classical theatre gives them an edge that American actors sometimes lack. Thirdly, Straczynski also has a fondness for using actors whom he saw and liked in other genre series – Michael Ansara (a *Star Trek* veteran) is one example, as is June Lockhart (of *Lost in Space*) and David McCallum (of *The Man From U.N.C.L.E.*). Straczynski has also spoken of his wish to cast Tom Baker (the fourth Doctor in *Doctor Who*), Patrick McGoohan (the eponymous star of the cult Sixties series *The Prisoner*) and Paul Darrow (Avon from *Blake's 7*) in the future. Where an actor whose face is familiar from other programmes has appeared more than once in the series, I've listed their previous genre credits the first time they appear, and just referred back to their first appearance the second time they appear.

Accidents Will Happen: I've always loved bloopers in television programmes, ever since I saw an episode of *Doctor Who* in which a character accidentally pulled a lever off a control panel and kept on talking without missing a beat while trying to force the lever back into its hole. Accidents can reveal a lot about the televisual process: the constraints of time and money, and the last-minute creative improvisations that can make a good episode great but can leave flaws in their wake. And besides, they're frequently funny. I'm not claiming by any means that I've spotted everything that's gone wrong in an episode, but the fourth or fifth time I've watched certain of them I've stopped concentrating on the dialogue and the acting and started watching the little things in the background, and it's almost like watching the episode for the first time.

A note on precedence: if information in two televised episodes is contradictory, the information in the episode televised first is assumed to be correct. Information in televised episodes is always assumed to be more accurate than information in the comics, which is itself assumed to be more accurate than the information in the books. This reflects the level of participation by Straczynski in the three different media incarnations of the series.

Questions Raised: Many of the episodes raise questions which, we hope, will be answered during seasons 4 and 5. I've listed some of the more obvious ones here, along with some unresolved threads which are unlikely ever to be answered but still keep me awake at night. No, really, they do.

Thematic Episode Lists

You've got a spare day at home: you're bored and you want to watch some *Babylon 5*. But which episode? Well, how about tracing one particular plot strand through all of the episodes in which it appears? Not every episode is about the Shadow War: not every episode mentions Psi Corps. Here, to save you fighting your way through the next 300 pages, is a list of which episodes from the pilot to episode 407 contribute in a major way to the five major plot strands in the series.

Telepathy and Psi Corps

106	'Mind War'
109	'Deathwalker'
116	'Eyes'
206	'Spider in the Web'
207	'Soul Mates'
208	'A Race Through Dark Places'
Comics Issue 8	'Shadows Past and Present' part 4: 'Silent Enemies'
219	'Divided Loyalties'
Books	*Voices*
Comics Issue 11	'The Psi Corps and You!'
301	'Matters of Honor'
306	'Dust to Dust'
314	'Ship of Tears'
318	'Walkabout'
407	'Epiphanies'

Minbari and Human Souls

Pilot Episode	'The Gathering'
102	'Soul Hunter'
108	'And the Sky Full of Stars'
122	'Chrysalis'
201	'Points of Departure'
Comics Issues 1–4	'In Darkness Find Me'
202	'Revelations'

President Clark and Nightwatch

The Narn/Centauri War

The Shadow War

Recurring Characters

More than in most shows, the complexity of *Babylon 5*'s plot structure has meant that many characters – some major, some minor – have recurred over the first three seasons. This is a list of the ones that get credits on screen. They may have been credited in various different ways – the character of David Corwin, for instance, was down as Tech No. 1, Tech No. 2, and Dome Tech No. 2 before being given a name – but I've tried to list them under their most commonly recognised title.

Most of this section has been drawn up using the opening and closing credits of the episodes, but some characters may have appeared in episodes without getting a credit for it. Macaulay Bruton, for instance, plays Garibaldi's aide in episode 112 ('By Any Means Necessary') but doesn't get an on-screen credit. I've tried to catch all these occurrences wherever possible.

Note that I've left out some of the more uncertain characters. Kim Strauss, for instance, has appeared as a Drazi on numerous occasions, but it's difficult to tell whether it's meant to be the same Drazi every time. Others, such as a certain Minbari telepath, turn up once or twice but never get an on-screen credit.

Note also that I have not included the books or the comics here, just the televised episodes. This list is accurate up to episode 407.

Character	Actor	Episodes
Alexander, Lyta	Patricia Tallman	The Pilot, 219, 304, 318, 401, 403, 404, 406, 407
Allan, Zack	Jeff Conaway	206, 209, 212 to 214, 216, 219, 222, 302, 304, 305, 308, 309, 312, 316, 319, 321, 401, 403, 404, 407

Character	Actor	Episodes
Bartender	Kathryn Cressida	118, 208, 212
Bester, Alfred	Walter Koenig	106, 208, 306, 314, 407
Brother Theo	Louis Turenne	302, 304, 320
Centauri Emperor	Wortham Krimmer	401 to 405
Centauri Official	Damien London	121, 312, 401 to 403, 406, 407
Clark, Morgan	Gary McGurk	122, 202, 305
Corwin, David	Joshua Cox	113, 117, 119, 201, 203, 206, 210 to 213, 215, 217, 219 to 222, 303, 305, 307, 309 to 311, 316, 321, 322
Cotto, Vir	Stephen Furst	101, 103, 105, 107, 115, 122 to 203, 205, 207, 209, 212, 214, 216, 217, 221, 222, 303, 306, 309, 312, 315, 317, 320, 322, 401, 403 to 406
Cramer, Mary Anne	Patricia Healy	104, 112
Delenn	Mira Furlan	The Pilot to 102, 105, 107, 108, 110, 113, 115, 117 to 120, 122 to 202, 204, 207, 208, 210 to 212, 214 to 216, 218 to 306, 308, 310, 312 to 404, 406, 407
Delvientos, Eduardo	José Rey	112, 215
Draal	Louis Turenne/ John Schuck	118 to 119, 220, 305

Character	Actor	Episodes
Franklin, Dr Stephen	Richard Biggs	102, 104, 107 to 111, 115, 117, 119, 121 to 205, 207 to 220, 301 to 304, 306, 307, 311, 313 to 315, 318 to 322, 402 to 404, 406, 407
Garibaldi's Aide	Macaulay Bruton	106, 108, 112, 122, 202
Garibaldi, Michael	Jerry Doyle	The Pilot to 316, 319 to 322, 402 to 405, 407
G'Kar	Andreas Katsulas	The Pilot, 101, 103, 105 to 107, 109 to 113, 122 to 202, 205, 207, 209, 212, 215, 220 to 303, 305, 306, 308 to 311, 313, 314, 317, 318, 320, 322 to 404
Hague, General	Robert Foxworth	201, 211
Hampton, Lise	Denise Gentile	119, 120
Hidoshi, Senator	Aki Aleong	109, 112, 119
Hobbs, Dr Lilian	Jennifer Balgobin	315, 318
ISN Reporter (1)	Maggie Egan	101, 111, 122, 210, 218, 309, 310
ISN Reporter (2)	Lenore Kasdorf	114, 118 to 119
Ivanova, Susan	Claudia Christian	101 to 401, 403 to 407
Keffer, Warren	Robert Rusler	201, 205, 209, 214, 218, 222

Character	Actor	Episodes
Kosh	Ardwright Chamberlain	The Pilot, 101, 107, 109, 110, 113, 115, 122, 202, 209, 211, 213, 214, 216, 219, 221, 222, 301, 304, 306, 315 to 318, 322 to 404
Krantz, Major	Kent Broadhurst	120, 317
Lennier	Bill Mumy	105, 109, 115, 116, 121 to 202, 207, 209, 214, 216, 218, 221 to 302, 304, 308, 311, 314, 316 to 319, 322 to 403, 405, 406
Lorien	Wayne Alexander	401 to 404, 406
Medlab Technician	James Kiriyama-Lem	122, 124, 205, 313
Mollari, Londo	Peter Jurasik	The Pilot, 101, 103, 105, 107, 109 to 113, 115, 118, 119, 121 to 203, 205, 207, 209, 212, 214 to 217, 220, 222 to 304, 306, 309 to 312, 315 to 318, 320, 322 to 407
Morden	Ed Wasser	113, 122, 202, 216, 301, 311, 315, 322, 401, 404, 406
Na'Kal	Robin Sachs	222, 318
Na'Toth	Caitlin Brown/ Mary Kay Adams	105, 109, 112, 117, 122, 201, 212
Neroon	John Vickery	117, 211, 319

Character	Actor	Episodes
Psi Cop	Judy Levitt	208, 306
Rathenn	Time Winters	316, 319
Refa, Lord	William Forward	203, 217, 220, 311, 320
Sakai, Catherine	Julia Nickson	105, 106, 122
Sheridan, Anna	Beth Toussaint/ Melissa Gilbert	202, 321, 322
Sheridan, David	Unknown/ Rance Howard	216, 310, 315
Sheridan, John	Bruce Boxleitner	201 to 407
Sinclair, Jeffrey	Michael O'Hare	The Pilot to 122, 209, 316, 317
Ta'Lon	Marshall Teague	211, 303, 309
Tech No. 1	Marianne Robertson	101 to 109, 111 to 120
Welch, Lou	David L. Crowley	111, 116, 202, 203, 207, 210
Wellington, Ombuds	Jim Norton	115, 121
Winters, Talia	Andrea Thompson	101, 103, 106, 109, 117 to 119, 121 to 202, 206 to 208, 214, 216, 219
Zathras	Tim Choate	120, 316, 317

The Rep Company

Certain actors turn up again and again in *Babylon 5*, but under different make-up. They form a small team whose voices can often be recognised when their faces aren't (to the point where at least one of them was dubbed by another actor for one episode because he had played a different alien in the previous episode and his voice was so distinctive). In a strange way, they have become the real stars of *Babylon 5*: after all, the commander of the station can change and the series goes on, but the Drazi wouldn't be the Drazi without Kim Strauss.

'We're trying to do this show in a more responsible fashion than has been done in the past,' J. Michael Straczynski has said, 'and that means planning on every conceivable level. One thing we decided to do was form an alien repertory company to whom we add and subtract people, but we have a few constant players. The main expense used in bringing a new alien character in for a one-shot is the head mould. It's very expensive to do it – but we already have their head moulds and we can sculpt the head to match requirements. It's also kinda fun to see the same actor play a different alien character – they're familiar but different at the same time.'

Here's a list of the five main players in this little company, and the aliens they have played. Please note that this list is based on their actual credited appearance – if any of them have turned up in episodes without saying anything (and thus been bereft of a credit) then it hasn't been noted (or even noticed).

Jennifer Anglin

Centauri:
> probably 205 ('The Long Dark') – she's just credited as an alien, but there aren't that many obviously 'female' aliens in the episode

Minbari:
> 201 ('Points of Departure')

Narn:
> 212 ('Acts of Sacrifice')

Neil Bradley

Drazi:
> 203 ('The Geometry of Shadows');
> probably 205 ('The Long Dark') – he's credited just as
> an alien, but there aren't many aliens to choose from

Minbari:
> 214 ('There All the Honor Lies')

Narn:
> 209 ('The Coming of Shadows');
> 220 ('The Long, Twilight Struggle')

Jonathan Chapman

Brakiri:
> 315 ('Interludes and Examinations');
> 321 ('Shadow Dancing');
> 403 ('The Summoning')

Drazi:
> 203 ('The Geometry of Shadows');
> 301 ('Matters of Honor')

Minbari:
> 214 ('There All the Honor Lies')

Narn:
> 209 ('The Coming of Shadows');
> 220 ('The Long, Twilight Struggle')

Other:
> an alien ambassador in 201 ('Points of Departure'), but
> it's difficult to tell which race in particular

Mark Hendrickson

Drazi:
> 107 ('The War Prayer');
> 109 ('Deathwalker');
> 321 ('Shadow Dancing');
> 401 ('The Hour of the Wolf')

Markab:
> 214 ('There All the Honor Lies')

Minbari:

    108 ('And the Sky Full of Stars');
    120 ('Babylon Squared')

Narn:

    101 ('Midnight on the Firing Line');
    105 ('The Parliament of Dreams');
    122 ('Chrysalis');
    202 ('Revelations');
    221 ('Comes the Inquisitor');
    222 ('The Fall of Night')

Other:

    an alien ambassador in 201 ('Points of Departure'), but
    it's difficult to tell which race in particular;
    a long-haired alien with a hat in 111 ('Survivors')

Kim Strauss

Drazi:

    203 ('The Geometry of Shadows');
    222 ('The Fall of Night');
    306 ('Dust to Dust')

Human:

    201 ('Points of Departure')

Markab:

    205 ('The Long Dark');
    218 ('Confessions and Lamentations')

Minbari:

    311 ('Ceremonies of Light and Dark')

Narn:

    209 ('The Coming of Shadows');
    221 ('Comes the Inquisitor');
    310 ('Severed Dreams');
    405 ('The Long Night')

Military Ranks in Earthforce

The thinking behind the unified military rank structure of the Earth Alliance is that the military arms familiar to us in the twentieth century have blended into a larger structure. 'We're assuming that the navy and airforce have more or less merged into Earthforce,' J. Michael Straczynski has said, 'so there's influences from both sides.'

Earthforce as portrayed in *Babylon 5* is effectively divided into two arms: the arm that operates in space (the one whose officers wear blue uniforms) and the arm that operates on planets (the Marines – whose officers wear olive/brown uniforms). Of necessity, the vast majority of the military personnel we've seen on the programme are members of the space division. They're the ones who operate the military spaceships, man the Starfuries and command the space stations. We've seen members of the Marines only a few times, primarily in episodes 116 ('Eyes') and 210 ('GROPOS').

To avoid confusion, it's worth remembering that not everyone wearing a uniform on Babylon 5 is a member of Earthforce. The Security section is technically under the jurisdiction of Earth Alliance, and is commanded by a serving Earthforce NCO (Mr Garibaldi) but they are a separate component, staffed under Babylon 5's own financing. These and medical, scientific and environmental, and other areas have their own symbol, which is worn on the chest and shoulder. You can tell who works for Earthforce because they have the Earth Alliance symbol on the chest and the left shoulder: those who are employed directly by Babylon 5 have a specialisation patch on the chest and the stylised '5' symbol on the shoulder.

The following sections discuss some of the more visible means of telling who is who amongst the military personnel stationed on, or passing through, Babylon 5.

Rank Bars: All Earthforce officers have rank bars on the epaulettes of their jackets. Earthforce commanders have one bar below a triangle: Earthforce captains have two bars below a triangle. Majors have three pips spaced out along the length of the epaulette (although Sinclair had three pips grouped at the end of his epaulette in the pilot episode – 'The Gathering'). General Franklin had three stars in episode 210 ('GROPOS'). General Hague had five in episode 201 ('Points of Departure').

If you examine it closely, the Earthforce system of military ranks is an approximate cross between the twentieth-century US Navy and US Air Force/US Army rank structures, meaning that, like *Star Trek*, *Babylon 5* does display some unfortunate signs of unconscious American imperialism. After all, given that Earthdome is located in Geneva, why not base the ranks on the Swiss Army? **Table 1** lists the current US Army/USAF ranks and their equivalent US Navy ranks. **Table 2** takes all the Earthforce military personnel we've seen during the course of *Babylon 5* and attempts to map them into this structure so you can get some idea of who outranks whom.

A close examination of **Tables 1** and **2** will throw up some inconsistencies, which only serve to prove that the Earthforce military structure isn't entirely understood by us or (horrifyingly) by the makers of the programme. For instance, why is it that there are two Earthforce rank structures in parallel up to the rank of Captain/Colonel, both wearing blue uniforms (i.e. Major Ryan and Lieutenant Commander Ivanova)? Why do the Naval-equivalent ranks disappear above the rank of Captain (i.e. why do we never see an Admiral?)? Why does Captain Hiroshi defer to Major Ryan in episode 310 ('Severed Dreams') when she should outrank him?

Uniform: All Earthforce uniforms in the spacegoing division (i.e. Earthforce) are primarily blue, whereas Earthforce Marines have an olive/brown uniform, and security personnel and non-commissioned officers wear grey. The standard uniform for all these divisions has a darker leather strip set vertically down the right-hand side of the chest, a leather belt, leather epaulettes and leather cuffs. Note that the uniform changed slightly between 2259 and 2260: the cut was altered slightly and the leather features gained red piping.

Earthforce dress uniform is more of a grey colour, and is missing the brown leather features. In their place, there's a dark, braided trim with red piping extending down the front of the jacket and around the cuffs. A diagonal dark strip runs from the left shoulder to the centre of the waist, edged on the right in braid and red piping. Epaulettes are also dark and edged with red piping. A loop of gold braid is worn on the right shoulder. Decorations are worn on the left-hand side of the chest.

Braid is worn on the right shoulder for members of the President's entourage (i.e. Major Kemmer in episode 111 – 'Survivors') and for members of the Joint Chiefs of Staff (i.e. General Hague in episode 201 – 'Points of Departure').

Earth Alliance Badge: This is worn on the left-hand side of the chest (standard and dress uniform), and comprises the EA symbol: a stylised 'E' in the form of an inverted triangle over a stylised 'A', again in the form of a triangle.

Status Bars: The status bar ('stat bar') is the horizontal bar located directly beneath the Earth Alliance badge on the left-hand side of the standard uniform. It indicates the general area that the member of staff works in. Gold bars indicate commanders; silver bars indicate command staff; red indicates medical staff; green indicates security personnel; yellow indicates science staff. Note that Ivanova, being in between Command and Command Staff, has a divided bar, half gold and half silver. Note also that Generals have (by and large) a small gold star set in the centre of their status bars.

Arm Patches (left): These patches are worn on the left arm of the uniform jacket, close to the shoulder. They consist of an Earth Alliance symbol, but with a special design woven inside the stylised 'E'. These designs, like the status bars, denote which area the personnel are working in. Command is a starburst with lines that radiate into every area; security is a crosshair symbol; medical is a stylised caduceus inside a galaxy. You can spot which members of the Babylon 5 staff work for Earthforce and which don't: those that do (Sheridan,

Ivanova, Garibaldi and so on) have the Earth Alliance badge as their arm patch: others (Zack Allen, for instance) have the stylised '5' representing Babylon 5.

Arm Patches (right): Some personnel have a patch on the right shoulders of their uniform jackets: a winged shield surmounted by a five-pointed star. This signifies that the person in question is a qualified pilot: Sheridan has one, as does Ivanova and Garibaldi, but Franklin doesn't. Neither did General Hague. These patches came in during the course of the series: nobody wears them in season one.

Patches (assorted): Those people working in an official capacity on Babylon 5 but who are not members of Earthforce – security staff, medical staff etc. – have patches on the left-hand side of their jackets, where the Earth Alliance badge is on Earthforce personnel uniforms. The patch contains the same symbol as their Earthforce equivalents wear on the left arms of their jackets: security is a crosshair symbol; medical is a stylised caduceus inside a galaxy, and so on.

Other patches are worn on flying suits and fatigues. Usually they're issued to commemorate an event or mark membership of a particular unit. Some examles are:

Earthforce Off-World patch: a gold-handled sword against a starburst within what looks like a cross between a Möbius strip and a human DNA molecule

Earthforce Command patch: similar to the Earth Forces Off-World patch, but minus the starburst and with transverse red stripes against a black background

Babylon 5 Fighter Wing Squadron (Flying Nightmares) patch: the initials 'B5FA-1013' on the outer ring, with a Babylon 5 symbol on the left side outlined by up-and-down red stripes, and on the right a black up-and-down stripe bordered by the year of the Wing's formation: 2256

Earth Alliance Fighter Identification patch: a five-pointed command insignia circled by red and gold, overlaid with gold wings over the pilot's name

The insignia worn by those on the Battle of the Line: a triangular patch with 'Star Fury' on the upper left angle in silver on black, 'FA-23E' in silver on black on the right upper angle, with the inner part of the triangle divided in two by a vertical silver stripe, blue on the left, gold on the right, over which is the design of one of the fighters in full acceleration, leaving trails behind it, with the squadron number '361st – TFS', and the word 'UGLY' beneath it, and on the lower left angle of the patch, in black on silver, the words 'BUT WELL HUNG' (that being their motto)

USAF US ARMY	US NAVY
Officers	
General of the Army	Fleet Admiral
General	Admiral
Lieutenant General	Vice Admiral
Major General	Rear Admiral (upper half)
Brigadier General	Rear Admiral (lower half)
Colonel	Captain
Lieutenant Colonel	Commander
Major	Lieutenant Commander
Captain	Lieutenant
1st Lieutenant	Lieutenant (junior grade)
2nd Lieutenant	Ensign
Warrant Officers	
Warrant Officer Grade Four	Warrant Officer W-4
Warrant Officer Grade Three	Warrant Officer W-3
Warrant Officer Grade Two	Warrant Officer W-2
Warrant Officer Grade One	—
Non-Commissioned Officers	
Sergeant Major of the Army	Master Chief of the Navy
Sergeant Major	Master Chief
Master Sergeant	Senior Chief
Sergeant First Class	Chief Petty Officer
Staff Sergeant	1st Class Petty Officer
Sergeant	2nd Class Petty Officer
Corporal	3rd Class Petty Officer
Other Enlisted	
Private First Class	1st Class Seaman
Private (E-1)	2nd Class Seaman
Private (E-2)	3rd Class Seaman

1. **20th-century American military rank structure**

USAF US ARMY	US NAVY
Officers	
—	—
General *Franklin, Hague, Miller Netter, Smits*	—
—	—
—	—
Colonel *Ben Zayn*	Captain *Hiroshi, Maynard, Pierce, Sheridan*
—	Commander *Ivanova, Sinclair*
Major *Kemmer, Krantz, Ryan*	Lieutenant Commander *Ivanova*
—	Lieutenant *Keffer*
—	Lieutenant (j.g.) *Corwin*
2nd Lieutenant *Corwin*	—
Warrant Officers	
—	Warrant Officer W-4 *Garibaldi*
—	—
—	—
—	—
Non-Commissioned Officers	
—	—
—	—
Sergeant Major *Plug*	—
—	—
—	—
—	—
—	—
Other Enlisted	
Private First Class *Derman, Large*	—
Private (E-1) *Kleist*?	—
Private (E-2) *Yang*?	—

2. **Earth Alliance military personnel mapped on to 20th-century American military rank structure**

The Pilot

'I was there, at the dawn of the Third Age of Mankind. It began in the Earth year 2257 with the founding of the last of the Babylon stations, located deep in neutral space. It was a port of call for refugees, smugglers, businessmen, diplomats and travellers from a hundred worlds. It could be a dangerous place, but we accepted the risk because Babylon 5 was our last, best hope for peace.

'Under the leadership of its final commander, Babylon 5 was a dream given form . . . a dream of a galaxy without war, where species from different worlds could live side by side in mutual respect . . . a dream that was endangered as never before by the arrival of one man on a mission of destruction.

'Babylon 5 was the last of the Babylon stations. This is its story.'

– Ambassador Londo Mollari

Regular and Semi-Regular Cast:

Commander Jeffrey Sinclair: Michael O'Hare
Lt. Commander Laurel Takashima: Tamlyn Tomita
Security Chief Michael Garibaldi: Jerry Doyle
Ambassador Delenn: Mira Furlan
Ambassador Londo Mollari: Peter Jurasik
Ambassador G'Kar: Andreas Katsulas
Dr Benjamin Kyle: Johnny Sekka
Lyta Alexander: Patricia Tallman
Carolyn Sykes: Blair Baron

Observations: Series creator and co-Executive Producer J. Michael Straczynski had intended for the pilot episode to begin in a very different way. The episode would have started with a black screen which faded up to a grainy video image of Babylon 5. The voice of an unseen Interplanetary News

Network presenter would have said that the Earth Alliance station Babylon 5 was celebrating its first year of operation with the arrival of an ambassador from the Vorlon Empire. Over a montage of shots from inside Babylon 5, the INN presenter would have added that the five-mile-long station had been so successful in dealing with the many life forms that had passed through it that Earth Central had approved an appropriations bill to keep it operating for another five years. The montage of Babylon 5 interior shots would have receded into a star field while the unseen INN presenter moved on to another news item: the naming of a newly discovered star after President John F. Kennedy. The shrinking montage would have been replaced with a picture of Kennedy speaking before the Democratic convention on the eve of his presidential nomination, and on the soundtrack we would have heard Kennedy saying: 'I believe that the times require imagination, and courage, and perseverance. I'm asking each one of you to be pioneers toward that New Frontier. My call is to the young at heart, regardless of age; to the stout of spirit, regardless of party; to all those who respond to the scriptural call, "Be strong and of good courage. Be not afraid, neither be dismayed." For courage, not complacency, is our need today.' The image would have vanished into the star field, the shot would have panned across to where Babylon 5 sat in full, glorious colour, and we would have heard Laurel Takashima telling Delta Gamma Niner that it was clear for docking, as in the transmitted version.

The proposed opening was refused by Warner Brothers, who felt that it tied the series too much to the past (that, of course, being the point). Had it been used, Londo Mollari would have voiced a briefer closing narration.

The 'unused' opening sequence is interesting for several reasons: some minor, one major. The minor points are that Interplanetary News Network later became Interstellar News Network (ISN) and that Earth Central later became Earthdome or EarthGov. The major point is the explicit reference so early to a president who was later assassinated as part of what many believe to be an inside conspiracy, setting up the assassination of President Santiago in episode 122 – 'Chrysalis'.

It's a common misconception that Londo says, 'Under the leadership of its final commander, Jeffrey Sinclair, Babylon 5 was a dream given form . . .' He doesn't. There is no mention of the final commander's name.

Until a month or two before filming started, Ambassador G'Kar was actually Ambassador Jackarr and Lyta Alexander was Lyta Kim. Babylon 5's head of Medlab was, at one stage, supposed to be an Indian named Chakri Mendak. It was later changed to an African/American named (of course) Benjamin Kyle.

Welsh actor John Rhys-Davies was one of the people who auditioned for the role of Commander Jeffrey Sinclair. Rhys-Davies came to prominence as Patrick Stewart's right-hand man Macro in the historical drama, *I, Claudius*, although his face became known worldwide as Indiana Jones's friend Sallah in *Raiders of the Lost Ark* and *Indiana Jones and the Last Crusade*. More recently he has taken the role of Professor Maximillian Arturo in the US SF series *Sliders*.

J. Michael Straczynski's brief to conceptual designer Steve Burg on Kosh's encounter suit specified only that it had to be very mysterious, and that it had to be very massive in the upper shoulders. The latter requirement was, one presumes, in order to hide the wings that we hear in episodes 122 ('Chrysalis') and 219 ('Divided Loyalties') and see in 222 ('The Fall of Night') and 306 ('Dust to Dust'). Burg also had a hand in designing Babylon 5 itself, as well as the Starfuries, the Minbari cruisers and various other ships, making him one of the major influences on the look of the show.

'The Gathering'

Transmission Number: Not applicable
Production Number: Not applicable

Written by: J. Michael Straczynski
Directed by: Richard Compton

Del Varner: John Fleck   **The Senator:** Paul Hampton

Date: 3 January 2257 (as we discover in episode 219 – 'Divided Loyalties').

Plot: There's a lot of plot going on here, so much so that some bits of it don't make any sense, but the background information about the station and the political situation in the galaxy is set up almost undetectably and there's even (ambitiously) a lot of groundwork laid for the arc plot. Offhand, I can't think of any SF series pilots I've enjoyed more.

The 'A' Plot: A Narn supply ship refuses to submit to a weapons search, and is held outside the station while its captain fumes. A one-being short-range transporter is covertly ejected from it, attaches itself to the hull of Babylon 5 and cuts a hole. Meanwhile, a human named Del Varner arrives through more normal means and conspicuously avoids the station's new resident commercial telepath, Lyta Alexander. The being who arrived via the covert transporter uses the ID code of Laurel Takashima to gain entrance to Del Varner's quarters. Varner is expecting the being, but isn't expecting to be killed by it. Meanwhile, the fourth ambassador from the major spacefaring powers – Ambassador Kosh of the Vorlon Empire – arrives early. A welcoming committee is hastily arranged, but Sinclair is delayed getting to the docking bay. By the time he arrives, Kosh is lying comatose on the floor of the bay. Despite injunctions from the Vorlon Empire not to remove his encounter suit, Dr Kyle manages to get inside it and stabilise Kosh's condition, but he can do no more until they find out what has happened. Telepath Lyta Alexander is persuaded to scan Kosh, and determines that Kosh was poisoned by Commander Sinclair. Sinclair is relieved of command, and a meeting of the Babylon 5 Advisory Council, called to determine whether he should face trial, votes that he should be tried on the Vorlon homeworld. Dr Kyle finds traces of a poison named florazine, and starts creating an antitoxin. Garibaldi discovers the dead body of Del Varner as well as the covert transporter with which the assassin gained access to Babylon 5. Evidence in Del Varner's quarters indicate that the assassin is using a changeling net – a mechanism which allows beings to change their apparent form using a holographic field. Disguised as Lyta Alexander, the assassin makes another attempt on Kosh's life but is foiled by Dr Kyle, who wounds it with a medical laser. The assassin flees. Garibaldi and Sinclair track it by reconfiguring Babylon 5's external sensors to scan the interior of the station. As a Vorlon fleet appears and threatens to destroy the station if Sinclair is not handed over, Sinclair confronts the assassin and throws it into an electrical field, where it is badly injured. Its changeling net malfunctions, revealing it to be a Minbari. Rather than be captured, the assassin activates a bomb built into its own body and blows itself up. Delenn tells Sinclair that the assassin was a member of a branch of the Warrior caste that split off from the Minbari government after the Earth–Minbari war. Retracing Del Varner's movements, Sinclair realises that the assassin was on the Narn transport, and was supposed to rendezvous with Varner to pick up the changeling net (on the basis that a Minbari leaving a Narn transport ship would have attracted attention). Varner missed the rendezvous, so the Narn had to smuggle the assassin onto Babylon 5 using the covert transport and meet up with Varner there. Their intention was, presumably, to neutralise the growing threat of humanity. Sinclair confronts G'Kar with his knowledge. Kosh, meanwhile, recovers and joins the other ambassadors.

The Arc: Babylons 1, 2 and 3 were sabotaged and destroyed. Babylon 4 vanished twenty-four hours after becoming operational. We discover part of what happened to Babylon 4 in episode 120 ('Babylon Squared'), and most of the rest in episodes 316 and 317 ('War Without End' Parts One and Two).

Delenn claims that she has given Sinclair 'everything we have' on the Vorlons. She patently hasn't, as revelations in episodes 217 ('In the Shadow of Z'ha'dum') make clear. Given that Minbari do not lie except to help another save face (episode 121 – 'The Quality of Mercy') we should be charitable and assume what she is giving Sinclair is all she has with her on the station.

When what we later discover to be the Minbari assassin enters Del Varner's quarters, he does so using Laurel Takashima's security code. The scanner outside Varner's quarters clearly reads, 'Laurel Takashima Cleared' when he puts his hand on it. The intention was that Laurel Takashima was in on the assassination, giving support from inside Babylon 5 (as Garibaldi points out later on, *someone* is providing support from inside the station). Later, in episode 122, she would have been implicated in the assassination of President Santiago and the shooting of Garibaldi, and at the beginning of season 2 it would have been revealed that she was an agent of Psi Corps (almost certainly with a secondary personality). Most of the plot function that she would have served was transferred to Garibaldi's aide, Jack, when it was decided that actress Tamlyn Tomita would not carry on to the series, although some of it later went to the character of Talia Winters.

G'Kar offers Lyta Alexander money if she will either mate with him or provide the Narn regime with some of her genetic material. The Narn have no telepaths, and desperately want to breed some. This seemingly throwaway line gains significance in episode 314 ('Ship of Tears').

Sinclair was present at the Battle of the Line – the climactic moment of the Earth–Minbari war. The situation was hopeless, and the Minbari forces were poised to completely destroy the Earth. He set his Starfury to ram the nearest Minbari cruiser, but blacked out. When he awoke, twenty-four hours had passed and the Minbari had surrendered for no adequately explained reason. Sinclair could never remember what happened during those missing twenty-four hours.

When he confronts the Minbari assassin at the end of the episode, the assassin tells him, 'You have a hole in your mind,' indicating that others also know about his missing time. This is one of the most important plot threads to run through the series, and will crop up again in episodes 102 ('Soul Hunter'), 108 ('And the Sky Full of Stars') and 109 ('Deathwalker') before being partially explained in episode 201 ('Points of Departure') and further explained in episode 317 ('War Without End' Part Two).

Vorlon encounter suits are shielded against telepaths. Kosh later appears to take action to neutralise another telepath in episode 109 ('Deathwalker').

When Kosh walks into the reception at the end of the episode, he bows only to Sinclair and to Delenn. The bow to Delenn indicates that relations between the Vorlons and the Minbari are stronger than anybody else suspects, as detailed in episodes 219 ('In the Shadow of Z'ha'dum') and 316 ('War Without End' Part One).

Observations: Lyta Alexander is the first commercial telepath to be assigned to Babylon 5. She is either a sixth-generation or an eighth-generation telepath – the dialogue conflicts with her biography displayed on screen as she arrives.

Kosh's ship docks in Bay 8. By episode 213 ('Hunter, Prey') it's taken up residence in Bay 13.

G'Kar is married – he refers to his mate at one stage. He also has gill implants that enable him to breathe the atmosphere in the alien sector.

Laurel Takashima was stationed on Mars just before the Food Riots. Sinclair was her commanding officer at the time. That is when she would have run foul of Psi Corps and had her secondary personality implanted.

Florazine is a poison found in only one system in the Damocles Sector.

A changeling net is a mechanism which allows beings to change their apparent form using a holographic field. The energy field created is strong enough to cause death if used too much, and every civilised society has banned their use.

The Minbari assassin was, we are told, a member of a branch of the Warrior caste that split from the Minbari government after the Earth–Minbari war. We see more of these rogue Minbari in episode 201 ('Matters of Honor').

The title of the episode – 'The Gathering' – never appears on screen. Nonetheless, this is the official title.

Around 20 minutes of material was cut from this episode to bring it down to an acceptable 90 minutes. Most of the scenes cut added little or nothing to the central plot – Dr Kyle talking about a nurse he had to get rid of, a dust smuggler trying to get on board the station, getting caught, taking a hostage and getting shot, and a conversation between Delenn and Londo in which Delenn tells Londo off – but one in particular would have added an extra layer to what was going on. The scene (which appeared in a documentary about the making of 'The Gathering' broadcast on American television) had Sinclair's girlfriend Carolyn Sykes confronting Delenn in Delenn's quarters. Sykes asks Delenn how she could lie to Sinclair, and Delenn replies that she did not know the truth herself. This scene implies that Sykes now knows something that Sinclair doesn't, and that there is a connection of some kind between Sykes and Delenn.

'When the director had done his cut of the episode,' J. Michael Straczynski has said, 'there were things I wasn't sure about as far as the pacing, the timing, things left in, things that were taken out, but the director said, "I love it, this is terrific," and I didn't know enough and wasn't confident enough in my abilities as an editor at the time to do anything. I made two or three suggestions on the director's cut and let it go, deferring to his approach, and have bitterly regretted it ever since. If I were to go through today – going back to the original footage and recutting the entire movie – we could put back every single one of those scenes without a problem. It would be faster, you would get more out of the characters, and it would be a much better movie. That's a very sore point with me because of my own personal failure.'

Changes were made to the pilot episode before broadcast following responses from people who saw previews of it. Originally, it was intended that Delenn would have been male, that Mira Furlan's voice would have been electronically processed to make it more masculine, and that Delenn would have changed sex during the course of the series.

Some additional voiceover was done by Patricia Tallman to clarify a scene with Kosh in the Medlab.

Early versions of the script had a real shape-shifting alien rather than a Minbari with a changeling net. This was dropped when *Star Trek: Deep Space Nine* suddenly went into production with its own shape-shifting alien.

Early versions of the script also had a line from Sinclair indicating that there *was* an Earth ambassador on Babylon 5, but the ambassador fell ill and had to return home. During the interim, Sinclair is nominally filling that role.

A well-known science fiction writer (probably David Gerrold) was approached to novelise the script for 'The Gathering', and agreed. For various reasons it never got written. During the making of season one, Straczynski was publicly talking about novelising it himself.

This episode won the 1993 Emmy award for Special Visual Effects.

This episode is, so far, the only one to have been released on laserdisc, although this was in Japan. Despite repeated rumours to the contrary, the laserdisc is *not* in widescreen. I know, I've got it. And besides, unlike the rest of the series, the pilot episode was not filmed in widescreen. The episode was also released as a one-off rental video in the UK before the series itself was transmitted. This was prior to its release as part of the *Beyond Vision* video series.

Dialogue to Rewind For: G'Kar to Lyta Alexander: 'Would you prefer to be conscious or unconscious during the mating? I would prefer conscious, but I don't know what your . . . pleasure threshold is.'

Ships That Pass In The Night: United Spaceways Transport Delta Gamma Nine. Trading vessel *Ulysses* (belonging to Carolyn Sykes). And, of course, the entire Vorlon fleet.

Other Worlds: The Centauri Republic conquered the Beta System in only nine days (at least, according to Londo Mollari).

Del Varner's encyphered records mention planets such as Antares, Andat and what looks like the Hutchinson Colony.

Culture Shock: No human has ever seen a Vorlon, although there are legends of one who did and was turned to stone. Vorlons breathe an atmosphere which is poisonous to humans – methane, carbon dioxide and some form of sulphur compound. The body which rules the Vorlon Empire is referred to as the Vorlon High Command.

The Centauri conquered the Narn many years before and subjugated them for a long time. Now the Narn Regime is becoming more powerful, while the Centauri Republic is sliding into depravity and dissolution. The Centauri Republic used to own most of the sector of space in which Babylon 5 is located, but now they only have control of twelve worlds.

Station Keeping: Babylon 5 is a free trading post run by Commander Sinclair, who also chairs the Babylon 5 Advisory Council, comprising representatives from the Narn, Centauri, Minbari and Vorlon Governments.

Telepaths are forbidden to gamble in the Babylon 5 casinos.

Literary, Mythological and Historical References: 'Sooner or later,' Sinclair tells Lyta Alexander, 'everyone comes to Babylon 5.' This is a deliberate nod towards the Humphrey Bogart film *Casablanca*, which is about a bar in Morocco during the Second World War where people from all sides can come to drink. 'Sooner or later, everyone comes to Rick's bar,' is the relevant line from the film. *Babylon 5* is quite consciously *Casablanca* in space.

Sinclair's explanation to Delenn concerning why Babylon 5 was built when the first four Babylon stations were destroyed deliberately echoes comments made by Winston Churchill during the Second World War when someone asked him what would happen if a V-2 rocket destroyed Big Ben. In essence, his answer was that it would be rebuilt, and rebuilt again if it was destroyed again, and rebuilt as many times as were necessary.

Sinclair quotes from Alfred, Lord Tennyson's poem *Ulysses* at the end of the episode.

I've Seen That Face Before: John Fleck, the actor playing Del Varner, played an ongoing character in the legal drama *Murder One*.

The Stewart Copeland who composed the music for this episode is the same Stewart Copeland who used to be the drummer for rock band the Police.

A number of production staff appear in the opening sequences of the story. Production designer John Iacovelli is in the bar (he's the one with the beard) with another production designer (perhaps they hadn't finished designing the set when the filming started). Christy Marx (writer of episode 115 – 'Grail') can be seen, barely, in a couple of casino shots. John Stears (Special Effects Supervisor) is running the wheel of fortune in the casino. Ron Thornton (Visual Effects Designer) can be seen as one of the two homeless people sitting on the floor in the Brown Sector (he's the one on the right). One of the show's production assistants plays a hooker just visible behind them.

Accidents Will Happen: Dr Kyle says that Kosh's atmosphere is composed of methane, sulphur and carbon dioxide. This is obvious nonsense: while methane and carbon dioxide are gases, sulphur is a yellow powder. He probably means sulphur dioxide, which *is* a gas.

It's stated that it will take Ambassador Kosh's ship two hours to decelerate from hyperspace after it has left the jumpgate. This technological limitation was dropped when the series proper was made – note that in episode 318 ('Walkabout') it takes a ship almost identical to this one just a few moments before it is able to dock with the station.

G'Kar points out that Lyta Alexander is a sixth-generation telepath, and she doesn't correct him, but her computer record (as seen when she arrives on the station) says she's an eighth-generation telepath.

All monitors showing Kosh are meant to be turned off while his encounter suit is open, and yet some are very clearly turned on later in the episode while there is still a hole in his chest.

Questions Raised: 'Why is it called Babylon 5?' Lyta Alexander asks Sinclair. Doesn't she know? Where has she been for the past few years?

Why does Delenn give Sinclair her files on the Vorlons? He makes no use of the information – there's obviously not enough there to help when Kosh is poisoned.

If Carnellian bed sheets are completely frictionless, does this mean that Sinclair and Carolyn Sykes spend all night sliding out of bed and getting back in again, only to slide out of the other side?

The only two people in the docking bay when Kosh is poisoned are Kosh and the assassin. Which one of them raises the station alarm that blares out? Not the assassin, one presumes, but if it's Kosh, how does he know which button to push?

Why use a Minbari assassin and then try to smuggle him on to Babylon 5 from a Narn ship? Why not use a Narn assassin? Alternatively, why not put the Minbari assassin on to an ordinary liner at some planet where he won't be as obvious?

If the assassin planned to kill Kosh, why use a changeling net? The assassin had no way of knowing that a telepath would break all rules and injunctions and scan the Vorlon, thus seeing the image of the assassin. If the assassin *didn't* plan to kill Kosh, but only injure him and use the changeling net to ensure he blamed Sinclair for the attack, then why did the assassin make a second attempt and blow his own cover?

Why is such a play made about Lyta Alexander meeting Del Varner on a number of occasions?

Why, if the assassin is armed, does he jump on Sinclair's back rather than burn a hole in it?

What, exactly, are the Narn hoping to get out of all this?

Season 1:
'Signs and Portents'

'It was the dawn of the Third Age of Mankind, ten years after the Earth–Minbari War. The Babylon Project was a dream given form. Its goal: to prevent another war by creating a place where humans and aliens could work out their differences peacefully. It's a port of call, a home away from home for diplomats, hustlers, entrepreneurs and wanderers: humans and aliens wrapped in two million, five hundred thousand tons of spinning metal, all alone in the night. It can be a dangerous place, but it's our last, best hope for peace.

'This is the story of the last of the Babylon stations.

'The year is 2258. The name of the place is Babylon 5.'

– Commander Jeffrey David Sinclair

Regular and Semi-Regular Cast:

Commander Jeffrey Sinclair: Michael O'Hare
Lt. Commander Susan Ivanova: Claudia Christian
Security Chief Michael Garibaldi: Jerry Doyle
Ambassador Delenn: Mira Furlan
Ambassador Londo Mollari: Peter Jurasik
Ambassador G'Kar: Andreas Katsulas
Dr Stephen Franklin: Richard Biggs
Talia Winters: Andrea Thompson
Vir Cotto: Stephen Furst   **Lennier:** Bill Mumy
Na'Toth: Caitlin Brown   **Catherine Sakai:** Julia Nickson
David Corwin: Joshua Cox
C&C Technician: Marianne Robertson

Observations: Certain characters have vanished between the pilot and the start of the first season. Primarily this was done in order to get the balance right between the individual members of the ensemble cast. 'We wanted to raise the energy level,' J. Michael Straczynski has said, 'and we recast different actors with different energy levels.' Johۦny Sekka, who played the idiosyncratic Dr Benjamin Kyle, was replaced by the more viewer-friendly Richard Biggs as Dr Stephen Franklin. Tamlyn Tomita's Laurel Takashima left to make way for Claudia Christian's Susan Ivanova. Patricia Tallman, who played station telepath Lyta Alexander in the pilot episode, has claimed that she would have liked to continue but negotiations with her fell apart. Andrea Thompson took over as Talia Winters. The planned semi-regular character of Sinclair's girlfriend Carolyn Sykes (played by Blaire Baron) was also ditched in favour of another girlfriend named Catherine Sakai.

Many actresses were considered for the new regular character of Susan Ivanova, including supermodel Iman (who had previously appeared as a shape-changing alien in *Star Trek VI: The Final Frontier*). Claudia Christian was offered the part almost as soon as she walked in. 'I went in by twelve,' she recalls, 'and by three o'clock I had got the role.'

Three new regular characters were introduced in the form of aides for the three ambassadors: Stephen Furst as the Centauri Vir Cotto, Bill Mumy as the Minbari Lennier and, after a couple of false starts, Julie Caitlin Brown as the Narn Na'Toth.

Richard Compton – director of the pilot episode ('The Gathering') – is credited as Co-Producer for the first nine episodes made (which aren't, of course, the first nine episodes shown). After that, his credit vanishes. All Straczynski would say was: 'We initiated a parting of the ways with Richard.'

The voice at the end of each episode saying '*Babylon 5*, produced by Babylonian Productions Inc. and distributed by Warner Bros. Domestic Television Distribution' is that of Co-Producer George Johnson.

Two possible scripts by David Gerrold – 'Target Unknown' and 'Metaphors and Body Counts' – went to outline stage only. Two possible scripts by Harlan Ellison were discussed, although nothing was ever written down – 'Midnight in the Sunken Cathedral' and 'Demon on the Run'. Both scripts were delayed due to his health problems and the 1994 Los Angeles earthquake. 'Demon on the Run' would have been a sequel to his 1964 second season episode of *The Outer Limits*, 'Demon With A Glass Hand', and would have featured Robert Culp reprising his role as Trent – the man with the fate of humanity in the palm of his hand. It would have gone after episode 120 ('Babylon Squared'). 'Midnight in the Sunken Cathedral' would have gone between episodes 112 ('By Any Means Necessary') and 113 ('Signs and Portents'). Harlan Ellison later reused the title 'Midnight in the Sunken Cathedral' for a story in his *Harlan Ellison's Dream Corridor* comic anthology.

'Midnight on the Firing Line'

Transmission Number: 101
Production Number: 103

Written by: J. Michael Straczynski
Directed by: Richard Compton

Senator: Paul Hampton   **Carn Mollari:** Peter Trencher
Narn Captain: Mark Hendrickson

Date: According to J. Michael Straczynski, it's been around six months since the events of the pilot episode.

Plot: The episode is, quite rightly, functional rather than decorative, but it does the job and does it well. It's a shame that none of the four plots connect with each other, but they do give the impression that there's a lot happening on the station on a regular basis.

The 'A' Plot: Narn forces attack a Centauri colony on the planet Ragesh 3, destroying its defences and taking captive the 5,000 or so Centauri colonists (one of whom is the nephew of Londo Mollari – the Centauri Ambassador to Babylon 5). The Centauri Republic decide to do nothing because they do not wish to provoke a war. Londo, acting against instructions, attempts to get the League of Non-Aligned Worlds to take action against the Narn, but G'Kar outmanoeuvres him by showing a message from Londo's nephew claiming that the colonists asked for Narn intervention. Data crystals discovered on a Narn command and control ship that has been helping Raiders attack transport ships prove that the Narns were not invited to Ragesh 3 by the colonists and that the attack on the colony was unprovoked. Sinclair embarrasses G'Kar into arranging for a withdrawal of Narn forces.

The 'B' Plot: Babylon 5 receives a long-range distress call from a ship attacked by Raiders, but by the time any scrambled Starfuries can get there the ship is gutted, the crew dead and the Raiders gone. This is the third ship in a month to be attacked in that sector, and the Raiders appear to be using heavier weapons than usual. Garibaldi wonders how the Raiders get their information about the locations of the ships, and discovers that one company has been responsible for selling the jumpgate routes for all the ships that have been attacked. Their information has somehow been hacked by the Raiders. Only one ship on their list hasn't been attacked, but it is carrying 500 refugees. If the Raiders attack it, the loss of life will be devastating. Sinclair leads a group of Starfuries out to the ship's current location and finds it being attacked by Raiders. He fights them off, rescues the ship and discovers a Narn command and control ship coordinating the Raider attack.

The 'C' Plot: (a) Talia Winters has been trying to register her arrival with Ivanova for several weeks with no success. It almost seems as if Ivanova has been avoiding her. Garibaldi tells Talia when to catch Ivanova off-duty in the bar, and Talia strikes up a conversation. Ivanova tells Talia that she doesn't like Psi Corps – Ivanova's mother was a telepath, and, rather than join Psi Corps or go to prison, she elected to take telepathy-suppressing drugs. The drugs affected her mind and her body to the point where she eventually committed suicide. (b) The election of the new Earth Alliance President is going on, with incumbent Louis Santiago fighting challenger Marie Crane. Santiago wins.

The Arc: Londo knows that he will die in twenty years' time with G'Kar's hands around his neck and his hands around G'Kar's. We see the truth of this prophecy in episode 317 ('War Without End' Part Two).

Kosh is temporarily out of his encounter suit in this episode, but all we see is a bright light behind a screen. We see what exactly it is that's glowing in episode 404 ('Falling Toward Apotheosis').

There are scenes in this episode of Delenn working on the device she uses in episode 122 ('Chrysalis') to transform herself.

We discover in this episode that Ivanova's mother was a telepath, and committed suicide as a result. The legacy of this family connection will return to haunt Ivanova later in the series, most particularly in episode 219 ('Divided Loyalties'). We also get a hint in this episode that Talia Winters is attracted to Ivanova – a plot strand that will also be concluded in episode 219 ('Divided Loyalties').

The Narn attack on Ragesh 3 is the spark that will later ignite a war in episode 209 ('The Coming of Shadows').

Observations: This episode marks the first appearance of Ivanova, Talia Winters and Vir Cotto.

We hear in this episode that terrorists detonated a nuclear device in San Diego at some stage in the past. We see the results in episode 206 ('Spider in the Web').

The Narn sold weapons to humanity during the war with the Minbari but, as Sinclair points out, the Narn would sell weapons to anyone.

The photo of the Earth Alliance president, Louis Santiago, is actually of co-Executive Producer Douglas Netter. The photograph of Marie Crane, the woman running against him, is of the *Babylon 5* wardrobe designer, Anne Bruice (later Anne Bruice-Aling).

This episode was originally entitled 'Blood and Thunder'.

G'Kar is eating spoo when Londo confronts him. Spoo was the subject of a running joke in the animated series *He-Man and the Masters of the Universe*, on which J. Michael Straczynski and Larry DiTillio worked. This is what Straczynski has said about spoo:

'Spoo is/are (the plural of spoo is spoo) small, white, pasty, mealy critters, rather wormlike, and generally regarded as the ugliest animals in the known galaxy by just about every sentient species capable of starflight, with the possible exception of the Pak'ma'ra, who would simply recommend a more rigorous programme of exercise. They are also generally considered the most delicious food in all of known space, regardless of the individual's biology, almost regardless of species, except for the Pak'ma'ra, who like the flavour but generally won't say so simply to be contrary.

'Spoo are raised on ranches on worlds with a damp, moist, somewhat chilly climate so that their skin can acquire just the right shade of paleness. Spoo travel in herds, if moving a total of six inches in any given direction in the course of a given year can actually be considered moving. They stay in herds ostensibly for mutual protection, but the reality is that if they weren't propped up against one another, most of them would simply fall down. They do not howl, bark, moo, purr, yap, squeak or speak. Mainly, they sigh. Herds of sighing spoo can reportedly induce unparalleled bouts of depression, which is why most spoo ranchers wear earmuffs even when it's only mildly cold, damp, wet and dreary outside. If there is any life-or-death struggle for dominance within the spoo herd, it has not yet been detected by modern science.

'Spoo ranching is one of the least-regarded professions known. Little or no skill is required, once you've got a planet with the right climate. You bring in two hundred spoo, plop them down in the middle of your ranch, and go back to the nearby house. Soon you've got more. When it comes time to cull out the ones ready for market (the softest, mealiest, palest, most forlorn-looking spoo of the pack), little physical effort is required since they're incapable of rapid movement without falling over (see above). They do not resist, fight, or whine; they only sigh more loudly. When spoo harvest time comes, the air is full of the sound of whacking and sighing, whacking and sighing. Even an experienced spoo rancher can only harvest for brief periods at a time, due to the increased volume of sighing, which even the sound of whacking cannot altogether erase (also see above). Some have simply gone mad.

'Spoo are the only creatures of which the Interstellar Animal Rights Protection League says, simply, "Kill 'em."

'Fresh spoo (served at an optimum temperature of 62 degrees) is served in cubed sections, so that they bear as little resemblance as possible to the animal from which they have just been sliced. Spoo is usually served alongside a chablis, or a white zinfandel.

'Further information on the care, feeding, eating and whacking of spoo can be found in the second edition of the Interstellar Guide to Fine Dining.'

So – now you know.

J. Michael Straczynski had intended to refer to the intestinal beacon (the one Sinclair claims to have implanted into G'Kar) in a later episode. The idea would have been for G'Kar and Garibaldi to have been trapped somewhere and G'Kar not to be concerned since he knew Sinclair would be able to track him down via the beacon.

Andrea Thompson's first scene as Talia Winters was the one where she calls for a lift, the doors open and Garibaldi is standing there. During rehearsals, everything went OK. When it came time to shoot the scene for real, Andrea Thompson walked up to the lift doors and they opened to reveal Jerry Doyle with his trousers around his ankles.

Koshisms: Kosh: 'They are alone. They are a dying people. We should let them pass.' Sinclair: 'Who – the Narn or the Centauri?' Kosh: 'Yes.'

It's interesting to note that a scene dropped from the script had Kosh in the Observation Dome, looking out through the window as a ship passed overhead with its lights shining down at him. 'Ahhh . . . beautiful,' he would have said, followed by a long pause as he looked around the Dome. 'I will miss this . . . when it is gone.'

Ivanova's Life Lessons: 'Mr Garibaldi, you're sitting at my station, using my equipment. Is there a reason for this or should I just go ahead and snap your hands off at the wrist?'

Dialogue to Rewind For: Londo Mollari: 'We thought your world was Beta 9, it was actually Beta 12. OK, we made a mistake. I'm sorry. Here, open my wrist.'

Londo: 'We should have wiped out your kind when we had

the chance.' G'Kar: 'What happened – run out of small children to butcher?'

G'Kar: 'I confess that I look forward to the day when we have cleansed the universe of the Centauri and carved their bones into little flutes for Narn children.'

Other Worlds: Beta 9 and Beta 12 are two in a series of Centauri colonies. Note that in the pilot episode ('The Gathering') Londo refers to the Centauri conquering the Beta System.

Culture Shock: Centauri don't have major arteries in their wrists. They do, however, have DNA (deoxyribonucleic acid doesn't have to be the only chemical that life is based on).

Centauri know how, and sometimes when, they are going to die. The knowledge comes to them in a dream.

I've Seen That Face Before: Paul Hampton recreates his role as the Senator back on Earth with whom Sinclair has direct dealings.

Accidents Will Happen: When Vir shows Londo the pictures of Narn forces attacking Ragesh 3, Londo spots a Narn Heavy Fighter and instructs the computer to isolate and expand it. Unfortunately, a rectangular highlighting box appears around the fighter before Londo actually says anything. Should that computer join Psi Corps?

'Soul Hunter'

Transmission Number: 102
Production Number: 102

Written by: J. Michael Straczynski
Directed by: Jim Johnston

Soul Hunter: W. Morgan Sheppard
Soul Hunter No. 2: John Snyder

Plot: A strong episode with a very creepy performance from W. Morgan Sheppard. The moral questions are sidestepped rather when we discover that the Soul Hunter is mad, but there's still a lot to think about in the clash between saving souls and setting them free.

The 'A' Plot: An unidentified ship comes through the jumpgate, out of control and on a collision course with Babylon 5. Sinclair takes a Starfury out and puts a grapple on to the ship, which has been the subject of weapons fire. The ship is towed into Babylon 5 and its sole occupant, close to death, is moved to medlab. Delenn, visiting medlab, recognises the alien as a Soul Hunter and tries to kill it, but is stopped by Sinclair. She explains that Soul Hunters are drawn to the moment of death of important beings ('leaders, thinkers, poets, dreamers, blessed lunatics' as the Soul Hunter later puts it) and attempt to steal the soul of the one who has died. As soon as word gets out that there is a Soul Hunter on board the station, the alien sector closes down and a number of ships attempt to leave. A second Soul Hunter arrives and tells Sinclair that the first Soul Hunter is deeply disturbed – driven mad by a succession of failures to preserve important souls and the consequent disgrace of their order. The first Soul Hunter had decided to take matters into his own hands – rather than wait for beings to die, he went out and killed them himself. By this time the first Soul Hunter has escaped from medlab and has kidnapped Delenn – having recognised her as a member of the Minbari Grey Council, he has decided to add her to his collection. Hidden away in the bowels of the station, he connects her up to his soul-catching machine and starts draining her blood to kill her painlessly. The Soul Hunter's location is pinpointed by the second Soul Hunter – who can sense Delenn's dying feelings – and Sinclair interrupts. The Soul Hunter is shot and injured by Sinclair and, while his previously captured souls form a wall preventing him from intruding, Sinclair turns the soul-catching machine away from Delenn and towards the Soul Hunter. He dies, Delenn is saved and the second Soul Hunter leaves. Delenn destroys the containers holding the Soul Hunter's collection of souls, freeing them.

The Arc: The Minbari believe in the reincarnation of souls, whereas the Soul Hunters believe that souls die if not preserved. This Minbari fascination with souls – and in particular with Sinclair's soul – will echo through the series, and will be addressed again primarily in episodes 201 ('Points of Departure') and 317 ('War Without End' Part Two). The key line here is when the Soul Hunter says to Sinclair, 'Why do you fight for her? Don't you understand? She is Satai. She is *Satai*. I have seen her soul. They're using you. They're *using* you.' They're not actually using Sinclair, of course – just watching him.

When he looks into her soul, the Soul Hunter says to Delenn, 'You would *plan* such a thing? You would *do* such a thing? Incredible!' He's referring to the transformation that Delenn chooses to undergo, starting in episode 122 ('Chrysalis') and ending in episode 202 ('Revelations').

When Delenn is in medlab after Sinclair has rescued her, she looks up at him and says, 'I knew you would come. We were right about you.' This links to two different later episodes. On the one hand, 'I knew you would come,' is later explained when Delenn tells a story in episode 218 ('Confessions and Lamentations') about a mysterious figure that appeared to her when she was lost as a child and said, 'I will not allow harm to come to my little ones, here in my great house.' The figure J. Michael Straczynski has said, was the revered historical Minbari figure Valen, and the connection between Sinclair and Valen is explored further in episode 317 ('War Without End' Part Two).

Delenn was present at the death of Dukhat, and the Minbari formed a wall of bodies to prevent the Soul Hunters getting to Dukhat's body. Dukhat was on board the Minbari ship that was fired upon by the Earth Alliance ship *Prometheus*, thus starting the Earth–Minbari war.

Observations: Sinclair has known Delenn about two years. Since the pilot episode was just over six months ago, we can assume they first met between a year and eighteen months before the events of the pilot episode took place.

In this episode Sinclair can't determine whether the Soul Hunter is alive or dead inside his ship until they get it inside Babylon 5 and open it up. In episode 218 ('Confessions and

Lamentations') however, a Starfury's sensors can distinguish between living Markab and dead Markab. Being charitable, the Soul Hunter's ship has better shielding.

The Soul Hunter claims to have been to Earth.

A typical human lifetime in 2258 is almost 100 years.

J. Michael Straczynski has said that we will see more Soul Hunters – eventually.

According to Straczynski, 'There was a version of "Soul Hunter" which went out as a first draft, which when I read it again, I realised was just *wrong*. So I had all copies of the script recalled, sending a memo explaining that "I had been momentarily possessed by an idiot".'

Ivanova's Life Lessons: Franklin: 'You're a pessimist.' Ivanova: 'I'm Russian. We understand these things.'

Ships That Pass In The Night: Star Liner *Asimov* arrives at the station.

Culture Shock: The Minbari call the Soul Hunters *Shag Toth* (pronounced 'shag tot'). It's an unfortunate name . . .

Minbari have almost translucent red blood, and they can lose an awful lot of it without dying.

Literary, Mythological and Historical Reference: The star liner *Asimov* was, of course, named after the famed SF author Isaac Asimov, who died shortly before the episode was written.

I've Seen That Face Before: W. Morgan Sheppard is a British actor who has appeared in a number of television series on this side of the Atlantic before transferring his talents to America. His primary genre credits are as Blank Reg in *Max Headroom*, as Dr Ira Graves in the *Star Trek: The Next Generation* episode 'The Schizoid Man' and as the Klingon in charge of the Rura Penthe penal colony in *Star Trek VI: The Undiscovered Country*.

Accidents Will Happen: When Delenn is strapped to the Soul Hunter's table and he is draining her blood, there is a shot where the camera pans from Delenn to the glass jar holding her blood. If you look carefully, her blood is dripping *upward* from the container into the tubes leading from her body. The shot has been played backward to get the pan the way the producer wanted it.

Questions Raised: On what charge is Sinclair holding the Soul Hunter in medlab? He refuses to let it leave, but it's not under arrest and it hasn't committed any crime. Isn't this an abuse of the legal system?

The second Soul Hunter talks about his 'order' rather than his race, and their disgrace when they failed repeatedly to obtain souls they were trying to get. This implies that the Soul Hunters are only a part of a larger alien culture, rather than an entire race in their own right, otherwise there would be nobody in whose eyes they were disgraced.

How did the Soul Hunter carry his collection of souls, his table, his glass jars and his impressively massive soul-collecting machine all the way from his ship to the level where he hides without anyone noticing him?

When the *Prometheus* fired on the Minbari ship and started the war, didn't anybody notice the sudden flurry of Soul Hunter ships in the vicinity?

'Born to the Purple'

Transmission Number: 103
Production Number: 104

Written by: Lawrence G. DiTillio
Directed by: Bruce Seth Green

Adira Tyree: Fabiana Udenio   **Trakis:** Clive Revill
Ko'Dath: Mary Woronov
Andrei Ivanova: Robert Phalen

Plot: A fun little episode with a wonderful turn from Clive Revill as Trakis. It gives us a perspective on Londo as an incurable romantic and a tired republican that is worth looking back on as he descends deeper into the abyss later in the series.

The 'A' Plot: Londo Mollari should be engaged in important diplomatic negotiations with the Narn, but instead he is spending all his time with Adira Tyree, a Centauri dancer

93

with whom he is smitten. Unfortunately for him, Adira is a slave owned by the rather slimy Trakis. Trakis is using Adira to get to Londo's Purple Files – a collection of blackmail information Londo has collected on all the Centauri houses. Trakis can sell that information to the Narn, who can use it to topple the entire ruling class of the Centauri Republic. Adira drugs Londo and uses a mind probe to retrieve his computer access codes from his mind. She copies the Purple Files, and arranges to meet Trakis on the Zocalo, but can't go through with the exchange and runs off instead. Waking, Londo panics when he finds out that Adira has gone and his files are missing. He confides in Commander Sinclair, and together they scout the underbelly of the station until they discover where Adira is hiding. Trakis has had Londo bugged, however, and as soon as he hears where Adira is he goes looking for her himself, distracting Londo and Sinclair with gunfire. Sinclair arranges for G'Kar to set up a meeting with Trakis, ostensibly to buy the data crystal with the Purple Files on, with Talia Winters monitoring the discussion. Talia mentions Adira's name in passing, and scans Trakis's mind to discover where she has been hidden. Trakis is arrested, and Adira leaves Babylon 5 after Londo has arranged for her to be given her freedom. She promises to come back to him one day.

The 'B' Plot: Garibaldi is monitoring unauthorised transmissions on the station's official gold channel, but he can't trace who is making them. Eventually he manages to intercept a call while it is being made, and discovers that Ivanova is using the gold channel to talk to her dying father. While Garibaldi watches the call, her father dies. Knowing that Ivanova won't be making any more calls, he gently lets her know that she's been rumbled, and offers to buy her a drink.

The 'C' Plot: Ko'Dath, the new head of G'Kar's diplomatic staff, arrives early on the station, and is shocked by G'Kar's lax attitude and by the general tone of moral depravity on the station.

The Arc: Adira returns to Babylon 5 in episode 315 ('Interludes and Examinations'), where she becomes a pawn in the power struggle between Londo and the mysterious Shadows.

Observations: Londo's three computer access codes are, 'wine', 'women' and 'song'. Three access codes, three wives . . . anyone would think he was a Minbari.

Trakis's race are never named on screen, but there's a distinct similarity between him and Caliban from episode 114 ('TKO'). According to J. Michael Straczynski he is meant to have originally been a Centauri slave, thus causing his resentment of them, but this was never explored in the episode.

Ko'Dath, played by Mary Woronov, was originally meant to be a regular member of the cast, and her name appears in the opening credits to prove it. Unfortunately she had huge problems with the Narn make-up and had to leave the series. Rather than recast the part, her plot function was switched to the new character of Na'Toth.

Straczynski has said, 'We *did* have a thing in mind where Londo sits up in bed, having just had wonderful sex, and his hair is now hanging limp . . . but in a sudden burst of sanity we decided against it.'

This episode was originally entitled 'Amaranth'.

Dialogue to Rewind For: Londo to Vir: 'What do you want, you moon-faced assassin of joy?'

Dialogue to Fast Forward Past: When Londo is told that he has to discuss the Euphrates Treaty with the Narn, he says that 'I would rather kiss a Jovian treeworm.' This has the definite ring of a Larry DiTillio line. Only he seems to refer to Jovian things (Jovian treeworms, Jovian Sunspots . . .)

Trakis, telling Adira how to get the information he needs from Londo's mind: 'Use the mind probe.' To which every *Doctor Who* fan watching choruses, 'No, not the mind probe!'

Ships That Pass In The Night: The *Piraeus*, and an unnamed Balosian freighter. The Greek port of Piraeus was originally a port of ancient Athens, and thus contemporary with ancient Babylon.

Other Worlds: The planet Davo is (probably) in the Aries Sector.

Culture Shock: *Jala*, a Centauri drink usually served hot, is bright blue in colour.

Centauri writing goes from left to right and from top to bottom.

Trakis has been described as a Golian in documents connected with the series.

Station Keeping: Fresh Air is, allegedly, the finest restaurant on Babylon 5.

I've Seen That Face Before: Clive Revill, who plays Trakis, is a stalwart of British film. He may be *least* known, however, as the voice of the Emperor in the 1980 *Star Wars* film *The Empire Strikes Back*. As far as I'm concerned, he uttered one of the ten best lines in cinema history when he played the Russian ballet impresario Rogozhin in Billy Wilder's 1970 film *The Private Life of Sherlock Holmes*. Introducing Holmes to a ballet dancer who wants to sleep with him, he says, 'Madame is great admirer of yours. She has read every story. Her favourite is *Big Dog From Baskerville*.' Holmes (Robert Stephens) can only murmur, 'I'm afraid it loses something in translation.'

Mary Woronov, who played Ko'Dath, began her career as an artist in 1960s New York and appeared in several of Andy Warhol's experimental films, including the 1966 *The Chelsea Girls*. She moved into the mainstream via Roger Corman's 1975 SF movie *Death Race 2000*, and has recently appeared in the 1989 film *Scenes From the Class Struggle in Beverly Hills*.

Robert DiTillio, who plays the alien thug named Norg, is the brother of writer and script editor Lawrence DiTillio.

Director Bruce Seth Green has also directed a number of films, including *Laker Girls* (1990). The only distinguishing feature of that film is that it also starred Shari Shattuck, who later played Babylon 5's political officer Julie Masante in episode 305 ('Voices of Authority').

Accidents Will Happen: There's a clumsy cut in the scene where Adira drugs Londo's drink. She leans forward to kiss one cheek, but when it cuts to the reverse shot she's kissing his other cheek.

'Infection'

Transmission Number: 104
Production Number: 101

Written by: J. Michael Straczynski
Directed by: Richard Compton

Vance Hendricks: David McCallum
Nelson Drake: Marshall Teague
Mary Ann Cramer: Patricia Healy

Date: It's the second anniversary of Babylon 5 going operational.

Plot: A worthy, albeit preachy, episode, 'Infection' suffers from the early perceived need to make the series 'user-friendly' for *Star Trek* fans. The central plot could easily have been done as, for instance, an episode of *Star Trek: Deep Space Nine*.

The 'A' Plot: Vance Hendricks – an old tutor of Stephen Franklin – arrives on Babylon 5. He brings with him a consignment of artefacts dug up on a dead alien planet named Ikarra. The artefacts have been smuggled through Babylon 5 customs by Hendricks's assistant Nelson Drake after Drake has killed a customs inspector. Hendricks asks for Franklin's help in examining the artefacts, which have a biological basis. He intends selling them to an industrial group who will develop organic technology for Earth, like the Minbari and the Vorlons. Drake opens a box alone, and an energy discharge infects him with something. He begins to change, his skin thickening to resemble the Ikarran artefacts and his left arm developing into a weapon. He attacks Franklin and goes on a rampage through Babylon 5, getting stronger all the time. Franklin and Hendricks determine from information encoded in the remaining artefacts that Ikarra was invaded over half a dozen times, and that the Ikarrans developed organic weaponry to try to fight their invaders. They encapsulated one of their researchers' brain patterns in the artefacts, which were designed to turn Ikarrans into killing machines which would wipe out anything on the planet except pure Ikarrans. The war machines' definition of pure was too restrictive, however, and they ended up wiping out the entire Ikarran race. Sinclair uses this knowledge to goad the war machine that was Drake into following him, then forces it to face up to what it has done. The war machine, shamed by Sinclair, pulls its central component off Drake's chest, and crushes it. Drake, still alive, is rushed to medlab, and Hendricks is arrested after Franklin realises he condoned the death of the customs inspector. The Ikarran artefacts are confiscated by Earthforce.

The 'B' Plot: Sinclair is trying to avoid being interviewed by an ISN reporter – Mary Ann Cramer. Finally he has to talk to her, and extols the virtues of being in space.

The Arc: On the face of it, nothing, although it's suspicious that the Ikarrans have been dead for over a thousand years following a number of invasions of their world, and the last great war with the Shadows was around a thousand years ago.

Observations: Garibaldi tells Mary Ann Cramer about the time he and Sinclair walked fifty miles to make it out of a desert after an unspecified incident. This is a reference to the time the two of them crash-landed in the Martian desert and discovered signs of Shadow activity tied in to Psi Corps (although neither of them knew about the Shadows then). The full story is recounted in issues 5 to 8 of the *Babylon 5* comics ('Shadows Past and Present', 'Against the Odds', 'Survival the Hard Way' and 'Silent Enemies').

This was the first episode of the series to be made. J. Michael Straczynski has gone on record as saying that it's probably the worst episode in season 1.

According to a medlab screen, the chemical make-up of the Ikarran artefacts includes traces of dinoribonucleic acid, thiamine, riboflavin, niacin, xanthan, maltodextrin and okudazin. Dinoribonucleic acid may or may not be a misprint for deoxyribonucleic acid – the building block of life on Earth. Thiamin is vitamin B1, riboflavin is vitamin B2, niacin (or nicotinic acid) is another vitamin in the B complex, xanthan is a gum, and maltodextrin is a starch compound derived from lactose products. They can all be found in many breakfast cereals. That just leaves okudazin – and it can't be a coincidence that Michael Okuda is the scenic art supervisor on *Star Trek: The Next Generation* and *Star Trek: Deep Space Nine* and the man responsible for putting the in-jokes onto the viewscreens of the USS Enterprise and the space station Deep Space Nine.

Ivanova's Life Lessons: A warning to Mary Ann Cramer as she stays in C&C after being ordered not to: 'Don't – you're too young to experience that much pain.'

Other Worlds: The planet Ikarra 7. Proxima 3 also gets a name-check.

Culture Shock: According to J. Michael Straczynski, living creatures affected by the Ikarran artefacts aren't actually 'turned into' Ikarran war machines. The process is more akin to a living armour-like compound growing over the being's body and influencing the being. The being's biology is not changed underneath.

Station Keeping: There's a passing reference to the Babylon 5 C&C night shift – run by the occasionally mentioned but never seen Major Atumbe.

All organic material arriving on Babylon 5 is subject to a forty-eight-hour quarantine period.

Literary, Mythological and Historical References: Sinclair partially quotes Shakespeare's *King Lear* when he says: 'How sharper than a serpent's tooth . . .' The quotation finishes, '. . . it is to have a thankless child.'

Vance Hendricks tries to attract Franklin's attention by telling him that there's a Martian War Machine outside that wants to have a word about the common cold. This refers to H. G. Wells's novel *The War of the Worlds*, in which Martian invaders are killed by Earth's bacteria. If I was being really picky, I'd point out it's not the War Machines that want the word, it's the Martians inside them, but I'm not *that* sad. No, really.

Ivanova quotes American philosopher George Santayana's

phrase, 'Those who cannot remember the past are condemned to repeat it.' That phrase comes from his 1905–1906 book *The Life of Reason*.

I've Seen That Face Before: David McCallum was the pin-up of a generation when he played the Russian U.N.C.L.E. agent Ilya Kuryakin in the 1960s American TV series *The Man From U.N.C.L.E.* He was slightly less well known for his role as the time-travelling force of nature named Steel in the cult British SF series *Sapphire and Steel* and should be shot for appearing in the dire 1970s American TV series *The Invisible Man* (supposedly 'based on the novel by H. G. Wells').

Accidents Will Happen: Not an accident, but a clumsy shot – the scene when Drake's body returns to an unmarked state mere seconds after the central controller has been ripped from his chest, shedding a large amount of armour with no trace, is a dramatic conceit equivalent to the mysterious 'wind from nowhere' that always scatters the ashes of a staked vampire. In other words, it's a cliché.

Questions Raised: Were the Ikarrans wiped out by the Shadows? Or, perhaps, the Vorlons?

'The Parliament of Dreams'

Transmission Number: 105
Production Number: 108

Written by: J. Michael Straczynski
Directed by: Jim Johnston

Catherine Sakai: Julia Nickson
Tu'Pari: Thomas Kopache   **Du'Rog:** Mark Hendrickson

Plot: A fun episode in which a linear plot is rendered more ornate by Andreas Katsulas's performance. This is the first time Katsulas has been allowed to let himself go in the role of G'Kar, and you can see he's having fun.
The 'A' Plot: Courier Tu'Pari arrives on Babylon 5 with a message for Ambassador G'Kar. The message is from Councillor Du'Rog, an old enemy of G'Kar. Du'Rog is now dead,

but before dying he liquidated all his assets to hire an assassin from the Thenta Makur – the Assassins' Guild – to kill G'Kar. G'Kar immediately suspects his new aide – Na'Toth – and hires a bodyguard from the criminal boss N'Grath. The bodyguard is killed, and the assassin turns out to be Tu'Pari – he had killed the real courier, Ru'Dak, before arriving. Tu'Pari kidnaps G'Kar and takes him to a deserted area of Babylon 5, where he will torture and finally kill him as per instructions. Na'Toth locates them and manages to free G'Kar from his restraints. Together they overpower Tu'Pari and render him unconscious. When he wakes up, he discovers that the time allotted to him to kill G'Kar has passed by. Worse still, G'Kar claims to have deposited enough money in Tu'Pari's account to make it look as if he has been bribed not to kill G'Kar. Tu'Pari leaves Babylon 5 as soon as he can, aware that the Thenta Makur will be after him.

The 'B' Plot: Earth Central has decided to hold a week of religious celebrations, during which each of the major races will demonstrate its dominant belief systems to the others. The Centauri hold a feast, the Minbari hold a mystical ceremony and the humans show just how many different religions they have.

The 'C' Plot: Catherine Sakai – one of Sinclair's former lovers – arrives on the station. She didn't know he was there, but they pretty soon end up back together again.

The Arc: According to J. Michael Straczynski, during the Minbari ceremony Delenn quotes the words that Valen said as he formed the first Grey Council. Those words are, in part: 'Then do this in testimony to the One who will follow, who will bring death couched in the promise of new life and renewal disguised as defeat.' Given that we find out in episodes 120 ('Babylon Squared') and 316 and 317 ('War Without End' Parts One and Two) that the One is an amalgam of Sinclair, Sheridan and Delenn, who are these words referring to? Probably Delenn, who is the One that is to come. So – whose renewal is disguised as defeat?

The Minbari ceremony is, we discover, either one of marriage or of renewal. Given the looks exchanged by Delenn and Sinclair during it, many people assumed that it was a ceremony of marriage. However, following what happens to Delenn in episodes 122 ('Chrysalis') and 202 ('Revelations'), it makes more sense to assume it is a ceremony of renewal.

Observations: The Centauri goddess Li (goddess of passion) has a number of tentacles emerging from her sides. These, as we discover in episodes 121 ('The Quality of Mercy') and 312 ('Sic Transit Vir') are Centauri male genitalia – implying that Li displays both male and (presumably) female characteristics.

Sinclair's brother is mentioned.

Na'Toth's father is named Sha'Toth, giving us some idea of how Narn names are formed.

Antarean flarn is mentioned. Flarn also turns up in episodes 218 ('Confessions and Lamentations') and 312 ('Sic Transit Vir').

Durinium and quantium-40 are both elements. Quantium-40 was a name invented by SF fans on GEnie after J. Michael Straczynski asked for suggestions. The person who came up with the name quantium-40 was called David Strauss, hence the reference in this episode to a waiter named David.

Catherine Sakai and Sinclair had been at the Academy together and lived together for a year. She asks Sinclair about his previous girlfriend, Carolyn Sykes. Sinclair replies that they split up a year ago. Note the coincidence of initials, by the way – Carolyn Sykes, Catherine Sakai, 'CS'. Given the Jeff Sinclair–John Sheridan–Joe Straczynski link, one does wonder if the show's creator is trying to get something out of his system.

Julia Nickson's full name is Julia Nickson-Soul.

After Mary Woronov (Ko'Dath) walked out of the series, Caitlin Brown was cast as the new character, Na'Toth. Time was so pressing that she is wearing the Ko'Dath mask in this episode. A cast was subsequently made of her face and a new mask created for Na'Toth for future episodes. Ko'Dath's disappearance was explained as being due to an airlock accident.

A scene in which Sinclair talks about Kosh's poisoning

(from the pilot episode – 'The Gathering') was originally filmed for this episode. When this episode was found to be overrunning slightly, the scene was moved to episode 107 ('The War Prayer') and slightly redubbed.

This episode is the first one to have been written after filming on the series started, meaning that Straczynski could actually write for the characterisations he was seeing the actors bring to their roles rather than to an abstract ideal.

G'Kar's song was intended to have a 'Gilbert and Sullivan' feel to it. The words are:

> I'm thinking of thinking of calling her right,
>   after my afternoon nap.
> I'm thinking of thinking of sending her flowers,
>   right after Bonnie gets back.
> So many fishies left in the sea,
>   so many fishies – but no one for me . . .
> I'm thinking of thinking of hooking a love,
>   soon after supper is done.

Andreas Katsulas ad-libbed his 'Stay put' line to his dinner, as the crawfish had a tendency to wander off the plate.

The alien bodyguard hired by G'Kar has seashells embedded in its mask, running in a line up its forehead and getting smaller as they go.

This episode marks the first appearance of Billy Mumy as Lennier. At one point during the filming of his first scene, as he and Delenn are walking off camera, Delenn asks him: 'Now tell me of home; I have been away far too long.' Mumy immediately ad-libbed the response: 'Beatlemania is back.'

This episode won the 1994 Emmy award for makeup.

This episode was originally entitled 'Carnival!'

Dialogue to Rewind For: Tu'Pari: 'Are you Ambassador G'Kar?' G'Kar: 'This is Ambassador G'Kar's quarters. This is Ambassador G'Kar's table. This is Ambassador G'Kar's dinner. What part of this progression escapes you?'

Londo, on the fate of Centauri Prime's other dominant species: 'Do you know what the last Xon said, just before he died? Aaaargh!'

Catherine Sakai to Sinclair after his hidden comlink starts calling his name: 'I hate to alarm you, but your trousers are talking to you.'

Na'Toth to G'Kar after he finds a black flower in his bed: 'Ambassador, it is not my place to speculate on how *anything* gets into your bed.'

Ships That Pass In The Night: Earth Alliance Transport *Southern Passage*, Transport *Alpha Seven*.

Other Worlds: There used to be two dominant species on Centauri Prime – the Centauri we have come to know and love and a species known as the Xon, whom they wiped out. According to J. Michael Straczynski, 'The Xon did evolve into a fair amount of intelligence. There are a very few land masses on Centauri Prime, separated by huge oceans. The two species evolved pretty much separately, on different continents that were absolutely unreachable until one or both sides developed sufficient technology for extended sea travel . . . and that's when all hell broke loose.'

Arcturus 4 is mentioned as an inhabited world.

Culture Shock: The Centauri have a number of household gods, much as the ancient Romans did. They also have massive feasts which alternate bingeing and purging – also much like those of the Romans.

The Narn have an Assassins' Guild (the Thenta Makur) with formal rules of business etiquette.

We discover in episode 311 ('Ceremonies of Light and Dark') that the Minbari ceremony of marriage and rebirth is called the *nafak'cha*.

Literary, Mythological and Historical References: Sinclair is listening to a poem by Alfred, Lord Tennyson being read. The poem in question is *Ulysses* – the same poem he quoted from in the pilot episode ('The Gathering'). Interestingly enough, the same poem also contains a reference to household gods, much like the Centauri's. Another poem by Tennyson – *The Lady of Shalott* – contains the line, 'I am half-sick of shadows, said/The Lady of Shalott.'

During the demonstration of the range of human religious

beliefs at the end of the episode, the Australian Aborigine is introduced as Mr Blacksmith. *The Chant of Jimmy Blacksmith* is a novel by Thomas Keneally about a half-caste Aborigine who is pushed around by white men until he finally explodes into violence. The novel was filmed in 1978.

I've Seen That Face Before: Thomas Kopache (who plays Tu'Pari) subsequently appeared in the episode of *Star Trek: Voyager* entitled 'The Thaw'.

Questions Raised: Why is it that every race has one or two dominant religions whereas humanity has a whole mass of them?

'Mind War'

Transmission Number: 106
Production Number: 110

Written by: J. Michael Straczynski
Directed by: Bruce Seth Green

Bester: Walter Koenig   **Kelsey:** Felicity Waterman
Jason Ironheart: William Allan Young
Catherine Sakai: Julia Nickson
Garibaldi's Aide: Macaulay Bruton

Plot: The fact that both the 'A' plot and the 'B' plot concern super-powered beings is obviously deliberate, but the lack of a 'C' plot means that the entire thing is pretty relentless. Just when you get tired of seeing an amazingly powerful being on the rampage, the episode cuts to another amazingly powerful being on the rampage.

The 'A' Plot: Jason Ironheart – a rogue telepath – is on his way to Babylon 5, and destroys a squadron of Black Omega Starfuries with the power of his mind to get there. Once he arrives, he takes a room and tries to contain his thoughts – which have a habit of shaking his surroundings when he's not concentrating. Two Psi Cops – Bester and Kelsey – arrive on the station in search of him, and forcibly scan Talia Winters's mind to find out whether she has had any recent contact with him. Ironheart was Talia's tutor in the Psi Corps, and they were lovers for a time. When she leaves their presence, Ironheart contacts her. He tells her that he volunteered for a series of Psi Corps experiments which he thought were to boost telepathic powers. He was genetically altered, and given 'mutated' serotonin and acetylcholine, and when his powers started developing he realised that Psi Corps were trying to develop a stable telekinetic. Their ultimate aim was to develop an agent who could carry out covert assassinations by, for instance, squeezing the victim's carotid artery until he or she was dead, but Ironheart's powers kept on developing until he could move individual atoms and molecules. Knowing that Psi Corps would misuse his power he killed the only researcher who could replicate the work, and fled. His powers are still developing, and every time they do the station shudders – what Kelsey refers to as a 'mind quake'. Ironheart seals off the area he is in so that the Psi Corps agents cannot get to him, and asks Sinclair to clear a path to his ship so that he can get away – he only came to say goodbye to Talia. Sinclair, who has heard some of Ironheart's story, complies, but Bester and Kelsey interrupt them on their way to the docking bays. They attempt to send a telepathic shut-down code into Ironheart's mind, and when that fails Kelsey tries to kill him. Sinclair knocks Bester out, and Ironheart rips Kelsey's body apart on the atomic level. Reaching his ship, he leaves the station, but before he can get to the jumpgate his body and his ship transform together into a being on a higher plane of existence. After saying goodbye to Talia Winters, and giving her a parting gift of telekinetic ability, he disappears.

The 'B' Plot: Catherine Sakai is offered a contract by Universal Terraform to survey a planet named Sigma 957. The planet is in an area of space contested by the Narn, and the company is obliged to seek the permission of Ambassador G'Kar before she can leave. G'Kar tries to persuade her not to go, telling her that strange things happen near that planet. She ignores his advice, and leaves. Arriving at Sigma 957 she begins her survey, but a disturbance in nearby space heralds the arrival of a bizarre object that may be an alien creature or may be a ship of amazingly advanced design. It vanishes as quickly as it has appeared, without apparently even noticing her, but her ship suffers a 90-per-cent energy loss and begins an irreversible descent to the surface of the planet. She is rescued by two Narn fighters which have been sent by G'Kar to help her. When she returns to Babylon 5 she asks G'Kar why he was willing to help. His answer effectively boils down to, 'Why not?'

The Arc: Jason Ironheart tells Talia Winters that they all thought Psi Corps was controlled by the government, but now Psi Corps is beginning to control the government. Telepaths make the ultimate blackmailers, and they are apparently trying to develop new weapons for their armoury – such as telekinetic assassins. The interaction between Psi Corps, the government (especially the current Vice-President, Morgan Clark) and the as-yet-unknown third party, the Shadows, is a theme that runs through the entire series. Important episodes in terms of explaining what's going on are 122 ('Chrysalis'), 301 ('Matters of Honor'), 314 ('Ship of Tears') and 322 ('Z'ha'dum').

The bizarre and amazingly powerful alien creatures that live around Sigma 957 make a reappearance in episode 305 ('Voices of Authority') and episode 406 ('Into the Fire').

Notice that Ivanova hands Talia a glass of water after she is forcibly scanned by Bester and Kelsey. This gesture of sympathy is a step on the path of their growing closeness, a path that will end in episode 219 ('Divided Loyalties').

Talia's telekinesis is not the only gift that Jason Ironheart gave her. His legacy becomes important to the plot in episode 208 ('A Race Through Dark Places').

Observations: Universal Terraform is an Earth Alliance megacorporation.

Bester can project thoughts into the minds of non-telepaths.

Duridium is usually (although not always) a by-product of quantum-40. Quantum-40 is mentioned in the previous episode (105 – 'The Parliament of Dreams').

One in every thousand human beings has telepathic powers. One in every ten thousand telepaths has telekinetic powers – and half of them are clinically insane.

J. Michael Straczynski has said that Jason Ironheart will not return – Straczynski doesn't like having characters with that much power running around the storyline.

Walter Koenig had originally been offered the part of Knight Two in episode 108 ('And the Sky Full of Stars') but could not accept as he was recuperating from a heart attack. He was then offered the part of Bester in this episode, which was filmed after episode 108 but shown before it.

The episode was originally scheduled to be broadcast around tenth in the running order, but Warner Brothers were so pleased with the final version that they asked for it to be broadcast earlier.

The company named Universal Terraform was invented by fans on GEnie.

Dialogue to Rewind For: G'Kar: 'No one here is exactly what they seem – not Mollari, not Delenn, not Sinclair and not me.'

Jason Ironheart: 'You cannot harm one who has dreamed a dream like mine,' (apparently a Native American prayer of protection against one's enemies).

Dialogue to Fast Forward Past: Jason Ironheart: 'I look at you, Commander, and I see not a man . . .'

Ships That Pass In The Night: We get our first sight of the Black Omega Starfury fighter squadron in this episode. We discover in episode 314 ('Ship of Tears') that the Black Omega Starfuries are assigned only to Psi Corps.

The stolen vessel that Jason Ironheart arrives at Babylon 5 in only has the designation Seven-Tango-Seven.

Catherine Sakai's ship is called the *Sky Dancer*.

Earth Transport *Spinoza* has brought Bester and Kelsey to Babylon 5. Spinoza was a philosopher who wrote, 'I have striven not to laugh at human actions, not to weep at them, nor to hate them, but to understand them', which might well be the theme for the series.

The Narn fighters we see regularly are *Frazi*-class.

Other Worlds: Sigma 957 – a supposedly deserted world in space contested by the Narn. It may have deposits of quantium-40, but there are strange beings that live in space nearby.

Station Keeping: A standard guest room on Babylon 5 costs 500 credits per standard Earth week.

Literary, Mythological and Historical References: Ivanova asks Bester, 'Who watches the watchmen?' She's quoting the Roman satirist and poet Juvenal, who wrote, '*Sed quis custodiet ipsos custodes?*' The entire sense of Juvenal's phrase has to do with husbands guarding their wives to stop them having affairs. 'But who is to guard the guards themselves?' he asks. 'Your wife arranges accordingly and begins with them.'

Bester's farewell to Sinclair – the forefinger and thumb salute and the words 'Be seeing you' – are a nod towards the cult 1960s TV series *The Prisoner*, which is itself about mind control and power games.

Bester himself is named after the famed science fiction writer Alfred Bester (we discover in issue 11 of the *Babylon 5* comic – 'Psi Corps and You!' – that Bester's first name is Alfred, and this is confirmed by episode 314 – 'Ship of Tears'). Alfred Bester wrote various books involving telepathy, one of which – *The Demolished Man* – had at its core a Guild of telepaths not entirely unlike a nice version of Psi Corps.

I've Seen That Face Before: Do I need to tell you that Walter Koenig played Ensign Pavel Chekov in the original series of *Star Trek* and the first seven spin-off films, as well as writing an episode of the *Star Trek* animated series? I thought not.

Accidents Will Happen: Ironheart refers to the drugs that were used on him – mutated serotonin and acetylcholine. Neither of those chemicals has any DNA, so the term 'mutated' has no meaning.

In the original CGI shots of the pre-title sequence, a binary star could be seen through Jason Ironheart's ship. The shot was redone for US repeats, although the international versions sent out contained it.

Questions Raised: What exactly did Catherine Sakai tell Universal Terraform about Sigma 957?

Why don't Bester and Kelsey take their gloves off when they're scanning Talia?

'The War Prayer'

Transmission Number: 107
Production Number: 107

Written by: D. C. Fontana
Directed by: Richard Compton

Shaal Mayan: Nancy Lee Grahn
Malcolm Biggs: Tristan Rogers
Kiron Maray: Rodney Eastman
Aria Tensus: Danica McKellar
Roberts: Michael Paul Chan   **Mila Shar:** Diane Adair

Plot: The episode is fun, but lightweight, and it's spoilt by the biggest cliché in American television – the handsome former lover who has returned after X years and for whom our hero or heroine still has feelings just happens to be the prime mover in whatever villainy is afoot, thus tying two plots neatly together and providing a good tug on the heartstrings. The word 'contrived' was invented for plot elements like this.

The 'A' Plot: Shaal Mayan, a Minbari poet and friend of Delenn, is stabbed and branded with a racist symbol during a visit to Babylon 5. The immediate suspect is the Home Guard – a militant, racist organisation that's gaining strength on Earth. A potential Home Guard recruit is watched by Garibaldi, and the surveillance pays off when the man is approached by the newly arrived Malcolm Biggs – an old lover of Ivanova. Sinclair asks Ivanova to introduce them, and goes out of his way to insult aliens and generally make himself look like prime recruiting material for Home Guard. Biggs indeed attempts to recruit Sinclair, and sets him a test – he must kill the head of the Abbai agricultural delegation who has arrived for a series of meetings and tours. Refusing,

110

Sinclair has Biggs and the other Home Guard members arrested after a fire fight.

The 'B' Plot: Kiron Maray, a cousin of Vir's, arrives on the station with Aria Tensus – the Centauri girl he loves. They have both been affianced to other people by their respective Houses on Centauri Prime, but they love each other and they have run away to get married. Londo's first inclination is to send them back to Centauri Prime, but the knowledge that he married for political advantage rather than love, and that his father always grieved for the experiences he never had, forces him to change his mind. He arranges for both of them to be fostered by a Centauri family who owe him a favour. They will be allowed to marry when they get older.

The 'C' Plot: Malcolm Biggs, an old lover of Susan Ivanova, arrives on the station. He claims to be setting up business there and wants to resume their relationship, but in reality he's a senior member of the Home Guard, there to coordinate an attack on Babylon 5's ambassadors. When Ivanova finds out she arranges to have him betray himself. He's arrested and shipped back to Earth.

The Arc: It suddenly occurs to Sinclair that the poison tab stuck on Kosh's hand in the pilot episode ('The Gathering') shouldn't have penetrated his encounter suit, but did. He also voices his concern that the only two people to have any experience of the inside of a Vorlon encounter suit – Dr Ben Kyle and Lyta Alexander – were both recalled to Earth shortly afterwards.

Observations: The scene in which Sinclair talks about Kosh's poisoning was originally filmed for episode 105 ('The Parliament of Dreams'), but as that episode overran slightly, the scene was moved to this episode and redubbed.

The branding of Shaal Mayan was thought by J. Michael Straczynski to be too close to events in an episode of *Star Trek: Deep Space Nine*. He had intended removing the brand via computer effects in the shots in which it appeared, but fan pressure changed his mind.

Mark Hendrickson (a regular *Babylon 5* background face) appears in this episode as a character called Thegras. His character (a Drazi) appears for only a few seconds, beating up a human. Why the credit? It's possible he appeared for longer, but that his scenes were cut for time.

Koshisms: 'We take no interest in the affairs of others.'

To Sinclair, when the Commander asks why he is watching images of Earth. 'I am studying.'

Dialogue to Rewind For: Londo about his wives: 'Do you think I married them for their personalities? Their personalities could shatter entire planets!' (This exchange, along with the designations of Londo's wives as Pestilence, Famine and Death, were inserted in Fontana's script by Straczynski).

Dialogue to Fast Forward Past: Sinclair: 'I want these scum, Michael – I want them bad.'

Londo's purple-prose explanation of why he is helping the two star-crossed young lovers: 'My shoes are too tight and I have forgotten how to dance.' (This is one of Straczynski's lines).

Ships That Pass In The Night: There's a Centauri liner that sounds like it's called the *Carvo*, as well as the Earth Alliance Transport *Wolfsbane* and the Earth Alliance Special Transport *Normandy Beach*.

Other Worlds: Centauri Prime is seventy-five light years from Babylon 5 (but is that Centauri light years or human light years?).

Abbai 4 is the home world of the vaguely aquatic Abbai race.

Literary, Mythological and Historical References: *The War Prayer* is also the title of a short piece of fiction by the American cultural icon Mark Twain. The piece concerns a small town whose inhabitants pray for victory in a war, until a mysterious stranger who may or may not be an angel stands up in church and rephrases their prayer to make explicit the horrors that they are actually praying for.

I've Seen That Face Before: Or rather, I've heard that voice before. Tristan Rogers, who plays Malcolm Biggs, was one of the voices on the 1990 Walt Disney film, *The Rescuers Down Under*. So, now you know.

Danica McKellar (Aria Tensus) played a regular character in the sitcom *The Wonder Years*.

Dorothy C. Fontana, the writer of the story, wrote many of the best episodes of the original series of *Star Trek*. She also wrote for *The Fantastic Journey*, but we'll do our best to ignore that.

Accidents Will Happen: When Biggs is in Ivanova's quarters, her door opens before he moves towards it.

'And the Sky Full of Stars'

Transmission Number: 108
Production Number: 106

Written by: J. Michael Straczynski
Directed by: Janet Greek

Knight One: Judson Scott
Knight Two: Christopher Neame   **Aide:** Macaulay Bruton
Benson: Jim Youngs   **Mitchell:** Justin Williams
Grey Council No. 1: Mark Hendrickson

Plot: An intense, *Prisoner*-esque episode which has a strong 'A' plot and also contributes a lot to the overall arc. One of the best stories of season 1.

The 'A' Plot: Two secretive men – Knight One and Knight Two – arrive on Babylon 5. They kidnap Commander Sinclair and strap him into a cybernet – a device that creates virtual scenes inside the mind with the appearance and the feel of reality. When Sinclair wakes up he finds himself inside the cybernet in a deserted replica of Babylon 5. Knight Two is also with him, and tells him that people on Earth are suspicious. During the Battle of the Line, ten years before, Sinclair vanished for twenty-four hours. There is a growing feeling that, during that time, he made a deal with the Minbari to betray Earth if they would spare his life. Knight Two forces Sinclair to remember the missing twenty-four hours of his life, and Sinclair recalls trying to ram a Minbari cruiser when

113

an energy beam immobilises his Starfury. He is taken into the Minbari cruiser and tortured by nine cowled figures. After they have examined him, he manages to rip the cowl off one of them. He now realises that the Minbari whose face he saw was Delenn. Sinclair has been keeping his sense of his physical body by clenching his fist, and he manages to break free of the cybernet and rip Knight Two's connections out – frying the man's brain. Sinclair escapes, believing himself to be still on the Minbari cruiser. He gets a gun and kills Knight One on the promenade before Delenn talks him out of his hallucination. Knight Two is shipped back to Earth on the orders of EarthGov before anyone can question him.

The 'B' Plot: Knight One and Knight Two bribe a debt-ridden security guard named Benson into getting them an energy pod with which they will power their cybernet. Garibaldi, trying to find Sinclair, stumbles across Benson's involvement, but Knight One kills Benson and shoves his body out of an airlock.

The 'C' Plot: Delenn is concerned about the possibility that Sinclair might regain his memory. She is instructed by a senior member of the Grey Council to kill him if he does remember.

The Arc: Delenn refuses to tell Dr Franklin what she did during the Earth–Minbari war, and she has at least one very good reason. It turns out that she and the Grey Council kidnapped Sinclair during their final assault on Earth and subjected him to some kind of examination before wiping his mind of the encounter, putting him back in his Starfury and surrendering. Under pressure from Knight Two, Sinclair remembers some of what happened, and manages to fill in the 'hole in your mind' that he was told about in the pilot episode – 'The Gathering' (we get a flashback from 'The Gathering' as well). Sinclair also remembers that Delenn was on the Minbari cruiser as a member of the Grey Council when he was tortured.

When he is on the Minbari ship during the Battle of the Line, Sinclair is scanned by a triangular device held by one of the Minbari. The results cause some consternation among the

Grey Council. This is undoubtedly the point at which they realise he has a Minbari soul.

At one point, Garibaldi is reading a newspaper (the *Universe Today*). The main headlines read:

'PSI-CORPS IN ELECTION TANGLE', with a sub-headline 'Did Psi-Corps Violate Its Charter By Endorsing Vice-President?' This foreshadows the Psi Corps association with President Clark as revealed in episode 122 – 'Chrysalis'.

'NARNS SETTLE RAGHESH 3 CONTROVERSY', referring back to episode 101 – 'Midnight on the Firing Line' (note the misspelling of 'Ragesh').

'HOME GUARD LEADER CONVICTED', with a sub-headline 'Jacob Lester Found Guilty in Attack on Minbari Embassy'. This refers tangentially back to episode 107 – 'The War Prayer'.

'SAN DIEGO STILL CONSIDERED TOO RADIOACTIVE FOR OCCUPANCY', setting up our first view of the radioactive San Diego wastes in episode 206 – 'Spider in the Web'.

'IS THERE SOMETHING LIVING IN HYPERSPACE?', a question that is raised again in episodes 204 ('A Distant Star'), 222 ('The Fall of Night') and 301 ('Matters of Honor').

The Grey Council member who gives Delenn her orders has a triangular metal emblem on his forehead. This is the same emblem that appears on Delenn's forehead when Morden asks her what she wants in episode 113 – 'Signs and Portents'. According to J. Michael Straczynski, it's symbolic of the fact that the wearer is a member of the Grey Council, and it manifests itself only for specific reasons at specific times.

Straczynski has indicated that Garibaldi's aide – the one who shoots him in episode 122 ('Chrysalis'), is implicated in the conspiracy, and helps Knight One get Benson's body out of the airlock.

Observations: Dr Franklin refused to hand over his medical notes on the Minbari to Earthforce during the war. He knew that they would be used to create genetic weapons, and he couldn't square that with his Hippocratic Oath.

The Grey Council comprises nine Minbari in Sinclair's flashback. This means they must have replaced the dead Dukhat.

Metazine is a psychotropic drug.

Talia Winters is a level-P5 telepath.

Other headlines on Garibaldi's copy of the *Universe Today* include 'COPYRIGHT TRIAL CONTINUES IN BOOKZAP FLAP', with a sub-headline 'Books Downloaded Directly Into Brain: Who Owns Them?', 'EA PRESIDENT PROMISES BALANCED BUDGET BY 2260' and 'NEW BINARY STAR DISCOVERED'. There's also a sub-headline reading, 'MINBARI PIRATE ACCORDED HONORS'. This is a misprint – it should read 'MINBARI *POET* ACCORDED HONORS'. The poet in question is almost certainly Shaal Mayan from the previous episode (107 – 'The War Prayer') as she was on her way to Earth from Babylon 5.

It is made clear in the headline concerning the continued uninhabitability of San Diego that the nuclear explosion that devastated it was an act of terrorism (see episode 101 – 'Midnight on the Firing Line').

A slight cut was made to this episode during the first UK showing on Channel 4. During the flashback to the Battle of the Line, the word 'bastards' was excised from Sinclair's line, 'Not like this, not like this, if I'm going out I'm taking you bastards with me.'

Walter Koenig was originally cast as Knight Two, but was prevented from taking the part by a heart attack. The part was offered to Patrick McGoohan, who loved the script but was going to be out of the country when it was filmed. Christopher Neame accepted the part, and Walter Koenig was later recast as the Psi Cop Bester. We're still waiting for Patrick McGoohan to turn up.

Ivanova's Life Lessons: 'Mr Garibaldi, there are days I'm very glad I don't have to think the way you do.'

Dialogue to Rewind For: Knight Two: 'It's a shadow play – without form or substance.'

Dialogue to Fast Forward Past: Knight Two: 'Then why did they surrender?' Sinclair: 'I don't know. Maybe the universe blinked. Maybe God changed his mind.'

Station Keeping: Earthforce security personnel are forbidden to gamble on duty. Off duty they are limited to risking fifty credits a week.

Babylon 5's security scanners are capable of detecting any energy pods which are being smuggled through customs.

Garibaldi's security card can open any door on the station without his having to enter a security code or an override of any sort.

The Babylon 5 edition of the *Universe Today* costs 50 millicredits.

Literary, Mythological and Historical References: In a way, this episode is a kind of off-hand homage to *The Prisoner* – the quintessentially sixties TV series about a retired spy held in a bizarre prison whose captors try everything possible to get information out of him.

I've Seen That Face Before: Judson Scott, who plays Knight One, was in *Star Trek II: The Wrath of Khan*, as Khan's sidekick Joachim. Christopher Neame, who plays Knight Two, is a British actor whose main genre credit is as the villainous Time Lord Skagra in the untelevised *Doctor Who* story 'Shada' (written by Douglas Adams).

Accidents Will Happen: When Sinclair is rushing around the virtual-reality station, we see a shot of the outside of a lift after he gets in. It's understandable that he could see the *inside* of the lift in his virtual-reality vision, but who is seeing the outside?

Is it my imagination, or does Delenn's door open before Sinclair moves towards it at the end of the episode?

The *Universe Today* newspaper that Garibaldi is reading refers to 'Psi-Corps' with a hyphen. Elsewhere on this show, and in the official documentation, Psi Corps is written without a hyphen.

Questions Raised: If Garibaldi's security card can open any door on the station without his having to enter a security code or an override of any sort, what happens if it gets stolen?

It's taken ten years for people on Earth to worry about whether Commander Sinclair is a traitor. Why so long?

If what happened to Sinclair on board the Minbari ship is so secret, how come the Minbari assassin knows about it in the pilot episode?

Is it a coincidence that, of all the Minbari cruisers Sinclair tried to ram, he had to choose the one carrying the Grey Council?

'Deathwalker'

Transmission Number: 109
Production Number: 113

Written by: Lawrence G. DiTillio
Directed by: Bruce Seth Green

Jha'Dur: Sarah Douglas
Ambassador Kalika: Robin Curtis
Abbut: Cosie Costa   **Senator Hidoshi:** Aki Aleong
Ambassador No. 1: Robert DiTillio
Vakar Ashok: Mark Hendrickson

Plot: An excellent story that balances action neatly against a rather nasty philosophical conundrum, and tops it all with a true *deus ex machina*.

The 'A' Plot: Awaiting a Narn in the customs hall, Na'Toth sees a familiar face arrive on the station. It is Jha'dur, the last surviving member of the Dilgar – a race who committed ghastly atrocities against the Narn and various members of the League of Non-Aligned Worlds some twenty-seven years before. The Dilgar were finally defeated by an alliance of worlds, and most of them died a few years later when their sun went nova. Na'Toth attacks Jha'dur, but is pulled off before she can kill her. Sinclair discovers rapidly that the Minbari have been sheltering Jha'dur, that she has developed a serum that can halt ageing and promote healing in all races, and that she is on Babylon 5 to give this serum to humanity. The Narn are also negotiating for the serum, and Sinclair is ordered by Senator Hidoshi to send Jha'dur to Earth as soon as possible. The League of Non-Aligned Worlds, alerted by G'Kar, blockade the station and prevent Jha'dur leaving. They want her tried for her crimes against sentient species, but Sinclair negotiates a solution by suggesting that they can share the serum she has developed. On her way to her ship, Jha'dur tells Sinclair that the serum contains an ingredient that can only be obtained from living beings, and that one being must die for every one that wants to live. This is her legacy to the races that defeated the Dilgar. Her ship leaves Babylon 5 but is destroyed by a Vorlon ship before it can enter hyperspace. 'You are not ready for immortality,' Ambassador Kosh tells Sinclair.

The 'B' Plot: Ambassador Kosh hires Talia Winters to oversee business negotiations between him and a small humanoid named Abbut, but the negotiations are gibberish and she is unable to read the mind of either party. As the negotiations go on, she starts having flashbacks to a time three years before when she was asked to read the mind of a convicted killer. After the negotiations are complete, Abbut removes a data crystal from his head and gives it to Kosh. Talia asks him what it is and why he wants it, but his answer isn't helpful. When she tells Sinclair and Garibaldi what has happened, Garibaldi identifies Abbut as a Vicker – a cybernetic creature capable of recording sounds, pictures and thoughts. They point out to her that Vorlons are 'leery' of telepaths, and suggest that Kosh wanted to know what frightened her.

The Arc: Jha'dur is familiar with Commander Sinclair, having resided with the Minbari clan of the Wind Swords for so long. 'The Wind Swords are right to fear you,' she tells him. 'They speak of you often, Sinclair. They say you have a hole in your mind.' This recurring plot point of the hole in Sinclair's mind is first raised in the pilot episode – 'The Gathering' – and is explained in episode 201 – 'Points of Departure'.

Kosh's recording of Talia's mind is referred to again in episode 219 – 'Divided Loyalties'. We still don't know why he wants it, but we know he has a reason.

Observations: At one point in the episode, a voice on a tannoy in the background announces that there will be a signing session at the Book Universe store. It sounds suspiciously like it's Harlan Ellison who will be doing the signing . . .

It was Harlan Ellison's suggestion that Deathwalker be female, rather than male. The original idea, with a male Dilgar, was felt to be too close to ground covered by the *ST:DS9* episode 'Duet'.

The UK's Channel 4 cut several seconds from the scene where Na'Toth beats Jha'dur with a metal pipe, as they considered it too violent for the timeslot in which they were showing the programme.

The role of Abbut was originally written with Gilbert Gottfried in mind, although he was later discovered to be unavailable on the dates required for filming. He's best known as the voice of Iago in Disney's *Aladdin*, although he also appeared as a host during season one of the US comedy series *Saturday Night Live*.

Koshisms: This episode is full of them. 'We will meet in Red 3 at the Hour of Scampering.' 'Understanding is a three-edged sword' (the three edges being, according to J. Michael Straczynski: your side, my side, and the truth in between). 'The willows must scuttle carefully.' 'We will commence again at the Hour of Longing.' 'A stroke of the brush does not guarantee art from the bristles.'

When Talia Winters protests that she doesn't understand what is going on, he says, 'Then listen to the music, not the song.' When she asks what is on the data crystal Abbut has given him, he replies, 'Reflection . . . surprise . . . terror . . . For the future . . .'

And, of course, his parting shot. 'You are not ready for immortality.'

Dialogue to Rewind For: Jha'dur's parting shot to Sinclair is quite chilling. Having told him that the immortality serum she has developed requires one living creature to die so that another may live for ever, she sneers, 'Not like us? You will *become* us.' (This dialogue was added by J. Michael Straczynski.)

Ships That Pass In The Night: Transport *Altera*; Liner *Callisto*; Minbari Flyer 969.

The Drazi, the Ipsha and the Vree all send ships to Babylon 5 in an attempt to force Sinclair to place Jha'dur on trial. The Drazi ship is known generically as a Sunhawk. The Vree ships look like flying saucers. The Ipsha ship is referred to as a Battleglobe.

Other Worlds: Sector 47 is in Minbari space.

Hyach 7 is a Narn colony that was conquered by the Dilgar.

Jha'dur was born on the planet Omelos, in the Caliban Sector. She later laid waste to the planets Comac 4, Latec 4, Halax and Tirolus, before being defeated, along with the rest of the Dilgar, at Balos.

Culture Shock: Vickers are cybernetic creatures capable of recording whatever they experience – sights, sounds, thoughts, biorhythms and so on. Abbut, the Vicker hired by Kosh, looks human, except that the top half of his head has been removed to expose his brain and various mechanical components, including a data-crystal port. Presumably there is no reason why a Vicker can't be from another race. Abbut claims to have a telepathic rating of P23 (compared with Bester's P12), but he may be lying.

The Minbari clan structure gets a mention in this episode, with the Wind Swords being the clan who sheltered Jha'dur without the Grey Council knowing until the Battle of the Line. According to Straczynski, the Minbari have a number of clans, the primary five being the Star Riders (the oldest), the Moon Shields, the Wind Swords, the Night Walkers and the Fire Wings. The first four names refer to the early Minbari version of a mounted force, for which you need mounted cavalry who can navigate by the stars followed by foot soldiers with shields and swords and soldiers who move primarily by night. The Fire Wings clan is made up of those Minbari whose clan first used flying machines in battle.

Although Ambassador Kalika's race are never identified on screen, they are, in fact, the Abbai.

I've Seen That Face Before: Sarah Douglas, who plays Jha'dur, appeared as the villainous Kryptonian Ursa in *Superman II*.

Robin Curtis, who plays Ambassador Kalika, took over the role of the Vulcan Lieutenant Saavik from Kirsty Alley in the films *Star Trek III: The Search For Spock* and *Star Trek IV: The Voyage Home*, as well as playing another Vulcan – Tallera – in the *Star Trek: The Next Generation* episodes 'Gambit' Part I and 'Gambit' Part II (alongside Caitlin Brown, oddly enough).

Robert DiTillio, who plays Ambassador No. 1, also played the alien thug Norg in episode 103 ('Born to the Purple').

Questions Raised: So, why *did* the Dilgar's sun go nova? Bit of a coincidence if it was an accident.

'Believers'

Transmission Number: 110
Production Number: 105

Written by: David Gerrold
Directed by: Richard Compton

Tharg: Stephen Lee   **M'ola:** Tricia O'Neill
Shon: Jonathan Charles Kaplan
Dr Maya Hernandez: Silvana Gallardo

Plot: There's something almost too worthy about this episode. It's a talky-feely plot with no redeeming action or tension, and it's unbalanced by the fact that we can't possibly sympathise with Franklin's position given that he's being so arrogant and uncaring.

The 'A' Plot: Shon, an alien child, is in medlab with an obstruction in his internal air bladder. His parents, Tharg and M'ola, are very concerned, and ask Dr Franklin to help, but when he tells them that surgery is the only answer they refuse their permission. Their religious beliefs forbid the opening of their bodies, lest their souls escape. Franklin tries to get them to change their minds, but they are resolute. Franklin wants to operate anyway, and can't see the sense in letting religious considerations overrule the right of his patient to live. He asks Sinclair to suspend Tharg and M'ola's parental authority. Tharg and M'ola, meanwhile, ask for help from the Narn Regime, the Centauri Republic, the Vorlon Empire and the Minbari Federation. Each race refuses for different reasons. When Sinclair finds out that Shon himself is refusing the operation he forbids Franklin from carrying it out, but Franklin goes ahead and does it anyway. After the operation, Shon's parents initially respond to him as if he were a demon, but they later appear to accept him as their child. It's a ploy to get him away from Franklin; as soon as they are alone they kill him like the animal they believe him to be.

The 'B' Plot: Starliner *Asimov*, on its way to Babylon 5, has a fire on board which wipes out its navigational ability. Flying blind in territory known to be a haunt of Raiders, its captain contacts Babylon 5 and asks for help. Ivanova and another pilot take two Starfuries and head for the *Asimov* in order to escort it back to the station. A single Raider ship approaches the *Asimov* and Ivanova gives chase, jamming it so it can't warn other Raiders, while her wingman stays to guard the *Asimov*. She destroys the Raider but comes across a large Raider fleet heading for the *Asimov*. She manages to either destroy them or escape from them (we don't see which) and make it back to Babylon 5 intact, along with the *Asimov*.

Observations: We discover in episode 307 ('Exogenesis') that Dr Franklin has the authority to open the door to any set of quarters on the station if he thinks there might be a medical emergency in progress, but he is not allowed to enter. He opens the door to Tharg and M'ola's quarters in this episode and enters, but he's under a lot of stress so he can be excused.

Delenn, talking about souls, tells Tharg and M'ola, 'We have suffered the interference of others in this area.' She is probably referring to the Soul Hunters (episode 102 – 'Soul Hunter').

J. Michael Straczynski (who developed the basic story for 'Believers') assigned the script to writer David Gerrold because he had adopted a child of Shon's age shortly before. Straczynski himself wrote the entire 'B' plot, as Gerrold's script ran too short.

Koshisms: 'The avalanche has already started. It is too late for the pebbles to vote.'

Ivanova's Life Lessons: A bored Ivanova: 'I think I'll just walk to and fro for a while, maybe over to my console. After that, maybe I'll try pacing fro and to, you know, just for the kick of it.' (This line was written by Straczynski.)

Dialogue to Rewind For: Londo: 'How much justice can you afford?'

Ships That Pass In The Night: Starliner *Asimov* hits Babylon 5 again. We first saw it in episode 102 ('Soul Hunter').

Other Worlds: Tharg, M'ola and Shon come from the planet Thalatine.

Culture Shock: Inhabitants of the planet Thalatine are oviparous (i.e. they lay eggs rather than hatch their young live).

Station Keeping: Senator Gant is one of the members of the Babylon 5 Oversight Committee.

Literary, Mythological and Historical References: The Pfingle eggs which get a passing mention are a reference back to writer David Gerrold's *War Against the Chtorr* series of novels.

I've Seen That Face Before: David Gerrold wrote, co-wrote and rewrote several episodes of the original series and the animated series of *Star Trek*, including the classic 'The Trouble With Tribbles'. He also contributed heavily to the development of *Star Trek: The Next Generation*.

Questions Raised: What happened to Tharg and M'ola?
Ivanova fires on the Raider ship and destroys it when all it

has done is turn and flee. It hasn't fired on her, or on the *Asimov*. It could have been going about its business quite peacefully. Is this standard Earthforce operating procedure – shoot first and ask questions afterwards?

'Survivors'

Transmission Number: 111
Production Number: 111

Written by: Mark Scott Zicree
Directed by: Jim Johnston

Lianna Kemmer: Elaine Thomas
Young Lianna Kemmer: Robin Wake
Cutter: Tom Donaldson   **Nolan:** José Rosario
General Netter: Rod Perry

Plot: It's fun seeing Garibaldi put into the position that he's put so many others in, and surprisingly distressing to see him fall off the wagon at the first sign of pressure. A good one.

The 'A' Plot: President Santiago is on his way to visit Babylon 5. An explosion in Cobra Bay 11 makes Garibaldi suspect that an assassination attempt is planned against him, and Major Lianna Kemmer – who has arrived ahead of the President – agrees. Pursuing a personal vendetta against Garibaldi, whom she blames for the death of her father seventeen years before, she takes control of the investigation. She questions Nolan, an injured survivor of the explosion, and he tells her before he dies that Garibaldi planted the bomb. Garibaldi is suspended from duty and his quarters are searched. Cutter, Major Kemmer's second-in-command, discovers a large quantity of Centauri ducats and schematic diagrams of the Cobra Bays in there. Garibaldi goes on the run and seeks assistance from Londo, G'Kar and N'Grath. Caught in a seedy bar, he is captured and locked up by Major Kemmer. A search of Nolan's quarters ordered by Sinclair turns up detonators and Home Guard literature. Garibaldi realises that Nolan got caught in his own bomb by mistake and implicated Garibaldi deliberately. When Major Kemmer asks about the incriminating material found in Garibaldi's quarters, he points out that only Cutter could have planted them. When Garibaldi and Kemmer confront him, Cutter knocks Kemmer out and fights with Garibaldi. Cutter has rigged the Cobra Bays to explode when the Starfuries launch as an honour guard for the President. Garibaldi knocks him out and alerts Ivanova to the imminent explosion a few seconds before the Starfuries launch.

The 'B' Plot: Major Lianna Kemmer, an Earthforce officer who is acting as security liaison for the President, knows Garibaldi from her childhood on Europa. Garibaldi was a local security man at the time, and was making things unpleasant for the local criminals. Lianna's father, Frank Kemmer, was a shuttle pilot who was killed as part of the criminals' attempts to get rid of Garibaldi. She has blamed him ever since, and when she discovers that he may be involved in a plot against the President she sees it as a chance to get revenge for her father's murder.

The 'C' Plot: President Santiago is visiting Babylon 5 to present a new wing of Starfuries and to make a speech encouraging greater contacts between Earth and alien governments.

The Arc: The unhappiness of certain sections of human society with the liberal attitudes of President Santiago towards aliens manifests itself again in episode 122 ('Chrysalis').

Observations: Seventeen years ago, Garibaldi was working in security on Europa (one of Jupiter's moons). Since then he has worked on Orion 4 and Mars.

This episode marks the arrival of Zeta Wing of Starfuries aboard Babylon 5.

Londo refers to the Narn occupation of Ragesh 3 (see episode 101 – 'Midnight on the Firing Line').

Garibaldi mentions the trouble they've recently had with the Home Guard (episode 107 – 'The War Prayer').

The addictive drug dust is mentioned (see episode 306 – 'Dust to Dust').

General Netter is named for Doug Netter, the show's co-Executive Producer.

This episode was originally entitled 'A Knife in the Shadows'.

Dialogue to Rewind For: G'Kar: 'The universe is run by the complex interweaving of three elements – energy, matter and enlightened self-interest.' (This line was written by J. Michael Straczynski, by the way.)

Ships That Pass In The Night: *Earthforce 1* – the President's personal transport – makes its first appearance.

Other Worlds: Garibaldi used to work on Orion 4 and Europa.

Culture Shock: The Vree are, apparently, messy eaters (their ships look like flying saucers, and have turned up in a number of episodes, most notably 109 – 'Deathwalker' – and 321 – 'Shadow Dancing').

Ilarus is the Centauri Goddess of Luck and Patron of Gamblers.

Accidents Will Happen: Garibaldi uses Cutter's comlink to alert Ivanova to the bombs, but we find out in episode 307 ('Exogenesis') that comlinks are biogenetically keyed to one person only and can't be used by other people.

Questions Raised: A big thing is made of these Centauri ducats – at first they seem to indicate that Londo has bribed Garibaldi and then, when it is discovered that G'Kar has some Centauri ducats, he is immediately suspected of arranging it all. However, we find out at the end of the episode that Cutter just drew a whole load of money out of his account in Centauri ducats and planted them in Garibaldi's quarters. If anyone can just draw Centauri ducats out of a bank, why the big fuss about them earlier?

'By Any Means Necessary'

Transmission Number: 112
Production Number: 114

Written by: Kathryn M. Drennan
Directed by: Jim Johnston

Neeoma Connelly: Kate Boyer   **Orin Zento:** John Snyder
Eduardo Delvientos: José Rey
Senator Hidoshi: Aki Aleong
Mary Ann Cramer: Patricia Healy

Plot: A nicely realised, well-written episode. Nice to see the little guy getting a look in – *Babylon 5* is the only series that's ever bothered to ask who builds and maintains these wonderful toys that the heroes play with all the time.

The 'A' Plot: Equipment failure in Docking Bay 8 results in the accidental destruction of a Narn cargo ship. The dock workers complain through their Dockers Guild representative, Neeoma Connelly, that they are working double and triple shifts with unreliable, outdated equipment for low rates of pay. The EarthGov response is that they are under contract, and can neither expect a pay rise nor go on strike. The latest round of budget cuts has left them with no pay rise, despite promises given to them during the previous set of negotiations. The dockers start reporting in sick to register their unhappiness, and EarthGov send top negotiator Orin Zento to the station to sort things out. Zento aggravates the dock workers by being inflexible, and they declare an official strike. Ships are stacking up outside the station, and Sinclair is getting more and more irritable as he tries to find a solution. On Earth, the Senate has been persuaded by Zento to invoke the Rush Act and declare the strike illegal. Sinclair is authorised to use any means necessary to break the strike – the clear implication being that he should use force. Instead he transfers 1.3 million credits from the military budget to pay for new docking bay equipment and to hire extra workers to take the strain off the ones already there. The dockers go back to work, satisfied, but Sinclair is warned that he has made important enemies back on Earth.

The 'B' Plot: G'Kar is going through the Days of G'Quan – a Narn religious festival in which abstinence figures strongly. In order to complete the ceremony, G'Kar is required to burn a G'Quan Eth plant when the sun rises above the G'Quan mountains on Narn, but the G'Quan Eth plant he had on order was destroyed when the Narn cargo ship

Talquith exploded. There is no time to ship another plant to the station, even if the dock workers weren't on strike, and the only other plant on the station belongs to Londo Mollari. Londo offers to sell it to G'Kar for 50,000 credits, but backs out of the deal when G'Kar raises the money. G'Kar breaks into Londo's quarters but cannot find the plant. When Sinclair's intercession fails to elicit any cooperation from Londo, G'Kar steals a Centauri religious statuette and offers to exchange it for the plant. Forced to intervene, Sinclair points out to Londo that the G'Quan Eth plant is a controlled item, and can only be used for legitimate religious and medical purposes. He forces Londo to hand the plant over, but G'Kar claims that it is too late – the required time for the ceremony has already passed. Sinclair points out that the sunlight that rose over the G'Quan mountain from ten years before will be passing the station within twelve hours, and that G'Kar can conduct his ceremony using that light instead. G'Kar gratefully agrees.

The Arc: 'Things are changing on Earth,' Sinclair says, 'and not all for the best.' This episode continues and develops Sinclair's troubles with certain forces in EarthGov, and sets up the events of episode 116 ('Eyes') and probably prefigures the rise of Morgan Clark to President in episode 122 ('Chrysalis').

Observations: Dockers Guild representative Neeoma Connelly refers during the course of the episode to various labour disputes in history. Most are fictional, but Matewan isn't. During 1920, Matewan (a town in West Virginia, USA) was the site of a confrontation between townspeople, miners and mine company detectives. The United Mine Workers of America had been attempting to organise the area's coal miners, but those who joined were fired and evicted from the company-owned homes. John Sayles made a film about the confrontation (*Matewan*) in 1987.

When Sinclair is working through the night on his budget calculations in the middle of the episode, various company names are listed on his computer screen, along with the amounts that Babylon 5 is paying them. One company is

McAuliffe Computational. This is a tribute to schoolteacher Sharon Christa McAuliffe, a Payload Specialist who died aboard the Challenger space shuttle on 28 January 1986. There is another tribute to her in episode 119 ('A Voice in the Wilderness' Part Two).

Kathryn M. Drennan, the writer of the episode, is married to J. Michael Straczynski. More restrictions were placed upon her than upon any other writer, to avoid accusations of nepotism – she had to write a complete spec script, and that script had to have the unanimous approval of all the in-house personnel and of Warner Brothers.

The Rush Act doesn't exist – it's a piece of legislation that will, in *Babylon 5*'s future history, be enacted at some stage between now and the year 2258. It was probably named for the right-wing American talk-show host Rush Limbaugh.

This episode was originally entitled 'Backlash'.

Ships That Pass In The Night: Earthforce ship *Omega*, shuttle *Copernicus*, Narn cargo ship *Talquith*, cargo ship *Seattle*, transport *Moroder*.

Other Worlds: Ganymede – the largest moon of Jupiter – apparently suffered a notable strike back in 2237 (the last time the Rush Act was invoked). Another strike occurred on or at New California, but we don't know whether this is a planet or a city.

The Narn homeworld is 12.2 human light years from Babylon 5 (or just over 10 Narn light years).

Culture Shock: Londo says of the Narn: 'They're all pagans, still worshipping their sun.' Coming from a culture that worships an entire pantheon of deities, this is a bit rich.

Station Keeping: There are over a thousand dockers working on Babylon 5 (we're told that the figure is around 1,500 in episode 215 – 'And Now For a Word' – but there's probably been a budget increase in the interim.

I've Seen That Face Before: John Snyder, who plays the rather touchy negotiator, previously played the second Soul Hunter (the sane one) in episode 102 ('Soul Hunter').

Garibaldi's aide Jack appears in this episode (played by Macaulay Bruton) but doesn't get any lines or, indeed, a credit.

The docker who yells 'Strike!' at the meeting of the Dockers Guild is the director of the episode, Jim Johnston. Most of the production crew appear in the episode at various points.

Questions Raised: It's a hell of a coincidence that Babylon 5 happens to be almost exactly ten Narn light years from the Narn homeworld, thus allowing G'Kar to complete his ceremony within twelve hours rather than having to wait for several months, but hey! that sort of crazy coincidence happens all the time on Babylon 5, doesn't it?

'Signs and Portents'

Transmission Number: 113
Production Number: 116

Written by: J. Michael Straczynski
Directed by: Janet Greek

Lord Kiro: Gerrit Graham   **Lady Ladira:** Fredi Olster
Morden: Ed Wasser   **Raider No. 1:** Whip Hubley
Reno: Robert Silver

Date: Wednesday 23 August 2258.

Plot: The significance of the story should be obvious from the fact that the overall title for season one is also 'Signs and Portents'. Essentially it acts as a pivot, changing the direction of the series, but unlike many later such episodes it has a story in its own right as well as setting up others yet to come. As with all the best *Babylon 5* stories, the 'A', 'B' and 'C' plots are all interlinked and come together with a satisfying 'click' at the end of the episode.

The 'A' Plot: Raider activity is on the increase and Sinclair puts Delta Wing on alert. Nobody can work out how the Raiders are able to conduct their raids without using jumpgates. An Earth transport ship – the *Achilles* – is attacked and Delta Wing are sent out to defend it, but Sinclair realises it's a ruse and recalls them. The Raiders' mothership – big enough to create its own jumpgates – appears and launches wave after wave of fighters, but Sinclair boxes them in between Alpha Wing, Delta Wing and the station's own guns. The Raider mothership retreats, its fighters annihilated, but the attack was a ruse to steal a valuable Centauri artefact known as the Eye.

The 'B' Plot: Londo Mollari has brokered a deal between the Centauri and what appears to be a group of high-class art thieves who possess the Eye – the oldest symbol of Centauri authority and the property of the first Emperor, missing for over a hundred years since the Battle of Nu'Shok. Lord Kiro and his seer aunt Lady Ladira arrive on Babylon 5 to take it back to the Emperor, but Kiro obviously has designs on the throne himself, and believes the Eye could help him. Raiders steal the Eye and take Kiro hostage, but once about their ship it is clear that Kiro is in league with them. They double-cross him, but a huge and terrifying alien ship of unknown design appears and carves the Raider ship up like a chunk of cheese. Londo believes the Eye is lost for ever, but a mysterious stranger named Morden returns it to him.

The 'C' Plot: A man named Morden arrives on Babylon 5 and arranges to see all the Ambassadors with the exception of Kosh. He asks them one simple question – 'What do you want?' – which they answer in a variety of ways. Only Londo Mollari's request seems to satisfy him, and he leaves after returning an ancient Centauri artefact that was stolen by Raiders.

The Arc: This story marks the first appearance of both the mysterious but boyishly charming Morden and of his demonic 'associates' – the Shadows. When Morden first appears he has just disembarked from Earth Transport *Spinoza*. Perhaps the owners of the *Spinoza* have a contract with Villains Inc.: they also brought Bester to the station in episode 106 ('Mind War'). Morden tells the Customs Guard, 'I've been out of circulation. Spent the last few years doing some exploration out on the Rim.' When the Guard asks him if he found anything interesting, he smiles, hesitates, then simply says, 'Yes.' This prefigures the explanation about his association with the Shadows, the *Icarus* and Captain Sheridan's wife given later in episode 217 – 'The Shadow of Z'ha'dum'.

Londo's reply to Morden's question 'What do you want?' is worth repeating in full, as it triggers the events that shape the rest of the series. 'Do you really want to know what *I* want? Do you really want to know the truth? I want my people to reclaim their rightful place in the galaxy. I want to see the Centauri stretch forth their hand again and command the stars. I want a rebirth of glory – a renaissance of power. I want to stop running through my life like a man late for an appointment, afraid to look back or look forward. I want us to be what we used to be. I want . . . I want it all back the way it was. Does that answer your question?' G'Kar is the only other ambassador who gives Morden a verbal answer, but he hasn't thought through exactly what it is that he *does* want. His vision is too small. Londo, by contrast, wants it all, and that is why the Centauri, not the Narn, are chosen by the Shadows.

Sinclair reveals to Garibaldi that he is starting to fill in the hole in his mind, and that he remembers being taken onto a Minbari ship during the Battle of the Line and seeing Delenn there. He asks Garibaldi to try to find out what happened to him during that time (not the hardest assignment Garibaldi's ever been given, but close). Garibaldi discovers that the Minbari rejected every name suggested to them as Commander of Babylon 5 until Earthforce got down to Sinclair. They obviously wanted him and only him. This picks up from events in the pilot episode and episode 102 ('Soul Hunter') and prefigures many later episodes, especially the discussion of Minbari souls in 201 ('Points of Departure') and later in 316 and 317 ('War Without End' Parts One and Two).

Lady Ladira has a premonition that 'Babylon will fall – the place will be destroyed . . . Fire . . . death . . . pain.' The picture she sees is obviously Babylon 5, but her words could have been referring to any Babylon station. In fact, we discover that her vision is probably of something that would have happened had Sheridan and Sinclair failed to send Babylon 4 back in time to the first Shadow War, as we discover in 'Babylon Squared' (120) and 'War Without End' Parts I and II (316 and 317).

Delenn is still building the device that she later uses in episode 122 ('Chrysalis').

When Delenn confronts Morden, a metal triangle appears on her forehead for a few moments. This panics her, and well it should: it's the symbol worn by Grey Council members, as seen in episode 108 ('And the Sky Full of Stars'). It only manifests itself for specific reasons at specific times, and its manifestation now shocks her.

Delenn recognises what Morden is, and as she does so a shadow passes across his face.

Morden avoids Kosh once, early on, but is confronted by him later. We do not see what happens, but we later hear that Kosh's encounter suit has been damaged. No doubt this damage was inflicted by the invisible Shadows that accompany Morden, as we saw in episode 217 – 'The Shadow of Z'ha'dum'. The battle was only a skirmish – the next time their paths cross, the outcome is a lot more dramatic (episode 315 – 'Interludes and Examinations').

Two seasons later, in episode 309 ('Point of No Return'), another Centauri seer – Lady Morella – prophesies the three opportunities Londo Mollari will have to 'avoid the fire' that awaits him at the end of his journey. One is 'save the eye that does not see'. It is generally accepted that this is a reference to the Eye which the Shadows return to Londo in this story, although it might well refer to something else.

Observations: Is this the first time in mainstream American television that two main characters have held a conversation while urinating? I like to think so.

When Ladira has her first vision, she stands before an electronic bulletin board on which the words 'BABYLON 5 TO HOST NATIONAL CONFERENCE' appear. Next to this is another board with a list of events occurring that day in the conference. The events include: Zero-G Shuffleboard, a Gravity Loss Safety seminar, a Flea Market and something called a

Mojo Mind Rave ('Mojo' being the nickname of Adam Leibowitz, a visual effects artist on the show).

This episode was originally entitled 'Raiding Party'.

The role of Morden was written with Ed Wasser in mind – he was already working on the series behind the scenes.

Koshisms: Kosh to Morden (and his 'associates'): 'Leave this place. They are not for you. Go. Leave. Now.'

Ivanova's Life Lessons: Ivanova: 'Why does my mouth always taste like old carpet in the morning?' Computer: 'Unknown. Checking medical log.'

Sinclair: 'Morning Lieutenant Commander. Problem sleeping?' Ivanova: 'Sleeping is not the problem. Waking up – *that* is the problem. I've always had a hard time getting up when it's dark outside.' Sinclair: 'But in space it's always dark.' Ivanova (with feeling): 'I know. I know.'

Dialogue to Rewind For: Morden's repeated refrain, posed best to Ambassador Mollari – 'I'm not allowed to leave here until you answer my question – so, what do you want?'

Delenn's horrified response after Morden has left – 'They're here . . .', and Lady Ladira's equally chilling, 'The Shadows have come for us all.'

Ships That Pass In The Night: Earth Transport *Spinoza*, the *Marie Celeste* (mentioned in 'walla' in the background), Earth Transport *Achilles*. The *Spinoza* previously appeared in episode 106 ('Mind War').

I've Seen That Face Before: The actor playing Morden – Ed Wasser – previously appeared in the pilot episode ('The Gathering') as Guerra, an Earthforce operative working in Babylon 5's Command and Control area. Given the backstory now established for Morden, it is unlikely that the two characters are connected. He had also worked on the show as a prompter – sitting off stage and reading lines for characters off screen or prompting characters on set with the proper lines.

Gerrit Graham, who played Lord Kiro, later appeared as a member of the Q Continuum in the *Star Trek: Voyager* episode 'Death Wish'.

Questions Raised: Morden says he has been given an introduction to Ambassador G'Kar by Councillor To'Bar of the First Circle. Is he lying, did he have to go to Narn first to arrange a meeting with G'Kar or are there already links between the Shadows and the Narn?

Delenn obviously has a spy network on the station, because she knows that Morden has seen G'Kar. And she seems so harmless, as well . . .

Lady Ladira can let other people share her visions. Is this a standard ability for Centauri seers?

What exactly *does* Delenn want?

'TKO'

Transmission Number: 114
Production Number: 119

Written by: Lawrence G. DiTillio
Directed by: John Flinn

Rabbi Joseph Koslov: Theodore Bikel
Walker Smith: Greg McKinney
The Muta-Do: Soon-Teck Oh
Caliban: Don Stroud   **Gyor:** James Jude Courtney

Plot: The central plank of this episode – a human fighting in an alien tournament – almost totally sabotages the suspension of disbelief the audience have entered into over *Babylon 5*'s aliens. Yes, they're just men in make-up, but we try to pretend they're not. Most of the time this works, but the sight of the different races in 'TKO' all using the same set of martial arts movements ruins the illusion. And it makes no sense: the various races should all have different physical characteristics – strength, speed, coordination, body movement – and would be completely unmatched. With the core of the episode so insubstantial, the rather sweet subplot involving Rabbi Koslov snaps beneath the weight of the audience's attention.

The 'A' Plot: Walker Smith – an old friend of Garibaldi – arrives on the station. He is a professional fighter – or at least he was until Sport Corp made sure that he failed a drugs test before a fight they didn't want him to compete in. He has come to Babylon 5 to compete in the *mutai* – a no-holds-barred alien fighting competition that no human has ever been allowed to enter. When he asks if he can take part, he is rejected by the *Muta-Do* – the ninety-year-old alien master of the *mutai*. When he insists, the *Muta-Do* knocks him down. Dejected, he is offered hope by the alien Caliban, who tells him that Gyor, the champion of the *mutai*, is obliged by the rules to fight any challenger. During a *mutai* session, Smith challenges Gyor, and the fight commences. It results in a draw when the two combatants are too exhausted and battered to hurt each other any more. Walker Smith leaves the station, triumphant, having proved that humanity can stand and inflict as much punishment as any of the races taking part in the *mutai*.

The 'B' Plot: Rabbi Joseph Koslov – an old friend of the Ivanova family – arrives on the station on the same liner as Walker Smith. He has come to give Ivanova her father's samovar – his legacy to her. When he discovers she has not sat *shiva* (the Jewish ceremony of mourning) for her father, he tries to persuade her that she should. She rejects his advice, and he tells her that he will leave. She changes her mind, and takes part in the ceremony.

Observations: Rabbi Koslov says *'Bohze moi'* at one stage. This roughly translates from Russian as 'My God!'. He also says, 'What *meshugas*!' when he arrives on the station, meaning, 'What madness!'

Walker Smith is the real name of Sugar Ray Robinson, US boxer and world welterweight champion from 1946 to 1951. Robinson fought 202 fights.

The Jewish *shiva* ceremony is a ceremony of mourning and remembrance for the dead. It should last for seven days, and the name is derived from the Hebrew word *sheva* meaning 'seven'. The deceased's close family sit on low stools and talk about them for a number of days, attended by friends and relatives. The *shiva* ceremony as portrayed in this episode differs from the classic Orthodox ceremony as performed in the twentieth century, but things change in three hundred years.

At one point in this episode, Ivanova is reading a book by Harlan Ellison entitled *Working Without a Net*. Ellison is, of course, the show's Creative Consultant, and the book is his (as yet unwritten) autobiography. He apparently plans on writing the book in about three years' time.

Larry DiTillio goes in to *Star Trek* emulation overdrive in this episode, what with Traxian ale, Jovian tubers and Zoomburgers.

As with a number of DiTillio's scripts, the title of this episode requires some decoding. 'TKO' stands for 'Technical Knock Out'.

The episode was not shown during the first UK showing of *Babylon 5*'s first season. Channel 4, the channel transmitting the programme, claimed that it was too violent for an 18.00 spot, and that cutting the violence out (as they did with episode 109 – 'Deathwalker') would have been impractical. It was subsequently aired at a later hour.

Caliban may be from the same race as Trakis in episode 103 ('Born to the Purple').

Ships That Pass In The Night: Earth Liner *White Star* (not *the White Star*, just *a White Star*.)

Other Worlds: Orion 4 (where Garibaldi was once stationed) and Cestus (where the waitresses all had three breasts).

Culture Shock: A treel is a Centauri fish.

Literary, Mythological and Historical References: Caliban is the bestial and villainous slave of Prospero in Shakespeare's last play, *The Tempest*, but there are no parallels between the play and this episode. Presumably DiTillio used the name because he liked it.

I've Seen That Face Before: Theodore Bikel, who gives such a warm performance as Rabbi Koslov, is an old hand at character acting in the USA. He has appeared in more than thirty films and been nominated for an Academy Award for Best Supporting Actor (for the 1958 film *The Defiant Ones*). Highlights of his film career include *My Fair Lady*, *The African Queen* and (my personal favourite) *Darker Than*

Amber. He is probably best known to SF TV fans as Worf's adoptive human 'father' in the *Star Trek: The Next Generation* episode 'Family'.

Soon-Teck Oh can also be seen in those classic movies *Death Wish 4* (with Charles Bronson) and *Missing in Action 2* (with Chuck Norris).

If you want to see what Don Stroud looks like without a ton of make-up and a long wig (and before he gained a scar and lost an eye) he plays Heller – Sanchez's mercenary sidekick – in the 1989 James Bond film *Licence to Kill*. He's the one who gets impaled on the fork-lift truck towards the end of the film.

Questions Raised: If the news that Walker Smith was taking part in the *mutai* was so important that ISN broadcast it, why weren't there any journalists trying to interview him on the station?

What was Caliban's motive in telling Walker Smith about the loophole in the rules of the *mutai*? We're set up to expect that he's getting something out of it, but we never find out what it is.

Why aren't humans allowed to participate in the *mutai*? It's not as if we're anything special in the *Babylon 5* universe, after all.

'Grail'

Transmission Number: 115
Production Number: 109

Written by: Christy Marx
Directed by: Richard Compton

Aldous Gajic: David Warner   **Deuce:** William Sanderson
Jinxo: Tom Booker   **Ombuds Wellington:** Jim Norton

Plot: On the one hand, the episode is complex and all the plots twine together in a satisfying manner, but on the other hand the plot device of someone looking for the Holy Grail in space is an early example of the series' occasional and unfortunate flirtation with British mythic archetypes.

139

The 'A' Plot: A petty extortionist named Deuce is about to be put on trial by the Ombuds for his crimes. He kidnaps the main witness and wipes her mind clean using a mysterious alien in a Vorlon encounter suit. With her effectively catatonic, the case against him collapses. Annoyed at the personal comments made about him by Ombuds Wellington, Deuce kidnaps the man and threatens to wipe his mind clean as well. Garibaldi realises that Deuce is using a semi-sentient life form known as a Nakaleen Feeder. He and Sinclair lead an armed team to the Downbelow area where Deuce is keeping Ombuds Wellington, where they kill it and wound Deuce.

The 'B' Plot: A traveller named Aldous Gajic arrives on Babylon 5 to be greeted by an honoured Delenn and Lennier and a confused Sinclair and Garibaldi. Gajic is searching for the Holy Grail – the vessel supposedly used to catch Christ's blood during the crucifixion, which then became an icon linked to the legend of King Arthur. Gajic refers to it as the Cup of the Goddess and the Sacred Vessel of Regeneration, and believes that it could be the salvation of the human race. He is the last representative of an order dedicated to finding it, and controls all their wealth. His wallet is stolen by a petty thief, Jinxo, who is arrested by Garibaldi and sentenced to five years' banishment from the station by Ombuds Wellington. Gajic offers to take responsibility for Jinxo's actions, but Jinxo owes Deuce a lot of money and Gajic is kidnapped by Deuce when he stops Deuce's men from taking Jinxo. Jinxo goes to warn Sinclair and Garibaldi what is happening. Gajic manages to distract the Nakaleen Feeder that Deuce is using as a weapon of terror, but is shot by accident when Deuce tries to shoot Jinxo. Before dying, he hands responsibility for finding the Holy Grail to Jinxo. Jinxo leaves the station to seek the Grail.

The 'C' Plot: Jinxo was a construction worker on the original Babylon station, as well as Babylons 2, 3, 4 and 5. He believes that the original Babylon station and its two successors were destroyed because he left, and that Babylon 4 vanished for the same reason. He doesn't want to leave Babylon 5 because he is terrified of what might happen to it if

140

he does. When he finally leaves, nothing happens. Not yet, anyway.

The Arc: Delenn describes Aldous Gajic thus: 'Among my people, a true seeker is treated with utmost reverence and respect . . . What matters is that he strives for the perfection of his soul and the salvation of his race, and that he has never wavered or lost faith.' Later dialogue makes it clear that she thinks of Sinclair as a true seeker too. Later, Sinclair tells her, 'It's a hard thing to live your life searching for something and never find it.' These are both oblique references to the Minbari soul thread that began in the pilot episode ('The Gathering') and was hinted at in various episodes, including 102 ('Soul Hunter'), 108 ('And the Sky Full of Stars') and 109 ('Deathwalker') before being partially cleared up in episode 201 ('Points of Departure') and fully explained in episode 317 ('War Without End' Part Two).

Observations: Deuce's real name is Desmond Mosichenko. Jinxo's real name is Thomas Jordan.

The Nakaleen Feeder is a semi-sentient life form from Centauri-controlled space. The planet it originated from has been quarantined, but the quarantine has recently been lifted. The Nakaleen Feeder is sentient enough to speak.

The Nakaleen Feeder's tentacle is oddly similar to the Centauri sexual organs. There is, apparently, no connection – the prosthetics people just built them that way.

There is some really hideous and inappropriate 'funny' music over the scene where Vir gives Gajic a data crystal. All J. Michael Straczynski has said about the subject is: 'After "Grail" we had a discussion with Chris about funny music. We do not anticipate further discussions.'

The man in the courtroom at the beginning of the episode who is demanding damages over the alien abduction of his ancestor is John Flinn, the show's Director of Photography and occasional director. Appropriately enough, the character's name is Mr Flinn. The trial scene itself was scripted by Straczynski because the episode was running short.

'Gajic' is the last name of Mira Furlan's husband.

Christy Marx's description of the Feeder in her script was

as a kind of flying jellyfish that moved using air jets.

In an earlier draft of the episode, Kosh appeared at the end and destroyed the Nakaleen Feeder with the explanation, 'Some things we do not allow.' It was felt that this was too like the end of episode 109 ('Deathwalker'), so the idea was dropped.

At one point, Deuce gives Jinxo 'three hundred cycles' to get him what he wants. Early in the run of the series, cycles were the local equivalent of hours. This was dropped for later episodes.

Ivanova's Life Lessons: When the station hasn't blown up after Jinxo leaves, and it's pointed out to her that there has been no 'boom!', Ivanova replies. 'No "boom" *today*. "Boom" tomorrow. There's always a "boom" tomorrow.'

Dialogue to Fast Forward Past: Londo's muttered comment, 'Fools to the left of me, Feeders to the right,' just calls out for a convention audience to sing, 'Here I am, stuck in the middle with you.'

Ships That Pass In The Night: Transport *Von Braun*, named after the Nazi rocket scientist who worked on the V1 and V2 weapons and was relocated to America after the war to help the Americans win the space race. There's also a Minbari Liner with a name that sounds like *Falkori*. Jinxo leaves Babylon 5 on the Transport *Marie Celeste* (which was first mentioned in episode 113 – 'Babylon Squared').

Literary, Mythological and Historical References: The first appearance of the Holy Grail in literature is in the *Conte del Graal* (or *Perceval le Gallois*) written by Chrestien de Troyes around AD 1180. The tale, which recounts the adventures of a knight named Perceval, was itself based on earlier Welsh tales that did not mention the Grail. Chrestien did not explain what the Grail actually was – that was left to later writers such as Gautier and Wolfram von Eschenbach (AD 1200). The Holy Grail was the receptacle used to catch Christ's blood at the crucifixion, and was supposedly brought to England by Joseph of Arimathea. There are no obvious references to its being called the Cup of the Goddess or the Sacred Vessel of Regeneration.

I've Seen That Face Before: David Warner, who plays Aldous Gajic, is a familiar face on both sides of the Atlantic. In Britain his stage presence is still fondly remembered, especially his performance as Hamlet, while in America he regularly pops up in film and television roles with some fantasy element to them. It's difficult to pick any one genre credit above the others, although his role as Ultimate Evil in the 1981 film *Time Bandits* was a masterpiece of straight-faced minimalism ('Tell me again about digital watches'). Never afraid to take the mickey out of himself, he played two villains in the 1982 film *Tron* (alongside Bruce Boxleitner and Peter Jurasik, of course) and a lunatic brain surgeon named Dr Necessiter in the 1983 Steve Martin vehicle *The Man With Two Brains*. He keeps popping up in *Star Trek*'s various incarnations – having played an alcoholic human diplomat in *Star Trek V: The Final Frontier* (1989), a Klingon Chancellor in *Star Trek VI: The Undiscovered Country* (1991) and a Cardassian torturer in the *Star Trek: The Next Generation* episodes 'Chain of Command Part I' and 'Chain of Command Part II'. He also had a recurring role in the second season of David Lynch and Mark Frost's cult TV series *Twin Peaks* as Thomas Eckhardt and in the first season of the TV series *Lois and Clark: The New Adventures of Superman* as Superman's father, Jor-El.

William Sanderson, who plays the villain Deuce, is best known for his role as the android toy designer J. F. Sebastian in the 1982 film *Blade Runner*. He also appeared in the *X Files* episode 'Blood'.

Jim (Ombuds Wellington) Norton appeared as Albert Einstein in the *Star Trek: The Next Generation* episode 'Descent Part I'.

Writer Christy Marx was editor of the in-house *Babylon 5* newsletter during season one of the show.

Accidents Will Happen: Lennier tells Gajic: 'There are two castes of Minbari – the Warrior caste and the Religious caste.' In those immortal words, what about the Workers?

Questions Raised: Who raised the quarantine on the home planet of the Nakaleen Feeders, and why?

'Eyes'

Transmission Number: 116
Production Number: 122

Written by: Lawrence G. DiTillio
Directed by: Jim Johnston

Colonel Ari Ben Zayn: Gregory Martin
General Miller: Frank Farmer
Harriman Gray: Jeffrey Combs
Tragedy: Macaulay Bruton   **Comedy:** Drew Letchworth
Sophie Ivanova: Marie Chambers

Plot: It's a taut, claustrophobic little story, but it suffers somewhat in relation to episode 108 – 'And the Sky Full of Stars' – whose plot it copies (a covert organisation inside Earthforce send an embittered veteran undercover to Babylon 5 in order to investigate Sinclair's loyalty).

The 'A' Plot: Colonel Ari Ben Zayn from Earthforce Internal Affairs arrives on Babylon 5, accompanied by Psi Cop Harriman Gray. Ben Zayn claims to be investigating command staff loyalty, but he appears to have Sinclair firmly in his sights. As justification for Gray's presence he quotes new Earthforce regulations that all command staff have to submit to telepathic scanning as part of any investigation. Sinclair gets Gray dismissed on a technicality, but Ben Zayn has Sinclair relieved of command in order to get him to submit to a mind scan. Ben Zayn assumes command of the station himself, and starts proceedings against Sinclair. Garibaldi discovers that Ben Zayn is a friend of Psi Cop Bester, humiliated by Sinclair during the Jason Ironheart business, and that Ben Zayn was in the top ten officers selected to command Babylon 5 but was rejected by the Minbari in favour of Sinclair. Sinclair confronts Ben Zayn with this latter fact. Ben Zayn is so furious with Sinclair that Harriman Gray telepathically picks up the real reason for his actions – a festering hatred and jealousy. Ben Zayn pulls a gun and attempts to take command by force, but Gray disables him with a psychic burst of pain. He is returned to Earth for psychiatric investigation.

The 'B' Plot: Knowing she will have to submit to a telepathic scan, but unwilling to have her mind invaded, Ivanova is in a quandary over what to do. She tries to resign from Earthforce, but Sinclair refuses to accept her resignation. She gets drunk and starts a fight, but Garibaldi sobers her up. She has bad dreams. She is about to refuse to undergo a scan, knowing that she will be dishonourably discharged from Earthforce, when Sinclair exposes Colonel Ari Ben Zayn's real motives, and the necessity for her scan vanishes.

The 'C' Plot: Garibaldi is building a 1992-vintage motor-cycle in his quarters when Lennier arrives. Garibaldi has been scrounging parts for the bike for five years, but hasn't got very far with building it. Lennier offers to help, but while Garibaldi is tied up with Colonel Ben Zayn, Lennier completes it – replacing the polluting hydrocarbon engine with a Minbari power source. Garibaldi is a little upset at first, but when he sees how despondent Lennier is, he takes the Minbari for a ride.

The Arc: Psi Corps and some factions within EarthGov are not happy with the way Sinclair has been running the station, and they want him removed. The factions in question are, presumably, those represented by Vice-President Clark, and the threads which we begin to sense dimly in this story will end, much later, in episodes 308, 309 and 310 – 'Messages From Earth', 'Point of No Return' and 'Severed Dreams.'

Ivanova has a dream in which she sees two masked figures who represent Psi Corps injecting her mother with a telepathy-suppressing drug. One of the figures is played by Macaulay Bruton – the actor who has already played Garibaldi's aide and who will be revealed as a Psi Corps agent in episode 202 – 'Revelations'. The 'coincidence' of casting has been described by J. Michael Straczynski as, 'An Easter egg left where it can be found on later viewings.'

In Ivanova's dream, her mother becomes her in a clear foreshadowing of Ivanova's latent telepathic powers (as revealed in episode 219 – 'Divided Loyalties'). In addition, during a conversation with Psi Cop Harriman Gray, Ivanova can tell that he is scanning her. This ability of hers is later used to check whether Bester is scanning her in episode 313 – 'Ship of Tears'. The real reason she does not want to be scanned is because she wants to hide her latent abilities, as she finally admits to Sheridan in episode 219 ('Divided Loyalties').

Observations: Delenn's friend, the Minbari poet Shaal Mayan, is said to be returning to Babylon 5, and Delenn is worried about her safety. Quite right too: the last time she turned up (episode 107 – 'The War Prayer') she was beaten up by a pro-Earth group.

The character of Harriman Gray also turns up in the first *Babylon 5* novel, *Voices*.

We get the recurring *Babylon 5* line – 'When the time is right' – twice during this episode. Colonel Ben Zayn tells Harriman Gray they will begin their task when the time is right, and General Miller tells Sinclair, 'I promise I'll do all I can to help – when the time is right.'

An Orion slitch is a creature with an ugly rear end.

Some telepaths can send psychic bursts of pain to selected victims.

Lennier learns a little Japanese while building Garibaldi's bike: '*domo arigato*' means 'thank you'.

When Harriman Gray mentions Psi Corps to Ivanova, he is surprised that her first thought is of Talia Winters. This foreshadows the relationship between Ivanova and Talia that starts and stops in episode 219 – 'Divided Loyalties' – and is admitted to in episode 311 – 'Ceremonies of Light and Dark'.

'Eyes' was the last episode filmed in season 1. As with most Larry DiTillio scripts, the title is slang. In this case, 'Eyes' is the derogatory term for the Internal Investigations (the IIs) branch of Earthforce.

This episode has a short clip from episode 109 – 'Death-walker' – playing on a computer screen (it's the Vorlon ship blowing up the ship Jha'dur is on). There are also references to Ragesh 3 (episode 101 – 'Midnight on the Firing Line'), the dockers' strike (episode 112 – 'By Any Means Necessary'), Jason Ironheart (episode 106 – 'Mind War') and the sabotage attempt during the President's visit (episode 111 – 'Survivors').

At one stage, when Ivanova leaves Command and Control, she pages Major Atumbe to take over. According to J. Michael Straczynski: 'I think the third in command would be Major Atumbe, who we've referenced in dialogue on the show, but have never shown. I keep meaning to do so, but it always ends up feeling forced, and it's hard to work in new recurring characters when we have something like sixteen as it is.'

Dialogue to Rewind For: Sinclair: 'Enough people have played with my brain already this year.'

Harriman Gray to Ivanova: 'You're very charming, in an odd sort of way.'

Ships That Pass In The Night: The *Epsilon* – a trader from an unspecified planet.

Other Worlds: Station Phobos has been the location for a terrorist attack. Presumably this is a base located on Mars's moon.

Ari Ben Zayn and Harriman Gray arrived on Babylon 5 from LaGrange 22. This is located near Mars, and is presumably a colony or space station in a stable gravitational ('LaGrangian') point with respect to the sun.

Colonel Ben Zayn has fought battles on New Jerusalem and Cyrus III.

Station Keeping: Arms trading is allowed under Babylon 5 rules, but only if the arms in question are not traded on the station itself but in ships outside.

Oxy-pills are used for sobering up humans.

I've Seen That Face Before: Gregory Martin can also be seen in the John Carpenter semi-SF film *Memoirs of an Invisible Man*.

Jeffrey Combs has become something of a horror fan's dream actor, after his excellent performances in the low-budget H. P. Lovecraft films *Re-Animator* and *Bride of Re-Animator* (as Herbert West) and *From Beyond*. He has also made three appearances as the Ferengi liquidator Brunt in the *Star Trek: Deep Space Nine* episodes 'Family Business', 'Bar Association' and 'Body Parts' and also appeared as the Vorta named Wayaun in the episode 'To The Death'.

Macaulay Bruton, the man in the tragedy mask in Ivanova's dream, also plays Garibaldi's aide in episodes 106 ('Mind War'), 108 ('And the Sky Full of Stars'), 122 ('Chrysalis') and 202 ('Revelations').

Questions Raised: If Ben Zayn's mission was so important to Bester, why did Bester assign him a Psi Cop whom he had never met and whose loyalty to Bester personally was uncertain?

'Legacies'

Transmission Number: 117
Production Number: 115

Written by: D. C. Fontana
Directed by: Bruce Seth Green

Shai Alyt Neroon: John Vickery   **Alisa Beldon:** Grace Una

Plot: A neat little episode with some nice character interplay between Sinclair and Neroon, but spoilt ultimately by the rather diffuse resolution. After all, when Delenn first stole Branmer's body, it didn't occur to any Minbari that it might have been transfigured. Why, suddenly, should they accept it when Neroon and Delenn tell them?

The 'A' Plot: Branmer, the greatest warrior leader the Minbari race ever had, has died during a diplomatic tour. His body is carried in state back to Minbar by Shai Alyt Neroon – the aide who served him for fifteen years. The Minbari war cruiser carrying Branmer's body stops off at Babylon 5 so that it may be displayed, but the body disappears. A search of the entire station turns up nothing, and neither does a stomach-pump of all the Pak'ma'ra on the station. Eventually, a telepathic girl named Alisa Beldon reads the mind of Delenn and discovers that she took Branmer's body. Sinclair confronts Delenn, who admits

148

what she has done. She tells him that Branmer was a member of the Religious caste before he became a warrior, and that he had told her that he did not want his body to become a monument to war. Delenn decided to steal his body to stop Neroon's triumphant procession. She has had it cremated. Under pressure from Sinclair, she blackmails Neroon into backing up her story that Branmer's body was transformed miraculously and has vanished.

The 'B' Plot: Alisa Beldon, a young girl living in Downbelow, steals food from a stall in the market, but before she can escape she collapses. Talia Winters recognises the symptoms as being those of someone whose latent telepathic powers have just sprung into life – effectively Alisa is suffering from the sudden shock of being able to read everybody's mind. She is taken to medlab, where she becomes the subject of an argument between Ivanova and Talia. Talia wants her sent straight to Psi Corps: Ivanova wants her to have a choice about where she goes. While Talia tells Alisa how good Psi Corps will be for her, Ivanova arranges interviews with most of the major ambassadors. After a bad experience with the rapacious Narn, Alisa decides to accept sanctuary on Minbar.

The Arc: The Narn have no telepaths, and make Alisa a very generous offer if she will allow them to sample her genetic material. This was originally set up in the pilot episode ('The Gathering'), and becomes an important factor in the Shadow War in episode 314 ('Ship of Tears').

Alisa manages to read Delenn's mind, and sees the word 'chrysalis'. Neither she nor Sinclair knows what it means, but it's a forward reference to what happens to Delenn in episode 122 ('Chrysalis'), and 202 ('Revelations').

Observations: The Minbari War Cruiser pitches up at Babylon 5 with its gun ports open. To the Minbari this is a sign of respect, but to Sinclair it's a threat. One would have thought he had learnt by now: after all, the war started that way.

We get a flashback to the Battle of the Line during this episode.

Jason Ironheart (from episode 106 – 'Mind War') gets a name check.

Interestingly enough, Delenn can tell when Alisa Beldon is reading her mind.

At the end of the episode: Talia buys Ivanova a coffee. This is the first obvious move in the developing relationship between them – a relationship that ends abruptly in episode 219 ('Divided Loyalties').

'Legacies' is the only episode of *Babylon 5* that has been pitched cold by a freelance writer – i.e. the story was not assigned by J. Michael Straczynski to D. C. Fontana, but pitched to him by her.

Dialogue to Rewind For: Neroon to Sinclair: 'You talk like a Minbari, Commander.'

Neroon to Sinclair again: 'Perhaps there was some small wisdom in letting your species survive.'

Culture Shock: Alyt is a Minbari rank. Shai Alyt is a step above Alyt.

Minbari with psi powers are considered to be blessed.

In Minbari culture, the caste of the mother takes priority over the caste of the father when a baby is born.

The Llort are collectors of souvenirs and trinkets.

The Pak'ma'ra are scavengers, and prefer eating flesh that's been dead for some time.

'A Voice in the Wilderness' Part One

Transmission Number: 118
Production Number: 120

Written by: J. Michael Straczynski
Directed by: Janet Greek

Draal: Louis Turenne **Varn:** Curt Lowens
Dr Tasaki: Jim Ishida

Plot: The episode is unbalanced by the number of strings left hanging from it, waiting to be picked up in later episodes, but it's still fun to watch.

The 'A' Plot: A sudden series of seismic disturbances on Epsilon 3 – the planet nearest to Babylon 5 – results in Commander Sinclair dispatching a shuttle to the planet's surface with a scientific team on board. A beam of energy suddenly erupts from the supposedly dead planet's surface, and the shuttle is forced to return to the station. Sinclair sees a mysterious alien figure appear in his quarters and ask for his help. The shuttle makes a return journey, escorted by Starfuries, but is attacked by missiles and has to abandon its mission again. Images taken from the shuttle indicate that the missiles were fired from a five-mile-deep fissure on the planet's surface, and Sinclair and Ivanova – aware that this might be a first-contact situation – take a shuttle down themselves, using Starfuries to distract the missiles. On the station, Londo too has seen a vision of the alien asking for his help. On the planet, Sinclair and Ivanova discover an artificial opening in the fissure leading to a landing pad. From there they evade defence systems and discover a chasm, some ten or twenty miles deep, lined with vast, glowing alien equipment. They also find a chamber with an alien – the alien who has appeared to Sinclair and Londo – strapped into more of the equipment. He seems to be ill, so they remove him and take him back to the station. As they do so, the jumpgate opens and a large ship appears through it . . .

The 'B' Plot: An open revolt against the provisional Earth government on Mars has broken out. Earthforce are trying to contain the rebellion, but there's little or no news coming off the planet. Garibaldi is worried about an old lover – Lise Hampton. He tries to get a clear Earthforce channel through to her, but can't, so he tries to get Talia Winters to contact the secret Psi Corps base in Syria Planum on Mars. She does, but they refuse to let Garibaldi use their communications equipment. They do, however, discover that she is not on the list of survivors. They relay this information to Talia, who tells Garibaldi. He refuses to give up hope.

The 'C' Plot: Delenn's old mentor and friend Draal comes visiting. Distressed at the way the Minbari race is lost and drifting, he has decided to make a pilgrimage out into 'the sea of stars' and has come to say goodbye.

The Arc: Garibaldi discovered the secret Psi Corps base in Syria Planum when he was stationed on Mars – a story told in issues 5 to 8 of the *Babylon 5* comic series: 'Shadows Past and Present'. He tells something of this story in episode 308 ('Messages From Earth').

Observations: Jeffrey Sinclair was born and brought up on Mars.

Rathenn, one of Delenn's teachers, is first mentioned in this episode. He later appears in issue 1 ('In Darkness Find Me') of the *Babylon 5* comic, then in episodes 316 ('War Without End' Part One) and 319 ('Grey 17 is Missing').

Draal's continued reaffirmation of the Third Principle of Sentient Life is a terribly clumsy way of foreshadowing the fact that he's going to sacrifice himself at the end of this two-part story.

Garibaldi was fired from four security jobs before arriving on Mars. We discovered in episode 111 ('Survivors') that one of these jobs was on Europa and one was on Orion 4.

Londo tells Garibaldi that he married a dancer with a nagging voice. According to J. Michael Straczynski, he's talking about a previous wife whom he was forced to divorce. It's worth noting that in some early pre-production documents for the series, Straczynski wrote that Londo had only one wife (although she was his third) and seven children.

Following the success of the ninety-minute pilot episode on video in Germany and England and on laserdisc in Japan, Warner Brothers asked Straczynski to write a two-parter that could be re-edited into a ninety-minute film for the foreign video market. This episode and the following one are the result.

Ivanova's Life Lessons: Ivanova to Dr Tasaki when he refuses to follow her orders and puts himself in danger: 'On your way back I'd like you to take the time to learn the Babylon 5 mantra: "Ivanova is always right. I will listen to Ivanova. I will not ignore Ivanova's recommendations. Ivanova is God. And, if this ever happens again, Ivanova will personally rip your lungs out".'

Dr Tasaki: 'What better way to go out than in the cause of advancing scientific knowledge?' Ivanova: 'Is this a multiple-choice question, because I have some ideas.'

Dialogue to Rewind For: Londo: 'If the Narns all stood together in one place and hated all at the same time, that hatred would fly across dozens of light years and reduce Centauri Prime to a ball of ash – that is how much they hate us.'

Other Worlds: Dr Tasaki's wife lives on Proxima (Proxima 3, one assumes, based on the fact that it's the only planet in the Proxima system mentioned in any other episode of the show).

Literary, Mythological and Historical References: The chasm filled with vast alien machines that Sinclair and Ivanova have to cross is a deliberate visual reference to the Krell machinery in the 1956 film *Forbidden Planet*.

The title of the episode is a nod towards the Bible, specifically Isaiah chapter 40 verse 3: 'The voice of him that crieth in the wilderness, Prepare ye the way of the Lord.'

'A Voice in the Wilderness' Part Two

Transmission Number: 119
Production Number: 121

Written by: J. Michael Straczynski
Directed by: Janet Greek

Draal: Louis Turenne   **Varn:** Curt Lowens
Captain Ellis Pierce: Ron Canada
Lise Hampton: Denise Gentile
Senator Hidoshi: Aki Aleong   **Takarn:** Michelan Sisti

Plot: As with the previous episode, there's a lot left unresolved by the end of it, and the extensive plot leaves little room for character development, but it's still fun to see Londo looking for the landing thrusters.

The 'A' Plot: The starship coming through the jumpgate is the Earth Alliance Starship *Hyperion*, commanded by Captain

Pierce. Pierce has been sent to Babylon 5 to ensure that no other alien race gets control of the alien technology which Sinclair and Ivanova have discovered on Epsilon 3. Pierce tries to take control of the situation, but Sinclair refuses to relinquish control unless ordered to directly by the President. The ships from the *Hyperion* are prevented from getting to the surface by an increased level of automated missile defences, and the increased seismic activity beneath the planet's surface leads Ivanova to believe that the vast fusion reactors they've discovered beneath the planet's surface will explode within forty-eight hours. Draal, Delenn's mentor, sees a vision of the alien from Epsilon 3, and follows it to sickbay. A second ship, this one of unknown alien design, appears through the jumpgate. It's commanded by an alien named Takarn, who appears to be of the same race as the alien Sinclair and Ivanova rescued from the planet, and who claims that the planet belongs to his race and that they have been searching for it for five hundred years. Having just received the beacon the planet has started broadcasting, they have returned. The alien in medlab (whose name, we discover, is Varn) regains consciousness and tells his rescuers that the arriving aliens are violent outcasts from his own race. Varn is the last of his race, and the custodian of the Great Machine. He is dying, and he says that the outcasts cannot be allowed to gain access to the power represented by the Machine. Draal realises that his destiny is linked to Varn, and so he and Delenn kidnap Varn, and Londo pilots them all down to the Great Machine. Draal knows that Varn needs someone to take his place in the Machine, but cannot ask anyone to do it. Draal volunteers, and Varn helps to connect him up. Draal calms the seismic disturbances – which were caused by the failing of Varn's health – and uses the immense power of the Machine to give an ultimatum to Pierce and Takarn: withdraw and leave the planet alone or face the consequences. He entrusts the fate of the planet to the Babylon 5 advisory council, under Commander Sinclair. Takarn leads his ship(s) towards the planet, so Draal destroys them with an energy beam.

The 'B' Plot: Garibaldi finally manages to get in touch with his old lover, Lise Hampton. She is alive – although injured – but she is also married. Garibaldi's hopes of a reconciliation are dashed.

The Arc: 'Do not let them take the Machine,' Varn implores Sinclair. 'It's not for them. It's not for this time.' We still haven't found out what time it *is* for, but the clear indication is that the machine is designed as a weapon in the Great War that is to come. The Machine's files have copious details of the last Great War, as we discover in episode 316 ('War Without End' Part One). Varn has been its custodian for 500 years, listening and watching.

After taking control of the Great Machine, Draal tells Sinclair that it is being kept in reserve. 'When the time is right we will be here, waiting for you.' That time might well be during the Great War, although Draal later influences events in episodes 220 ('The Long, Twilight Struggle') and 305 ('Voices of Authority').

Delenn tells Garibaldi that she let Draal take control of the Great Machine because otherwise Sinclair would have done it. 'His destiny lies elsewhere', she says. Indeed it does, as we discover in episode 317 ('War Without End' Part Two).

Observations: For piloting Delenn and Draal down to the surface of Epsilon 3, Londo tells Delenn that she now owes him a huge favour. He collects on this favour in episode 303 ('A Day in the Strife').

When Takarn's ship scans Babylon 5's computer linguistic files, twenty-six 'pages' of four words each flash up on the C&C computer screen. Most appear random and innocuous, but one particular 'page' displays, in order, the words ORAK, FORBIN, NOMAD and SKYNET. FORBIN could be a reference to the creator of the computer in the 1969 SF film *The Forbin Project*, NOMAD a reference to the computer in the *Star Trek* episode 'The Changeling' and SKYNET a reference to the computer that took over the world in Jim Cameron's 1984 and 1991 films *The Terminator* and *Terminator 2: Judgment Day*. That would suggest that ORAK might be a misspelt reference to the computer Orac in the British SF series *Blake's Seven*.

If the first words on nine sequential C&C screen 'pages' are read in order, we get: EYE AM KNOT A NUMBER AYE AMA FREE MAN – a cunning play on the defining phrase from the cult 1960s series *The Prisoner*: 'I am not a number, I am a free man!' This isn't the first reference to *The Prisoner* in this series – Bester's farewell comment in episode 106 ('Mind War'), 'Be seeing you', along with his little salute, is another tip of the hat.

Other interesting words on other computer screen 'pages' are UTEROUS (a misspelling of UTERUS, perhaps?) and MCAULIFFE (another reference to Sharon Christa McAuliffe, who died when space shuttle Challenger exploded in 1986. The other reference is in episode 112 – 'By Any Means Necessary'). The word SCRIM appears twice in the list. Is this completist, or what?

J. Michael Straczynski has said the following about these two episodes: 'During the dead of winter last year, I got hit by the flu as badly as I've ever been hit. Temperature so high that I was near delirious at times, but refused to go to the hospital (I don't like doctors, and I was under deadline and couldn't afford the potential time away). We're talking mondo sicko here. It was around this time – either at the top or bottom of the flu, I can't remember now – that I wrote the "Voice" two-parter. And here's the trivia part . . . this isn't the original two-parter that I wrote. My brain already deteriorating, I wrote something that even I could see wasn't up to par. Wrote the entire two-hour script. Printed it up, and gave it to Doug and John. Before they could even respond, I looked at it and decided it had to go. So I trashed the entire script. By now we were getting very close to pre-production, and I was getting sicker and sicker . . . but I more or less locked myself in my home office, swallowed down massive amounts of vitamins (as much as my stomach could handle), kept forcing down coffee, and wrote twelve hours a day for about six days, after which the original draft was finished. Turned it in; did some mild polishes thereafter, but what was filmed was essentially what I turned in in first-draft stage.' Episode 121 ('The Quality of Mercy') was also written during this period.

The Earthforce ship *Hyperion* was named for the Internet

site where *Babylon 5* files are stored: ftp.hyperion.com.

'A Voice in the Wilderness' Parts One and Two were released on rental video in the UK after the first season had been transmitted. They were later rereleased as part of Beyond Vision's *Babylon 5* series.

Ivanova's Life Lessons: Concerning Captain Pierce: 'Worst case of testosterone poisoning I've ever seen.'

Dialogue to Rewind For: Londo, gazing at the controls of the shuttle: 'If I were a landing thruster, which one of these would I be?'

Ships That Pass In The Night: The alien ship is a clunky object like a mass of skyscrapers thrown together that looks like it has the ability to split into separate parts, each of which can fight independently of the others.

Other Worlds: Captain Pierce and the *Hyperion* were on their way to the Vega Outpost before they were redirected to Babylon 5.

Frallis 12 was once attacked by the Centauri.

Questions Raised: How come Varn could suddenly breathe human atmosphere halfway through this episode, having been rescued from a planet with a poisonous atmosphere and kept in a medlab isolation room with the same atmosphere?

When Varn is unconscious in medlab and Sinclair is worried about what's happening on the planet below, why doesn't he ask Talia Winters to scan Varn's mind for the answers?

'Babylon Squared'

Transmission Number: 120
Production Number: 118

Written by: J. Michael Straczynski
Directed by: Jim Johnston

Major Krantz: Kent Broadhurst
Zathras: Tim Choate   **Lise Hampton:** Denise Gentile
Grey Council No. 2: Mark Hendrickson

Plot: A fast-moving episode that manages to set up a lot of things that will pay out two seasons down the line, and is clever enough to booby-trap certain assumptions that will blow up in our faces (like the identity of the One).

The 'A' Plot: Babylon 5 is picking up unusual tachyon readings from Sector 14. A Starfury is sent to investigate, and its pilot is amazed to see a mysterious object appear out of nowhere. His transmissions back to the station are cut off, and when his Starfury arrives back on autopilot, he is dead. According to Dr Franklin, there isn't a mark on the outside of his body, but his internal organs are three times as old as they should be. The only clue is the characters he scratched into his belt buckle – 'B4'. A distress call is received from Sector 14, from what appears to be the old Babylon 4 space station. The only problem is that Babylon 4 vanished mysteriously four years before – in Sector 14. According to the time stamp on the message, no time has passed for Babylon 4's inhabitants. Sinclair and Garibaldi lead a flotilla of spacecraft to evacuate them. When they arrive on the station, they find it subject to strange time slips. Sinclair is projected into his own body in the future, fighting alongside Garibaldi as mysterious invaders occupy the station. The future Garibaldi tells Sinclair that he has rigged the fusion reactors to explode, and that Sinclair must get off the station. Garibaldi will remain – it is what he was born for. Garibaldi slips back into his body on Mars just before he left for Babylon 5, just as his girlfriend Lise Hampton is telling him she can't leave with him. Babylon 4's commander, Major Krantz, tells them that the station is unstable, and shows them a mysterious alien who appeared suddenly in a conference room. The alien – Zathras – tells them that Babylon 4 is being moved through time to become a base in a great war, and that it has been stopped four years in the future to allow the crew to evacuate. He refers to a mysterious leader known as the One. The One appears – a figure in a blue space suit – and Zathras hands it an object, saying that the object is fixed. The One vanishes again. Zathras warns Sinclair to evacuate the station before it is too late. Krantz wants to take Zathras with them as evidence, but Zathras is caught beneath a falling beam. Sinclair wants to stay and help him, but Zathras tells him to go. 'You have a destiny,' he says. They leave. The One appears to rescue Zathras from beneath the beam. A few moments later, just before Babylon 4 vanishes again, the One watches the departing flotilla from a porthole. Removing its helmet, it is revealed as an older Sinclair with a scar on his cheek. He tells someone out of sight that he tried to warn them, but it all happened just as he remembered. The unseen person tells him it is time to go, and from her voice we know it to be Delenn.

The 'B' Plot: Delenn leaves Babylon 5 in her personal cruiser, summoned by the Grey Council. On board their space ship, she is welcomed by one of the Grey Council. He tells her that it is ten cycles since Dukhat died, and that it is time to choose a new leader of the Grey Council (and thus of the Minbari). Delenn has been chosen. When Delenn asks about the prophecy, she is told that 'The prophecy will attend to itself.' She refuses the offer, and is asked to leave while the Council consider their position – and hers.

The Arc: This episode is one of the core episodes of the series. Almost everything in it resonates either backward or forward in the story. One of the more important sections is where Delenn reminds the Grey Council about why they surrendered during the Earth–Minbari war and why she was sent to Babylon 5 in the first place. 'This Council stopped the war against the humans because of prophecy, because Valen said that the humans – or some among them – had a destiny which we could not interfere with. It was my place to study them – to determine if the prophecy was correct.' The surprising surrender of the Minbari was first mentioned in the pilot episode ('The Gathering') and has been occasionally referred to ever since. The prophecy will be a recurring theme in the rest of the series, being explicitly referred to in episodes 201 ('Points of Departure'), 310 ('Severed Dreams'), 311 ('Ceremonies of Light and Dark') and finally explained (at least, in part) in episode 317 ('War Without End' Part Two).

As she leaves the Grey Council chamber, Delenn is given a triangular piece of perspex by the Grey Council No. 1. She calls it a triluminary, and seems to be in awe of it. This is the device used on Sinclair in episode 108 ('And the Sky Full of Stars'). Delenn later uses it in episode 122 ('Chrysalis'), as does Sinclair in episode 317 ('War Without End' Part Two).

Sinclair's future flash ends with Babylon 5 blowing up as a shuttle makes a last-minute escape. This is the same precognitive vision that the Centauri seer Lady Ladira had in episode 113 ('Signs and Portents'), and that is also referred to heavily in episode 316 ('War Without End' Part One).

It's a fair bet that whatever is coming through the walls in Sinclair's future flash, it has something to do with the Shadows.

Observations: According to the Grey Council No. 1, there are three triluminaries. Unsurprising, really – everything on Minbar is done in threes.

Delenn says of humanity, 'They carry within them the capacity to walk among the stars like giants.' In episode 217 ('In the Shadow of Z'ha'dum') she describes the First Ones in similar terms. 'There are beings in the universe much older than either of our races ... Once, long ago, they walked among the stars like giants ...' Is she implying in this episode that humanity is destined to become like the First Ones?

J. Michael Straczynski has pointed out that Major Krantz was not the Commander of Babylon 4: he'd just been assigned to supervise its construction.

The Grey Council No. 1 tells Delenn: 'We are surrounded by signs and portents.' The overall title for the season is 'Signs and Portents', and it is also the title of episode 113.

The actor playing the Minbari Grey Council No. 1 doesn't get a credit on screen. It was his choice, according to Straczynski.

The blue spacesuit worn by the One originally appeared in the 1984 film *2010*. It was leased from a prop house for *Babylon 5* and redressed.

The identification code for Babylon 4 is Elvis Presley's birthday. J. Michael Straczynski did not realise the CGI animator had slipped this in, and was apparently angry when he found out.

Dialogue to Rewind For: Delenn's catechism before the Grey Council: 'I am Grey – I stand between the candle and the star. We are Grey – we stand between the darkness and the light.'

Zathras: 'Great war. Terrible war . . . A great darkness. It is the end of everything.'

Zathras again: 'We live for the One. We would die for the One.'

Zathras, explaining why it doesn't matter whether Krantz takes him off Babylon 4 or not. 'You take – Zathras die. You leave – Zathras die. Either way, it is bad for Zathras.'

Dialogue to Fast Forward Past: Sinclair trying to sound macho: 'Something fatal happened out there – I want to know what.'

Ships That Pass In The Night: Delenn's cruiser sounds like it is called the *Julit*.

Culture Shock: The Head of the Grey Council is, by default, the leader of the Minbari people. He or she never leaves the Council chamber, which is on a war cruiser kept distant from Minbar.

Literary, Mythological and Historical References: Sinclair compares Babylon 4 to the story of the Flying Dutchman. According to one story, the Flying Dutchman was a Dutch captain who tried to sail his ship around the Cape of Good Hope despite a violent storm and the pleas of his crew and passengers. When God appeared on his deck the captain was so incensed that he fired upon him, and was condemned to sail and be a torment to sailors until the Day of Judgement. According to another story, an outbreak of plague on board the ship meant that no harbour would let it in, and it was condemned to sail the seas for ever.

I've Seen That Face Before: Denise Gentile returns as Lise Hampton, Garibaldi's old girlfriend. She previously appeared in episode 119 ('A Voice in the Wilderness' Part Two).

Kent Broadhurst (Major Krantz) can also be seen (should you wish) in the 1990 Michael Caine film *A Shock to the System*.

Accidents Will Happen: If you watch very carefully during Garibaldi's final stand against the enemy that's coming through the walls, you can see his eyes flash a bright, glowing red (but not if you've got the UK video release, because the frame has been redone). It's best if you freeze-frame your way through it. Much critical energy was expended by fans on trying to explain this hidden moment. Had he suddenly been taken over by an alien force? Had a futuristic weapon been used against him? Had he gained undreamt-of mental powers? Alas, nothing so . . . plot-driven. What had actually happened was that a CGI technician working on Garibaldi's PPG gun blasts got bored, and added the glowing eyes for a laugh while he was waiting for his effects shots to finish. He thought he had erased the glowing eyes before he finished. He was wrong.

Questions Raised: Why is it that the Starfury pilot's internal organs have aged to death, but his skin is fine?

Why on Earth did the Starfury pilot scratch a clue into his belt buckle? Isn't there anything else on the Starfury he could have used instead like a voice recorder? And what did he scratch it with – his fingernails? Did he really scratch it during the three-hour trip back, or did time pass more slowly for him in the cockpit? Why does this bit look like something that just wasn't thought through properly?

'The Quality of Mercy'

Transmission Number: 121
Production Number: 117

Written by: J. Michael Straczynski
Directed by: Lorraine Senna Ferrara

Laura Rosen: June Lockhart
Janice Rosen: Kate McNeil   **Karl Mueller:** Mark Rolston
Centauri Senator: Damien London
Ombuds Wellington: Jim Norton

Plot: Given that the writer of the story cannot remember actually writing it (see later) this story stands up remarkably

162

well. The 'A', 'B' and 'C' plots are all equally balanced, and there's a decent subtext about the morality of punishment that doesn't get a pat answer – because there isn't one. The alien device is, quite literally, a plot device, but at least with the benefit of hindsight we know it will be important later in the series.

The 'A' Plot: Convicted murderer Karl Mueller is sentenced to the death of personality (i.e. mindwipe) for three murders. Garibaldi suspects he is also responsible for a whole lot more – a charge that the telepath Talia Winters confirms when she examines his mind. Mueller escapes from custody, getting shot in the process, and takes refuge in Downbelow, in the quarters of Laura Rosen. Rosen runs a clinic for people who can't pay medlab charges, using an alien device whose function she is investigating to transfer her life energy to them, thus healing them. Mueller orders Rosen to cure his wounded arm, and holds her daughter at gunpoint to force her to do so. Rosen begins, but manages to alter the settings of the device such that Mueller's life force is transferred to her. Mueller dies, and it is decided by the Ombuds that Rosen acted purely in self-defence and should face no charges.

The 'B' Plot: In Delenn's absence, Londo offers to show Lennier the *real* Babylon 5 for two days. They spend some time in a bar, where Lennier is fascinated by the scantily clad dancers, and then, when Londo discovers that Lennier is a Master Adept at probability, they become involved in a poker game. Londo uses one of his tentacular genitalia to interfere with other people's cards and is caught. Lennier demonstrates his remarkable martial arts abilities during the ensuing fight, but they are both arrested. Lennier takes full responsibility for what happened because Minbari believe that it is an honour to help another save face. Given that they are both protected by diplomatic privilege, Sinclair cannot punish them, but he orders them to pay for the damage to the bar.

The 'C' Plot: Franklin is running an unofficial medlab in Downbelow for those people who cannot afford to come to the official one. His patient base is dwindling, and when he investigates he discovers that Laura Rosen is running her own clinic in Downbelow using an alien machine which, she claims, can transfer life force between two entities using it. She suspects it was originally used as a means of punishment, but she can now use it to transfer her own life force to others, thus healing them. She is suffering from Lake's Syndrome – a chronically painful and ultimately fatal disease. By absorbing the life energy of the convicted murderer Karl Mueller to stop him from abusing her daughter, she cures her disease at the expense of his life. She is ordered by the Ombuds to give the alien machine to Earthforce personnel, and she goes off on a pilgrimage into the universe in an effort to absolve her guilt.

The Arc: The writing on Laura Rosen's alien device looks suspiciously like a primitive form of Vorlon (we see Vorlon writing on the side of their ships in episodes 213 ('Hunter, Prey') and 318 ('Walkabout').

Laura Rosen tells Franklin that she took stims, made mistakes and had her medical licence taken away from her. This foreshadows the path that Franklin himself will take in seasons 2 and 3.

Observations: J. Michael Straczynski has said of this story, 'Bit of B5 trivia: during the dead of winter last year, I got hit by the flu as badly as I've ever been hit. Temperature so high that I was near delirious at times, but refused to go to the hospital (I don't like doctors, and I was under deadline and couldn't afford the potential time away.) We're talking mondo sicko here. It was during this time that I wrote "The Quality of Mercy," a script which I have *no* memory of ever writing. I know it's here, and I know I wrote it on an intellectual level, but the process . . . gone in the fever.' Episodes 118 and 119 ('A Voice in the Wilderness' Parts One and Two) were also written during this time.

Londo's tentacular genitalia bear a remarkable resemblance to the limbs of the Nakaleen Feeder as shown in episode 115 ('Grail'). This is just a coincidence – Straczynski has said that there is no connection between the Feeders and the Centauri.

Also according to Straczynski, 'In the first season, in "The Quality of Mercy", we had Londo picking up playing cards using his tentacle-like genitalia. Larry, who was the story editor on the first season, came into my office when the script was published, apoplectic, and said, "Let me get this straight – you told me I can't do 'camp', and you've got a guy picking up cards with his dick?" And I said, "Well, you write what you know." '

J. Michael Straczynski has *also* said, 'The worst part was the prop girls who made up the tentacle. They kept bringing it to me and saying: "Is this right? Floppy or more stiff? You want blue veins visible, or just pink veins? Is it diamond- or spade-shaped?" '

The original title for this episode was 'The Resurrectionist'.

Dialogue to Rewind For: Lennier's description of his life: 'From birth I was raised in the temple and studied the ways of the Religious caste. Six months ago I came here. There is nothing else.'

Franklin, mistaking Ivanova for a patient: 'You can start by removing your clothes.' Ivanova: 'Not without dinner and flowers.'

Dialogue to Fast Forward Past: 'Stroke off' is not a workable alternative for 'fuck off'.

Culture Shock: Lennier tells Londo that Minbari do not react well to alcohol – they become subject to psychotic impulses and homicidal rages.

In Minbari culture it is an honour to help another person save face.

Centauri males have six external genitalia that take the form of tentacles emerging for a distance of several feet from their sides, terminating in a leaf-shaped . . . er . . . member. These genitalia are remarkably dexterous, and can function as secondary limbs if necessary.

Li, the Centauri Goddess of Passion, has both male and female characteristics.

Station Keeping: It costs money to visit medlab, rather than being paid for out of taxes. This is parochialism – the American medical system moved to the stars.

As a sentence, spacing (i.e. throwing someone out of an airlock) can be imposed only for mutiny or treason.

Literary, Mythological and Historical References: The title of this episode comes from Shakespeare's play *The Merchant of Venice*. The complete quotation is: 'The quality of mercy is not strain'd, it droppeth as the gentle rain from heaven upon the place beneath . . .' The meaning, given the courtroom setting in which that line is spoken, is that mercy should not be something that is hard to give: it should be as natural as rain.

I've Seen That Face Before: June Lockhart, the actress playing Dr Laura Rosen, also played Maureen Robinson in the 1960s SF TV series *Lost in Space*. Bill (Lennier) Mumy, of course, played her son Will. Bill Mumy had suggested a shot where he, dressed as a security guard, would walk past June Lockhart, and they would both half-recognise each other, but it never got filmed.

Questions Raised: Is the device Laura Rosen is using a Vorlon device?

'Chrysalis'

Transmission Number: 122
Production Number: 112

Written by: J. Michael Straczynski
Directed by: Janet Greek

Catherine Sakai: Julia Nickson
Garibaldi's Aide: Macaulay Bruton
Deveraux: Edward Conery   **Morgan Clark:** Gary McGurk
Morden: Ed Wasser   **Lurker No. 1:** Liz Burnette
Lurker No. 2: Gianin Loffler

Date: 30 December 2258 to 1 January 2259.

Plot: Arguably the best end-of-season episode the series has managed so far.

The 'A' Plot: Stephen Petrov – a lurker who has been feeding Garibaldi information – has been attacked on his way to see him. Before dying, he says, 'They're going to kill him . . .' Garibaldi discovers from other lurkers that Petrov had been doing some unofficial loading work for a man named Deveraux. Garibaldi takes Deveraux into custody, but at the same time he discovers that Deveraux's PPG doesn't have a serial number – meaning that it was made for an Earthforce special security agent. Deveraux vanishes from his holding cell. Garibaldi examines the crates that the lurkers were packing for Deveraux, and discovers them to be filled with jamming equipment set to the Gold Channel frequency used by the President and *Earthforce 1*. President Santiago is on *Earthforce 1* on a good-will tour of five planets. Just before passing through the jumpgate near Io he intends giving a speech which, it is rumoured, will lead to a greater cooperation between Earth and alien governments. Vice-President Clark leaves *Earthforce 1* shortly before they get to Io, claiming to have a virus. Realising that there is a plot to kill the President, Garibaldi rushes to tell Sinclair but is intercepted by Deveraux. During the confrontation, Garibaldi is shot in the back by his own aide – Jack. He crawls for help and manages to tell Sinclair about the plot before being wheeled into surgery, but too late. All communications to *Earthforce 1* are being jammed, and the President dies in a massive explosion. Deveraux and his companions are killed by Garibaldi's aide to cover his tracks.

The 'B' Plot: Londo and G'Kar are arguing about the disputed territory of Quadrant 37. The Centarum instruct Londo to agree to hand the area over to the increasingly aggressive Narn – who already have a military outpost there – but the mysterious stranger who previously retrieved the Centauri Eye for Londo reappears and offers to solve the problem. On the advice of this man – who says that his name is Morden – Londo tells the Centarum that he will solve the problem of Quadrant 37 himself. The Narn military outpost in Quadrant 37, along with its complement of 10,000 Narn, is completely wiped out by mysterious spaceships, and Londo becomes a hero to the Centauri people. G'Kar cannot believe that any known race has the power to do what has been done, and he heads for the Narn homeworld to investigate a disturbing possibility.

The 'C' Plot: Delenn relays a question to Kosh via Lennier.

When the answer comes back as 'Yes', she immediately goes to see Kosh. She tells him that she must be sure, and he shows her his true form. Thus reassured that her course is correct, she uses the device she has been building for several months to spin a chrysalis in one corner of her room. She tries to speak to Sinclair, but he is too busy dealing with Garibaldi's disappearance. Delenn enters the chrysalis and, with Lennier standing guard, begins to undergo a transformation.

The Arc: This episode is a major point for three major arc plots in *Babylon 5* (each of which is intertwined with the others). The first is the ongoing introversion of Earth, with the assassination of the alien-friendly President Santiago and his replacement with the increasingly fascistic President Clark. This plot strand will bubble away for a long time before reaching a major climax in episodes 308, 309 and 310 ('Messages From Earth', 'Point of No Return' and 'Severed Dreams'). The second plot strand involves the mysterious Shadows and their agenda. Again, this strand runs through a number of episodes throughout the series, although we find out a lot more about the Shadows and who Morden is in episode 217 ('In the Shadow of Z'ha'dum') and what the Shadows claim they want in episode 322 ('Z'ha'dum'). The third plot strand is Delenn's transformation which involves the whole story about Minbari souls and the missing twenty-four hours in Sinclair's life. This was first brought to our attention in the pilot episode ('The Gathering'), and is tied up temporarily in episode 201 ('Points of Departure') and 202 ('Revelations') and more or less permanently in episode 317 ('War Without End' Part Two).

We find out what Delenn's question to Kosh was in episode 217 ('In the Shadow of Z'ha'dum'). His response to the question is a simple 'Yes', but it's enough to send her to see him, where he shows his 'true' form to her (*we* get to see one version of this 'true' form in episode 222 – 'The Fall of Night' – and another in episode 404 – 'Falling Toward Apotheosis'). The answer, and the confirmation of his true form, is enough to send Delenn into her chrysalis.

We see the Shadow aliens for the first time in this episode, although only dimly. They enjoy the ability to make themselves invisible and insubstantial. They appear vaguely insectoid, in that they have six limbs – four of which they walk on and two of which they use as grasping limbs and hold like a preying mantis. Their spiky skin also gives the appearance of being an exoskeleton.

Observations: Sinclair asks Catherine Sakai to marry him.

Londo and Morden both talk about the Eye and the problem with Raiders. This, of course, is a reference to episode 113 ('Signs and Portents').

Morden uses the phrase, 'When the time is right . . .' A lot of people use this phrase in *Babylon 5*.

Prompted by Delenn, Sinclair has a flashback to episode 108 ('And the Sky Full of Stars').

The photograph of President Santiago is actually of Executive Producer Douglas Netter, as it was in episode 101 ('Midnight on the Firing Line').

Koshisms: In response to Delenn's unknown question: 'Yes.'

To Sinclair: 'And so it begins. You have . . . forgotten something.'

Dialogue to Rewind For: Londo, complaining about diplomacy: 'This is like being nibbled to death by . . . what are those Earth creatures called – feathers, long bill, webbed feet, go "quack"?' Vir: 'Cats.' Londo: 'Like being nibbled to death by cats.'

Londo: 'Is there something wrong with your hearing?' Vir: 'No, it's just for a moment I thought I had entered an alternate universe.'

G'Kar, realising that no known race had the ability and the will to wipe out the Narn military outpost so completely: 'There's someone else out there, Na'Toth.'

Ships That Pass In The Night: We see *Earthforce 1* again (it previously turned up in episode 111 'Survivors'). We also hear about *Earthforce 2*.

Culture Shock: There are currently fifty gods in the Centauri pantheon, although Vir isn't sure whether one of them should be included. As with the ancient Roman Empire, it is customary for dead emperors to become gods. We discover in episode 401 ('The Hour of the Wolf') that Emperor Cartagia is quite prepared to see this custom extended to living emperors as well.

Questions Raised: On what charge does Garibaldi arrest Deveraux?

It's a New Year's Eve party and you find someone lying in a lift. Do you assume (a) they've been shot, and scream, or (b) they're drunk, and find another lift?

Why is it so urgent that Delenn gets into her chrysalis *now*? Why can't she wait half an hour to talk to Sinclair?

What were the jammers in Deveraux's crates for? *Earthforce 1*'s communications were jammed effectively without them, and they weren't actually held up in shipment at all. Come to that, why ship them through Babylon 5 in the first place? It's a long way from Earth.

Why give Earthforce special security personnel PPGs with no serial numbers? Doesn't it just draw attention to them if someone takes their PPG apart? And yes, I believe this *is* what currently happens with special forces and intelligence operatives, but reality is no defence.

Isn't Vice-President Clark's excuse for getting off *Earthforce 1* a bit flimsy and prone to backfire? If the President and Vice-President of the United States were on a good-will tour together and the Vice-President said, 'I've got a cold, please let me off,' there's a good chance the President would say, 'No way – this is important. Take an aspirin and sit by the window.'

If it comes to that, isn't the whole point of having a vice-president that he should never be at risk at the same time as the president? That way, if the president is assassinated the vice-president can carry on. The President and Vice-President of the USA *never* go on good-will tours together.

Season 2:
'The Coming of Shadows'

'The Babylon Project was our last, best hope for peace. A self-contained world, five miles long, located in neutral territory. A place of commerce and diplomacy for a quarter of a million humans and aliens. A shining beacon in space, all alone in the night.

'It was the dawn of the Third Age of Mankind – the year the Great War came upon us all.

This is the story of the last of the Babylon stations.

The year is 2259. The name of the place is Babylon 5.'

– Captain John Sheridan

Regular and Semi-Regular Cast:

Captain John Sheridan: Bruce Boxleitner
Commander Susan Ivanova: Claudia Christian
Security Chief Michael Garibaldi: Jerry Doyle
Ambassador Delenn: Mira Furlan
Ambassador Londo Mollari: Peter Jurasik
Ambassador G'Kar: Andreas Katsulas
Dr Stephen Franklin: Richard Biggs
Talia Winters: Andrea Thompson
Vir Cotto: Stephen Furst   **Lennier:** Bill Mumy
Na'Toth: Mary Kay Adams   **Zack Allen:** Jeff Conaway
Warren Keffer: Robert Rusler   **David Corwin:** Joshua Cox

Observations: During the filming of season 1, J. Michael Straczynski said that he was considering having Ivanova narrate the title sequence dialogue for season 2. The change in lead actor necessitated Captain Sheridan doing it instead.

The voice at the end of each episode saying '*Babylon 5*, produced by Babylonian Productions Inc. and distributed by Warner Bros. Domestic Television Distribution' is Harlan Ellison's.

The title sequence for the first two episodes of season 2 showed Delenn in full Minbari make-up, in order to keep the surprise of her transformation to half human, half Minbari in episode 202 – 'Revelations'. From episode 203 ('The Geometry of Shadows') onward, the title sequence showed her with hair.

Anthony Andrews, Roger Rees and James Earl Jones were all under consideration for the role of Captain John Sheridan. Andrews first made his mark on British television as Sebastian Flyte in *Brideshead Revisited*, although his genre credentials stretch only as far as an almost forgotten BBC play set after a nuclear holocaust called *Z for Zachariah*. Roger Rees is an ex-Royal Shakespeare Company actor who sprang to fame when he appeared in their stage production of Dickens's *Nicholas Nickleby*, although the highlight of his career since then has been a semi-regular appearance in *Cheers*. James Earl Jones is one of the grand old men of American drama. He has, perhaps, the greatest genre credential of all, as he provided the voice for Darth Vader in all three *Star Wars* films.

Caitlin Brown left the role of Na'Toth at the end of season 1. At the time, J. Michael Straczynski said of Caitlin Brown, 'She came in without being under the five-year option that generally exists in these situations. Did one year, about nine episodes, as Na'Toth. And had to turn down a couple of leading-female parts. During the hiatus, she did a romantic lead character in a film with Jack Nicholson and Meryl Streep. And had to ask the hard question: do I continue to grow as a romantic lead actor in feature films, or play Na'Toth? She is a *very* gorgeous woman, and felt awkward hiding behind the mask and cutting herself out of leading female parts in feature films to do it. We went round and round about this for some time. It was a very difficult decision for her because she likes the show and everyone here, but finally opted out. On one level it's a pain in the butt, but we respect her decision. And it *is her* call, not ours.' Straczynski added, 'We are recasting Na'Toth. By the end of season one, Na'Toth knows stuff that I need that character, G'Kar's aide, to know. (Though I was briefly tempted to do the *Murphy Brown* Secretary line, with G'Kar getting a new aide every so often due to terrible airlock accidents . . . but I went to lay down for a while and the notion passed.)'

Mary Kay Adams was cast as Na'Toth for season 2. Until then her best-known genre credit was probably her role under equally heavy make-up as the Klingon Grilka in the *Star Trek: Deep Space Nine* episode 'The House of Quark'. She played the same part more recently in the episode, 'Looking For par'Mach in All the Wrong Places.'

Two more newcomers to the regular cast in season 2 were security guard Zack Allen, played by Jeff Conaway (previously familiar as a regular character in the sitcom *Taxi*) and Robert Rusler as the ill-fated Starfury pilot Warren Keffer.

Bruce Boxleitner's opening narration was re-recorded for episode 204 ('A Distant Star') onward. His original narration was weak and hesitant, while the re-recorded version was firmer and more decisive. This was because he was unable to see the visuals for the opening sequence when he recorded the first version. At the same time, the shot reflected in the CGI spaceman's faceplate was also redone to improve it.

Composer Christopher Franke rearranged the first half of the opening title music – the section running beneath the narration – to fit in with the new, darker slant of the series and the revised visuals.

Episodes which were originally announced as being in this season but, for one reason or another, were never made, include 'The Customer is Always Right', 'Unnatural Selection' (by D. C. Fontana, later retitled 'All Our Songs Forgotten'), 'Expectations' (by David Gerrold) and 'The Very Long Night of Susan Ivanova' (by J. Michael Straczynski). The last episode was eventually rewritten for season 4.

'Points of Departure'

Transmission Number: 201
Production Number: 201

Written by: J. Michael Straczynski
Directed by: Janet Greek

Kalain: Richard Grove   **Hedronn:** Robin Sachs
General William Hague: Robert Foxworth

Date: 8 January 2259.

Plot: There's a lot of plot to get over, but Boxleitner makes an impressive start and the *Trigati* plot works nicely. A good season opener.

The 'A' Plot: A Minbari named Kalain arrives on Babylon 5 and makes for Ambassador Delenn's quarters. Another Minbari – Hedronn – recognises him and warns the new captain – John Sheridan – that he is a danger to the station. Kalain seems to be about to kill the chrysalid Delenn when he is arrested by Babylon 5's security guards. A Minbari warship – the *Trigati* – arrives through the jumpgate and demands Kalain's release. The *Trigati* is a rogue Minbari ship whose crew went into exile after the Minbari surrendered during the Earth–Minbari war. They have been wandering around the galaxy for over ten years. Kalain commits suicide in his cell to make it look as if the humans have killed him, and a confrontation between the *Trigati* and Sheridan seems to be about to erupt into another war when Sheridan realises that what the crew of the *Trigati* really want is to be destroyed. They have become tired of their exile, but things have gone too far and they can never go home. Sheridan refuses to attack, and the *Trigati* destroys itself rather than be captured by another Minbari cruiser, which had arrived after Sheridan had warned it about the *Trigati*'s presence.

The 'B' Plot: Jeffrey Sinclair has been recalled to Earth and permanently reassigned as the first human ambassador allowed to live on Minbar. Captain Sheridan – currently in command of the *Agamemnon* – is to take over the post. Sheridan was the late President Santiago's second choice for the post should anything have happened to Sinclair. Sheridan is not a popular choice with the Minbari, as he scored one of the major successes of the Earth–Minbari war when he destroyed their ship, the *Black Star*. Sheridan arrives on Babylon 5 and does his best to settle in while the *Trigati* crisis is going on around him – a crisis brought on by the fact that many Minbari hate him.

The ' C' Plot: Lennier reveals to Sheridan and Ivanova the truth about the end of the war, and what happened to Sinclair during his missing twenty-four hours. When the Minbari captured and examined Sinclair, they discovered that he had a Minbari soul. Other pilots captured also had Minbari souls, to a greater or lesser extent. As no Minbari has killed another Minbari for thousands of years, they had to stop the war straight away. Only the Grey Council knew. The Warrior caste took the surrender especially hard, and one of their number – Sineval – killed himself. The crew of his ship – the *Trigati* – went into self-imposed exile, until they turned up at Babylon 5 looking to die.

The Arc: The revelation that Minbari souls are being reborn in human bodies, and have been doing so for one thousand years, caps an arc thread that has been going on since the pilot episode ('The Gathering'). Other major stories in the soul arc are episodes 102 – 'Soul Hunter' – and 108 – 'And the Sky Full of Stars'. It is also glancingly referred to in episode 109 – 'Deathwalker'. The arc vanishes for a long time, surfacing later in episode 317 ('War Without End' Part Two) in which we get some indication *why* the souls started being reborn in humans. The only humans to know about this are Sheridan, Ivanova, Sinclair and President Clark.

Hedronn is a member of the Grey Council. He tells Lennier that they advised Delenn not to proceed with her plan, and that the Prophecy would attend to itself.

Lennier, talking to Delenn's cocoon, mentions the Great Enemy, and the prophecy that both sides of their spirit must unite against the darkness.

Observations: Sheridan shows himself in this episode to be a bit of a food obsessive. Alas, this character trait gets lost after an episode or two.

The original plan was to have President Clark notify Ivanova of the change in Babylon 5's command, but J. Michael Straczynski introduced the character of General Hague with the intention of using him further down the line. This led to a slight inconsistency with the comics, where President Clark tells Ambassador Sinclair that he will notify

Ivanova himself, but hey! he's a busy man.

Sheridan mentions that his father is (or was) a diplomatic envoy.

This episode, along with much of episode 202 ('Revelations'), was originally entitled 'Chrysalis' Part II but during the writing process J. Michael Straczynski realised he would need two episodes to tie up the loose ends, not one.

Bruce Boxleitner's lines are redubbed by him during his 'Starkiller' speech.

Ivanova's Life Lessons: 'And if you're not happy with the seating arrangements I will personally order your seats to be moved outside, down the hall, across the station and into the fusion reactor. Am I absolutely, perfectly clear about this?'

Sheridan: 'I can only conclude that I'm paying off karma at a vastly accelerated rate.'

Dialogue to Fast Forward Past: Sheridan: 'The last time I made "personal contact" with a Minbari warship I sent it straight to Hell.'

'It's amazing what two years on the rim can do to you.'

Ships That Pass In The Night: Earth Alliance Starship *Agamemnon*. Minbari cruiser *Trigati*. Minbari warship *Black Star*.

Literary, Mythological and Historical References: John Sheridan is in command of the *Agamemnon* at the beginning of the episode. Agamemnon was the king who (according to legend) led the Greek side during the Trojan War. Agamemnon was later murdered by his wife. We find out in episode 202 ('Revelations') that Sheridan's wife is missing, presumed dead, but revelations in episode 217 ('In the Shadow of Z'ha'dum') suggest that she may not be. These revelations finally pay off in episodes 321 ('Shadow Dancing') and 322 ('Z'ha'dum'). History is not on Sheridan's side.

The presidential speech Sheridan quotes from at the end of the episode is Abraham Lincoln's annual message to Congress, as delivered in December 1862. Sheridan leaves those sections out which are specific to the time at which Lincoln was speaking and the audience he was addressing. The original text of that section of the speech is as follows (the italicised sections are the sections Sheridan left out, the words in square brackets are words spoken by Sheridan instead of the actual words):

'The dogmas of the quiet past are inadequate to the stormy present. The occasion is piled high with difficulty, and we must rise with [to] the occasion. *As our case is new, so we must think anew, and act anew. We must disenthrall ourselves, and then we shall save our country.*

Fellow citizens, we cannot escape history. We *of this administration,* will be remembered in spite of ourselves. *No personal significance or insignificance can spare one or another of us.* The fiery trial through which we pass will light us down, in honor or dishonor, to the *latest* [last] generation. *We say we are for the Union. The world will not forget that we say this. We know how to save the Union. The world knows we do know how to save it. We – even we here – hold the power, and bear the responsibility. In giving freedom to the slave, we assure freedom to the free-honorable alike in what we give, and what we preserve.* We shall nobly save, or meanly lose, *the* [our] last best hope of earth. *Other means may succeed; this could not fail. The way is plain, peaceful, generous, just – a way which, if followed, the world will forever applaud, and God must forever bless.'*

Station Keeping: Babylon 5 uses XV-7 tracking units to locate objects in nearby space.

Command and Control is left unmanned for short periods every 36–48 hours for maintenance, backups, etc. Presumably there's a secondary control room somewhere.

I've Seen That Face Before: Robert Foxworth (General Hague) was in the failed Gene Roddenberry pilot *The Questor Tapes* and, subsequent to this episode, has appeared as authority figures in two episodes of *Star Trek: Deep Space Nine* ('Homefront' and 'Paradise Lost') and an episode of the new *The Outer Limits* ('Worlds Apart').

Robin Sachs (Hedronn) is a British actor with credits in a number of TV series and films. You may wish to find a copy of the rather stylish horror film *Vampire Circus* if you want to see him without the prosthetics. He plays the vampire acrobat Heinrich.

Questions Raised: If, as he says, Hedronn doesn't recognise Sheridan's authority, why does he request Sheridan's help in the first place?

The XV-7 tracking units on Babylon 5 are the same type as were used in the Earth–Minbari war, twelve years before. Haven't they been improved since then? What's the pace of technological development on Earth?

Lennier tells Sheridan and Ivanova that Commander Sinclair was the first human that the Minbari had ever had contact with – and this was right at the end of the war. However, in episode 108 – 'And the Sky Full of Stars' – we discover that Franklin took extensive notes on the Minbari during the war. In episode 311 – 'Ceremonies of Light and Dark' – we're told that humans had captured and tortured Minbari behind enemy lines. If the humans were doing all this, why weren't the Minbari?

How's this laser-beam message to the Minbari ship in hyperspace supposed to work? Laser beams travel in straight lines, right? Unless the Minbari ship is directly within line of sight of the line joining Babylon 5 to the jumpgate, the laser beam is just going to keep on going for ever. Or can you swivel jumpgates to point in whatever direction you want?

'Revelations'

Transmission Number: 202
Production Number: 202

Written by: J. Michael Straczynski
Directed by: Jim Johnston

Morden: Ed Wasser   **Elizabeth Sheridan** Beverly Leech
Anna Sheridan: Beth Toussaint
Narn Captain: Mark Hendrickson
Medlab Technician: James Kiriyama-Lem
President Clark: Gary McGurk

Plot: A good episode, with plenty of arc material to get one's teeth into. It's a shame that Bruce Boxleitne. has to give a performance of this depth so early in his tenure: given a few more episodes to get under Sheridan's skin, his reaction to Anna's message would have been even more heart-rending than it already is.

The 'A' Plot: G'Kar has been leading a Narn reconnaissance mission to the rim of the galaxy, examining dead worlds for signs of life. On numerous worlds that should be dead and deserted he has found signs of activity, and at a world named Z'ha'dum he and his companions are attacked by Shadow vessels. The other fighters sacrifice themselves so that G'Kar can escape with the news. G'Kar returns to Babylon 5 and arranges for the Kha'Ri to send a heavily armed ship to Z'ha'dum for a swift reconnaissance mission. He tells Sheridan, Londo and Lennier what he is doing, and Londo repeats the message to Morden straight away. When the Narn ship comes out of hyperspace, a Shadow ship is waiting for it. The ship's destruction is blamed on an accident with the hyperspace engines, and G'Kar momentarily suspects that Londo had something to do with it.

The 'B' Plot: Dr Franklin has tried almost everything to get Garibaldi out of his coma, with no success. The only option left is the alien device he confiscated from Dr Laura Rosen. He uses it to drain some life energy from himself and from Captain Sheridan, and Garibaldi revives. He cannot remember who shot him, but Talia Winters retrieves a forgotten memory from his mind that proves to his satisfaction that it was his aide, Jack, who fired. Jack is arrested, but refuses to say who he was working for, although he indicates to Garibaldi that Psi Corps are involved. On the direct orders of President Clark, Jack is returned to Earth along with all the recordings and transcripts of the interviews with him. En route, he is transferred to a ship with Earthforce markings but one that does not appear on any register.

The 'C' Plot: Captain Sheridan's sister, Elizabeth, arrives for a visit. Sheridan tells her that he feels responsible for his wife Anna's death because he was responsible for her taking the post on an archaeological dig aboard a ship that exploded. She gives him the last message she received from Anna, in which Anna says she took the post of her own accord but never got a chance to tell Sheridan.

The 'D' Plot: Delenn emerges from her cocoon. After some initial uncertainty over what she really looks like, it appears that she has taken on some human characteristics, although to what extent is uncertain. She takes back her position on the Babylon 5 Advisory Council.

The Arc: When Londo is talking to Morden, he expresses some disbelief that Morden's associates can do what they claim. 'Why don't you eliminate the entire Narn homeworld while you're at it?' he sneers. 'One thing at a time, Mr Ambassador,' Morden replies seriously. Well, they get around to helping the Centauri do it eventually, in episode 220 ('The Long, Twilight Struggle').

Morden asks Londo to let him know if anything unusual is happening out on the Rim. The Shadows are obviously worried after G'Kar discovered their base on Z'ha'dum.

The legendary Narn figure G'Quan wrote about a great war, long ago, against a foe that dwelled in a star system at the rim of known space. That foe is the race whose presence we first felt in episode 113 ('Signs and Portents'), whom we first saw in episode 122 ('Chrysalis') and whose presence will be felt more and more as this series progresses. They are known as the Shadows (see the essay 'Between the Essence and the Descent' earlier in this book).

Garibaldi's aide tells Garibaldi, 'There's a new order coming, back home.' He's referring to Nightwatch, whom we first hear about in episode 217 ('In the Shadow of Z'ha'dum'), who start flexing their muscles in episode 222 ('The Fall of Night') and whose story peaks in episodes 308 to 310 ('Messages From Earth', 'Point of No Return' and 'Severed Dreams'). He salutes Garibaldi with the same 'Be seeing you' salute used by Bester in episode 106 ('Mind War'), implying for the first time that Psi Corps are linked with President Clark and Nightwatch.

We hear in this episode that Sheridan's wife was on an archaeological expedition to a world out on the rim of the galaxy, where ancient ruins had been discovered. It's a throwaway line at the time, but it will come back to haunt us in episode 217 ('In the Shadow of Z'ha'dum') when we discover that the expedition awoke an ancient race known as the Shadows. The seventh *Babylon 5* novel, *The Shadow Within*, tells this story in more detail.

Observations: The alien device used by Franklin to save Garibaldi's life is the one he confiscated from Dr Laura Rosen in episode 121 ('The Quality of Mercy').

The man in charge of the archaeological expedition to Z'ha'dum was Dr Chang.

When G'Kar reads the poem 'The Second Coming' (which, as the title suggests, concerns the appearance of the Antichrist) we see shots of Delenn looking at herself in a mirror. Is this an implication that she is, somehow, evil? Or that she will give birth to something monstrous?

J. Michael Straczynski has said that if the character of Laurel Takashima had been retained from the pilot episode ('The Gathering'), rather than having been replaced by Ivanova, then she would have been involved with the attempted murder of Garibaldi, either by pulling the trigger herself or by setting him up for the person who did.

Dialogue to Rewind For: Londo talking about G'Kar and Delenn: 'One deserts his post without any explanation, the other one picks the most breathtakingly inconvenient moment possible to explore new career opportunities – like becoming a butterfly!'

Dialogue to Fast Forward Past: Sheridan tells his sister about his wife – her best friend: 'She died on a deep-space exploration vessel that exploded.' Like, his sister didn't already know that?

Officer Lou Welch to Garibaldi's aide: 'Make my fraggin' solar year!'

Ships That Pass In The Night: This is the first mention of the *Icarus* – a deep-space exploration vessel (that exploded, you'll remember).

Transport *Von Braun* returns Sheridan's sister to Earth. The ship was first mentioned in episode 115 ('Grail').

Other Worlds: Z'ha'dum – a dark, deserted world on the rim of known space – is mentioned for the first time. But not the last.

Culture Shock: Shadow fighters 'pulse' in order to expel their munitions.

Narn sleep on stone slabs (the stone itself is called bloodstone).

I've Seen That Face Before: James Kiriyama-Lem, who played the medlab technician, also played General Ming in the episode of *Space: Above and Beyond* entitled 'Sugar Dirt'.

Literary, Mythological and Historical References: After G'Kar gets back to the station, he says to Na'Toth, 'I have looked into the abyss, Na'Toth. You cannot do that and ever be quite the same again.' This is a nod towards the German philosopher Friedrich Nietzsche, who said, 'And if you gaze for long into an abyss, the abyss gazes also into you.'

G'Kar also quotes from a book of Earth poetry he has in his possession. Specifically, the poem he reads is 'The Second Coming', by the Irish poet William Butler Yeats. The poem is a prophecy concerning the rising of a new dark God and the fall of Christian values.

The first two lines of the poem invoke the image of a falcon flying in larger and larger orbits around its falconer, but eventually moving so far away that it cannot hear the falconer's shouted commands. The implication is that some things (such as Empires and Alliances) grow so large they cannot maintain control. This theme is made explicit by the lines that G'Kar quotes:

> Things fall apart; the centre cannot hold;
> Mere anarchy is loosed upon the world,
> The blood-dimmed tide is loosed, and everywhere
> The ceremony of innocence is drowned;

The two lines taking the poem up to the end of the stanza suggest that even the best people lack fire and spirit, while the worst people have a messianic zeal that outshines their opponents. This echoes themes in the Tennyson poem *Ulysses* as quoted by Sinclair in the pilot episode and Sheridan in episode 405 ('The Long Dark').

The first two lines of the second stanza convey an image of hope: a revelation, a Second Coming that might unite the world again. However, the next seven lines convey a deeper sense of unease when the poet receives a vision suggesting that the Second Coming might be of an evil, Sphinx-like creature born out of the desert. In the three following lines, the poet wakes from his vision with the realisation that the two thousand years since the birth of Christ have been leading to a nightmare. The poem concludes with the lines also quoted by G'Kar:

> And what rough beast, its hour come round at last,
> Slouches toward Bethlehem to be born?

The poem also gives the episode its title – 'Surely some revelation is at hand' is the first line of the second stanza.

Accidents Will Happen: Wasn't it amazingly fortunate timing that Sheridan walked in on Franklin just as Franklin was connecting himself up to the alien equipment in order to transfer some of his energy to Garibaldi?

'The Geometry of Shadows'

Transmission Number: 203
Production Number: 203

Written by: J. Michael Straczynski
Directed by: Mike Laurence Vejar

Elric: Michael Ansara   **Lord Refa:** William Forward

Plot: Don't worry about how a race like the Drazi survived to the space age with such an archaic way of settling leadership issues, it's still a good episode.

The 'A' Plot: A group of Techno-mages – mystics who use technology to achieve the effect of magic – arrive on Babylon 5. They wish to leave human space for an unnamed destination, and Captain Sheridan is under orders from EarthGov to determine where they are going and why before he lets them go. Londo Mollari is also interested in them – Lord Refa has indicated that Londo might get a crack at the throne at some stage, and he thinks an endorsement from the Technomages will boost his chances. Vir tries to arrange a meeting for him, and is rebuffed, so Londo manipulates Sheridan into setting up a conference with Elric – the chief Technomage. Londo tries to record the meeting, but Elric destroys his camera and plagues him with various technological curses. Elric and the Technomages finally leave without telling Sheridan where they are going.

The 'B' Plot: Once every five years, all members of the Drazi race split into two camps – purple and green (denoted by scarves) – whose members are chosen at random, and who fight for a year. The camp that notches up more victories gets to rule for the next four years. It's that time, and all over Babylon 5, the Drazi are fighting each other. A newly promoted Ivanova is put in charge of sorting the situation out. During a fight in a conference room she breaks her foot. When things turn nasty and the Drazi start killing each other, she is kidnapped by the green Drazi and her comlink is used to send a message to the purple Drazi telling them to assemble in a spot that will be used for an ambush. She is rescued by Garibaldi, who became suspicious when he discovered that the message to the purple Drazi didn't come directly from her but was uplinked remotely. Together they confront the green Drazi, and Ivanova suddenly finds herself in charge of them when she rips the green scarf from around their leader's neck. She leads the green Drazi off to somewhere she can dye all their scarves purple.

The 'C' Plot: Garibaldi is still recovering after being shot, and is uncertain about returning to duty. He doesn't know who to trust any more, and he contemplates suicide. Sheridan is concerned, but gives him enough space to make his own decision. Saving Ivanova's life brings it home to him that nobody knows Babylon 5 like he does and that nobody is as suspicious as he is, and he returns to work.

The Arc: At one stage, Sheridan says of Babylon 5, 'If we went back in time a thousand years and tried to explain this place to people, they could only accept it in terms of magic.' Of course, in episode 317 ('War Without End' Part Two) they *do* take Babylon 4 back a thousand years. This line has been sitting in plain sight all this time, and (if we had only known) would have told us what was going to happen.

The Technomages are leaving because they sense something dangerous will soon happen. 'There is a storm coming,' Elric tells Sheridan, 'a black and terrible storm.' What they sense is, of course, the Shadow War that we first began to glimpse in episode 113 ('Signs and Portents') and which finally gets going for good in episode 314 ('Ship of Tears').

Elric tells Londo Mollari that he sees Londo's hand reaching out from the stars. Londo later has this dream in episode 209 ('The Coming of Shadows').

Observations: Garibaldi makes reference to a changeling net (see the pilot episode – 'The Gathering').

Turhan Bey, who was eventually cast as the Centauri Emperor in episode 209 ('The Coming of Shadows'), had originally auditioned for the part of Elric in this episode, but it was felt that he was too nice.

Originally this episode was written so that Ivanova solved the entire Drazi crisis without being rescued by Garibaldi. Claudia Christian broke her ankle just before filming began and the script was rewritten so that she was injured in a fight with the Drazi, and some of the action was transferred to Garibaldi.

Elric's technocurses end up with Londo owning 200,000 shares in a spoo ranch. Spoo first get a mention in episode 101 ('Midnight on the Firing Line').

The Drazi make-up was redesigned for this episode. Previously their skulls had been smooth apart from the frontal plate, but from here on most Drazi we see have small scales covering their heads. Some smooth-headed Drazi still turn up, indicating that there are two types of Drazi rather than that their entire race has spontaneously mutated (as *Star Trek*'s Klingons did).

Ivanova's Life Lessons: To Dr Franklin: '*Now* you can give me something for the pain. Where were you when I was going through puberty?'

Dialogue to Rewind For: Vir to Londo: 'I believe there are currents in the universe, eddies and tides that pull us one way or the other. Some we have to fight, some we have to embrace. Unfortunately, the currents we have to fight look exactly like the currents we have to embrace. The currents that we think are the ones that are going to make us stronger are the ones that are going to destroy us – they're the ones we have to avoid. And the ones we think are going to destroy us – they're the ones that are going to make us stronger . . .'

Elric's description of what Technomages know: 'Fourteen words to make someone fall in love with you. Seven words to make them go without pain. How to say goodbye to a friend who is dying. How to be poor. How to be rich. How to rediscover dreams when the world has stolen them from you.'

The purple Drazi leader apologetically explains to Ivanova why her scarf-snatching trick worked: 'Rules of contest older than contact with other races – do not mention aliens. Rules change caught up in committee – not come through yet.'

Elric to Londo: 'As I look at you, Ambassador Mollari, I see a great hand reaching out of the stars. The hand is your hand. And I hear sounds – the sounds of billions of people calling your name.' Londo, awestruck: 'My followers?' Elric: 'Your victims.'

Dialogue to Fast Forward Past: Sheridan about the Technomages: 'Part of me says we'll not see their like again, but the part of me that still believes in magic says, "Don't be so sure".'

Culture Shock: A Drazi week is equal to six Earth days, and a Drazi year is equal to 1.2 Earth years. The Drazi are an aggressive, warlike species, and this episode only goes to confirm our opinion of them.

Literary, Mythological and Historical References: The name Elric is a nod towards Michael Moorcock's fantasy hero – or rather, to the reinterpreted version named Elrod in Dave Sim's comic masterpiece *Cerebus*.

Elric's line, 'Do not try the patience of wizards, for they are subtle and quick to anger,' is a quotation from J. R. R. Tolkien's fantasy trilogy *The Lord of the Rings*.

I've Seen That Face Before: Michael Ansara, who plays Elric, has a long association with science fiction series. He played the eponymous 'Soldier' in 1964 in the first episode of the second season of *The Outer Limits* – written by Harlan Ellison – and also appeared as the Klingon warrior Kang in the *Star Trek* episode 'The Day of the Dove' – a role he has recently reprised in an episode of *Star Trek: Deep Space Nine* entitled 'Blood Oath'. He also took part in the 1970s series *Buck Rogers*, but we can safely ignore that, as we can his appearances in *Abbott and Costello Meet the Mummy* (1955) and the film of *Voyage to the Bottom of the Sea* (1961).

Accidents Will Happen: It looks like Elric is reading off cue-cards when he makes his 'Fourteen words to make someone fall in love with you' speech.

The Drazi use Ivanova's comlink to send a fake message in this episode. Alas, in episode 307 ('Exogenesis') we're told that comlinks are biogenetically keyed to their users, and cannot be used by anyone else.

Questions Raised: Will the Technomages be back?

'A Distant Star'

Transmission Number: 204
Production Number: 204

Written by: D. C. Fontana
Directed by: Jim Johnston

Captain Jack Maynard: Russ Tamblyn
Ray Galus: Art Kimbo   **Patrick:** Daniel Beer
Orwell: Miguel A. Nunez, Jnr   **Teronn:** Sandey Grinn

Plot: A fun, but rather pedestrian, episode with some major-league logical flaws.

The 'A' Plot: The *Cortez*, an Explorer-class Earthforce ship, arrives at Babylon 5 after more than five years exploring the galactic rim. It's reprovisioning before heading off to build some more jumpgates for humanity to use. The *Cortez* leaves, but an accidental explosion while in hyperspace blows out its tracking systems. Without a firm lock on any jumpgate beacons, it can't get out of hyperspace. When he receives its distress signal, Sheridan arranges for a chain of Starfuries to extend into hyperspace – the first one close enough to the jumpgate to receive its beacon signal, the next one close enough to the first to remain in contact with it, and the entire chain extending towards the *Cortez*'s last reported position in the hope that Maynard will be able to pick up the beacon from the last one in the chain. He does, and the *Cortez* determines its direction back to the jumpgate, but the last two Starfuries in the chain are damaged when a Shadow ship suddenly jumps into hyperspace near them and moves rapidly away without noticing them. The pilot of one of them – Ray Galus – is killed when his ship explodes, but the pilot of the other – Warren Keffer – gets his bearings from the path of another Shadow vessel and finds his way back to the jumpgate.

The 'B' Plot: Dr Franklin draws up diet plans for all senior officers. His recommended daily intake doesn't meet with the wholehearted approval of Sheridan, Garibaldi and Ivanova, but Franklin is watching to ensure that they don't eat anything they shouldn't. Garibaldi tries to circumvent Franklin by smuggling high-cholesterol items on to the station for a birthday meal, but he's caught. He talks his way out of trouble, and ends up cooking for Franklin as well.

The 'C' Plot: The visit of his friend Jack Maynard, Captain of the *Cortez*, causes Sheridan to rethink what he is doing on Babylon 5. He always wanted to command an explorer vessel, and he's angry that he's been turned into a paper-shuffling bureaucrat. A conversation with Ambassador Delenn convinces him, however, that everyone is in the right place at the right time for the universe's purposes, even if they do not realise it themselves.

The Arc: Warren Keffer mentions a story in the *Universe Today* asking whether there was something strange living in hyperspace. We saw this edition of the *Universe Today* in episode 108 ('And the Sky Full of Stars'). We now realise, of course, that the reports of strange things in hyperspace are actually reports of Shadow ships.

Observations: Delenn mentions the Minbari belief that living beings '. . . are the universe made manifest, trying to figure itself out.' This is later echoed in episode 319 ('Grey 17 is Missing').

After the death of Ray Galus, Warren Keffer is made commander of Zeta Wing (or Zeta Squadron, as it is called in this episode).

Captain Maynard was John Sheridan's commanding officer on the Moon–Mars run.

The kilometre is a measure of distance in hyperspace as well as real space.

The *Cortez* is the first ship lost in hyperspace ever to be found again.

Ivanova's Life Lessons: On the subject of Franklin's diet plan, which involves her eating *more* food than usual, rather than less: 'Figures. All my life I've fought against imperialism. Now, suddenly, I *am* the expanding Russian frontier.' In the background, Franklin quietly adds, 'But with very nice borders.'

Dialogue to Fast Forward Past: Sheridan: 'Hell, I always thought the opposable thumb was overrated.'

Ships That Pass In The Night: The *Cortez*, of course, named after the Spanish explorer Ferdinand Cortez (or Hernándo Cortés), the man who overthrew the Aztec empire and secured Mexico for Spain.

Culture Shock: An alien race named (I think) the Tokadi are mentioned in passing as having a delegation on Babylon 5.

I've Seen That Face Before: Russ Tamblyn, who plays Captain Maynard, was a familiar Hollywood figure in his youth, having starred in such films as *Seven Brides For Seven Brothers* (1954), *tom thumb* (1958), *West Side Story* (1961), *The Haunting* (1963) and *Dracula Versus Frankenstein* (1971). He was nominated for the Academy Award for Best Supporting Actor in 1957 for (of all things) *Peyton Place*. More recently he played the part of Dr Lawrence Jacoby in David Lynch's cult TV series *Twin Peaks*.

Accidents Will Happen: The communications officer on the *Cortez* is badly dubbed during her scene shortly after the accident. Her words are completely out of sync with her lips.

Questions Raised: At one point in the episode, Garibaldi sentences a shoplifter to community service. Isn't this an abuse of his power? What do the Ombuds do for a living?

The *Cortez* is huge and it's designed to operate as an exploration vessel – isn't it big enough to create its own jumpgate, get into real space and take a star reading, rather than hang around in hyperspace waiting to be rescued?

'The Long Dark'

Transmission Number: 205
Production Number: 205

Written by: Scott Frost
Directed by: Mario DiLeo

Amos: Dwight Schultz
Mariah Cirrus: Anne-Marie Johnson
Markab Ambassador: Kim Strauss
Medlab Tech: James Kiriyama-Lem

Plot: A neat little episode with ramifications extending into the arc, but the absence of any 'B' plot makes it seem rather slight.

The 'A' Plot: A century-old Earth ship – the USS *Copernicus* – drifts past Babylon 5 broadcasting a greetings message. It was sent from Earth with a frozen crew as an attempt to contact alien life forms, but it was sent through normal space just before the Centauri contacted Earth and provided jumpgate technology. The ship is brought to the station, but one of the crew is dead – murdered by evisceration. When the other crewmember – Mariah Cirrus – is removed from her cryogenic tube, something gaseous escapes. A lurker named Amos – the only survivor of a massacre during the Earth–Minbari war – tells Garibaldi that something is loose on the station. Together they track down an invisible beast, using

190

Amos as bait, and destroy it with heavy PPG fire. Amos dies in the encounter.

The 'C' Plot: Dr Franklin falls in love with Mariah Cirrus, but he feels that she needs to see something of the future before she can return and make a commitment.

The Arc: The Minbari command and control post that Amos's troop were spying on during the war set up their base in the middle of old ruins on an uninhabited moon. In episode 202 ('Revelations') we heard that the archaeological expedition Sheridan's wife was on did the same thing on an alien planet. In episode 217 ('In the Shadow of Z'ha'dum') we discover that Sheridan's wife's archaeological expedition woke something that had been asleep in the ruins for a thousand years or so. The Minbari mentioned in this story must have done the same thing. The moral is, of course, leave alien ruins well alone.

Amos's cry when he first senses the approach of the 'Dark Soldier' – 'They're coming through the walls!' – is more or less the same thing Garibaldi yells in the future flash in episode 120 ('Babylon Squared'). Amos is recalling the Shadow attack on the listening post he was stationed at, and he later expands on what happened. 'It came right through the walls like a hot wind.' Not like any hot winds in Britain, though.

The 'Dark Soldier' is, we presume, a kind of Shadow foot soldier or servant. It's about fifteen feet tall, biped, and has horns of some kind. It's also invisible, but most of the other Shadows we've seen are, when they want to be. There's an illustration of the 'Dark Soldier' in the Book of G'Quan that shows it to have a snouted face rather like a wolf's.

The 'Dark Soldier' feeds on internal organs and can render itself incorporeal enough to hide 'inside' a human being in some sense. Those within whom it has hidden have a psychic connection to it. It is intelligent enough to reprogram the *Copernicus*'s course so that it is heading towards Z'ha'dum.

Interestingly, the Markab seem to know a fair bit about the Shadows and their defeat a thousand years ago. Their ambassador tells the League of Non-Aligned Worlds, 'The forces of

Darkness do not move openly. They work through others – use others. When the Darkness was defeated, long ago, they scattered, hid themselves away in secret places and waited. Now the Dark hand is reaching out and recalling them from their sleep.' Remember, this is several episodes before Delenn tells anyone the same information. Is this why the Markab were so conveniently wiped out by a plague?

There are two indications in this season that one of the heroes of the series will turn to the Darkness. One is the use of W. B. Yeats's poem, 'The Second Coming', as narration over a shot of Delenn (although it would, perhaps, be too obvious for Delenn to be the one to turn) in episode 202 ('Revelations'). The other is the Markab Ambassador's throwaway line, 'Evil sometimes wears a pleasant face.'

Observations: Garibaldi still sees councillors about his traumatic experiences during the Minbari war.

Dialogue to Rewind For: G'Kar: 'The future isn't what it used to be.'

Dialogue to Fast Forward Past: Medlab technician, looking at the unconscious Mariah Cirrus: 'Looks like a dream.' Franklin: 'Or a nightmare.'

Garibaldi: 'Lousy way to die, huh?' Franklin: 'Last I checked, there weren't too many good ways.'

Amos, about the 'Dark Soldier': 'It looked like it had come straight from hell.' Hardly surprising: on this show everything either came straight from hell or is going straight to hell.

Ships That Pass In The Night: The USS *Copernicus* – an Earth ship sent out into normal space a century or so before Babylon 5 was built with a frozen crew as an attempt to contact alien races. Nicolaus Copernicus (1473–1543) was a Polish astronomer who was the first person in Europe to openly claim that the Earth went round the sun, not vice versa.

Culture Shock: The Drazi eat food so live that it sometimes tries to escape.

Station Keeping: Devalera is a drug used to treat cardiac arrest in humans.

I've Seen That Face Before: Dwight Schultz became a household Face in *The A-Team*, but his major genre credit to date is as the socially challenged Lieutenant Reginald Barclay in various episodes of *Star Trek: The Next Generation*, one episode of *Star Trek: Voyager* and the film *Star Trek: First Contact*.

Scott Frost is the brother of the Mark Frost who co-created the cult US TV series *Twin Peaks* and wrote two supernatural thrillers in which Arthur Conan Doyle was the hero – *The List of Seven* and *The Six Messiahs*. Scott Frost has also written for *The X Files*.

Questions Raised: How is it that the 'Dark Soldier' can exist inside living creatures and then leave them? Why did it let Amos go when it could have killed him? Was it just a coincidence that the *Copernicus* drifted past Babylon 5 when Amos was there?

'Spider in the Web'

Transmission Number: 206
Production Number: 206

Written by: Lawrence G. DiTillio
Directed by: Kevin G. Cremin

Abel Horn: Michael Beck
Amanda Carter: Adrienne Barbeau
Taro Isogi: James Shigeta
Senator Elise Voudreau: Jessica Walters
Thirteen/Psi Cop: Anne Grindlay

Plot: This episode is too heavy on the 'A' plot and too light on everything else.

The 'A' Plot: Taro Isogi, an old friend of Talia Winters and a representative of the independent company FutureCorp, has arrived on Babylon 5 to talk to Amanda Carter, a member of the Business Affairs Committee of the Mars Provisional

Government. The deal he proposes would be in both their interests and would help guarantee peace on Mars, but EarthGov believe that he is financing a Martian rebellion against Earth. Isogi is assassinated – electrocuted, in fact – by a man with a prosthetic hand. Talia gets a flash of memory from the assassin – an exploding spaceship – but no emotion at all. The assassin downloads recorded data of the killing from his prosthetic hand to a mysterious controller, and is ordered to kill Talia as well. He tries, killing a security guard in the process, but sees the same memory flash as she does – an Earth Alliance ship blowing up the ship he was in. He staggers off, but Garibaldi identifies him by his DNA as Abel Horn, a former Free Mars terrorist who was killed during the Mars Rebellion. Horn hides out in Amanda Carter's quarters (she was in Free Mars too) and gets her to ask Talia Winters to come and see her. Sheridan and Garibaldi, meanwhile, have discovered that Horn might have been a part of an old Earthforce experiment into grafting computer controllers into human brains. To avoid problems with rejection, the subjects were rescued from near-certain death and their minds fixated on that moment, so that their minds would cycle through their deaths again and again, leaving the computers free to control their bodies. Sheridan reconfigures Babylon 5's internal sensors to detect the iranium radiation given off by Horn's prosthetic arm. Horn is about to kill Talia when Sheridan and Garibaldi burst in. He releases her, but manipulates Sheridan into killing him. His body self-destructs, removing all evidence. Talia later identifies a face she saw in his mind – one of the people responsible for carrying out the operation on him – as a Psi Cop listed as being dead. Meanwhile, in the San Diego headquarters of Horn's mysterious controllers (identified only as Bureau 13) the dead Psi Cop receives a report from her agent on Babylon 5 . . .

The Arc: Captain Sheridan is asked by Senator Voudreau to spy on the negotiations between FutureCorp and the Mars Provisional Government. His objections that this would be illegal are overridden. 'Practicalities are more important than principles,' the senator tells him. This is an early indication of the sort of thing the Nightwatch will be asking people to do later in the series, and the senator's bland assurance could well be their motto.

When Ivanova discovers that Talia Winters has been attacked, she is very concerned – more concerned than one would expect considering she hates telepaths. This is a subtle nod towards the developing relationship between the two of them – a relationship that will come to fruition and then self-destruct in episode 219 ('Divided Loyalties') and be acknowledged by Ivanova in episode 311 ('Ceremonies of Light and Dark').

It's difficult to tell whether Bureau 13 is part of the arc or not. This is the first and last time they get a mention. Perhaps they will come back, perhaps they won't. All we know for sure is that they are a dirty-tricks organisation within the Earth Alliance government, that one of their controllers used to be in Psi Corps, that they have a base in the devastated wasteland of San Diego and that they have a ghoulish tendency to use people who have been declared dead as agents. Oh, and they still have an agent on Babylon 5, and that agent is male. The final discussion between the mysterious '13' and 'Control' refers to an agent on Babylon 5 who assures them that their security has not been compromised. That agent is referred to as 'he'.

Talia lies to Sheridan when she says she didn't recognise any uniforms in the flashback she caught of Abel Horn being operated on. She recognised a Psi Corps uniform. Did she not tell him out of misplaced loyalty to the Corps, or for reasons which will be revealed in episode 219 ('Divided Loyalties')?

This episode was originally entitled 'A Trick of the Mind'.

Observations: Whatever happened to Sheridan's hobby of collecting information on secret organisations, black projects and conspiracies? Given what's happened with the Nightwatch, the Ministry of Peace and the Psi Corps, he's had ample opportunity to reveal more information since, but he's said nothing. Perhaps it was one of those youthful hobbies that get abandoned soon after being taken up . . .

Sheridan orders a Jovian Sunspot in the bar for the first

and, we devoutly hope, the last time. The Jovian Sunspot was introduced in episode 109 ('Deathwalker') – which was also written by Lawrence DiTillio.

Despite appearances, the doctor performing the prosthetic surgery in Abel Horn's flashback is *not* Stephen Franklin. J. Michael Straczynski has said so.

Clumsy scripting and/or editing has rendered some of the ramifications of this episode confusing. Firstly, the DECEASED flag on the computer file of the Bureau 13 agent Talia Winters is checking out at the end of the episode doesn't mean that she has been killed, brought back to life and reprogrammed, even though the person working for her has. Secondly, the Bureau 13 agent is not Talia's old friend Abby, even though Talia talks about Abby in a conversation with Garibaldi that serves no other dramatic function.

There will probably not be any more references in the series to Bureau 13. Neither Larry DiTillio nor J. Michael Straczynski was aware that there was already a CD-ROM computer game by that name involving a covert government organisation. Although there was never any threat of legal action, Straczynski decided to drop the organisation out of courtesy.

Dialogue to Fast Forward Past: Sheridan, remembering the Tikar: 'I spent two days with them, and what I learned in that time made me realise just how wondrous this galaxy of ours really is.'

Ships That Pass In The Night: The Earthforce Star Cruiser *Pournelle* killed Abel Horn (or thought it did) above Mars. The ship is named for the noted SF author Jerry Pournelle (who has co-written some recent books with a Martian theme).

The transport ship *Matheson* gets a mention. Richard Matheson is a highly respected author and screenwriter in the fields of SF and horror. His one specific 'Martian' credit in a long and distinguished career is the script for the TV adaptation of Ray Bradbury's *The Martian Chronicles*.

The Tikar ship looks like a large, green cloud. Perhaps sensibly, the guys doing the special effects didn't try to show it on screen.

Culture Shock: We discover in this episode that San Diego is a nuclear wasteland. This was set up in a newspaper headline in episode 108 ('And the Sky Full of Stars'). Sinclair said in episode 101 ('Midnight on the Firing Line') that a terrorist bombing was the cause.

Station Keeping: Private negotiations are not subject to official scrutiny on the station. There is no legal mechanism to force anyone to divulge the content of their negotiations.

Literary, Mythological and Historical References: See **Ships That Pass In The Night** for references to writers Jerry Pournelle and Richard Matheson.

Amanda Carter's great grandfather was John Carter. John Carter was also the hero of many of Edgar Rice Burroughs's *Barsoom* series of novels set on Mars, starting with *A Princess of Mars* and passing through nine more books before ending with *John Carter of Mars*.

I've Seen That Face Before: Adrienne Barbeau, the actress who plays Amanda Carter, made her name in the early horror films of John Carpenter (to whom she was married for a time). Look for her in *The Fog* and *Escape From New York* as well as Wes Craven's *Swamp Thing*.

Accidents Will Happen: When Talia Winters arrives at Amanda Carter's quarters, she makes her presence known. The door opens, but Amanda Carter is unconscious. Who gave the command for the door to open (a procedure that has been set up in previous and subsequent episodes)? Was it Abel Horn – and, if so, does this mean that rooms are not voice-coded to their occupants?

Questions Raised: What is Bureau 13?

Who is the Bureau 13 agent on Babylon 5?

Why does Sheridan – the man in charge of the entire Babylon 5 station – go all the way to Amanda Carter's quarters to ask her two trivial questions, then leave?

'Soul Mates'

Transmission Number: 207
Production Number: 208

Written by: Peter David
Directed by: John Flinn

Timov: Jane Carr   **Daggair:** Lois Nettleson
Mariel: Blair Valk   **Matthew Stoner:** Keith Szarabajka
Trader: Carel Struycken

Plot: A fun romp with a serious side, with a performance from Jane Carr that ascends above everything else. The things that aren't being said between her and Londo at the end of the episode are far more important than anything that is.

The 'A' Plot: It's the thirtieth anniversary of Londo Mollari's Day of Ascension, and the Emperor has granted him whatever wish he wants. His wish is to divorce all three of his wives, but the Emperor has persuaded him to keep one for state occasions. Londo has called his wives to Babylon 5 so he can decide which one to keep. Timov arrives first – a shrew with a voice that could cut glass and no patience at all for Londo's games. Daggair arrives next – a social climber whose hostess manner conceals a bitchy nature. Mariel is last – a sultry seductive who can't be as innocent as she acts. During a party to celebrate Londo's anniversary, he is given a gift by Mariel that she bought from a trader on the station. The gift is a Minbari statuette, but it fires poisoned darts into Londo's forehead when he touches it and he falls into a coma. The statuette is apparently a Narn booby trap left on a Centauri colony world during their previous conflict and not discovered until now. Londo's wives realise that he has not had time to finalise the details of their separation yet, and so if he dies they will still inherit his money, but Timov offers a blood transfusion on the understanding that Dr Franklin won't tell Londo that she saved his life. She tells Franklin that beating Londo that way wouldn't seem fair. Londo's life is saved, and he chooses Timov as his remaining wife, on the basis that he knows exactly where he is with her. Meanwhile, G'Kar has worked out that Mariel deliberately bought the

198

statuette knowing it would kill Londo.

The 'B' Plot: Matt Stoner, Talia Winters's ex-husband, arrives on Babylon 5. He claims to have been working on an archaeological dig, and sells a trader a Centauri statuette (the one that is later bought by Mariel and poisons Londo). Stoner wants Talia to come back to him, and tells her that he knows a way out of Psi Corps. They conducted drug experiments on him that accidentally erased his telepathic powers, and he can replicate the effect on her. Although she initially rejects Stoner, she quickly changes her mind and decides to leave with him. Garibaldi, worried, discovers that Stoner has the power to control people's minds – a result of the drug experiments conducted upon him. Garibaldi suspects that Psi Corps want Stoner and Talia to breed telepathically enhanced children, and have sent Stoner to get her back. Garibaldi reveals this to Talia, and throws Stoner off the station.

The 'C' Plot: Delenn is having problems being human, and asks Ivanova's help. It turns out that she didn't know she had to wash her hair, and so Ivanova lends a hand and a set of curlers for the sake of diplomatic relations. Now all Ivanova has to do is explain the function of periods and all will be fine . . .

Observations: G'Kar has worked with Mariel before, but we never find out what on.

Londo referred to his three wives previously in episode 107 ('The War Prayer'), calling them Pestilence, Famine and Death (and indeed 'Pestilence, Famine and Death' was the working title for this episode). The reference is to the Bible, specifically the Revelation of St John the Divine. Writer Peter David has said that Daggair is meant to be Pestilence, Timov is Famine and Mariel is (of course) Death. That leaves Londo as War, of course.

Timov's name is 'Vomit' spelt backwards. This was a deliberate joke on Peter David's part.

Writer Peter David has written a number of *Star Trek* novels, one *Alien Nation* novel and a whole slew of comics. He appears in Londo's party scene, talking with Delenn and Lennier.

Director John Flinn appeared as a man whose ancestor had been abducted by aliens in episode 115 ('Grail').

This episode and the next episode were made in the reverse order to the way they were shown. They make more sense if considered that way. On the UK video releases, they're swapped around.

One of the *Babylon 5* blooper tapes has the moment during the filming of the dart attack on Londo when Bruce Boxleitner yelled into his link, 'Medlab, this is Sinclair,' bringing production to a halt while everyone recovered.

Dialogue to Rewind For: When Dr Franklin asks Londo if he knows where he is, Londo replies, 'Either in medlab or in hell. Either way, the decor needs work.' The second sentence was added by J. Michael Straczynski.

G'Kar, warning Mariel that her plot to kill Londo might be discovered: 'If I were married to Londo Mollari, I'd be concerned.' Mariel: 'G'Kar, if you were married to Londo Mollari, we'd *all* be concerned.'

Ships That Pass In The Night: Centauri Liner *Melourian*.

Culture Shock: Minbari do not sweat – they secrete a fluid while they are asleep that serves a similar purpose. Let's hope Sheridan is understanding about Delenn's physical peculiarities.

Station Keeping: Medlab have problems synthesising Centauri blood.

I've Seen That Face Before: Jane Carr (Timov) is a former Royal Shakespeare Company actress. Her only major film credit is as one of the students in *The Prime of Miss Jean Brodie* (1969).

Carel Struycken (who plays the Trader) has one of those instantly recognisable faces. You may have seen him in the 1985 *Star Wars* film *Ewoks: The Battle for Endor* or the 1987 Jack Nicholson vehicle *The Witches of Eastwick*, but more probably in the 1991 film *The Addams Family* and its sequel *Addams Family Values*. He also appeared in the David Lynch and Mark Frost TV series *Twin Peaks*.

Accidents Will Happen: Medlab's magic door strikes again. Even though it's supposed to open if people go up to it and close after them, it stays open so that Timov can make a dramatic entrance.

The three wives we see photographs of in episode 107 ('The War Prayer') are not the wives who turn up in this episode.

Questions Raised: Why do Psi Corps send Matt Stoner to control Talia's mind and get her to return to them? Given the events of episode 219 ('Divided Loyalties') they could just call up and ask her to come back and she would.

'A Race Through Dark Places'

Transmission Number: 208
Production Number: 207

Written by: J. Michael Straczynski
Directed by: Jim Johnston

Bester: Walter Koenig **Psi Cop:** Judy Levitt
Rick: Brian Cousins **Telepath 1:** Apesanahkwat
Telepath 2: Diane Dilasco **Lurker:** Gianin Loffler

Date: From 14 March 2259 onward.

Plot: The episode has the feel of something important, but looking back it's difficult to see why it should. The only major effect the events have is on Talia Winters, and later stories (especially 219 – 'Divided Loyalties') manage to completely disrupt the character arc that this story supports.

The 'A' Plot: An underground organisation is smuggling unregistered and unhappy telepaths to safety via Babylon 5, and Psi Cop Bester arrives on the station to investigate. After an attempt on his life, Talia Winters is kidnapped by the underground. They explain to her exactly what they are afraid of, and convince her that Psi Corps is A Bad Thing. Captain Sheridan arranges a meeting with the head of the underground, and is shocked to discover that it's Dr Stephen Franklin. Bester confronts the underground telepaths and believes that he and Talia Winters have killed them all, but it's just an illusion planted in his mind by their combined powers. He leaves, happy, and Talia makes the first hesitant move towards Ivanova.

The 'B' Plot: Earthforce order Sheridan and Ivanova to move to smaller quarters and to start paying rent. Sheridan refuses, and persuades Ivanova to do the same. Garibaldi is ordered to lock them out of their quarters. They both sleep in Sheridan's office until it occurs to him to pay their rent directly from the combat-readiness budget (on the basis that he can't be expected to fight if he hasn't had a good night's sleep).

The 'C' Plot: Delenn asks Sheridan's help in becoming more 'human'. He takes her to dinner and they discuss humour.

The Arc: Little obvious arc-related material occurs in this episode, despite the gloom and the presence of Bester. Even Talia Winters's realisation that Psi Corps is abusing its powers is a red herring, as 'Divided Loyalties' (episode 219) disrupts the path her character is tentatively following. Dr Franklin's telepaths lifeline does, however, prove to be of some use towards the end of season 3.

Observations: No official business is allowed to be discussed in Earhart's bar. Anybody who flouts this rule has to buy a round for everyone present.

P11 is the highest rating one can get in Psi Corps without being a Psi Cop.

Jason Ironheart didn't just give Talia Winters the gift of telekinesis in episode 106 – 'Mind War' – he also gave her the ability to shield her mind from more powerful telepaths (unless this is a latent ability of her secondary personality as revealed in episode 219 – 'Divided Loyalties').

When Delenn and Sheridan have dinner Sheridan is drinking wine but Delenn isn't. We found out in episode 121 ('The Quality of Mercy') that alcohol causes Minbari to become violently psychotic.

When the rogue telepaths implant the vision in Bester's mind, part of it is Talia Winters betraying them and siding with Bester. This is, of course, exactly what she does in episode 219 – 'Divided Loyalties'. Is this Straczynski pre-figuring events again, or is it merely coincidence?

Stephen Franklin has been involved with the underground telepath escape route since before he arrived on the station.

Judy Levitt, who plays a Psi Cop, is Walter Koenig's wife.

Dialogue to Rewind For: Sheridan on the Minbari: 'One day they're shooting at you, the next day they're taking you out to dinner. What a universe.'

Delenn: 'In temple we spend one whole year just learning how to appreciate humour.'

Sheridan's joke: 'How many Minbari does it take to screw in a lightbulb? None – they always surrender right before they finish the job and they never tell you why.' (Compare this with Londo's similar joke in episode 302 – 'Convictions').

I've Seen That Face Before: Gianin Loffler, who plays the telepathic Lurker in this story and in episode 122 – 'Chrysalis' – also appeared in the SF blockbuster movie *Stargate*.

Literary, Mythological and Historical References: At one point, Doctor Franklin quotes the American orators and opponents of British rule Patrick Henry ('. . . give me liberty or give me death!') and James Otis (although Franklin says, 'No taxation without representation,' whereas Otis actually said, 'Taxation without representation is tyranny.' Franklin's version is the commonly remembered one, and became the catchphrase of the American Revolution).

Questions Raised: Why isn't this episode as important as it seems to think it is?

'The Coming of Shadows'

Transmission Number: 209
Production Number: 209

Written by: J. Michael Straczynski
Directed by: Janet Greek

Jeffrey Sinclair: Michael O'Hare
Centauri Emperor: Turhan Bey
Centauri Prime Minister: Malachi Throne
Lord Refa: William Forward
Ranger: Fredric Lehne   **Kha'Mak:** Neil Bradley

Plot: One of *Babylon 5*'s best stories, this has it all – political intrigue, complex characterisation, a guest-star performance from an actor who has nothing to prove and a gut-wrenchingly tragic scene with G'Kar trying to buy Londo a drink without knowing – as we do – that Londo has just unleashed the dogs of war. It just takes your breath away.

The 'A' Plot: The Centauri Emperor is making a visit to Babylon 5 in order to give a speech, and G'Kar is furious. When Sheridan refuses to cancel the visit, G'Kar seeks permission from the Kha'Ri – the Narn ruling council – to kill the Emperor. The Emperor arrives, but before he can make his speech he collapses. There are no suspicious circumstances, but Franklin diagnoses that even a move to his royal yacht could kill him. He asks Franklin to take a message to G'Kar – the message he was going to give in his speech. He wants to say he is sorry. He wants to be the first person to apologise on behalf of the Centauri for what was done to the Narn. Meanwhile, back on Centauri, various families are jockeying to get their preferred candidate on the throne, and Lord Refa recommends that Londo do something to attract attention. Londo chooses to destroy a Narn colony and listening post in Quadrant 14 on the border of Centauri space with the help of Morden and his mysterious associates. The colony is destroyed and the Centauri are blamed. The Emperor dies shortly after being told the news. Shortly after that, the Centauri Prime Minister is assassinated. The Narn declare war on the Centauri, and the Emperor's nephew – the choice of Lord Refa – is crowned Emperor.

The 'B' Plot: A stranger arrives on Babylon 5 and tails Garibaldi. He is arrested and locked up, but gives Garibaldi a data crystal. The crystal contains a message from Ambassador Jeffrey Sinclair, telling Garibaldi that he is leading a network of 'Rangers' – mainly human but some Minbari –

whose job it is to patrol the frontier, to listen, to watch and to report back anything suspicious. Sinclair asks Garibaldi to give aid to any Ranger who requires it. The Ranger tells Garibaldi that there is a link between the Centauri and a previously unknown alien race. Garibaldi tells Sheridan about the link between the mysterious alien race and the Centauri, and Sheridan uses the information to force Londo into agreeing to release the Narn prisoners from Quadrant 14, rather than sending them to slave labour camps.

The 'C' Plot: There is no room for a 'C' plot.

The Arc: This story marks the transition between the veiled Centauri/Narn hostilities of episodes 101 ('Midnight on the Firing Line') and 122 ('Chrysalis') and the all-out, open war that will change the face of the series.

After he has called for Morden's allies to destroy the Narn colony, Londo has a dream that may be a remembrance of his past and a premonition of his future. He dreams about the destruction of the Centauri colony orbiting Ragesh 3 (episode 101 – 'Midnight on the Firing Line'), then sees a hand coming out of the sun (a possible reference to the hand that Elric the Technomage talks about in episode 203 – 'The Geometry of Shadows'). He sees Shadow ships flying across a blue sky (a prediction we see coming true in episode 401 – 'The Hour of the Wolf') and then sees himself crowned Emperor (as Lady Morella predicts in episode 309 – 'Point of No Return'). He sees an older version of himself, wizened and white-haired, slumped on a throne (a vision, in fact, of seventeen years in the future, as later revealed in episodes 316 and 317 – 'War Without End' Parts One and Two). Finally he sees a wizened G'Kar, one eye covered with a strip of cloth, first half hidden in the shadows of the throne room and then strangling him (a prophecy he first mentioned in episode 101 – 'Midnight on the Firing Line' – and which comes true seventeen years in the future in episode 317 – 'War Without End' Part Two).

In episode 309 – 'Point of No Return' – the Centauri seer Lady Morella tells Londo that he has already had two chances to turn away from the path he is following. This might be one of them – he specifically asks for Morden's help, even though Vir begs him not to.

Observations: The Centauri Emperor says goodbye to his old friend the Prime Minister as if he knows he is not coming back.

We never get to hear what Sinclair had to say to Delenn.

We don't find out the Emperor's name in this story, but in episode 309 – 'Point of No Return' – we discover that he is Emperor Turhan, named after the actor who played him – Turhan Bey. We also discover in episode 320 ('And the Rock Cried Out, No Hiding Place') that the Prime Minister's name is Malachi. He's *also* named for the actor who plays him – Malachi Throne.

J. Michael Straczynski has pointed out that, in many ways, this episode serves as a dark reflection of episode 101 ('Midnight on the Firing Line'). To give just two examples, there is an attack on an outpost (Narn against Centauri in 101, Centauri against Narn here), and a character decides to kill another (Londo decides to kill G'Kar in 101, G'Kar decides to kill the Emperor here).

The major image of Londo's dream, and the one that will come back to haunt him later, was based on a recurring dream that Straczynski has. 'Ever since I was a kid,' he has said, 'I've had that image in my dreams, of standing out in the open and looking up as strange dark ships pass overhead. It's always been an unnerving image, and I really wanted to use it here to see if it would have the same effect on others.'

The shot of Londo looking up into the blue sky was shot outside the *Babylon 5* studio. That makes it the first (and, excluding a couple of model shots, only) piece of outside location filming done for the series.

This episode won the 1996 Hugo Award for Best Dramatic Presentation, beating 'The Visitor' (*Star Trek: Deep Space Nine*), Ron Howard's *Apollo 13*, the animated movie *Toy Story* and Terry Gilliam's *12 Monkeys*.

A shot of the knife entering the Centauri Prime Minister when he is assassinated was cut by Channel 4 during the first UK showing of the episode.

The scene between Londo, Vir and Lord Refa had an additional line of dialogue which was cut from the final transmission. After Londo says, 'For once we have something in common,' he pauses and then adds, 'I am an old man. What is lost by trying? As the humans say, "Who Dares Wins".' Vir replies, 'Who dares sometimes gets his head cut off and stuck on a pike.'

The complete script for this episode was published in J. Michael Straczynski's *The Complete Book of Scriptwriting* (Writer's Digest Books) in October 1996. The published script includes scenes omitted from the transmitted episode for reasons of time.

Koshisms: Centauri Emperor to Kosh: 'How will this end?' Kosh: 'In fire.'

Dialogue to Rewind For: Sinclair: 'There is a great darkness coming.'

Sinclair's advice to Garibaldi: 'Stay close to the Vorlon, and watch out for Shadows – they move when you're not looking at them.'

Londo's version of the Emperor's last words: 'Continue. Take my people back to the stars.'

Londo admitting to Lord Refa what the Emperor's last words *really* were: 'He said that we were both damned.'

Culture Shock: The Centauri Emperor usually wears a wig to cover his balding scalp. Centauri women are not naturally bald – they shave their heads.

The Centauri throne is hereditary.

The Centauri Emperor is accompanied at court by four female telepaths who are constantly linked. When he travels, two go with him and two remain behind, so that he always knows what is going on back on the homeworld. The fact that they can remain in contact over so many light years is more because they have been raised together to become almost one entity, rather than because they are telepaths *per se*.

I've Seen That Face Before: Malachi Throne, who plays the Centauri Prime Minister, is a familiar face on American TV. Probably his best known genre roles are as Commodore

Mendez in the original *Star Trek* episodes 'The Menagerie' Part I and 'The Menagerie' Part II and as the Romulan senator Pardek in the *Star Trek: The Next Generation* episodes 'Unification I' and 'Unification II'.

Turhan Bey – born Turhan Gilbert Selahettin Saultavey – is a Viennese actor who appeared in some thirty-one Hollywood films between 1941 and 1953 (including, prophetically, one entitled *Shadows on the Stairs*). He had originally auditioned for the part of Elric in episode 203 ('The Geometry of Shadows'). He failed to get that part, and this part was written for him by J. Michael Straczynski.

Accidents Will Happen: Well, a verbal blooper anyway. A quadrant is a quarter of something: how can there be a Quadrant 14?

Questions Raised: What, exactly, is the Ranger arrested and locked up for? Is 'tailing the security chief' an indictable offence? If not, is this an abuse of Garibaldi's powers?

The Rangers are patrolling human space, listening and watching for anything suspicious and reporting it to an unaccountable higher authority. Does this ring a bell? Isn't it exactly what the Nightwatch end up doing at the end of the season?

Was this one of Londo's two missed chances to redeem himself?

'GROPOS'

Transmission Number: 210
Production Number: 210

Written by: Lawrence G. DiTillio
Directed by: Jim Johnston

General Franklin: Paul Winfield
Sgt Major Plug: Ryan Cutrona   **PFC Large:** Ken Foree
PFC Derman: Marie Marshall   **Pvt Kleist:** Morgan Hunter
Pvt Yang: Art Chudabala   **Tonia Wallace:** Mowava Pryor

Date: Lois Tilton's *Babylon 5* novel *Accusations* is set between episodes 209 ('The Coming of Shadows') and 211 ('All Alone in the Night'), putting it almost coincident with this episode. The action of the book begins on 18 April 2259 and continues for some days, if not weeks. It's a fair bet that 'GROPOS' takes place in early April 2259.

Plot: It's been said that most American fiction is about the relationship between the lead character and his or her father. It's as true in this series as in most others, and this episode in particular showcases Dr Franklin's problems with his parenting. It's somehow hard to imagine an episode of *Blake's Seven* in which Blake or Avon meets his father and tells he loves him.

The 'A' Plot: Six Earthforce ships come through the jumpgate carrying 356 Infantry Division, comprising some 25,000 marines. They're on their way to the planet Akdor – a part of the Sh'lassan Triumvirate that's going through a rebellion at the moment. Earthdome have been asked to help fight the rebels and, given the strategic position of the Sh'lassan sector close to the Narn–Centauri war, they think it politic to help. The marines are quartered on the station for several days, during which time accommodation is stretched almost to breaking point and fights break out with alarming regularity in the bars and gambling establishments. They leave for Akdor and subdue the rebellion, but at the cost of numerous lives.

The 'B' Plot: The commander of 356 Infantry Division is General Richard Franklin – father to Dr Stephen Franklin. The two of them have communications difficulties, but with Sheridan encouraging the general and Ivanova encouraging Stephen, they eventually settle their differences for long enough to hug and make up.

The 'C' Plot: Private First Class Elizabeth Derman (better known as Dodger) tries to get Garibaldi into bed, but he wants a long-term relationship and he's still pretty screwed up about an old lover. They part with a suggestion that they'll see each other again, but she dies on Akdor.

Observations: Alfredo Garibaldi, Michael Garibaldi's father, was under General Franklin's command during the war against the Dilgar (this war was extensively talked about in episode 109 – 'Deathwalker').

Garibaldi tells Dodger that he's still trying to work through his feelings for an old lover. From what he says, it's obvious he's talking about Lise Hampton – who turned up in episodes 119 ('A Voice in the Wilderness' Part Two) and 120 ('Babylon Squared'). He also implies that he has strong feelings for Talia Winters, and mentions the fact that he was shot (episode 122 – 'Chrysalis').

There's a mention of Ms Connelly – the Dockers Guild representative. She turns up in episode 112 ('By Any Means Necessary').

There's a mention of the Mars Rebellion (which occurred in episodes 118 and 119 – 'A Voice in the Wilderness' Parts One and Two).

Warren Keffer recalls going head to head with a load of Minbari fighters. He's talking about episode 201 ('Points of Departure').

Jerry Doyle (the actor who plays Garibaldi) had problems with the script for this episode in terms of his relationship with Dodger. 'The original script had me going to bed with her,' he said. 'I just said, "No, I'm not going to do it, because it doesn't make sense." I had been chasing Talia, and my thinking on it was, for the sake of getting laid, why would you want to risk throwing away what could potentially be a phenomenal relationship with your absolute fantasy woman? We kind of battled on that for a few weeks, and I got a rewrite on it.' J. Michael Straczynski has pointed out that he sided with Doyle on the requested changes, although he did note that Doyle had been asking for his character to get laid for two years.

This episode went so far over budget that J. Michael Straczynski had to write two smaller-scale episodes to balance the books.

Dialogue to Fast Forward Past: Is 'stroking' really a workable euphemism (as in 'What the stroking hell are you guys doing?')? I think not.

Franklin to his dad: 'I love you, Dad. I always have and I always will.'

Ships That Pass In The Night: One of the six Earthforce ships that turn up is the *Schwarzkopf* (see **Literary, Mythological and Historical References** below).

Other Worlds: Akdor is the third planet of the Sh'lassan Triumvirate.

Orcha is a Markab fruit juice that Dr Franklin likes. He's obviously got a taste for things Markab – we discover in episode 218 that he's been to the planet and still has at least one friend from that time.

General Franklin is described as being 'the scourge of Janos 7'. One of the inhabitants of Janos 7 – a nasty flying reptile called a grylor – turns up in episode 216 ('Knives').

Station Keeping: General Franklin brings with him some upgraded weaponry for Babylon 5's defence grid in this episode.

There are over twenty species living on the station, according to this story, and more pass through every day. This just about squares with episode 215 ('And Now For a Word'), in which we are told that fourteen alien races live inside the 'alien sector', with its non-oxygen atmosphere. That leaves only six races living outside the 'alien sector', and a quick count gives us at least nine we can put names to (the Abbai, the Brakiri, the Centauri, the Drazi, the Hyach, the Llort, the Markab, the Minbari, the Narn) along with various races who turn up in the League of Non-Aligned Worlds conference room but haven't made much of an impact yet.

Literary, Mythological and Historical References: The Earthforce ship *Schwarzkopf* is named for General ('Stormin'') Norman Schwarzkopf, the in-theatre commander of the Coalition forces during the Gulf War.

I've Seen That Face Before: Paul Winfield, who plays General Richard Franklin, is a highly experienced American actor. He was nominated for an Academy Award for Best Actor in 1972. His SF film credits include *Damnation Alley* (1977), *Star Trek II: The Wrath of Khan* (1982, as Captain Terrell) and *The Terminator* (1984, as Lieutenant Traxler).

'All Alone in the Night'

Transmission Number: 211
Production Number: 211

Written by: J. Michael Straczynski
Directed by: Mario DiLeo

Hedronn: Robin Sachs   **Neroon:** John Vickery
Narn: Marshall Teague   **Lt Ramirez:** Nick Corri
General Hague: Robert Foxworth

Date: It's around six months since Sheridan took command of Babylon 5, so let's say early July, 2259.

Plot: The only saving grace this story has is the possibility that the Streibs are part of something bigger – like the Shadow War. Once that possibility is taken away from us, questions like 'What do the Streibs want?' dominate our minds. We never find out, and so the episode leaves us unsatisfied. A shame.

The 'A' Plot: Mysterious sightings in Sector 92, along with the disappearance of at least one ship, prompt Captain Sheridan to lead an investigative team of four Starfuries to that area. Shortly after they arrive, an alien ship pops out of hyperspace, destroys most of the Starfuries and picks up Sheridan's escape pod with some kind of tractor beam. He wakes up in the strangely organic alien ship, strapped to a table. Shortly after that, a robot arm tipped with scalpels and needles descends from a hole in the ceiling and proceeds to torture him. Abruptly released from the table, he is attacked by a homicidal Drazi who has artificial implants in his head. Sheridan kills the Drazi, and is confronted with a homicidal Narn with artificial implants in his head. During the fight, the Narn begs Sheridan to kill him. He is obviously being controlled by the implants. Sheridan knocks the Narn out, rather than kill him, and removes the implant. Back on Babylon 5, a returning Delenn has recognised images of the alien ship (brought back by a badly damaged Starfury and a dying pilot). The ship belongs to the Streibs, a race who collect specimens of alien races and test them, probably as a prelude to invasion. When they acquired Minbari samples the Minbari tracked them back to their home world and taught them a lesson. The *Agamemnon* – Sheridan's old ship – arrives at Babylon 5, and a rescue mission is mounted to retrieve Sheridan. On the Streib ship, Sheridan and the Narn have escaped from their cell, and when the *Agamemnon* attacks they leave the ship in a lifepod and are picked up. The Streib ship is destroyed.

The 'B' Plot: Delenn is summoned to a meeting of the Grey Council and is told that she has been removed from its ranks and replaced by another. The Grey Council have grave doubts about her loyalty to the Minbari race, given her change of form. Delenn is shocked when she discovers that her replacement – Neroon – is a member of the Warrior caste rather than of the Religious caste. This now gives the Warrior caste a numerical advantage in the Grey Council – it becomes the largest faction. Delenn asks to be allowed to return to Babylon 5 and remain in her post of ambassador, and her request is granted.

The 'C' Plot: General Hague – a member of the Joint Chiefs of Staff on Earth – arrives on Babylon 5 to talk to Sheridan. They discuss the belief amongst certain people on Earth that President Santiago was assassinated probably at the instigation of Psi Corps, and Hague asks Sheridan if he is willing to work towards proving it. Sheridan agrees, and discusses the subject secretly with Ivanova, Garibaldi and Franklin.

The Arc: Given that J. Michael Straczynski has said that the Streibs are not related to the Shadow plot, and will not be making a reappearance for a long time, if ever, we can safely assume they are not part of the arc plot.

Apart from Delenn's ongoing problems with the Grey Council, the only arc-related material in this story is the dream that Sheridan has while he's cooped up on the Streib ship. The dream is obviously pregnant with symbolism, and is explained in something of a rush in episode 321 ('Shadow Dancing'). Sheridan dreams of Ivanova standing with a raven on her shoulder, saying, 'Do you know who I am?' He then sees Garibaldi with a dove on his shoulder saying, 'The man in between is searching for you.' Ivanova dressed as for a funeral then says, 'You are the hand.' Sheridan then sees himself dressed in Psi Corps uniform. He sees Kosh, and asks him, 'Why are *you* here?' Kosh replies, 'We were never away. For the first time, your mind is quiet enough to hear me.' Sheridan asks, 'Why am *I* here?' to which Kosh responds, 'You have always been here.' Sheridan wakes up then, but when he is back on Babylon 5 Kosh tells him, 'You have always been here,' indicating that it was more than just a dream. See the essay on Jung and *Babylon 5* earlier in this book for further explanation of this dream.

Observations: Hedronn is now in charge of the Grey Council (well, he carries the big stick at least). Neroon has replaced Delenn, distorting the Grey Council so that there are now four members of the Warrior caste, three members of the Worker caste and two members of the Religious caste.

We discover in episode 303 ('A Day in the Strife') that the name of the Narn imprisoned with Sheridan is Ta'Lon.

Koshisms: Sheridan to Kosh: 'Why are *you* here?' Kosh: 'We were never away. For the first time, your mind is quiet enough to hear me.' Sheridan: 'Why am *I* here?' Kosh: 'You have always been here.'

Dialogue to Rewind For: Delenn: 'Have I mentioned recently how much I . . . appreciate you, Lennier?' Lennier: 'Not really, but it will give us something to discuss on our trip.'

Ships That Pass In The Night: The *Agamemnon* makes a welcome reappearance (it was first seen in episode 201 – 'Points of Departure').

Delenn's flyer is called the *Zhalen*. She must have traded her previous one in, because in episode 120 ('Babylon Squared') it sounded like her flyer was called the *Julit*.

Culture Shock: The Streibs seem to travel around abducting specimens of alien races and examining them for weaknesses – resistance to torture, stamina and so on. J. Michael

Straczynski has said that the aliens from the pre-title sequence of episode 115 ('Grail') are similar to, and distant relatives of, the Streibs, but they're not the same race. A closer examination of the Streibs would have revealed red slitted eyes instead of the black eyes of the ones in 'Grail'.

Literary, Mythological and Historical References: Naming the alien race Streibs is a clear nod towards the author Whitley Strieber, who claimed in his books *Communion: A True Story* (1987) and *Transformation: The Breakthrough* (1988) that he had been abducted by aliens. Note the subtly different spellings of Streibs and Strieber.

Sheridan misquotes the Greek philosopher Archimedes when he says, 'Give me a lever big enough and I will move the world.' What Archimedes really said was, 'Give me somewhere to stand and I will move the Earth.'

I've Seen That Face Before: John Vickery returns as Neroon (he first appeared in episode 117 – 'Legacies'). Robin Sachs returns as Hedronn (he first appeared in episode 201 – 'Points of Departure'). Robert Foxworth returns as General Hague (he also first appeared in episode 201 – 'Points of Departure').

Questions Raised: What do the Streibs want?

'Acts of Sacrifice'

Transmission Number: 212
Production Number: 212

Written by: J. Michael Straczynski
Directed by: Jim Johnston

Correlilmurzon: Ian Abecrombie
Taq: Paul Williams   **Narn No. 1:** Christopher Darga
Centauri No. 1: Paul Ainsley   **Franke:** Glenn Morshower

Plot: A bit of a time-wasting episode, with lots happening but little of it forming a cohesive whole. The 'A' plot is superficial (and emphasises the 'might makes right' solution), the 'B' plot is frankly embarrassing and the 'C' plot is the best thing about it all. Not a bad episode, by any means, but not one you would want to watch too often.

The 'A' Plot: Tensions are rising between the Narn and Centauri groups on Babylon 5, and G'Kar is having trouble keeping his people under control. He asks Sheridan and Delenn for aid from their respective governments, but they both reluctantly refuse. During a brawl in a corridor, a Narn is accidentally shot by Zack Allen. In retaliation, a group of hot-headed Narn stab the Centauri who started the fight. They are arming themselves in readiness for a riot, but G'Kar challenges their nominal leader to a fight, wins, and orders them to disperse. Sheridan and Delenn offer G'Kar 'unofficial' aid – medical supplies, food and a means of rescuing Narn populations at risk – and he reluctantly accepts.

The 'B' Plot: Representatives of a newly contacted alien race – the Lumati – arrive on the station, and Ivanova is detailed to show them around. Earth wants to negotiate an alliance with the Lumati, but the Lumati believe most other races to be their inferiors. Ivanova accidentally manages to persuade them that humanity is as 'superior' as they are. Correlilmurzon, the Lumati in charge, wishes to seal the agreement to open talks in the standard Lumati way – with sex – but Ivanova bluffs her way out of a nasty situation.

The 'C' Plot: Londo Mollari is realising that his new-found popularity has its drawbacks. Too many people who didn't want to know him before now want his help. When he tries to have a drink with the only person he considers a friend – Garibaldi – he finds that he may have lost more than he has gained.

The Arc: No obvious arc-related material appears in this episode, apart from the ongoing Centauri–Narn conflict.

Observations: Centauri have red blood.

Drazi knives come with poisoned blades as standard. They're a nasty race.

They eat whole lizards roasted on a stick in Downbelow. Yummy.

The character of Franke was named for the series' composer.

This episode marked the last appearance of G'Kar's aide Na'Toth in the series. Mary Kay Adams had been cast in the part after Caitlin Brown left, but after this episode Mary Kay Adams was asked to leave the series. J. Michael Straczynski has said, 'After Caitlin Brown decided to do other things we brought in Mary Kay, who we knew and who auditioned with the same attitude that Caitlin brought to it, and did an excellent job. When she took over the role she made a conscious decision to go in a different direction, and to play her almost more feminine, more subdued. I kept saying to her that it wasn't what we had discussed. If you're going to be in a scene with G'Kar you have to fight for every frame: you have to be as big as he is and go toe to toe. She wouldn't do it – she felt that "rather than push up against it I'll act zen-like and let it all go past me," but you can't do that with G'Kar – he'll eat you alive. And, after several performances, I said, "This is not what we really want to do" . . . and I dropped an asteroid on her.'

Ivanova's Life Lessons: 'Boom-shakalakalaka-boom-shakalakalaka!' You probably had to be there.

Dialogue to Rewind For: Franklin to Ivanova on her imminent sexual encounter with a Lumati: 'You could put a bag over his head and do it for Babylon 5.'

Ships That Pass In The Night: The Lumati ship is an impressive piece of software, but if it has a name then we never get to hear it.

I've Seen That Face Before: Paul Williams, who plays the diminutive Taq, is a well-regarded singer/songwriter. You can see him in Brian De Palma's 1974 film *Phantom of the Paradise* (alongside Gerrit Graham – Lord Kiro from episode 113, 'Signs and Portents').

'Hunter, Prey'

Transmission Number: 213
Production Number: 213

Written by: J. Michael Straczynski
Directed by: Menachem Binetski

Dr Everett Jacobs: Tony Steedman
Derek Cranston: Bernie Casey
Sarah: Wanda de Jesus   **Max:** Richard Moll

Plot: A tense, fast-paced episode that benefits from a vulnerable performance by Tony Steedman. The story encompasses everything on the station from heaven (Kosh's ship) to hell (Downbelow). Ah, but how much more satisfying would it have been if, instead of Tony Steedman as Dr Everett Jacobs, we had been given Johnny Sekka as Dr Benjamin Kyle?

The 'A' Plot: Dr Everett Jacobs, personal physician to President Clark, is on the run and heading for Babylon 5. Earthforce Special Intelligence Agent Derek Cranston is sent to intercept him, and tells Babylon 5's command staff that Jacobs knows about various black projects and covert operations that would adversely affect Earth's diplomatic endeavours if they ever got out. Garibaldi's security personnel are instructed to shoot to kill. Dr Franklin can't believe that Jacobs could be a threat – Jacobs taught him for two years at Harvard. Jacobs is captured by a criminal lurker in Downbelow who tries to ransom him back to Cranston. Garibaldi and Franklin rescue him and, while Cranston uses Babylon 5's own scanners to scan for Jacobs inside the station, he is smuggled off aboard Kosh's ship. Cranston leaves, seeking Jacobs elsewhere, and Sarah (one of General Hague's agents) arranges to get Jacobs to safety.

The 'B' Plot: Sheridan is contacted by Sarah – one of General Hague's agents – and told that Dr Jacobs can prove that President Clark did not have a virus when he disembarked *Earthforce 1*, as he said he did, and therefore probably knew it was going to blow up. Clark has waited this long to divert suspicion, but he wants Jacobs dead. Jacobs knows this, and is fleeing for his life. Sheridan has to send Garibaldi to find Jacobs before Cranston can while he distracts Cranston.

The 'C' Plot: Sheridan asks Kosh if they can spend some time together in order to understand one another better. Kosh initially refuses, apparently annoyed at Sheridan's misinterpretation of his obscure pronouncements, but finally relents. Kosh tells Sheridan that he will teach Sheridan about Sheridan himself to prepare him to fight legends.

The Arc: Dr Jacobs was Vice-President Clark's personal physician, and was the last person to examine him before he left *Earthforce 1* just before it exploded (see episode 122 – 'Chrysalis'). He knows that Clark wasn't suffering from any virus. That knowledge by itself isn't enough to prove that Clark was implicated in President Santiago's death, but it's a start. That's why Clark wants him dead. Unfortunately, Jacobs's testimony is overtaken by the events of episode 310 ('Severed Dreams'), but it may turn out to be important later on in the series. Or not, as the case may be.

When Sheridan asks Kosh, 'What do you want?' Kosh responds, '*Never* ask that question.' It's the question Morden asks in episode 113 ('Signs and Portents') – the question that leads directly to the Great War. Why does Kosh respond so strongly to it?

Kosh agrees in this episode to teach Sheridan about himself, to make him ready to fight legends. In effect, he is preparing Sheridan to take part in the Great War that is to come. We see little bits of Kosh's teachings in a few subsequent episodes – most notably 214 ('There All the Honor Lies') – and Kosh tells Sheridan in episode 315 ('Interludes and Examinations') that there was so much more he wanted to teach him.

Observations: Garibaldi, referring to Franklin's problematic relationship with his tutors, mentions the events of episode 104 ('Infection').

Sheridan reminds Kosh that Kosh touched his mind (in episode 211 – 'All Alone in the Night').

Dr Jacobs – one of Dr Franklin's mentors – is using stims to keep himself going. This is exactly what Franklin does, later in the series.

Max, the lurker who kidnaps Jacobs, mentions the drug dust. We get to see what dust does in episode 306 ('Dust to Dust').

There is a mention of the Dilgar war (see episode 109 – 'Deathwalker').

Derek Cranston points out that the command staff have previously used Babylon 5's sensors to scan the station's interior. This is a reference to the pilot episode ('The Gathering') and episode 206 ('Spider in the Web').

If you look carefully, Sarah leaves an object behind when she leaves the meeting with Sheridan. It's a flashlight. A sequence in which Sheridan and Sarah signal their presence to each other with flashlights was cut for time reasons, but the flashlight is still sitting there.

Koshisms: Kosh: 'I sought understanding. I listened to the song. Your thoughts *became* the song.' Sheridan: 'Has this ever happened before' Kosh: 'Once.'

Kosh to Sheridan after Sheridan has misunderstood him yet again: 'You do *not* understand.'

Sheridan to Kosh: 'What do you want?' Kosh's response: '*Never* ask that question.'

Kosh to Sheridan: 'I will teach you.' Sheridan: 'About yourself?' Kosh: 'About you. Until you are ready.' Sheridan: 'For what?' Kosh: 'To fight legends.'

Dialogue to Rewind For: The maintenance personnel who were working in Bay 13 refuse to go anywhere near Kosh's ship, according to Ivanova. 'They say it talks to them in their sleep.'

Dr Jacobs, after leaving Kosh's ship: 'While I was asleep, the ship . . . it sang to me.'

Dialogue to Fast Forward Past: Sarah's melodramatic parting shot to Sheridan: 'In this game, Captain, you only get one shot.'

Sheridan's response when Sarah asks the impossible: 'You want mayo on that?'

Garibaldi to Franklin: 'Maybe someone should've labelled the future, "some assembly required".'

Ships That Pass In The Night: Kosh's ship is kept in Bay 13 when not in use. The patterns on its side change subtly as they are being watched. The ship understands spoken messages (in Vorlon) and can reply by spelling out messages (in the Vorlon language, one presumes) on its hull. It has a self-protection system consisting of an energy beam with a targeting device on the end of an arm that extends from its hull. Kosh won't allow anybody on board unless they are in a coma. Effectively, the ship is alive. It is also telepathic, as it communicates with people in their dreams.

Culture Shock: Pak'ma'ra can see into the ultraviolet.

Station Keeping: All high-ranking Earthdome personnel are injected with a coded identification crystal as a precaution against kidnapping.

Ambassador Kosh's ship is berthed, rather aptly, in Bay 13. This isn't a regular berth – someone else is directed there in the third issue of the *Babylon 5* comic ('In Harm's Way') while Kosh is on the station, implying that his ship is berthed elsewhere.

Literary, Mythological and Historical References: Derek Cranston is the Earthforce security agent in this episode. Coincidentally, Lamont Cranston is the true identity of the 1930s radio-serial and pulp-magazine hero the Shadow.

I've Seen That Face Before: Bernie Casey, who plays Agent Cranston, has also been in the James Bond film *Never Say Never Again* (as Bond's CIA companion Felix Leiter) and, more recently, appeared in two episodes of *Star Trek: Deep Space Nine* ('The Maquis Part I' and 'The Maquis Part II') as a Starfleet officer named Cal Hudson.

Tony Steedman, who plays Dr Jacobs, is a stalwart of British television. Readers of a certain age may recall that he took over from Peter Vaughn as the father in the Robert Lindsay comedy series *Citizen Smith*, although he is probably more recognisable as Socrates in the 1989 film *Bill and Ted's Excellent Adventure*.

Accidents Will Happen: All high-ranking Earthdome personnel are injected with a coded identification crystal as a precaution against kidnapping, but the transmissions from the crystal can be blocked by something as simple as a lead door and have a range of a few hundred metres. Does this look like a sensible precaution against kidnapping to you?

Questions Raised: Was it originally meant to be Dr Benjamin Kyle who arrived on the station instead of Dr Everett Jacobs?

'There All the Honor Lies'

Transmission Number: 214
Production Number: 215

Written by: Peter David
Directed by: Mike Laurence Vejar

Guinevere Corey: Julie Caitlin Brown
Ashan: Sean Gregory Sullivan
Human Customer: Elliott Harold
Human/Alien Customer: Mark Hendrickson

Plot: A strangely unbalanced episode. On the one hand the 'A' plot is trite and obvious and none of the three other plots is very strong, but on the other hand it contains three priceless moments that sum up the ethos of *Babylon 5* for many people.

The 'A' Plot: Sheridan's comlink is stolen, and when he gives chase he is ambushed by a Minbari. Forced to defend himself, he kills the Minbari with a gun he finds on the floor, but Ashan – another Minbari – witnesses the event and claims that Sheridan fired with no provocation. The Minbari want him put on trial for murder, and Earthforce are inclined to agree, but Sheridan's lawyer tells him that even if he is found innocent his career is probably over. Lennier follows Ashan and sees him meet the person who stole Sheridan's comlink. He gets Ashan to admit in conversation that Sheridan is being framed by the clan they both belong to – the Third Thane of Chodomo. The clan still blame him for the loss of the *Black Star*, during the war. The conversation is overheard by Delenn and Sheridan, who find a way of clearing Sheridan without exposing the Third Thane of Chodomo and thus dishonouring Lennier.

The 'B' Plot: A Babylon 5 memorabilia emporium opens up in the Zocalo. Sheridan is initially enthusiastic, until he discovers a teddy-bear version of himself on sale. Londo too is unhappy when he finds dolls meant to represent him but without his distinctive genitalia.

The 'C' Plots: (a) Vir is recalled to Centauri Prime because the post of attaché to Ambassador Mollari isn't the joke it used to be, and more important people want it. Londo tells the homeworld that if Vir goes, he goes, and they rescind the order. (b) Kosh, as part of his attempt to open Sheridan's mind, shows him something beautiful and inexplicable.

The Arc: Delenn is having trouble with the Minbari on Babylon 5 – they refuse to recognise her as a Minbari now that she has undergone her transformation.

Observations: 'Minbari do not lie,' Sheridan is told by both Delenn and Lennier, but they are lying. Londo tells Sheridan that Minbari will lie if by doing so they can protect the honour of someone else. He fleetingly refers to the time in 'The Quality of Mercy' (episode 121) when Lennier takes the blame for a fight that Londo started.

During the baseball scene in the pre-title sequence, Sheridan is wearing a cap with a silhouette of his previous command – the *Agamemnon* – on the badge.

The episode contains three priceless moments. The first is when Ivanova takes a tour of the Babylon 5 emporium and is freaked out by the sight of a Markab wearing a human mask and a human wearing a Drazi mask – it's a scene that should completely break the spell of the make-up and force the viewer to realise that he or she is watching a television programme, but it's a tribute to the power of the series that it doesn't work that way at all. The second is the 'beauty in the dark' that Kosh shows Sheridan – a truly wondrous moment, quite impossible to describe. The third is the fate of the poor Bab-bear-lon teddy bear – thrown out into space by Sheridan and left to thump into the canopy of a passing Starfury.

The Bab-bear-lon teddy bear was a present from the wife of writer Peter David to J. Michael Straczynski, and Straczynski (who hates cute bears with a vengeance) wrote the tag scene in which it appears. In a bizarre case of revenge, the bear later makes a special guest appearance in an episode of the US kids

TV SF show *Space Cases*, written by Peter David and Billy Mumy (Lennier). A group of space-going children find the bear floating in the vacuum. 'Oh, he's so cute,' says one of them. 'What kind of dope would toss a perfectly good Earth bear into space?' The same episode has mention of an alien race named the Straczyns, and Minbar chess.

The whole 'beauty in the dark' sequence was written by J. Michael Straczynski. The music used is a Gregorian chant.

Koshisms: 'One moment of perfect beauty.'

Ivanova's Life Lessons: 'Welcome to Babylon 5 – the last, best hope for a quick buck.'

To Sheridan after he has tried to explain about Kosh's lesson: 'It must be working – you're beginning to talk just like a Vorlon.'

To Londo when he tries to explain about the lack of genitalia on his doll: 'So you feel like you're being symbolically cast– . . . in a bad light.'

Dialogue to Rewind For: Sheridan to Garibaldi: 'You have a suspicious mind. I like that.'

I've Seen That Face Before: Julie Caitlin Brown, who plays Guinevere Corey (Sheridan's lawyer) is the Caitlin Brown who played Na'Toth. Julie Caitlin Brown is her 'real' name.

Accidents Will Happen: Ashan tells Lennier all about the plot to frame Sheridan when they are alone in Delenn's quarters, not knowing that Sheridan, Delenn, Sheridan's lawyer and Garibaldi are all listening from the next room. He can't be very observant, because all four of them can clearly be seen silhouetted behind the translucent door between the rooms.

'And Now For a Word'

Transmission Number: 215
Production Number: 214

Written by: J. Michael Straczynski
Directed by: Mario DiLeo

Cynthia Torqueman: Kim Zimmer
Senator Ronald Quantrell: Christopher Curry
Psi Cop: Granville Ames   **Johnny:** John Christian Graas
Mother: Leslie Wing   **Eduardo Delvientos:** José Rey

Date: 16 September 2259 – this is the date that the ISN programme *36 Hours on Babylon 5* is supposedly transmitted, but the thirty-six hours in question were presumably recorded before this date.

Plot: This episode is hardly original in approach, and the first time it was shown the superficialities were off-putting to those of us who have been following the intricacies of the series for thirty-seven previous episodes. However, on repeated viewings the subversive undercurrents become apparent, and the episode becomes more and more watchable.

The 'A' Plot: An ISN news team led by unruffled reporter Cynthia Torqueman is making a 'warts-and-all' feature about the station – *36 Hours on Babylon 5*. During the course of their filming the Narn–Centauri war comes closer to the station than it has before, Ambassador Kosh is ambushed by a camera crew, Ambassador Delenn is reduced to tears, the Psi Corps transmit subliminal adverts and a clear picture is gained of the ambiguity with which Babylon 5 is viewed by the Senate on Earth.

The 'B' Plot: A Narn transport fires on a Centauri transport near Babylon 5. G'Kar claims that the ship was carrying fusion bombs, mass-drivers and ion cannons for use against Narn in the ongoing war, and investigations of the wreckage bear out his accusation. Suddenly the war comes to Babylon 5 as Narn ships start firing on Centauri ships and the Centauri ships start firing back. The appearance of a Centauri battle cruiser escalates matters significantly, especially when Londo tells Sheridan that if any Centauri ships are searched for weapons he will consider it an act of war. Earthdome rejects the Centauri demands and Sheridan tells the Centauri ship that any hostile action will be considered to be an attack on Babylon 5 itself. A Narn heavy cruiser appears on the scene and destroys the Centauri ship, but is so badly damaged that it explodes when it tries to enter hyperspace. Things return to normal – for a while.

The 'C' Plot: Psi Corps are using overt and covert advertising to influence public opinion of them.

The Arc: Earth now has an Office of Public Morale – prefiguring the rise of Nightwatch in episode 217 ('In the Shadow of Z'ha'dum') and the arrival of Babylon 5's Political Officer in episode 305 ('Voices of Authority').

The Centauri are transferring mass-drivers through Babylon 5's local space on their way to the war front. They later use these mass-drivers to bomb the Narn in episode 220 ('The Long, Twilight Struggle').

Observations: The documentary *36 Hours on Babylon 5* is sponsored by Interplanetary Expeditions – the company who financed the mission of the *Icarus* to Z'ha'dum.

Senator Hidoshi – an occasional character from the first season – is now *former* Senator Hidoshi. Presumably he vanished in a reshuffle after President Clark took power (although he turns up in issue 3 of the *Babylon 5* comic, 'In Harm's Way', which is set shortly after President Clark takes power).

During the Psi Corps advert in the middle of the *36 Hours on Babylon 5* documentary, there is a brief, almost subliminal, flash of words on the screen. The words read 'THE PSI CORPS IS YOUR FRIEND. TRUST THE CORPS.' The clear implication is that Psi Corps are attempting to influence the population of Earth, turning the general dislike of telepaths into admiration and liking. The flash lasts for four frames (i.e. one-fifth of a second) – that's two frames longer than the official American Government definition of subliminal influencing.

Dialogue to Rewind For: G'Kar: 'There are humans for whom the words "Never again" carry special meaning.'

Dialogue to Fast Forward Past: All of Franklin's speech concerning his friend's unfortunate accident with an airlock can be missed with equanimity.

Ships That Pass In The Night: Earth Transport *Heyerdahl*, Narn Transport *Na'Ton*, Centauri Transport *Molios*.

Sheridan tells Cynthia Torqueman that the *Agamemnon* – the ship he used to command – was one of the first Omega Class destroyers to come off the construction lines after the Earth–Minbari war.

Other Worlds: New Vegas is mentioned during this episode. According to J. Michael Straczynski, it's a city on Mars.

Minbar is the seventh planet out from its sun. Fully one quarter of the planet is covered by its northern ice cap, and there are heavy deposits of crystalline minerals.

Culture Shock: The Minbari race have three languages – one for each caste.

Station Keeping: Babylon 5 is 8.0645 kilometres long. Its casing weighs 2.5 million tonnes.

There are 1,500 Guild of Dockers workers and 6,500 Earthforce personnel on the station.

Aliens make up around 42 per cent of the station's population, and there are fourteen species of alien in the non-oxygen-breathing 'alien sector'. This just about squares with episode 210 ('GROPOS'), in which we are told that over twenty races live on Babylon 5. That leaves only six races living outside the 'alien sector', and a quick count gives us at least nine we can put names to (see 'GROPOS').

Literary, Mythological and Historical References: This episode is very similar in structure to the 'Blood and Guts' episode of *M*A*S*H*, which was also told entirely from the point of a camera crew and reporter doing a report on the Mobile Army Surgical Hospital. J. Michael Straczynski was aware of the parallels when he wrote the episode.

G'Kar's reminder – 'There are humans for whom the words "Never again" carry special meaning' – refers to a phrase often used after some great but avoidable human catastrophe such as a war. It's often used in reference to the Holocaust (the annihilation of some 11 million people by the Nazi regime before and during the Second World War) but the phrase was used previously about the First World War.

Accidents Will Happen: President Clark's first name is given as William in this episode, even though the credit in episode 122 ('Chrysalis') reads 'Morgan Clark'.

There must be something odd about names in this episode – Sheridan's middle initial is given as J even though we know his middle name is David.

'Knives'

Transmission Number: 216
Production Number: 216

Written by: Lawrence G. DiTillio
Directed by: Stephen L. Posey

Urza Jaddo: Carmen Arganziano
Lord Refa: William Forward

Plot: A difficult one to classify, this. Written by the series script editor, the episode should somehow encapsulate what *Babylon 5* should be all about, acting as a template of what DiTillio and Straczynski expect from other writers. Instead it's a slow and predictable trudge through familiar territory with no 'C' plot to lighten it up and a gratuitous continuity reference to keep the fans happy.

The 'A' Plot: Garibaldi lets slip to Sheridan that Grey Sector is referred to unofficially as 'the Babylon 5 Triangle', due to the high incidence of disappearances, malfunctions and odd noises. Intrigued, Sheridan pops down to investigate. He discovers a dead Markab, who briefly comes to life and transfers an alien force to Sheridan. Sheridan is plagued by hallucinations, but pieces together a message from them and realises that the alien force was picked up by accident in an unstable sector of space. Sheridan leaves the station in a Starfury and returns the alien to where it wants to go.

The 'B' Plot: Urza Jaddo, an old friend and duelling partner of Londo Mollari, arrives on the station. Back on Centauri Prime he and his House are accused of treachery, and face disgrace and death. Londo initially offers to help, but a conversation with Lord Refa convinces him that he

228

would be risking his own career and reputation. Angered by Londo's alliance with Refa – who is the man orchestrating the accusations against him – Urza challenges Londo to a duel. He deliberately lets Londo kill him, knowing that under the Centauri duelling rules he will die with honour and his House will become a part of House Mollari, and will be safe.

The Arc: The unstable sector of space in which the alien force was picked up, and to which Sheridan returns it, is Sector 14 – the sector in which Babylon 4 vanished. Sheridan is given the Babylon 4 files by Garibaldi (even though Earthforce supposedly confiscated them all).

Perhaps this is arc-related, and perhaps it isn't, but the scene of the alien force leaving Sheridan's body is almost identical to that of Kosh leaving Lyta Alexander's body at the end of episode 304 ('Passing Through Gethsemane') and of the new Vorlon Ambassador doing the same thing in season four. Is this a coincidence, or is the alien force in Sheridan an adjunct to or analogue of a Vorlon? Only time will tell.

One season later, in episode 309 ('Point of No Return'), Lady Morella tells Londo that he has already let two opportunities to change his fate slip through his fingers. This might have been one of them – Urza Jaddo begs him to reconsider his actions, and after Jaddo's death Vir expresses the same wish. Londo refuses, of course.

Observations: Londo refers back to his brief affair with Adira in 'Born to the Purple' (episode 103).

Dr Franklin mentions that he knows a good Markab doctor. This presumably is a reference to Lazarenn, who appears in episode 218 ('Confessions and Lamentations').

Sheridan has visions of the *Icarus* (the ship his wife was on) exploding and of his parents.

Urza Jaddo is a hero of Goraj – an epic battle of some kind.

Sheridan's hallucination of his wife's ship – the *Icarus* – is intended to prepare viewers for its use in the next episode (except that the episodes were shown in the wrong order in the USA).

Grey Sector is referred to as the Babylon 5 Triangle

because of the strange noises and disappearances that keep occurring there. It's not the alien force that's causing the noises and disappearances – it's only just arrived, and all it wants to do is go home. We discover what's *really* causing the noises and disappearances in episode 319 ('Grey 17 is Missing'), and we'll wish we hadn't.

Ivanova's Life Lessons: Sheridan: 'Do you always worry when things are going well?' Ivanova: 'I don't have time to worry about them when they're not.'

Dialogue to Rewind For: Vir to Londo: 'On rare occasions I am proud to be your attaché.'

Ships That Pass In The Night: A ship named the *Arkadi* appears through the jumpgate. It looks like it might be an Earth ship.

Other Worlds: Janos 7 (home of the grylor – a nasty flying reptile with no eyes). Janos 7 is also mentioned in episode 210 ('GROPOS') – also by Larry DiTillio.

Culture Shock: Young Centauri men join duelling societies, much as the German army officers did in the late nineteenth century. Much of their social status is derived from their position in these societies. Londo Mollari and Urza Jaddo both belonged to the Cour Prido ('the Proud Knives') where Urza Jaddo's nickname was Scotura ('the Silent Beast') and Londo's was Paso Leati ('Crazed Leati') – which sounds like something out of an Italian opera.

Vocator is a Centauri rank or title of some sort. Along the same lines, *bravari* is a Centauri alcoholic drink, the *morago* is a Centauri formal duel to the death and a *kutari* is a Centauri sword.

Accidents Will Happen: Nothing obvious (but note that this episode will lead to a blooper later, in episode 310 – 'Severed Dreams'.)

Questions Raised: What is the alien force? Is it a Vorlon?

Was this one of Londo's chances to avoid the fire that lies before him?

'In the Shadow of Z'ha'dum'

Transmission Number: 217
Production Number: 217

Written by: J. Michael Straczynski
Directed by: David Eagle

Morden: Ed Wasser   **Pierce Macabee:** Alex Hyde-White

Plot: A 'wow!' episode that sets up the dark heart of Sheridan very neatly. There is a very thin line between what Clark and Bester are capable of doing and what Sheridan finds he is capable of doing. The difference is, we know Sheridan is right. Don't we?

The 'A' Plot: When Sheridan sorts through some of his dead wife's possessions, Garibaldi recognises a face on the crew manifest of her ship, the *Icarus*. The face belongs to Morden, the mysterious associate of Londo Mollari. Records show that Morden is currently on the station. Sheridan orders his arrest, and interrogates him concerning what happened to the *Icarus* and how he escaped. Morden gives nothing away, claiming he has suffered amnesia ever since the *Icarus* blew up. Garibaldi points out that Sheridan is holding Morden illegally, but Sheridan has become obsessed by the idea that if Morden is alive then his wife might still be. Garibaldi resigns, but Sheridan continues. Vir Cotto relays a message from Londo Mollari to the effect that Morden is under Centauri diplomatic immunity, but Sheridan still refuses to release him. Ivanova tells him that he is acting irrationally, but he *still* refuses. Eventually Delenn and Kosh explain exactly why Morden must be released. He is the agent of an ancient and evil race known only as the Shadows, who were awakened from a thousand-year sleep by the arrival of the *Icarus* on their planet, Z'ha'dum. The Vorlons and the Minbari are aware that the Shadows are mobilising their forces, ready to continue their Great War, but if the Shadows become aware that their activities are being watched then they might strike before preparations can be made. Kosh reveals that the Vorlons are one of the last remaining races of First Ones left in the galaxy. Faced with this terrible knowledge, Sheridan is forced to let Morden go. Garibaldi rescinds his resignation.

The 'B' Plot: Pierce Macabee, Regional Director of the newly formed Ministry of Peace on Earth, arrives on the station. He explains during a series of talks that the ministry has been formed to promote the ideals of peace amongst humans. To that end, an organisation called the Nightwatch is being set up to keep an eye out for signs of sedition and loose talk.

The 'C' Plot: Vast numbers of injured Narn are being channelled through medlab, and Franklin is resorting to stimulants to keep himself going.

The Arc: This story contains the first major statement of the major *Babylon 5* arc strand – the ongoing war between the forces of light and dark. Delenn explains it to Sheridan thus: 'There are beings in the universe much older than either of our races . . . Once, long ago, they walked among the stars like giants – vast and timeless – taught the younger races, explored beyond the Rim, created great empires. But to all things there is an end. Slowly, over a million years, the First Ones went away. Some passed beyond the stars, never to return. Some simply disappeared . . .' Pressed by Sheridan, she admits that, 'Not all of the First Ones have gone away. A few stayed behind, hidden or asleep, waiting for the day when they may be needed – when the Shadows come again . . .' When Sheridan asks about the Shadows, she replies, 'The Shadows were old when even the ancients were young. They battled each other over and over across a million years. The last great war against the Shadows was ten thousand years ago. It was the last time the ancients walked openly among us. But the Shadows were only defeated, not destroyed. A thousand years ago the Shadows returned to their places of power, rebuilt them and began to stretch forth their hand. Before they could strike, they were defeated by an alliance of worlds including the Minbari and the few remaining First Ones who had not yet passed beyond the veil. When they had finished, the First Ones went away – all except one.' That one, of course, is Kosh – or, more properly, the Vorlon race.

Delenn tells Sheridan that the crew of the *Icarus* accidentally awoke the Shadows during their archaeological investigations. 'Those that would not serve were killed,' she says,
but she doesn't say how many served and how many were
killed. We now know, of course, that Morden is not the only
human servant of the Shadows.

We get a flashback to episode 122 – 'Chrysalis' – when
Delenn reveals that the question she asked Kosh in that
episode was, 'Have the Shadows returned to Z'ha'dum?' The
answer was, 'Yes.'

Delenn tells Sheridan that Morden is always accompanied
by Shadows. Sheridan and Zack both hear the Shadows
talking to Morden in his cell. By a judicious manipulation of
the scanners through various wavelengths, Sheridan is able to
see the Shadows briefly. This is the second time we have seen
the Shadows – the first was in episode 122 – 'Chrysalis'.

Sheridan arranges for Morden and telepath Talia Winters to
pass in the corridor. Talia reacts strongly to Morden without
even having to touch him – shying away and seeing a shadow
cross his face (as Delenn does in episode 113 – 'Signs and
Portents'). She also sees a half-materialised Shadow by Morden's side. The threatening reaction of the Shadows to Talia is
a hint of the importance of telepaths, as shown in episode 315
('Interludes and Examinations').

This episode marks the first appearance of the Nightwatch
– the organisation loyal to President Clark that is to become
important in episode 309 – 'Point of No Return'. Members of
Nightwatch are asked to wear the Nightwatch armband and
thus to raise public awareness of the aims of the Ministry of
Peace. They are also encouraged to be watchful for signs of
discontent.

Observations: Delenn and Kosh have known about the resurgence of shadow activity for three years.

Dr Franklin is taking stims in this story to keep himself
going. This occasional plot will resurface in episode 218
('Confessions and Lamentations') and 303 ('A Day in the
Strife') – and get resolved the last third of season three,
starting from episode 315 ('Interludes and Examinations').

A hundred and thirty-nine people died on board the *Icarus*, according to Sheridan. This implies that Morden is the 140th crew member.

At one point, Sheridan tells Garibaldi that interpreting regulations for a senior officer can be construed as insubordination. This is an almost identical line of dialogue to one used by Colonel Ari Ben Zayn to Sinclair in episode 116 – 'Eyes'. There is a distinct parallel being set up here, with Sheridan willing to break rules and ride roughshod over advice in pursuit of his goal, just as Colonel Ben Zayn was.

Reputable histories of military intelligence during the Second World War do not give any credence to the story that Churchill knew about the bombing of Coventry days before it happened – a story repeated by Sheridan in this episode. During November 1940, Enigma decrypts of German communications did refer to an unusually important bombing raid against a target in England, but they referred to the target and some alternative targets only by code names and numbers. Military intelligence analysts believed, based on a captured map, that those targets were all in the London and Home Counties area. A German pilot shot down over England did say that Birmingham and Coventry were the targets, but his information was disregarded in favour of the assessment based on the captured map. It was only at 15.00 on 14 November 1940 that Coventry was unambiguously identified as the target for the attack, when beams from German direction-finding equipment were detected crossing over the city. Within less than twelve hours, 449 German bombers were off-loading their ordnance above the city. The rest, as they say, is history.

This episode was shown before the previous one (216 – 'Knives') in the USA because the CGI work on the flying creature in that episode pushed its transmission date back. The use of the *Icarus* in that episode was intended to set up the explanation of Morden's origins in this episode.

On one of the *Babylon 5* blooper tapes, during a take of the scene where Sheridan says Morden is supposed to be dead, Ed Wasser clutches his chest and keels over in sync with Sheridan's dialogue.

Koshisms: When Delenn tells Sheridan that Kosh's encounter suit is designed to stop him being recognised, Sheridan asks, 'By whom?' Kosh replies, 'By everyone.'

To Sheridan: 'If you go to Z'ha'dum, you will die.'

Dialogue to Rewind For: Morden to Vir: 'What do *you* want?' Vir: 'I'd like to live long enough to be there when they cut off your head and stick it on a pike as a warning to the next ten generations that some favours come with too high a price. I want to look up into your lifeless eyes and wave – like this. Can you and your associates arrange this for me, Mr Morden?'

Dialogue to Fast Forward Past: Franklin, explaining to Ivanova that he can sometimes see God reflected in the eyes of dying patients: 'I've seen a lot of reflected Gods today, Susan.'

Ships That Pass In The Night: The *Icarus*, of course.

Other Worlds: The Vega Colony is mentioned.

Culture Shock: Franklin is a Foundationist – a new religion whose central tenet seems to be that God cannot be described in words. He talks more about his beliefs in episode 318 ('Walkabout').

I've Seen That Face Before: Alex Hyde-White, who plays Pierce Macabee, is the son of the British character actor Wilfred Hyde-White (whose genre credits include *Battlestar Galactica* and *Buck Rogers in the 25th Century*). Alex Hyde-White is himself best known for starring in the film *Biggles* as the time-travelling hero (but not as Biggles).

Questions Raised: How did Londo, back on Centauri Prime, know Morden had been arrested within ten hours of its happening? Are there other Shadow agents with whom he is in contact?

Why are the Shadows always with Morden? Don't they trust him?

'Confessions and Lamentations'

Transmission Number: 218
Production Number: 218

Written by: J. Michael Straczynski
Directed by: Kevin Cremin

Lazarenn: Jim Norton   **Markab Ambassador** Kim Strauss
Markab Mother: Diane Adair
Markab Girl: Bluejean Ashley Secrist

Plot: Distressing. There's no other word for it.

The 'A' Plot: A Markab transport vessel is ten hours overdue
at Babylon 5, and when Zeta Wing are sent to find out
what happened to it they discover it drifting in space, all
two hundred occupants dead. Meanwhile, on Babylon 5,
four Markab have died within three days, all apparently of
natural causes. Provoked into conducting deeper autopsies, Dr
Franklin discovers that the Markab are dying of a plague. An
old friend of his – a Markab doctor named Lazarenn – admits
the existence of the plague, which is called *drafa* and tells
Franklin that it is 100 per cent contagious and 100 per cent
terminal. An outbreak some years before was believed to have
been a punishment from the gods for immorality. Markab
people are failing to report this current outbreak for fear that
they too might be accused of immorality. Lazarenn himself has
been ordered to keep silent about the plague. Sheridan
quarantines the entire station – no ships are to enter or leave.
The Markab isolate themselves from the rest of the station to
pray for deliverance – all except for Lazarenn, who stays to
help Franklin. Delenn and Lennier go with them to minister to
the sick and the dying. A Pak'ma'ra is found dead of no
apparent cause, and Franklin orders an autopsy to determine
whether the *drafa* has crossed the species boundary. Lazarenn
is infected with the disease, but watching its progress until
Lazarenn dies means that Franklin is able to determine how it
attacks the body. The Markab and the Pak'ma'ra are the only
species vulnerable – unless it mutates. Armed with a drug that
will help the Markab bodies fight the disease, Franklin goes to
where they are isolated – but they are all dead.

The 'B' Plot: Delenn has invited Sheridan to a special Minbari meal, but the long, drawn-out formal procedures are too much for him and he falls asleep halfway through.

The Arc: Franklin takes stims to keep himself going during this episode – a problem that first raised its head in episode 217 ('In the Shadow of Z'ha'dum') and will again in episode 303 ('A Day in the Strife'), and will get resolved the last third of season three, starting from episode 315 ('Interludes and Examinations').

The relationship between Delenn and Sheridan deepens in this episode. Her having him for dinner is in response to his buying her dinner in episode 208 ('A Race Through Dark Places'). He asks her to call him John for the first time.

At one point during this episode, Delenn says she was in the temple as a child, lost and frightened, and someone appeared to her and said, 'I will not allow harm to come to my little ones, here in my great house.' This figure, J. Michael Straczynski has admitted, is Valen, adding a piquancy to Delenn's line back in episode 102 ('Soul Hunter') when she says to Sinclair, 'I knew you would come,' when he rescues her. Episode 317 ('War Without End' Part Two) explains her certainty further.

Observations: Sheridan is left-handed.

Franklin met Lazarenn when he visited the Markab homeworld, during his stint hitch-hiking around the galaxy.

J. Michael Straczynski has said about this episode, 'A man is shot by a gun. Now, you can either do a story about the guy and his life up to the moment he was shot and killed, or you can do a story about the people who are affected by his death. The former story ends kinda fast. But both are perfectly valid. The main thrust is how this story *affects* our main characters. Would they have been more affected if it were the Drazi rather than the Markabs? No. It would've been just the same. My job is not to sit here and say, "Hmm . . . do I think audience members like the Drazi or the Markabs more?" and thus base my decision on that. I write my stories based on what's right for the story, period. In this case, I knew it had to be one of the League races, and in particular, those prosthetics capable of expressing broad ranges of emotion, potentially sympathetic characters. That instantly cut out the Pak'ma'ra as primary characters. I considered the Drazi, but my sense was that the prosthetics couldn't convey the depth of emotion I needed. Finally, that led me to the Markabs.'

A certain amount of redesigning had to go on with the Markab masks to ensure that they *could* convey those emotions. Lazarenn's mask is different from many of the background ones.

Ships That Pass In The Night: The Markab transport which fails to turn up at Babylon 5 on schedule sounds like it's called the *Cortee*.

Culture Shock: The formal meal that Lennier arranges for Delenn and Sheridan takes two days to prepare. There are fifteen stages of cooking (including the blessing of spices), and if any one of them is done wrongly then the entire process must be started again. Lennier has not slept, and has eaten only bread and drunk only water, since he started.

Minbari flarn is green.

The Markab would appear to be (or to have been) a very religious and moral people.

Markab have red blood.

For formal meals, Minbari leave one place setting empty, ready for the return of Valen.

Station Keeping: Starfuries have sensors capable of detecting dead bodies.

Until this episode, there was a population of around 5,000 Markab on Babylon 5.

I've Seen That Face Before: Jim Norton, who plays Lazarenn, was Ombuds Wellington in episodes 115 ('Grail') and 121 ('The Quality of Mercy').

Diane Adair, who plays the Markab mother, also played Mila Shar, the head of the Abbai agricultural delegation in episode 108 ('The War Prayer').

Literary, Mythological and Historical References: Dr Franklin refers to the Black Death – the great epidemic of bubonic plague that ravaged Europe in the fourteenth century. Franklin confidently states that three-quarters of the population of Europe died in that epidemic. In fact, estimates of the actual death toll vary greatly, not least because there is no definitive way of determining what the population of Europe actually *was* at the time the plague struck. Recent work, using a variety of different estimation techniques, indicates that the death toll was somewhere between 30 per cent and 40 per cent of the entire European population. However, by Franklin's time they may know different . . .

Accidents Will Happen: Human surgical rubber gloves fit Markab perfectly. Isn't that lucky . . .

The sensors on a Starfury can distinguish between live Markab and dead Markab in this episode, but they can't distinguish between a live Soul Hunter and a dead Soul Hunter in episode 102 ('Soul Hunter').

Questions Raised: Were the Markab killed by the Shadows (see the entry for episode 205 – 'The Long Dark' – for a full discussion of why they might have been)?

'Divided Loyalties'

Transmission Number: 219
Production Number: 219

Written by: J. Michael Straczynski
Directed by: Jésus Treviño

Lyta Alexander: Patricia Tallman

Plot: One of the best and nastiest episodes yet made of this series, with the first tentative steps of a realistically portrayed love affair and a revelation that is truly shocking – the more so because of the emotional investment we've been led to make in the two people concerned. Not only that, we get 'A', 'B' and 'C' plots that seamlessly mesh into one.

The 'A' Plot: Lyta Alexander – Babylon 5's first commercial telepath – returns to the station in a badly shot-up spacecraft. She tells Sheridan that one of his command staff is

239

a 'traitor' with a secondary personality implanted by Psi Corps, but that she doesn't know who it is. While Sheridan is trying to decide whether to allow Lyta to test the command staff one at a time with the telepathic password, someone tries to kill her. She runs, and seeks the assistance of Ambassador Delenn. Sheridan agrees, over the objections of Ivanova, that all command staff can be tested. One by one, they are. No traitor is found. Through a fluke, Lyta tests Talia Winters and discovers that *she* is the 'traitor'. Talia is arrested and forced to leave Babylon 5.

The 'B' Plot: Talia Winters is looking for temporary quarters after the air recycling system in her usual quarters is being repaired. Ivanova offers to lend her a bed for a while. Talia moves in, and the two of them become emotionally very close, and probably lovers. Ivanova's feelings are rocked when the Talia she knows is destroyed by Lyta Alexander and replaced with a sarcastic and vicious secondary personality.

The 'C' Plot: Lyta tells Sheridan that ever since scanning Kosh she feels drawn to Vorlon space. Before leaving the station, she goes to see Kosh. She tells him she never told anyone what she truly saw when she scanned him, and she asks him to show her what she saw before – his true form. He opens his encounter suit, and she sees.

The Arc: Lyta Alexander tells the command staff that, after her experience scanning Kosh, she was recalled to Earth and questioned about what she saw. She claims she told 'them' everything she knew (although we later find out she was lying), but they didn't believe her. She escaped to Mars, and became involved in the revolutionary movement. One of the Martian revolution agents discovered that a Psi Corps installation in *Syria Planum* was creating covert agents by implanting secondary personalities deep inside people's minds. This is the installation we see in issue 8 of the *Babylon 5* comic series ('Shadows Past and Present' Part IV – 'Silent Enemies'), near where the Shadow ship was dug up (as we later discover in episode 308 – 'Messages from Earth'). The secondary personality can see and hear whatever the primary personality does, and can take control of the body

240

when the primary personality is asleep. On telepathic receipt of a password, the real personality is destroyed and the secondary personality takes over. Lyta knows there is one of these agents on Babylon 5, but she doesn't know who it is. It turns out to be Talia Winters, as indicated previously in issue 8 (Part IV of 'Shadows, Past and Present' – 'Silent Enemies') of the comic series.

Ivanova finally admits why she hates telepaths and won't submit to a telepathic scan (as shown in various episodes, including 101 – 'Midnight on the Firing Line', 106 – 'Mind War', 116 – 'Eyes' and 208 – 'A Race Through Dark Places'). She is a latent telepath herself – she could block her mother's telepathic scans, she could occasionally scan her mother, she can detect scans and she can sometimes pick up feelings from the people around her. Her mother helped her avoid Psi Corps by moving her from school to school.

Although Talia's primary personality has been destroyed and replaced with the Psi Corps agent personality, Kosh still has a recording of the original personality (made in episode 109 – 'Deathwalker'). Garibaldi remembers this. J. Michael Straczynski has said that Garibaldi has discussed the recording with Kosh.

Observations: Delenn refers to her unfortunate encounter with Earth reporters in episode 215 ('And Now For a Word'). Dr Franklin's underground telepath escape route is mentioned (episode 208 – 'A Race Through Dark Places'). Sheridan wonders whether Garibaldi's traitorous aide (episodes 122 – 'Chrysalis' – and 202 – 'Revelations') may have been a Psi Corps agent with a secondary personality. Ivanova refers to the events of episode 116 – 'Eyes'.

There's another conversation in a urinal (see episode 113 – 'Signs and Portents').

Lyta Alexander first arrived on Babylon 5 on 3 January 2257, and left six weeks later (see the pilot episode – 'The Gathering'). Talia Winters says that she and Lyta spent six months together on a Psi Corps internship. 'We were very close,' she says with an expression implying something more than just friendship.

There is a strong implication that, by the end of the episode, Talia and Ivanova have become lovers. There's one shot early on where it looks as if they move to kiss, and they sleep in the same bed late in the episode. In the scene where they move to kiss, it seems as though a few seconds of film have been cut out, but according to J. Michael Straczynski, 'No, nothing was edited out by C4 [Channel 4] or anyone; the footage we had to work with in editing had a *slight* matching problem.'

Psi Corps slang for telepaths is 'teeps', and for telekinetics is 'teeks'.

We get flashbacks within the course of this episode to the pilot episode – 'The Gathering' – and episodes 109 ('Death-walker') and 211 ('All Alone in the Night').

The Lumati want to open trade relations with the Minbari (see episode 212 – 'Acts of Sacrifice').

The character of Talia Winters was written out in this episode. Andrea Thompson, the actress who played her, left the series because, she has said, she felt she wasn't getting enough to do.

Ivanova's Life Lessons: 'Does the phrase, "No way in hell", ring a bell?'

Dialogue to Rewind For: Ivanova to Talia Winters: 'I've hidden things, Talia.' Talia to Ivanova: 'We all have secrets.'

Dialogue to Fast Forward Past: Sheridan's rather forced attempt at swearing: 'Abso-fraggin'-lutely.'

Culture Shock: On Minbar, the Minbari are told what they need to know and no more. Undue curiosity is frowned upon.

Minbari writing goes from left to right and from top to bottom.

Station Keeping: *Universe Today*, the Earth newspaper, can be tailored by individuals so that they get a printout only of the sections they want. The Sunday papers can presumably be distilled down to half a page of news if you take out the lifestyle sections.

I've Seen That Face Before: Patricia Tallman returns as Lyta Alexander. She was Babylon 5's resident telepath in the pilot episode – 'The Gathering'.

Accidents Will Happen: After they all find out Talia Winters has a secondary Psi Corps personality, Sheridan asks, 'Is there anything else that we can use to protect ourselves, if necessary?' Garibaldi remembers Talia's strange experience with Kosh in episode 109 – 'Deathwalker'. One of the scenes we see in his flashback is a scene he wasn't actually present at.

Questions Raised: When Lyta Alexander was recalled to Earth, she claimed to have told her questioners all she knew about Kosh, but they didn't believe her. Why didn't they have her scanned? It would have cleared up any doubt.

'The Long, Twilight Struggle'

Transmission Number: 220
Production Number: 220

Written by: J. Michael Straczynski
Directed by: John Flinn

Draal: John Schuck **Lord Refa:** William Forward
G'Sten: W. Morgan Sheppard

Plot: Tragic. Tragic and so horribly predictable in the way that the best tragedy is.

The 'A' Plot: G'Kar receives a visit from his uncle, G'Sten, who has a senior position in the Narn military forces. He tells G'Kar that the Narn are losing the war, and that they have decided to strike directly at the Centauri supply centre at Gorash 7. This will mean leaving the Narn homeworld undefended, but this is a risk they're prepared to take. Unfortunately, the Centauri have intercepted Narn communications discussing the attack. Lord Refa orders the Centauri defences away from Gorash 7 and throws them into a strike against the Narn homeworld, and asks Londo to get his 'associates' to defend Gorash 7 against the Narn. The Narns attack Gorash 7 and are wiped out by the Shadows. Meanwhile the Centauri

243

attack the Narn homeworld and flatten its cities by bombarding them with asteroids fired from mass-drivers. The Narn offer a complete and unconditional surrender. The war is over. The last order of the Kha'Ri is that G'Kar should ask Sheridan for sanctuary. He does so, and Sheridan grants it against the strong objections of Londo. G'Kar's position as ambassador and official representative of the Narn on Babylon 5 is, however, at an end.

The 'B' Plot: Draal, custodian of the Great Machine on Epsilon 3, makes contact with Sheridan and Delenn. He invites them down to the planet and tells them he will join forces with them against the Shadows.

The 'C' Plot: Draal suggests that Delenn introduce Sheridan to the Rangers. She does so, and gives him joint command over them.

The Arc: The war between the Narn and the Centauri that effectively started when the Narn attacked Ragesh 3 in episode 101 ('Midnight on the Firing Line') is now over, although the repercussions will take some time to die down.

Both Draal and the Great Machine on Epsilon 3 were first introduced in episodes 117 and 118 ('A Voice in the Wilderness' Parts One and Two), and both will crop up again in episodes 316 and 317 ('War Without End' Parts One and Two).

'I've learned that there are a few others living here who maintain the Great Machine,' says Draal. Later, Draal calls for Zathras, and complains he is never around when he is needed. Zathras is the alien with the lined face and the huge sideburns whom we first see in episode 120 ('Babylon Squared') and later encounter in episodes 316 and 317 ('War Without End' Parts One and Two).

The Rangers are first introduced in episode 209 ('The Coming of Shadows'), where we find out that they are under the overall command of Ambassador Sinclair. Locally they are commanded by Delenn, although Garibaldi knows about them. Their job is to patrol known space, watching, listening and occasionally acting on behalf of the forces of light.

Observations: One of the spiderlike Shadow ships fires a spiky ball at the Narn forces. This ball splits into hundreds of smaller Shadow 'fighters' which individually attack the Narn ships.

A Shadow ship has one of its spiderlike 'limbs' shot off by a Narn ship. Another Shadow ship joins with it and helps it away from the battlefield, almost as if they were alive . . .

Londo refers obliquely to his regret at the death of his friend Urza Jaddo (episode 216, 'Knives').

Louis Turenne, who originally played Draal, had a stroke not long before this episode was filmed. He was replaced with John Schuck, who had originally auditioned for the part of G'Kar's uncle G'Sten. Louis Turenne was eventually recast as Brother Theo in episode 302 – 'Convictions'. In order to explain Draal's different appearance, dialogue was added indicating that the Great Machine had given him back the body he had thirty years before.

Dialogue to Rewind For: Draal: 'You do not take custody of the planet – the planet takes custody of you.'

Sheridan to the Rangers: 'Tell them that from this place we will deliver notice to the parliaments of conquerors that a line has been drawn against the darkness, and we will hold that line no matter the cost.'

Dialogue to Fast Forward Past: G'Sten: 'There is always hope – at least, that is what I tell myself when I awake in the middle of the night and the only sound I can hear is the beating of my own desperate heart.'

G'Sten: 'But how could I go off without saying goodbye to my favourite nephew?'

Delenn, copying Sheridan's pathetic attempt at swearing from the previous episode: 'Abso-fraggin'-lutely, dammit!'

Ships That Pass In The Night: The *Valerius* is the flagship of the attacking Centauri fleet.

Other Worlds: Shi, Dras and Zok are Narn worlds. Gorash 7 is the site of a Centauri supply dump.

I've Seen That Face Before: John Schuck, who takes over the role of Draal from Louis Turenne, has a long track record within SF television and film. He was the robotic policeman

Yoyo in the deservedly short-lived comedy series *Holmes and Yoyo*, and later turned up as the Klingon Ambassador in the films *Star Trek IV: The Voyage Home* and *Star Trek VI: The Undiscovered Country* and as a Cardassian Legate in the *Star Trek: Deep Space Nine* episode 'The Maquis Part II'. We'll skip over his short-lived role as Herman Munster in the thankfully short-lived colour revival of *The Munsters* ('We went to sleep a long time ago, and now we're back with a brand-new show!').

W. Morgan Sheppard, who took the role of G'Sten, had previously appeared in episode 102 ('Soul Hunter') as the madder of the two Soul Hunters.

'Comes the Inquisitor'

Transmission Number: 221
Production Number: 221

Written by: J. Michael Straczynski
Directed by: Mike Laurence Vejar

Mr Sebastian: Wayne Alexander
Mr Chase: Jack Kehler   **Centauri No. 1:** Jim Chiros

Plot: Dark and nasty, but also rather confused, this episode suffers from a rather typical American trait of taking British archetypes and stripping them of all their symbolic and mythic overtones.

The 'A' Plot: Kosh tells Delenn that he has concerns over her suitability for the task ahead – she has placed herself in the centre of the coming storm, and he needs to be assured that the right people are in the right place at the right time. He has sent for an inquisitor to be sure. The inquisitor – a human named Sebastian who claims to have been taken from Earth by the Vorlons in the year 1888 – arrives on a Vorlon ship. Sheridan clears an area of Grey Sector for him, and Delenn goes to meet him. He asks her to wear a pair of bracelets, and tells her that if she takes the bracelets off she will be admitting defeat. His aim seems to be to break her spirit and get her to admit that she is fighting the Shadows for selfish reasons – because she wants the glory, or because she feels 'chosen' in some way. If she gives him an answer he does not approve of, he punishes her with pain administered through her bracelets. Meanwhile, Lennier has seen Delenn's brutalisation at the hands of Sebastian, and begs Sheridan to intervene. Sebastian has been waiting for Sheridan's arrival – his task appears to be to test them both – and it is only when he realises that each would be willing to die, alone and unremembered, to save the other that he knows they are the first people ever to pass the test. As Sebastian leaves the station, Sheridan reveals that he has identified him as Jack the Ripper, a killer of prostitutes in London in 1888.

The 'B' Plot: G'Kar is attempting to smuggle arms to the Narn underground through Babylon 5. Garibaldi finds out, and rather than stop the trade as he should he arranges an off-station transfer point for G'Kar. Meanwhile, the other Narn on the station don't believe that he can get the weapons to Narn, and challenge him to obtain messages from their families to prove that he has a line into the homeworld. G'Kar asks for Sheridan's assistance, and Sheridan uses the Rangers to obtain the messages.

The 'C' Plot: After listening to him ranting about Centauri atrocities, Vir attempts to apologise to G'Kar for the slaughter. G'Kar refuses to accept the apology.

The Arc: This story could not exist without the arc to support it, and yet you could remove it without damaging the arc at all. Essentially it acts as a validation of Sheridan and Delenn's motivations, and as a reminder that the Narn aren't going to lie down and accept occupation.

J. Michael Straczynski has said of the episode, 'Part of the reason for the story was to grey up the Vorlons a little; one shouldn't fall too easily for what other people *say* they are.'

Observations: In the opening sequence, where G'Kar is proclaiming from a balcony about Centauri atrocities, Vir is watching him. If you look at the expression on Vir's face, you might almost convince yourself that he decides then to help the Narn to the best of his abilities – a decision which results in the events of episode 312 – 'Sic Transit Vir'.

The spotlights illuminating Delenn in Grey 19 are a visual analogue of those in the Grey Council chamber.

A scene of G'Kar slicing his hand open with a knife in front of Vir was cut for the episode's first UK broadcast by Channel 4.

Koshisms: 'We have sent for an inquisitor . . . to be sure about you.'

Dialogue to Rewind For: Sebastian, about the Vorlons: 'The Vorlons have been to Earth. The Vorlons have been everywhere. The Vorlons *are.*'

Sebastian to Delenn and Sheridan: 'Are you willing to die, friendless, alone, deserted by everyone? Because that is what may be required of you in the war to come.'

Culture Shock: The Vorlons are able to preserve Sebastian when they have no use for him. This implies they cannot (or will not) extend his life, but effectively have to freeze him until they need him again.

Literary, Mythological and Historical References: Sebastian's line to Delenn – 'Have you nothing of your own, nothing to stand on that is not provided, defined, delineated, stamped, sanctioned, numbered and approved by others?' – resonates with a line from the cult British TV series *The Prisoner*: 'I will not be pushed, filed, stamped, indexed, briefed, debriefed or numbered. My life is my own.'

Another exchange of dialogue – Sheridan telling Sebastian, 'Go to hell' and Sebastian replying, 'This is hell' – is reminiscent of the moment in Christopher Marlowe's play *Doctor Faustus* when Faustus realises, 'Why, this is hell, nor am I out of it.'

Creative Consultant Harlan Ellison wrote a short story involving Jack the Ripper in the future entitled 'The Prowler in the City at the Edge of the World'. The story was first published in 1967.

Accidents Will Happen: Sheridan claims that the Ripper murders were carried out in London's West End. In fact they were carried out in London's East End, in the heart of

Whitechapel. The line was redubbed for American transmission and for subsequent airings and video releases.

Questions Raised: Why are Americans so much more fascinated with Jack the Ripper than the British?

'The Fall of Night'

Transmission Number: 222
Production Number: 222

Written by: J. Michael Straczynski
Directed by: Janet Greek

Fredrick Lantz: Roy Dotrice   **Mr Welles:** John Vickery
Na'Kal: Robin Sachs   **Narn No. 1:** Mark Hendrickson
Drazi Ambassador: Kim Strauss
Pak'ma'ra Ambassador: Donovan Brown
Human/Minbari Kosh: Joshua Patton

Date: Around a week before Christmas, 2259.

Plot: Based on the end of season 1, there was a certain amount of expectation that this episode would be a tense, action packed finale with a cliff-hanger climax. That's almost what we get, of course, but what we weren't expecting was the air of melancholy about the episode, of sadness for what has been lost and foreboding over what is to come. If *Babylon 5* is a symphony then rather than end the second movement with a triumphant resolution, J. Michael Straczynski has ended it with a muted discord.

The 'A' Plot: Fredrick Lantz, a representative of the Ministry of Peace, and his Nightwatch companion Mr Welles arrive on Babylon 5. Initially Lantz claims to be investigating the Centauri victory over the Narn, but he soon admits that his real task is to negotiate a non-aggression treaty between Earth and the Centauri. He is frustrated first when he discovers that Sheridan has been training his Starfury pilots to cope with Centauri flight tactics, and secondly by Sheridan offering aid and temporary sanctuary to a crippled Narn warship. Lantz tells Londo about the Narn ship, and

Londo immediately alerts Centauri Prime. A Centauri warship appears and attempts to engage the Narn ship, but Sheridan has offered it his protection, and when the Centauri ship attacks Babylon 5 as well he has no choice but to open fire. Babylon 5 takes a lot of damage, but the Centauri ship is destroyed. In revenge for their loss, a group of young Centauri plant a bomb on the monorail carriage in which Sheridan is travelling. Seeing the bomb, Sheridan flings himself out into the low-gravity interior of Babylon 5. At Delenn's request, Kosh reveals himself to be a winged life form (mistaken by many races present for their own deities) and rescues Sheridan.

The 'B' Plot: Some Starfury pilots report having seen bizarre things in hyperspace – things Warren Keffer recognises as similar to a ship which killed a friend of his. He obtains a copy of the neutrino trail left by the ship and programs his Starfury to scan for it. While he and the rest of Zeta Wing are escorting the crippled Narn war cruiser through hyperspace, his Starfury picks up those same readings. He gives chase, recording what he sees, but the ship turns on his and attacks him. All that gets back to civilisation is the recorder buoy he ejects. ISN broadcast it, complete with the alien ship.

The 'C' Plot: Are you kidding?

The Arc: After their victory over the Narn, the Centauri have invaded Drazi and Pak'ma'ra space. Londo claims they are just creating a buffer zone, but Centauri territorial ambitions have been reawakened.

Nightwatch, first established in episode 217 ('In the Shadow of Za'ha'dum') is beginning to flex its muscles. Mr Welles claims to have the power to influence Earthforce into promoting Ivanova early – if she cooperates with them by naming names. Nightwatch are beginning their crackdown on sedition, which means in practice that anyone criticising President Clark is assumed to be a traitor.

Shadow ships leave behind an unusual neutrino trail. They can be tracked that way. They have recently been seen in hyperspace in Sector 14 – the sector in which Babylon 4 vanished (episode 120 – 'Babylon Squared') and in which Sheridan's mind parasite was released (episode 216 – 'Knives'). Obviously a busy sector.

Keffer mentions that Commander Galus was killed by the Shadows (as we saw in episode 204 – 'A Distant Star').

Observations: Ivanova gives Sheridan an early Christmas present of some shrapnel from the *Black Star* – the Minbari ship he destroyed during the war, as first mentioned in episode 201 ('Points of Departure'). One imagines it might make a nice conversation piece for when Ambassador Delenn calls in. 'What is that piece of twisted metal, John?' 'Ah . . . I'm glad you asked, Delenn . . .'

We see the Shadow ship turn towards Keffer's ship while emitting an energy beam, and we see Keffer scream as his cockpit fills with light, but we never see his Starfury explode. It's been suggested that he has been taken for investigation rather than killed, but if you frame-advance through that scene you can (allegedly) see the flesh melting off his face.

Ivanova lights some Hanukkah candles, showing that she, too, is celebrating in her own faith.

There are slight differences between the UK and US versions of this episode. After the UK tape was mastered and sent, minor alterations were made to four scenes (including some extra 'glow' around Kosh's angelic form).

On one of the *Babylon 5* blooper tapes, when Londo is asked what he saw when Sheridan was saved, he replies, 'I tawt I taw a Putty Cat! I did!'

Dialogue to Rewind For: Sheridan, rehearsing his apology to Londo: 'I'm sorry we had to defend ourselves against an unwarranted attack. I'm sorry that your crew were stupid enough to fire on a station filled with a quarter million civilians, including your own people. And I'm sorry I waited as long as I did before I blew them all straight to hell.'

Ivanova's last speech: 'It was the end of the Earth year 2259, and the war was upon us. As anticipated, a few days after the Earth–Centauri treaty was announced, the Centauri widened their war to include many of the Non-Aligned Worlds. And there was another war brewing closer to home –

a personal one whose cost would be higher than any of us could imagine. We came to this place because Babylon 5 was our last, best hope for peace. By the end of 2259, we knew that it had failed, but in doing so it became something greater – as the war expanded, it became our last, best hope for victory. Because sometimes, peace is another word for surrender, and because secrets have a way of getting out . . .'

Dialogue to Fast Forward Past: Keffer's description of the Shadow ships: 'A spider big as death and twice as ugly, and when it flies past it's like you hear a scream in your mind.'

I guess we should also include Sheridan's '. . . blew them all straight to hell' line quoted above, because that's what he said he did to the *Black Star* as well.

Ships That Pass In The Night: Narn heavy cruiser *Ja'Dok*.

Culture Shock: It looks like Mr Lantz talks to the Brakiri ambassador, but we only see him from the back so it's difficult to be sure.

Kosh is seen by different races as being their own deities. The Minbari see him as the deity Valeria; the Drazi see him as Droshalla; G'Kar sees him as G'Lan.

Literary, Mythological and Historical References: Lantz's claim, 'We will, at last, know peace in our time,' echoes the words of Neville Chamberlain, Prime Minister of Britain in 1938, concerning the peace agreement he had just signed with Adolf Hitler: 'I believe it is peace for our time.' Despite popular belief, Chamberlain never actually said, 'Peace *in* our time.' The parallel goes a bit further, in that when Chamberlain signed a peace agreement with Hitler he sold Britain's former allies, particularly Czechoslovakia, down the river.

I've Seen That Face Before: Roy Dotrice, who played Fredrick Lantz, is a British actor whose genre credits include the part of Father in the US fantasy series *Beauty and the Beast*. He also provided the voice for Harvey Keitel's character in the SF film *Saturn Three*.

John Vickery, who played Mr Welles, has previously appeared in *Babylon 5* as the Minbari warrior Shai Alyt

Neroon in episodes 117 ('Legacies') and 211 ('All Alone in the Night').

Robin Sachs, who played the Narn captain Na'Kal, has also played the same Minbari on two occasions. In his case the character was Hedronn and the episodes were 201 ('Matters of Honor') and 211 ('All Alone in the Night').

Questions Raised: If no ship lost in hyperspace has ever been found apart from the *Cortez* (as we heard in episode 204 – 'A Distant Star') then what are the odds on finding a small recorder buoy?

Season 3:
'Point of No Return'

'The Babylon Project was our last, best hope for peace.

'It failed.

'But, in the year of the Shadow War, it became something greater – our last, best hope for victory.

'The year is 2260. The place: Babylon 5.'

– Commander Susan Ivanova

Regular and Semi-Regular Cast:

Captain John Sheridan: Bruce Boxleitner
Commander Susan Ivanova: Claudia Christian
Security Chief Michael Garibaldi: Jerry Doyle
Ambassador Delenn: Mira Furlan
Ambassador Londo Mollari: Peter Jurasik
Ambassador G'Kar: Andreas Katsulas
Dr Stephen Franklin: Richard Biggs
Vir Cotto: Stephen Furst
Lennier: Bill Mumy
Marcus Cole: Jason Carter
Zack Allen: Jeff Conaway
David Corwin: Joshua Cox

Observations: J. Michael Straczynski had said during the filming of season 1 that Garibaldi might be doing the opening narration for season 3. During the filming of season 2, he said that either Ivanova or Delenn would voice the opening narration for season 3. It turned out to be Ivanova.

The original overall title for season 3 was going to be 'I Am Become Death, the Destroyer of Worlds'. This is a quotation from the religious and philosophical Sanskrit poem *Bhagavad Gītā* ('The Song of the Blessed', a part of the sixth book of the *Mahābhārata* – one of the supreme religious works of Hinduism). The line is said in the *Bhagavad Gītā* by

Vishnu – one of the triad of Hindu deities (the *Trimurti*) along with Brahma and Siva. The glancing reference to a trinity is intriguing when compared with Zathras's description of Sinclair, Sheridan and Delenn in episode 317 – 'War Without End' Part II. The line was also allegedly quoted by American physicist J. Robert Oppenheimer when he saw the test explosion of the atomic bomb he helped develop in 1945.

When preview tapes of the first two episodes were sent out in the USA, the title sequence showed only a fleeting glimpse of the *White Star*, travelling head-on towards the viewer and firing its weapons. This was because the completed shot of the *White Star* that Foundation Imaging had delivered was considered inadequate by J. Michael Straczynski, and he asked them to redo it. The redone shot appears in the title sequence for the transmitted episodes.

Composer Christopher Franke rearranged the opening title music for this season to make it more sombre and discordant, in keeping with the darker themes of the episodes. Elements of the music are taken from episodes 108 ('And the Sky Full of Stars') and 220 ('The Long, Twilight Struggle'). The end title music was kept as in the previous season for the first four episodes, and then replaced with the rejigged sombre, discordant music. There's no deeply significant explanation for the alteration in the end title music after four episodes – Straczynski just forgot about it.

Stephen Furst, who plays Vir, has said he was originally contracted to be in all of the episodes of the third season. He was released from his contract after he was cast in a new comedy series *Misery Loves Company*, and was temporarily written out in episode 303 – 'A Day in the Strife'. *Misery Loves Company* ran for only eight episodes before it was cancelled, and Vir returned full-time to Babylon 5 in episode 312 – 'Sic Transit Vir'.

Neither Mary Kay Adams (Na'Toth) nor Andrea Thompson (Talia Winters) returned for season 3 (see the entries for episodes 212 and 221 for details). Following the shock death of pilot Warren Keffer (Robert Rusler), a new character was introduced in the form of Jason Carter's Ranger, Marcus Cole. Carter is a British actor who, shortly before taking on the part, had appeared as a rock musician in an episode of *The New Adventures of Superman* and a villain in *Viper*. He was also in an episode of *She-Wolf of London* and made several appearances on the cult US teen soap *Beverly Hills 90210*.

Lawrence DiTillio (Executive Story Editor on the series) left between seasons two and three. Given that all the scripts in season three were going to be written by J. Michael Straczynski, and given that Straczynski is notoriously reluctant to have his words rewritten by anyone, it had become obvious that DiTillio wouldn't have much work to do, and so he left to pursue other writing and editing opportunities.

Season 3 of *Babylon 5* was written entirely by Straczynski. This, he claims, means that he has written more consecutive episodes of a television show than any other writer (a difficult claim to check, it has to be said). Straczynski has claimed that the previous holder of this record was Terry Nation, with thirteen episodes of *Blake's Seven*. In fact, the 1960–61 season of the British police series *Dixon of Dock Green* ran to thirty 45-minute episodes, all of which were written by Ted Willis. It could be argued that, if the last four episodes of season two and all of season four are also included, then Straczynski will have written forty-eight consecutive 45-minute episodes. However, taking cross-season breaks into account, Ted Willis wrote every single episode of *Dixon of Dock Green* between July 1955 and March 1963. Given that the episodes up to 1961 were 45 minutes and the episodes after that were 30 minutes, that totals 113.5 consecutive hours of scripting by one man, as compared with Straczynski's 12 hours. It's probable, however, that Straczynski holds the record for most consecutive episodes of an *American* TV series written.

'Matters of Honor'

Transmission Number: 301
Production Number: 301

Written by: J. Michael Straczynski
Directed by: Kevin G. Cremin

David Endawi: Tucker Smallwood
Morden: Ed Wasser   **Senator:** Kitty Swink
Psi Cop: Andrew Walker   **Drozac:** Jonathan Chapman
Large Man: Nils Allen Stewart

Plot: It's a bit lightweight, but it has all the right ticks in the box – Shadows, Morden, space battles and intrigue.

The 'A' Plot: A Ranger named Marcus Cole arrives on Babylon 5 asking for Sheridan's help. A Ranger training camp on Zagros 7 – a Drazi colony world – has been blockaded by Centauri mines, and they anticipate an attack on the camp at any time. Sheridan agrees, and Delenn presents him with the *White Star*, a ship that blends Minbari and Vorlon technology. In the *White Star* Sheridan, Ivanova, Lennier, Delenn and Marcus travel to Zagros 7 and destroy enough of the Centauri mines to enable the Rangers to escape in their own ships. The absence of any Centauri ships is explained when a Shadow vessel appears and attacks them. Sheridan lures the Shadow vessel away and destroys it by emerging from hyperspace in a jumpgate and then forming a separate jump point inside the jumpgate. The *White Star* gets away just in time, but the Shadow ship is caught in the resulting explosion. They return to Babylon 5, and Sheridan sets up a War Council comprising himself, Delenn, Ivanova, Garibaldi and Franklin to discuss developments in the ongoing conflict with the Shadows.

The 'B' Plot: David Endawi, an agent of Earthforce Special Intelligence Division, arrives on Babylon 5. He has the gun-camera footage recorded by Warren Keffer's Starfury before it was destroyed, showing an alien ship of unknown configuration. Endawi shows the footage to Sheridan, Delenn, Londo and G'Kar in an attempt to discover the identity of the aliens in question – he claims that nobody on Earth knows. Delenn claims not to have seen that design of ship before, even though she later admits to Sheridan that she has read descriptions of it, and knows it to be a Shadow ship. Londo says that he has seen ships like that in a dream. G'Kar shows Endawi a page from the Book of G'Quan showing an illustration of the same ship. G'Quan wrote that the aliens who

257

owned those ships set up a base on the Narn homeworld over a thousand human years ago, and that G'Quan believed them to be fighting a war somewhere else in the galaxy. David Endawi returns to Earth to present his report to a Senator in Earthdome. When he leaves, the mysterious Mr Morden and a Psi Cop enter the room and discuss the way ahead with her.

The 'C' Plot: Londo suggests that the Centauri Republic can now go about their affairs without the help of Mr Morden or his mysterious 'associates'. Morden agrees, although it is clear that he has already been talking with Lord Refa back on Centauri Prime. He suggests to Londo that they carve up the galaxy between them – one half will belong to the Centauri, the other half to Morden's associates. Londo agrees.

The Arc: Kosh tells Sheridan two interesting things in the pre-title sequence. The first is that being seen by so many different beings was a strain. This implies that Kosh was actually expending energy – he wasn't just being seen, he was actually projecting what he wanted people to see. We had assumed in episode 222 ('The Fall of Night') that the different visions of Kosh seen by the various races were because their brains interpreted his appearance in different ways but, if we are to believe what he says in this episode, Kosh actually makes people see what he wants them to see. This implies that we *still* don't know what a Vorlon actually looks like – just what they want us to think they look like. As J. Michael Straczynski has admitted, 'That's the irony, in a sense . . . what's inside Kosh's biomechanical encounter suit . . . is a *perceptual* encounter suit.' The second interesting thing Kosh tells Sheridan is that he had to return to his ship to rest. Why? What's wrong with his quarters on Babylon 5? Presumably they cannot furnish him with what he needs, and this implies that the connection between Kosh and his ship is more convoluted than we had believed.

When Kosh says to Sheridan, 'I have always been here,' Sheridan responds, 'Oh yeah – you said that about me too.' He is referring to the events of episode 211 ('All Alone in the Night').

Londo had his dream of multiple Shadow ships crossing

the sky of Centauri Prime in episode 209 ('The Coming of Shadows'). It is a prophecy of the future – a prophecy that comes true in episode 401 ('The Hour of the Wolf').

'Do you know,' Marcus says of the Ranger badges, 'I've heard that when these are made they're forged in white-hot flame, then cooled in three bowls. The first is some kind of ancient holy water, the second Minbari blood, the third human blood. They say that when a Ranger dies, the figures on either side shed three tears – one of water and two of blood.' This is interesting more for what Marcus doesn't say than for what he does. We know from later episodes (primarily 319 – 'Grey 17 is Missing') that the Rangers actually date back a thousand years, to the time of the first Great War. We also know (from episodes 316 and 317 – 'War Without End' Parts One and Two) that the Vorlons have a representative on Minbar and that they were actively involved in the last Great War. We know from *this* episode that the Vorlons have allowed their technology to be used in the ships that are later (episode 321 – 'Shadow Dancing') piloted exclusively by Rangers. This all implies a close tie between the Rangers, the Minbari and the Vorlons. Is it not reasonable to assume, therefore, that the first bowl doesn't contain 'some kind of ancient holy water', but Vorlon blood?

G'Kar says of the Shadows, 'They came to our world over a thousand of your years ago – long before we went to the stars ourselves. They set up a base on one of our southern continents. They took little interest in us. G'Quan believed they were engaged in a war far outside our own world.' G'Quan was a great Narn spiritual leader, and we discover more about the connection between the Narn and the Shadows in episode 314 ('Ship of Tears').

David Endawi submits his report to a senator in Earthdome and departs happily. He clearly doesn't know anything about the Shadow ships, but the Senator does. She discusses the report with Morden and a Psi Cop, indicating very clearly that the Shadows have already been in contact with elements within EarthGov and the Psi Corps. This plot strand will be picked up again in episodes 305 ('Voices of Authority'), 308 ('Messages From Earth') and 322 ('Z'ha'dum').

When the Narn knowledge about the Shadow ships is raised by the senator, Morden says, 'I think we've neutralised that problem.' He's referring to the Shadows supporting the Centauri war against the Narn, a war that began in episode 209 ('The Coming of Shadows') and ended with the defeat of the Narn in episode 220 ('The Long, Twilight Struggle').

Delenn's potted history of the Shadows begins like this: 'There are beings in the universe billions of years older than any of our races. They walked amongst the stars like giants – vast and timeless. They created great empires, taught the new races, explored beyond the rim. The oldest of the ancients are the Shadows. We have no other name for them . . .' This is a virtual replay of what she tells Sheridan in episode 217 ('In the Shadow of Z'ha'dum').

Observations: Marcus knows about the effect alcohol has on a Minbari. It makes them psychotically violent, as we discovered in episode 121 ('The Quality of Mercy').

The jumpgate that Sheridan destroys is the one nearest the Markab homeworld. He refers to the fact that all the Markab have died out (as seen in episode 218 – 'Confessions and Lamentations') and that their world is being stripped bare by other races.

We get our first sight of Earthdome – the centre of Earth government – in this episode. Earthdome is based in Geneva, Switzerland. The design of the building itself is actually based on designs drawn up (but never used) for Gerry Anderson's *Space Precinct*.

Koshisms: 'Being seen by so many was a great strain. I returned to my ship to rest.'

In response to Sheridan asking why Kosh took the risk of being seen by so many beings: 'It was necessary.'

In response to Sheridan's point about not knowing whether this is the same Kosh as first arrived on the station: 'I have always been here.' Sheridan: 'Oh yeah – you said that about me too.' Kosh: 'Yes.' Sheridan: 'I really hate it when you do that.' Kosh: 'Good.'

Dialogue to Rewind For: Morden: 'And now that we've done everything that you've asked us to, you'd like us to just disappear?' Londo: 'I do believe you have got it surrounded, Mr Morden.'

Londo: 'We have danced our last little dance, Mr Morden.'

Dialogue to Fast Forward Past: Delenn talking about a seedy bar: 'A most unreasonable place for reasonable assumptions.'

Ships That Pass In The Night: The *White Star* – first in a line of ships that blend Minbari technology with Vorlon technology – is able to form its own jump point, a trick supposedly impossible for a ship its size. It is piloted by members of the Minbari Religious caste.

Other Worlds: Zagros 7 – a Drazi colony world on the edge of their territory.

Literary, Mythological and Historical References: The Zagros Mountains were a geographical feature near the ancient city of Babylon.

I've Seen That Face Before: Tucker Smallwood, the actor playing David Endawi, recently played the regular character of Commodore Ross on the short-lived SF TV show *Space: Above and Beyond*. He also recently appeared in *The X Files* episode 'Home'.

'Convictions'

Transmission Number: 302
Production Number: 302

Written by: J. Michael Straczynski
Directed by: Mike Laurence Vejar

Morishi: Cary-Hiroyuki Tagawa
Brother Theo: Louis Turenne
Robert Carlsen: Patrick Kilpath

Date: Uncertain, but Carlsen arrived on the station on 11 January 2260 and hasn't been working there long.

Plot: After the shocks and surprises of the last episode, we get a fairly run-of-the-mill story saved only by the two 'B' plots.

The 'A' Plot: A series of explosions on the station cause tensions to rise. Examination of security camera records by a newly arrived group of monks shows the same man present at each location – Robert J. Carlsen, a violent drifter who has been traumatised by losing his job and his wife. Sheridan confronts Carlsen, who is holding a dead man's switch rigged to explode Babylon 5's main reactor if he lets go. Garibaldi locates the bomb and has it ejected into space.

The 'B' Plots: (a) Lennier is injured while saving Londo Mollari from a bomb. Badly injured, and in a coma, he is comforted by Londo in medlab. A bad joke brings him round. (b) Another bomb traps Londo and G'Kar in a lift together. G'Kar refuses to help Londo escape because he wants Londo dead but can't take any overt action against Londo without attracting Centauri reprisals against his people. Eventually, to G'Kar's chagrin, they are rescued.

The 'C' Plot: A group of monks have arrived on Babylon 5 in order to find out more about the deities of other races. They believe that if they do this, they will know more about their own god.

The Arc: No major arc-related material appears in this story, and given what lies behind and ahead, it's probably a good thing. The only minor event is the first appearance of Brother Theo, who can be expected to play a significant role in future episodes.

Observations: There's a rather nice floating camera in the background when the first bomb-blast scene is being investigated. It has no relevance to the plot, but it's a neat touch.

Lennier claims to have the fatal disease Netter's Syndrome in order to escape an obnoxious drunk. Douglas Netter is co-Executive Producer on the series.

Captain Sheridan hides his comlink where the sun doesn't shine in order to stop Carlsen from finding it. Its location is given away when he sits down and his bottom beeps.

Brother Theo was named for Vincent Van Gogh's brother, according to J. Michael Straczynski.

G'Kar's little song – 'Not many fishes left in the sea, not many fishes – just Londo and me,' is a variation on the song he sang in episode 105 ('The Parliament of Dreams').

The immobile form of Lennier in medlab is actually a dummy with a life-cast of actor Billy Mumy's face attached. Mumy's father had died and Mumy was not on set for those scenes. Andreas Katsulas (the actor who plays G'Kar) apparently later congratulated Mumy on his stillness during the medlab scenes. Mumy claims that he doesn't have the heart to tell Katsulas it wasn't him.

Some dialogue was cut from the end of the episode by the UK's Channel 4 during the first UK showing. As broadcast, when Londo and G'Kar are being rescued from the lift Londo says, 'Fanatic!'; G'Kar retaliates with 'Murderer!'; Londo shifts ground by snarling, 'You're insane!'; and G'Kar tops him with, 'That's why we'll win!' The exchange should have been prefaced with Londo muttering 'Bastard!' and G'Kar replying, 'Monster!'

Dialogue to Rewind For: Garibaldi to his aide when two Drazi missionaries arrive at customs: 'Zack, do me a favour and explain the missionary . . . position . . . to these folks.'

Londo after a long and tortuous explanation: 'I'm not sure that made any sense, but I'm afraid that if I go back to figure it out I'll start bleeding from my ears.'

Londo's joke: 'How many Centauri does it take to screw in a lightbulb? Just one, but in the great old days of the Republic, hundreds of servants would screw in a thousand lightbulbs at our slightest command!'

Lennier on saving Londo's life: 'I fear I have served the present by sacrificing the future.'

Ships That Pass In The Night: Minbari liner *Zerphol*.

Other Worlds: Vega 7.

Literary, Mythological and Historical References: The performance of Patrick Kilpath as Carlsen contains echoes of John Malkovitch's performance as the mad bomber in the film *In The Line of Fire*. J. Michael Straczynski denies any connection.

I've Seen That Face Before: Louis Turenne, who plays Brother Theo, previously played Delenn's Minbari tutor Draal in episodes 118 and 119 ('A Voice in the Wilderness' Parts One and Two). When the character of Draal returned in charge of the Epsilon 3 machine in episode 220 ('The Long, Twilight Struggle') Turenne was recovering from a stroke and John Schuck was cast in the role. Straczynski reportedly told Turenne at the time that a better role awaited him when he recovered. This was it.

Cary-Hiroyuki Tagawa, who plays Morishi, appeared in the James Bond film *Licence to Kill* as a secret service agent. He also appeared in the Sean Connery thriller *Rising Sun* and the US teen SF series *Space Rangers*.

Accidents Will Happen: Most of the time Carlsen is nearly bald, except for his big fight scene when he has a full head of hair. Sheridan's hair suddenly turns black in the fight scene (I'm not proposing any sudden change in appearance of the actors – it's just that their stuntmen don't look anything like them).

Londo tells his joke to the comatose Lennier. Later, Dr Franklin tells the joke to Delenn within Lennier's earshot. Lennier joins in, but the words are slightly different (he says 'hundreds of servants would *leap to* screw in . . .' Yeah, it's picky, but the series is so perfect that I have to root around in the details to find bloopers.

'A Day in the Strife'

Transmission Number: 303
Production Number: 303

Written by: J. Michael Straczynski
Directed by: David Eagle

Na'Far: Stephen Macht   **Ta'Lon:** Marshall Teague

Plot: The simplistic 'A' plot of this episode could have been done by *Star Trek* but the 'B' plot is sufficiently complex to make up for it. As a result, the episode has a strangely unbalanced feel about it.

The 'A' Plot: A robotic alien probe arrives at Babylon 5 offering cures for every known disease, technological advances centuries ahead of anything humanity has and new jumpgate technology. All the crew have to do is answer six hundred-odd questions on various subjects, including physics, quantum mechanics, molecular biology and genetics. If the answers aren't forthcoming within a certain time, the probe will explode. Its builders, or so the speculation goes, are trying to weed stupid races out of the galaxy. Sheridan is about to send the answers when he realises the probe's story doesn't make any sense. In fact, it's designed to seek and destroy all those races intelligent enough to pose a threat to its creators. Sheridan doesn't send the answers, and the probe leaves without blowing up. Worried that it'll only pull the same stunt on another race, he transmits the answers when it's safely out of range, and it explodes.

The 'B' Plot: Councillor Na'Far arrives on the station to replace G'Kar. If G'Kar refuses to return to Narn and face the Centauri, the families of all those Narn on the station will be harassed, imprisoned and tortured. Na'Far's presence begins to split the Narn resistance on the station, and G'Kar realises that the only way he can keep them together is to go. He prepares to leave, but Ta'Lon – Na'Far's bodyguard – persuades the other Narn that continued resistance is preferable to submission. G'Kar stays.

The 'C' Plot: (a) Dr Stephen Franklin is becoming addicted to stimulants. Garibaldi tries to help him, but is rebuffed. (b) Londo Mollari arranges through Delenn for Vir to be transferred to Minbar as the Centauri diplomatic envoy. He does this because he does not want Vir involved in the troubles to come.

The Arc: The ongoing occupation of Narn by the Centauri is a strong theme in this episode.

Observations: In the initial confrontation between Sheridan and the Transport Pilots' Association, there's an extra in the background who's out-acting everyone.

After the confrontation, Sheridan tells Ivanova that he had removed the energy cap from the PPG he gave to the spokesperson of the TPA. If you look closely during the confrontation, you can see him do it.

When Londo talks to Delenn about sending Vir to Minbar, he refers to 'some trouble, I understand, with our last envoy'. He expands upon this later, in 'Sic Transit Vir' (episode 312). He also tells Delenn that he is cashing in a favour she owes him. This favour is in return for his taking her and Draal to Epsilon 3 in episode 319 ('A Voice in the Wilderness' Part Two).

A *katok* is a Narn sword that, once drawn, cannot be resheathed before it has drawn blood.

J. Michael Straczynski had this to say about the genesis of the episode: 'The US House Science Sub-Committee held a series of hearings into the question of extraterrestrial contact during the 1970s, to determine what we should do in the event of contact. The most likely scenario, the scientists agreed, was a probe coming into our solar system. So what do we do in response to a message asking if anybody's home? Believe it or not, it was the consensus of the sub-committee that we should not respond . . . in case it was a berserker, just as shown in the episode. That is our government's official policy on the subject.'

This is the first episode in which the young technician in Command and Control (usually credited as Tech No. 1, Tech No. 2 or Dome Tech No. 2) is given the name David Corwin.

During the first UK showing on Channel 4 a shot of Dr Franklin injecting himself with stims was cut. The cut was done so clumsily that it indicated Franklin had decided to inject himself and then changed his mind – the implication being that Franklin had his stim problem under control.

Koshisms: Yet again, Kosh is mysteriously absent. He probably knew all the answers to the questions asked by the probe, but nobody bothered to check with him. As J. Michael Straczynski has said, 'If you asked Kosh a question about the subject, he'd probably come back with, "The heart does not sing with its parts." Not exactly useful.'

Ivanova's Life Lesson: 'With all due respect, that was Grade-A stupid!'

'I don't want to get killed because of a typo – that would be stupid.'

'If I live through this job without completely losing my mind it will be a miracle of biblical proportions!' (To which Second Lieutenant Corwin mutters: 'There goes *my* faith in the Almighty.')

Dialogue to Rewind For: Franklin to Garibaldi and Ivanova: 'I've got to use the little officers' room – I'll be right back.'

Londo to Vir: 'I have always been alone.'

Ships That Pass In The Night: Earth Transport *Dionysus* is being held outside the station at the beginning of the episode (presumably with a cargo of wine).

Literary, Mythological and Historical References: Sheridan refers to the alien probe as a 'berserker'. The original berserkers were savage, reckless Scandinavian fighters. This probably isn't what he meant. On the other hand, Fred Saberhagen's *Berserker* series of SF novels and short stories are about robot probes left over from a long-ago alien war that are designed to search the universe and destroy all intelligent life that they find. This is probably what Sheridan meant.

David Corwin – the young Command and Control technician – was named for Norman Corwin, a prodigious and hugely literate American writer whose career was blighted by the Communist witch-hunts of the 1950s. J. Michael Straczynski has made a point of saying how much Corwin taught him about writing.

I've Seen That Face Before: Ta'Lon – the Narn who arrives on the station with Councillor Na'Far – is the same Narn whose life Sheridan saved on the Streib ship in 'All Alone in the Night' (episode 211). Marshall Teague, the actor who plays Ta'Lon, also appeared as Nelson Drake in episode 104 – 'Infection'.

Accidents Will Happen: The subjects of the questions sent by the alien probe include physics and quantum mechanics. Isn't quantum mechanics *part* of physics in the year 2260? It is nowadays.

How come the alien probe can offer cures for 'every known form of disease' when its builders have never come across humanity before? OK, maybe it's lying, but someone in C&C should have found this claim a little suspect.

Questions Raised: Both G'Kar and Londo are usually very hot on getting hold of new technology, especially when it looks like humanity might keep them at arm's length. Why didn't they demand that Sheridan give them access to all this free technology the alien probe was offering? One might have thought word would have got around the station.

'Passing Through Gethsemane'

Transmission Number: 304
Production Number: 305

Written by: J. Michael Straczynski
Directed by: Adam Nimoy

Lyta Alexander: Patricia Tallman
Brother Theo: Louis Turenne
Brother Edward: Brad Dourif   **Malcolm:** Robert Keith
Centauri Telepath: Mark Folger

Plot: This is as complex a theological argument as we're ever likely to see in an American drama series, taking in original sin, personal sacrifice, the legitimacy of revenge and the limits of personal responsibility. Again, as in episode 217 – 'In the Shadow of Z'ha'dum' – Sheridan's moral stance is questioned and found wanting. As is that of the audience. Straczynski cleverly leads us along a path, one step at a time, then makes us see that we have arrived at a place where we don't want to be.

The 'A' Plot: Brother Edward, one of the monks now living on Babylon 5, is experiencing strange events. First he discovers a black rose in his bag, then he finds a message – 'Death Walks Among You' – scrawled in blood across the wall of his room. The message disappears by the time Garibaldi arrives, but Brother Edward starts hearing accusing voices and seeing visions of a dead woman with a black rose stuffed in her mouth. He uses the Babylon 5 computer to search for some event that ties all these clues together, and discovers he used to be a murderer named Charles Dexter whose trademark was to stuff black roses in the mouths of his victims. He was captured and sentenced to the death of personality – in other words, mind-wipe. Somehow, he ended up in the order of monks. The knowledge of his past life horrifies him – how, he asks Brother Theo, can God forgive his sins if he cannot even remember them? Garibaldi discovers that some of the relatives of Dexter's victims are conspiring to force Brother Edward to remember his crimes, and then to kill him in vengeance. To break the mind-wipe they used a Centauri telepath who wasn't bound by Psi Corps's restrictive rules. Telepath Lyta Alexander forces the location of the planned murder from the Centauri telepath's mind and a rescue attempt is mounted, but too late. Brother Edward has been crucified. His murderer is captured, sentenced, mind-wiped and, in an irony unappreciated by Captain Sheridan, joins the order of monks so that he can help mankind.

The 'B' Plot: Lyta Alexander, Babylon 5's original registered commercial telepath, returns to Babylon 5. She is now an agent of Ambassador Kosh, and runs what she refers to as 'errands' for him. She warns off Ambassador Mollari, who wishes to find out what she knows about the Vorlons, and helps Sheridan and Garibaldi locate the site of Brother Edward's murder.

The 'C' Plot: Brother Edward asks Ambassador Delenn about the Minbari religion.

The Arc: At the beginning of the episode Ivanova is told to go to Bay 13, where Ambassador Kosh's ship is docking after having just come out of hyperspace. Kosh, however, hasn't left the station. This is more evidence that Kosh's ship can come and go without Kosh actually being on board (as we saw previously in episode 213 – 'Hunter, Prey').

Lyta Alexander returns to the station. During her previous return, Kosh let her see his true form, and we now discover that she has become so obsessed with Vorlons that she made her way to the edge of Vorlon space and was left there in an escape pod with only five days of oxygen, hoping that the Vorlons would agree to take her in. She broadcast telepathic messages, and she was on the verge of running out of oxygen when a Vorlon ship arrived and took her on board. This implies, of course, that Vorlons are either all telepathic or, like other races, they have telepathic members (as it were). Contrast this with episode 109 – 'Deathwalker' – in which it is speculated that Vorlons either don't have or don't trust telepaths. The latter is looking more likely. The connection between Vorlons and telepathy is addressed – at least partially – in episode 322 ('Z'ha'dum').

Lyta refuses to say anything about what happened to her on the Vorlon homeworld, but she appears to have come back changed. Her health is generally better (an inherited chronic iron deficiency has been cured, as has an enlarged appendix and an incipient hiatus hernia); the levels of oxygen in her blood are unusually high and she has methane-processing gills implanted in her neck (enabling her to breathe the atmosphere in Kosh's quarters unaided). We saw that Ambassador G'Kar had much the same thing in the pilot episode.

Some form of energy transfer occurs between Lyta and Kosh – or perhaps just Kosh's empty encounter suit. We know from episode 101 – 'Midnight on the Firing Line' – that Kosh's body is probably a noncorporeal energy form, and the energy transfer in this episode is very similar to the moment in episode 216 – 'Knives' – when an alien life form leaves Sheridan's body. Kosh has obviously been using Lyta's body as a convenient vehicle within which he can move around without suspicion – a habit the new Vorlon Ambassador continues in season four.

Delenn tells Brother Edward: 'We do not believe in any individual god or gods . . . We believe that the universe itself is conscious in a way we can never truly understand. It is engaged in a search for meaning, so it breaks itself apart, investing its own consciousness in every form of life. We are the universe, trying to understand itself.' This is a continuation of an important theme in the series which has been made explicit in the pilot episode, episode 102 ('Soul Hunter') and other later episodes, especially 201 ('Points of Departure') and will be addressed further in episode 317 ('War Without End' Part Two).

Lennier makes a very important statement when he describes the revered historical Minbari figure Valen thus: 'Valen was the greatest of us. A thousand years ago he came from nowhere, formed the Grey Council and brought peace to our people. They say he was a Minbari not born of Minbari . . .' This statement paves the way for revelations in episode 317 – 'War Without End' Part Two.

Observations: The 'A' plot of this episode was originally intended to appear as a 'B' plot in a second-season episode, but J. Michael Straczynski had to delay it after a similar idea was suggested on the internet by a fan of the show in August 1994. It was only after the fan sent Straczynski a legal statement allowing him to continue with the plot that he was able to complete the writing.

The newscast of the trial result that Garibaldi has been following mentions a twelve-person jury. We know from previous episodes (notably episode 121 – 'The Quality of Mercy') that justice on Babylon 5 is dispensed by solitary people called Ombuds. The jury system is used where there is a large enough pool of jurors – such as on Earth – whereas the Ombuds work like circuit court judges during the 1800s in America.

Delenn tells Brother Edward, 'Among my people it is considered an honour to aid any true seeker in his quest.' This is very similar to what she says to Aldous Gajic in episode 115 – 'Grail'.

Brother Theodore quotes a phrase from Delenn – 'Faith manages.' She used this line in episode 218 ('Confessions and Lamentations').

At a recent convention, Straczynski said, 'There's a convent in Chicago – I am not lying – where the nuns watch the show every week and they talk about it afterwards. I heard about this and sent them a copy of "Passing Through Gethsemane", autographed to them.'

The UK's Channel 4 made a slight cut to this episode for the first UK broadcast. During the scene where Garibaldi is talking to Delenn while listening to an ISN broadcast about a murderer being brain-wiped, he refers to the criminal as a bastard. Channel 4 cut the 'bastard' out.

Koshisms: 'Formality . . . ritual . . . you should be informed.'

Other Worlds: Brother Edward (when he was Charles Dexter) carried out his crimes on Earth Colony 3 in the Orion System.

Literary, Mythological and Historical References: Brother Edward defines the task of the monks as 'Learning all the names and faces of God from our non-human neighbours.' This, according to Straczynski, isn't a glancing reference to the Arthur C. Clarke short story 'The Nine Billion Names of God'.

I've Seen That Face Before: Brad Dourif is a well-known character actor whose previous genre credits include the 1984 David Lynch movie *Dune*. More recently he played a psychopathic Betazoid named Suder in the *Star Trek: Voyager* episodes 'Meld' and 'Basics' Parts I and II and the killer Luthor Lee Boggs in *The X Files* episode 'Beyond the Sea'. He was nominated for an Academy Award for Best Supporting Actor for the 1974 film *One Flew Over the Cuckoo's Nest*.

Lyta Alexander – the only telepath ever to have scanned a Vorlon – returns to Babylon 5. We first saw her in the pilot episode – 'The Gathering' – and then again in episode 219 – 'Divided Loyalties'.

Not that you actually see his face, but director Adam Nimoy is Leonard Nimoy's son.

Accidents Will Happen: When Kosh's ship docks, Ivanova is expecting him to disembark. When she realises he is actually standing behind her in the docking bay *before* his ship has docked, she doesn't seem in the slightest bit surprised.

Less of a blooper and more of a missed opportunity: in

order to remind viewers what a mind-wipe is, Garibaldi is watching the newscast of a trial he has been following. Wouldn't it have been nicer if the guilty party in the trial had been Robert Carlsen, the mad bomber from episode 302 – 'Convictions'?

How did Garibaldi manage to work out that Brother Edward was actually Charles Dexter? The mind-wiped Dexter was presumed dead in a fire, and the only piece of evidence Garibaldi had was the phrase written on the wall – 'Death Walks Among You'. Not much to go on. At least Brother Edward had the black rose and the name from his vision to help him.

How come Franklin didn't spot Lyta Alexander's whizzy new methane-breathing gills when he did his all-over medical examination? We know she didn't have them in either the pilot episode ('The Gathering') or the last time she turned up (episode 219 – 'Divided Loyalties').

Questions Raised: Is Kosh just a noncorporeal energy form, and is he using Lyta Alexander's body as a vehicle?

'Voices of Authority'

Transmission Number: 305
Production Number: 304

Written by: J. Michael Straczynski
Directed by: Menachem Binetski

Draal: John Schuck **Julie Masante:** Shari Shattuck
Voice of the First One: Ardwright Chamberlain

Plot: When you take out the massive arc references, the humour and the nudity, what is left? A chilling vision about what Earth has become, and the most massive coincidence ever seen in a science fiction series. Repeated viewings of this episode are not advised.

The 'A' Plot: Delenn suggests they need allies in their fight against the Shadows, and proposes contacting the First Ones. They have fought the Shadows before, and might help now if asked nicely. Marcus is unsure – he has been warned off the

First Ones – but Delenn is insistent. She asks Draal for his advice, and he suggests using the Great Machine on Epsilon 3 to find them. Sheridan is invited down to the planet, but has to cry off when Julie Masante – Babylon 5's new political officer – arrives unannounced. Ivanova takes his place and projects her mind to where the First Ones can be found – the planet Sigma 957. Her approach is noticed by the Shadows, who congregate to trap her. She pulls out in a hurry, but catches a fleeting glimpse of the past – the moment when *Earthforce 1* is destroyed – and intercepts a communication between Vice-President Clark and a mysterious other person in which Clark admits his complicity in the assassination. She ensures that Draal has recorded the message, and sets out to Sigma 957 in the *White Star* with Marcus. Once there, they locate the First Ones and get them to offer their help in the forthcoming war with the Shadows. Back on Babylon 5, Sheridan sends the recording of Clark's admission back to General Hague on Earth. Hague releases it to the public, where it causes widespread confusion.

The 'B' Plot: Julie Masante – a beautiful blonde – arrives on Babylon 5. She has been assigned as the station's political officer by the Nightwatch Division of the Ministry of Peace under the authority of the Babylon 5 Oversight Committee. Some of Sheridan's recent decisions have been frowned on back on Earth, and it has been decided he needs someone beside him to guide his actions in the light of the political situation. Masante tries to get Zack Allen to spy on Sheridan, and tries to get Sheridan into bed. She fails on the second, but Zack is getting increasingly worried about Garibaldi's secretiveness. When the Clark recording is released back on Earth she is recalled to help.

The 'C' Plot: G'Kar has been hearing rumours about the Rangers, and realises that a new alliance is being forged between Sheridan and Delenn. He approaches Delenn and tries to blackmail her into telling him what is going on, but she refuses. He then approaches Garibaldi and offers his help in whatever is going on. Garibaldi prevaricates, and G'Kar gives Garibaldi his own copy of the Book of G'Quan, suggesting he learn Narn and read it.

The Arc: Delenn gives a neat summation of the situation vis-à-vis the First Ones and the Shadows. 'Many times over the last million years the Shadows were fought to a standstill by the First Ones – races immeasurably older than our own. After the last war, a thousand years ago, we believed the First Ones went away for ever, passing beyond the galactic rim where no human or Minbari has ever ventured. But the Vorlons remained, so it is possible that some of the others may still be around . . . They have grown tired of constant warfare – lost interest in the affairs of the younger races. According to legend, some went to sleep in secret places deep beneath their ancient cities where no one can bother them. The rest walk among the stars on errands we can never hope to understand, barely aware of our existence.' This contains resonances of her speeches to Sheridan in episode 217 ('In the Shadow of Z'ha'dum') and to the newly formed War Council in episode 301 ('Matters of Honor'). It also prefigures the discovery of Lorien in episode 401 ('The Hour of the Wolf').

Draal and the Great Machine on Epsilon 3 were first introduced in episodes 118 and 119 – 'A Voice in the Wilderness' Parts One and Two – and again in episode 220 – 'The Long, Twilight Struggle'.

The First One ship that we see is identical to the one Catherine Sakai sees in the same place in episode 106 – 'Mind War'.

When Ivanova's mind is at Sigma 957, courtesy of the Epsilon 3 machine, the Shadows become aware of her. They are represented by parallel rows of glowing lights which are very similar to their glowing eyes as seen in episode 217 ('In the Shadow of Z'ha'dum') and the season 3 title sequence (and again in episode 401 – 'The Hour of the Wolf'). The noise Ivanova hears is similar to the noise they make when speaking to Morden in episode 301 ('Matters of Honor').

The 'voice' to whom Vice-President Clark admits his complicity in Santiago's death is recognisably Morden's.

When Ivanova retrieves Clark's conversation with Morden, Draal tells Ivanova that 'A normal human mind should not have been able to do that.' Can she do it because of her telepathic talents, as mentioned previously in episode 219 – 'Divided Loyalties'?

Julie Masante warns the Nightwatch that something big will be coming up on Earth – a purge in which all traitors will be cleared from the face of the planet. This prefigures the events of episode 310 – 'Point of No Return'.

The representation of the First Ones Ivanova sees – a stone mask with glowing eyes – reacts badly to the mention of the Vorlons. There may be some bad feeling there.

Observations: The First Ones absorb the power from the *White Star* when it gets too close to them.

In a line cut from the final transmitted version Draal admits that he once nearly blew up Babylon 5 when an insect landed on his nose while he was plugged into the Great Machine.

This episode was slipped from fourth to fifth because the heavy CGI effects were taking time to complete.

Jeff Conaway, who plays Zack Allen, had complained about his ill-fitting costume during season 2, and was surprised to find his character voicing almost the same words during this episode.

One of the infamous *Babylon 5* blooper tapes contains the moment when Shari Shattuck (playing political officer Julie Masante) refers to the Minibar War rather than the Minbari war.

The character of Julie Masante is named after a fan who helped raise money to reimburse Michael O'Hare, after money due to him for a convention he attended was not paid.

Ivanova's Life Lessons: Draal: 'I don't like surprises.' Ivanova: 'Really? Love 'em myself. To me, everything is a surprise. You're a surprise, this place is a surprise . . . You see this? Paper cut – hurts like hell. Anybody else would be upset, but to me it's just one more wonderful surprise. I mean, I even surprise myself sometimes, so I guess there's nothing wrong with me surprising you. Right?' Draal (laughing): 'I like you – you're trouble.' Ivanova: 'Why, thank you. That's the nicest thing anybody's said about me in days.'

Dialogue to Rewind For: Zack Allen on his badly fitting uniform jacket: 'I look like a circus tent. Any minute now a little teeny car with sixteen clowns in is gonna come flying outta my butt.'

Draal: 'I spend so much time out of my body I sometimes forget where it is.'

Ivanova, catching Sheridan being seduced by Julie Masante: 'Good luck, Captain – I think you're about to go where *everyone* has gone before.'

Draal: 'I must remember to dust myself once in a while.'

Sheridan, glancing down at the naked Julie Masante's nipples: 'Well, it must be colder in here than I thought.'

Marcus to Ivanova during the confrontation with the First Ones: 'I think you just hit a nerve. The Vorlons must owe them money or something.'

Ivanova to the First Ones: 'Will you join us in our fight against the Shadows?' The First Ones: 'Zog.' Ivanova: 'Zog? What do you mean, Zog? Zog yes? Zog no?'

Marcus on how to stop the First Ones from leaving: 'I'll put a bucket on my head and pretend to be the ancient Vorlon god Booji.' Ivanova, suddenly getting an idea: 'That's it!' Marcus: 'Fine, I'll get a bucket.'

Dialogue to Fast Forward Past: Ivanova: 'They were here – I can feel their footprints in the sand, hear their words whispered in the wind.'

Ships That Pass In The Night: Earth liner *Loki*.

Literary, Mythological and Historical References: The description given by Delenn of the First Ones and their possible locations is very reminiscent of H. P. Lovecraft's works. Lovecraft was an early-twentieth-century writer whose stories described an ongoing conflict between titanic cosmic forces: the Great Old Ones and the Elder Gods. Many of the Great Old Ones have been imprisoned by the Elder Gods – some, like great Cthulhu, beneath ancient cities – while others, like Hastur the Unspeakable, still walk among the stars.

The name of the ship Julie Masante leaves Babylon 5 on – Earth Liner *Loki* – is a reference to the Norse trickster god.

I've Seen That Face Before: Shari Shattuck, who plays Julie Masante, has been in a few highly forgettable films, including the 1986 entry in the 'women in prison' genre *The Naked Cage* and the 1990 'cheerleader audition' movie *Laker Girls*.

The latter film was directed by Bruce Seth Green, who also directed a number of episodes of *Babylon 5*. Shari Shattuck also appeared in the 1996 Leslie Nielson spoof *Spy Hard*. She *also* appeared in the April 1980 edition of *Playboy*.

Questions Raised: Ivanova tells Sheridan that she might be able to catch the First Ones at Sigma 957, but she'll have to move fast. Why? They've been there for some time and there's no indication they're going anywhere. Or do they have an urgent dental appointment?

The First Ones tell Ivanova, 'When it is time, come to this place. Call our name. We will be here.' So – what *is* their name? Zog, perhaps?

Isn't it an incredible coincidence that, of all the things in space and time Ivanova could have found, it had to be President Clark's confession? Admittedly her thoughts were influencing her direction, and President Clark was weighing heavily in her thoughts, but it's just as likely that she would have ended up watching her mother commit suicide, or her brother die during the Earth–Minbari war.

'Dust to Dust'

Transmission Number: 306
Production Number: 306

Written by: J. Michael Straczynski
Directed by: David Eagle

Bester: Walter Koenig   **Narn Image/Kosh:** Jim Norton
Lindstrom: Julian Neil   **Psi Cop:** Judy Levitt
Vizak: Kim Strauss

Plot: A satisfying and multi-layered story in which all the plots connect up and the final product looks deceptively simple. It has everything: arc material, a message and Bester. Oh, and Kosh as well.

The 'A' Plot: Psi Cop Bester returns to Babylon 5, on a mission to track down a criminal who is smuggling an addictive drug named 'dust'. Sheridan worries that Bester will scan the command staff and find out all their secrets.

Ivanova is worried too, and comes close to destroying Bester's spaceship before he can dock. Delenn suggests a compromise – using Minbari telepaths to shield the command staff. Sheridan, protected by the Minbari, forces Bester to agree to have his telepathic powers temporarily suppressed by drugs. Bester tells the command staff that dust can cause short-term telepathy in its users. Bester suspects the criminal intends selling a large quantity of dust to an alien government as a weapon. Dr Franklin reports an upsurge in cases of dust abuse on the station. Bester and Garibaldi question a known Babylon 5 criminal – Ashi – and Bester forces a confession out of him by pretending that his telepathic powers are still active. Together the two men arrest Lindstrom and impound his consignment of dust. Bester is forced to leave the station before the suppressant drugs wear off.

The 'B' Plot: G'Kar is Lindstrom's customer for the dust, and is given a small sample to test. He tests it on himself, gains a temporary burst of telepathic power, and bursts into Londo Mollari's quarters. He knocks Vir unconscious and invades Londo's mind, forcing him to reveal his shame at being sent to Babylon 5 as a joke. Probing deeper, he discovers Londo's connection with the mysterious Morden, and his central role in the invasion of the Narn homeworld. Still in Londo's mind, G'Kar encounters a vision of his own father, and meets a mysterious elderly Narn who asks him to change what he is doing. The elderly Narn warns him that if he continues to be distracted by his hatred of the Centauri, he will be unable to prevent a greater tragedy. The elderly Narn reveals himself to be the mythical Narn hero G'Quan, but G'Kar fails to see that behind G'Quan is Ambassador Kosh. G'Kar is sentenced to sixty days' imprisonment by an Ombuds.

The 'C' Plot: Vir returns from Minbar on a short visit to Babylon 5. He asks Londo to read his first report on the Minbari people. Londo suggests rewriting it with a more 'hawkish' slant, making the Minbari sound like a degenerate race of religious zealots who might pose a threat to the Centauri. As Vir makes his preparations to return to Minbar, Londo, mindful of the things G'Kar saw in his mind, advises him never to let the people back on Centauri think that his appointment is a joke.

The Arc: G'Kar tells Lindstrom that all Narn telepaths were exterminated long ago. This was originally set up in the pilot episode ('The Gathering'), and becomes an important factor in the Shadow War in episode 314 ('Ship of Tears').

Psi Corps developed dust themselves in order to 'create' telepaths from the normal population, but it has never produced one lasting telepath.

While he is in Londo's mind, G'Kar sees a discussion between Londo and a Centauri diplomat concerning Londo's forthcoming posting to Babylon 5, and two instances of Londo and Morden discussing attacks on the Narn. He then sees a series of short images. Most of these are of Londo himself – looking up, looking away, looking sad and looking angry. He also sees a hand emerging from the sun, Londo looking up at Shadow ships crossing the sky and Londo's premonition that he will be strangled by G'Kar (all of which first appeared in episode 209 – 'The Coming of Shadows'). There are some fifty shots in all.

Observations: Londo has never been to Minbar.

Bester says that what happened to Talia Winters was the result of an operation sanctioned by his predecessors. He also implies that Talia was dissected by Psi Corps after her cover was blown and her secondary personality revealed. He could well be lying on both counts.

The drug that suppresses telepathic powers takes effect only after three hours.

Dust is a human-made drug, a white powder in appearance, that accelerates neural processing and stimulates the latent telepathic gene in most humans. It bestows temporary telepathy, and allows a kind of mental rape to take place. The victims of this mental rape suffer some neural-pathway disruption, but recover in a few days unless they are telepaths, in which case they almost never recover. It can be altered to take effect on most non-human species.

Londo rewrites Vir's first report on the Minbari. This is the beginning of a joke that carries on in episode 309 ('Point of No Return') and pays off in episode 312 ('Sic Transit Vir').

G'Kar's father's death – hanging from a tree for three days – was originally described by G'Kar in episode 215 ('And Now For a Word').

Vir's gift to Londo of a packet of peanuts ('Ah, salted!') was improvised by actor Stephen Furst on set, based on the fact that free packets of peanuts are always handed out on aircraft.

For the filming of G'Kar's attack on Londo, actor Peter Jurasik was made up to look as if he'd been badly abused. At one point during the filming, while he was slumped on the floor, he glanced up at the camera and muttered, 'You wouldn't believe it but three wine coolers and I'm buzzed.'

Kosh's cryptic comment to G'Kar – 'I have *always* been here' – is what he says to Sheridan at the end of episode 211 – 'All Alone in the Night'.

The lettering on Vir's Coat of Welcome spells out 'Aloha' in the Minbari alphabet created for the show.

Koshisms: 'I have always been here.'

'We are not alone – we rise and fall together, and some of us must be sacrificed if all are to be saved, because if we fail in this then none of us will be saved.'

Kosh says both of these lines in the persona of the Narn image in G'Kar's mind. You can call it a Narn image as the credits do, you can call it G'Quan as G'Kar implies, but it's Kosh.

Dialogue to Rewind For: Bester, to Garibaldi: 'There are things going on out there that you know nothing about – threats to the human race that no one ever hears about because we stop them. There's danger all around us, and whether you like it or not, we may be all that stands between you and the abyss.' He's right, of course.

Londo, about Vir's report: 'I have only seen political *naïveté* this complete once before, in a speech before the Centarum by Lord Jarno. When he was finished we recommended that he be sterilised in the best interests of evolution, and then we remembered that he was married to Lady Jarno, so really there was no need.'

Dialogue to Fast Forward Past: Garibaldi: 'If I had a baseball bat we could hang you from the ceiling and play *piñata*.' Bester: 'A *piñata*, huh? So, you think of me as something bright and cheerful, full of toys and candy for young children?'

Culture Shock: The Minbari have given Vir a ceremonial coat of welcome.

I've Seen That Face Before: Jim Norton, who plays the Narn image seen by G'Kar (in other words, Kosh), has also appeared as Ombuds Wellington in episodes 115 ('Grail') and 121 ('The Quality of Mercy') and as the Markab doctor Lazarenn in episode 218 ('Confessions and Lamentations').

Judy Levitt (Walter Koenig's wife) returns as a Psi Cop. She played the same part in episode 208 ('A Race Through Dark Places').

Literary, Mythological and Historical References: Bester's comment about Psi Corps being all that stands between humanity and the abyss echoes the German philosopher Friedrich Nietzsche, who said, 'And if you gaze for long into an abyss, the abyss gazes also into you.' G'Kar makes reference to this in episode 202 ('Revelations'), as does Londo in episode 316 ('War Without End', Part One).

Accidents Will Happen: The door in Command and Control usually closes after people have passed through it, except in this episode in the scene where Ivanova is about to shoot Bester's ship. The dismissed command staff leave, and the door remains open for a while so that Sheridan can arrive without Ivanova hearing him.

Questions Raised: What reprisals did Londo take on the Narn population for G'Kar's attack on him? We never find out, but it must have been nasty.

What are the chances that four Minbari telepaths just happened to be passing through Babylon 5 just when they were needed?

'Exogenesis'

Transmission Number: 307
Production Number: 307

Written by: J. Michael Straczynski
Directed by: Kevin G. Cremin

Matthew Duffin: James Warwick **Duncan:** Aubrey Morris
Samuel: Eric Steinberg **Dr Harrison:** Carrie Dobro

Plot: It's an episode of two halves, both of which are halves of fine episodes. Unfortunately, they aren't halves of the same episode. We start off going in one direction and end up heading in another direction wondering how we got there. Still, sit back and enjoy the scenery (which is being chewed by one of the hammiest British actors around).

The 'A' Plot: Lurkers on Babylon 5 are being infected with what appear to be alien parasites that wrap themselves around the spinal column. Dr Franklin is conducting an autopsy on a dead lurker with one of these parasites in his body when Marcus asks for his help. Duncan – a lurker friend of Marcus's – has disappeared, and Marcus needs Dr Franklin to open Duncan's quarters for him. They find a web-encrusted hole in the wall of Duncan's room, leading to an area of Brown Sector where lurkers controlled by the aliens are infecting other lurkers. The aliens are called the Vendrizi, and the one that has taken control of Duncan explains they were created half a million years ago, and their function is to travel the galaxy memorising things – music, sunsets, landscapes – to ensure that these things are never forgotten. The lurkers have all volunteered to join with the Vendrizi, who require biological hosts. The host that died – the one Franklin was conducting the autopsy on – was polluted by drugs and was unsuitable. To prove to Marcus that they are benign, Duncan removes his Vendrizi 'controller'. Franklin agrees to help them on condition that everything is explained fully to him and nothing more is done without his consent. Duncan – unable to join with another Vendrizi – leaves Babylon 5 to see for himself some of the sights that the Vendrizi showed him.

The 'B' Plot: Sheridan and Ivanova are worried about Lieutenant Corwin – given the confrontation with the forces of President Clark that they are expecting, which side will Corwin support? Ivanova invites Corwin to her quarters for a chat, but he assumes she is propositioning him and brings flowers. During their discussions, he tells her that he can't just pick and choose which orders to obey and which not to obey. Reluctantly, Ivanova recommends to Sheridan that they should not bring Corwin in on their council of war.

The 'C' Plot: Marcus is romantically interested in Ivanova, and asks Franklin what his chances are. Ivanova assumes that the bunch of artificial roses given to her by Corwin are actually from Marcus, and hands them back. Marcus, who knows nothing about the flowers, assumes Ivanova is interested in him.

The Arc: Marcus receives a message from Ranger One (Ambassador Jeffrey Sinclair on Minbar) telling him that all Rangers in Earth space are being withdrawn because of something that will happen soon. This, of course, is a clear reference to the imposition of martial law and consequent problems which will happen in episodes 308, 309 and 310 ('Messages from Earth', 'Point of No Return' and 'Severed Dreams'). Sinclair also tells Marcus that the Shadows are gathering in Sector 800, creating a border on the edge of Centauri space. The last part of his message is that a 'package' is on its way to Marcus from Mars, and should take about a week to arrive. The 'package' in question is almost certainly Dr Mary Kirkish, who arrives in episode 308 – 'Messages From Earth'.

The Vendrizi are a clear analogue of the Technomages in episode 203 – 'The Geometry of Shadows'. The Technomages fled the galaxy to ensure that technical knowledge was preserved for after the Shadow War. The Vendrizi imply that they are preserving art and beauty for the same reason.

Observations: The pilot of Earth Transport *Dyson* sounds suspiciously like a bad impersonation of Sean Connery.

Earhart's bar is for use by Earthforce personnel only.

David Corwin – a regular face in Command and Control, is

promoted to Lieutenant (j.g.) – i.e. Lieutenant (junior grade) – during this story.

Marcus refers in passing to Dr Franklin's clinic for lurkers in Downbelow.

Synthetic blood is in common use by medlab, but they prefer using real blood where possible.

Dr Franklin refers to various drugs, including dust (see episode 306 – 'Dust to Dust') and morphazine.

Samuel is Marcus's regular Ranger contact on Babylon 5 until he is taken over by the Vendrizi.

Ivanova still has her coffee plant in hydroponics (as mentioned in episode 103 – 'Born to the Purple').

Marcus invents a Copeland J-5000 medical scanner during his attempts to escape from the Vendrizi. John Copeland is the show's producer.

J. Michael Straczynski was interrupted during the writing of this episode and, by the time he got back to it a week later, he has said that he lost track of where he was going with it.

Ships That Pass In The Night: Earth Transport *Dyson* is one of the Babylon 5 shuttles used for ferrying passengers to and from larger ships. It is named after the physicist Freeman Dyson, who suggested that an energy conscious and technologically advanced society would dismantle their solar system and arrange it in a sphere around their sun, ensuring that they collected all the energy it emitted.

Other Worlds: Orion 7 is mentioned (Orion 4 has been mentioned previously), and we find out that it harbours a life form known as a flamebird.

Culture Shock: The Vendrizi are an ancient form of life who were artificially created by an unnamed race half a million years ago. They consist completely of genetically neutral material (looking rather like a large earwig), and are able to infiltrate a host creature and join with its neural system, effectively forming a joint creature with the memories of both its components. The Vendrizi appear to have a collective mind, with everything known by one of them being accessible to all of them. Once a Vendrizi is removed from its host organism, the host cannot accept another Vendrizi without causing severe damage to its neural system. They are very sensitive to 'impurities' such as drugs in the host's blood. The 'purpose' of the Vendrizi is to travel through the galaxy memorising everything they see and hear. They are a mobile repository of knowledge, and when darkness falls across the galaxy and everything that was known is lost, they will keep the memories alive. They refer to themselves as 'keepers of the past, the present and the future'.

Station Keeping: Dr Franklin has the authority to open the door to any set of quarters on the station if he thinks there might be a medical emergency in progress, but he is not allowed to enter (so what does he do – throw a handful of pills in?)

Earthforce comlinks are biogenetically keyed to their users, and cannot be used by anyone else.

Literary, Mythological and Historical References: Marcus quotes from Shakespeare's *Macbeth* and refers in passing to Dickens's *A Christmas Carol*.

Duncan's paean to the memories shared with him by the Vendrizi – 'I saw flamebirds dying on Orion 7 . . . I saw cities floating in the air, five miles high' – may be a nod in the direction of the film *Blade Runner*, in which Roy Batty – the replicant played by Rutger Hauer – says something similar to Harrison Ford: 'I've seen things you people wouldn't believe. Attack ships on fire off the shoulder of Orion. I've watched c-beams glitter in the dark near the Tannhauser Gate. All those moments will be lost . . .'

Earhart's bar is named after Amelia Earhart, an American aviator who was the first woman to fly the Atlantic alone.

I've Seen That Face Before: James Warwick – who plays Matthew Duffin – is a familiar face on British television. His primary genre role was as Lieutenant Scott in the *Doctor Who* story 'Earthshock'.

Aubrey Morris – who plays Duncan – is another familiar

face on British television and films. His particularly hammy style of acting has graced genre films such as *Lifeforce* (where he played the Home Secretary). For those old enough to remember, he played the time-travelling Mr Zed in the 1971 British children's SF series *Jamie*.

Questions Raised: Duffin and Samuel are already on Babylon 5 and already joined with the Vendrizi when Earth Transport *Dyson* arrives with a cargo they have been waiting for. What's the cargo? More Vendrizi?

If Dr Franklin has the authority to open the door to any set of quarters on the station if he thinks there might be a medical emergency in progress, but isn't allowed to enter, what happens if someone has had a heart attack in the shower?

Why is there a web-encrusted hole in Duncan's quarters leading to where the Vendrizi are working? All of the humans who are hosting the Vendrizi are perfectly capable of walking, and Duncan accepted a Vendrizi voluntarily so they didn't have to break into his quarters.

A fair number of lurkers have agreed to host Vendrizi, but only one has died because his blood supply contained traces of drugs like dust and morphazine. Is it likely that such a small percentage of lurkers would be drug users?

Where did Duncan get the money with which to buy a ticket off Babylon 5? He was pathetically grateful for two credits at the beginning of the episode, and Marcus didn't give him the fare.

How come David Corwin is promoted from second lieutenant (a rank associated with the current US Army/ USAF) to Lieutenant (j.g.) (a rank associated with the current US Navy)? Earthforce's rank structure appears to be a bizarre cross between the services, and it's not consistent in the series.

'Messages From Earth'

Transmission Number: 308
Production Number: 308

Written by: J. Michael Straczynski
Directed by: Mike Laurence Vejar

Dr Mary Kirkish: Nancy Stafford
Security Guard No. 1: Vaughn Armstrong

Plot: It may be superficial in terms of motivation and internal struggle, but the plot is nail-biting enough to cover it. A genuine feeling of dread pervades this episode.

The 'A' Plot: Garibaldi and the Rangers smuggle Dr Mary Kirkish on board Babylon 5. She tells the War Council that she is an archaeologist, and seven years ago she was part of a team that discovered a Shadow ship buried beneath the surface of Mars. They notified the authorities, who told them to withdraw. A second Shadow ship arrived and excavated the first. The two ships left together. The team were split up after that, and told never to reveal what they had seen. Garibaldi backs up Kirkish's story – he was on Mars at the time, and he saw a Shadow ship as well, and found a Psi Corps badge near the scene. Dr Kirkish tells them that a similar ship has just been excavated on Ganymede – the largest moon of Jupiter – but that the Earth authorities don't want to give it back to its mysterious owners. Kirkish has escaped with the news, and people are trying to kill her. Delenn offers her safety in Minbari space, and tells the War Council that Shadow ships have to join with living creatures in order to operate. If the joining is done incorrectly, the resulting entity would go mad and pose an incredible danger to everyone. Sheridan decides the ship cannot be allowed to fall into President Clark's hands. Leaving all his identification and insignia behind, he and Delenn travel in the *White Star* to Jupiter. They are almost too late: the ship has been activated and goes on a rampage. The *White Star* opens fire on it, angering it and causing it to give chase. Sheridan lures it deep into Jupiter's atmosphere, where the pressure causes it to crumple and die. The *White Star* is attacked by the Earth Alliance Destroyer *Agamemnon*, but Delenn suggests opening a jumpgate inside Jupiter's atmosphere and escaping.

The 'B' Plot: The Nightwatch are gaining strength, and are suspicious of Sheridan's absence. They ask Zack to find out through Garibaldi where Sheridan has been. They believe there to be an alien-led conspiracy against President Clark, and laws are being changed to allow anonymous informants to pass information on friends, family and colleagues to the Nightwatch office. In order to forestall this conspiracy, President Clark declares martial law on Earth.

The 'C' Plot: G'Kar is writing a book while incarcerated in his cell. The book lists everything that has happened recently – the war, the fall of the Narn homeworld, the mistakes made by the Narn and how to correct them. Garibaldi tells him that people have complained about his singing.

The Arc: An ISN news broadcast mentions two headlines – President Clark blaming allegations that he conspired to kill President Santiago on alien conspirators, and the announcement that a ship belonging to a new alien race has been seen. These refer specifically, of course, to episodes 201 ('Chrysalis'), 301 ('Matters of Honor') and 305 ('Voices of Authority').

Dr Mary Kirkish is the 'package' that the Rangers told Marcus was on its way in episode 307 – 'Exogenesis'.

The Shadow ship was buried 300 feet beneath Mars's Syria Planum. It had been there for over a thousand years, which means it was left there during or after the last Great War. That also means that there were connections between the Shadows and senior government officials seven years ago. So, Earth Central wasn't trying to find out what the Shadow ship was in episode 301 – 'Matters of Honor' – it was trying to find out whether anyone else recognised it.

Garibaldi's story about seeing a Shadow ship on Mars seven years before, and his discovery of a burnt Psi Corps badge, seems to come from way out of left field. In fact it's a reference to issues 5 to 8 of the *Babylon 5* comic series: 'Shadows Past and Present'. The full story is that Garibaldi and Sinclair crash on the surface of Mars during a reconnaissance flight, and see a Shadow ship being excavated by a second Shadow ship. They also find a Psi Corps installation containing alien technology, in which humans are being mentally prepared for something unexplained. There is a fight, and they both escape. Garibaldi keeps one piece of evidence – a Psi Corps badge – but when they return with reinforcements the ships and the buildings are gone.

Observations: The Minbari crew of the *White Star* have obviously learnt English since episode 301 – 'Matters of Honor' – as they share a giggle when Sheridan calls them 'Ladies and gentlemen.'

This is the closest Sheridan has been to Earth in four years.

It *isn't* Morden's voice on the radio when the Shadow ship comes to life, for anyone out there who thinks it is.

The UK's Channel 4 allegedly made some minor cuts to the initial fight scene between Marcus and the people trying to kill Dr Kirkish for the first UK broadcast.

Ships That Pass In The Night: The Earth Alliance Destroyer *Agamemnon* (which first appeared in episode 201 – 'Points of Departure').

Culture Shock: Minbari sleep at an angle, because they believe sleeping horizontally to be tempting death.

Narn write from right to left (but see **Accidents Will Happen** below).

Station Keeping: Earth's solar system is covered by an early-warning system that can detect jumpgates forming.

Literary, Mythological and Historical References: Security Guard No. 1 – the Nightwatch's finest Aryan specimen – tells Zack that 'Eternal vigilance is the price of peace.' This is a misquotation on three counts. Firstly it is usually attributed to American president Thomas Jefferson, although he is never recorded as having said or written it. Secondly, the quotation erroneously attributed to Jefferson is actually 'The price of peace is eternal vigilance.' Thirdly, the real quotation (by an Irish judge named John Philpot Curran in 1790) is: 'The condition upon which God hath given liberty to man is eternal vigilance; which condition if he break, servitude is at once the consequence of his crime, and the punishment of his guilt.'

I've Seen That Face Before: Vaughn Armstrong, who plays Security Guard No. 1, recently appeared in the Harrison Ford movie *Clear and Present Danger* as a drunken helicopter pilot in Colombia.

Accidents Will Happen: When G'Kar is in his cell, writing his book, the long shot shows him holding the pen in his right hand and writing left to right, while the close-up has him holding the pen in his left hand and writing right to left. It looks as if the close-up has been reversed to make his writing look more alien, but it doesn't match the long shot.

In the middle of the *White Star*'s jump to hyperspace there is a single frame showing an alien cityscape from the TV series *Hypernauts*. Many of the creative team behind *Babylon 5* also work on *Hypernauts*, and the CGI effects are built up on the same computers. In this particular case, a software glitch caused a slight problem.

Questions Raised: Why do they still have garden hoses in the twenty-third century? Sheridan's dad still uses one. You would have thought there would be a better means of watering one's garden by then.

'Point of No Return'

Transmission Number: 309
Production Number: 309

Written by: J. Michael Straczynski
Directed by: Jim Johnston

Lady Morella: Majel Barrett   **Ta'Lon:** Marshall Teague
General Smits: Lewis Arquette
Security Guard No. 1: Vaughn Armstrong

Date: 9 April 2260.

Plot: The three-part story gathers steam here, with the humour of the Lady Morella scenes leavening the sense of betrayal we feel when Garibaldi's staff desert him for Nightwatch. The episode cranks up the series tension very neatly.

The 'A' Plot: Following his declaration of martial law, President Clark has dissolved the EarthGov Senate. Some senators are on the run; some have been arrested; some have barricaded themselves in their offices and are refusing to leave. Clark orders his Elite Guard to open fire on the Senate Building. General Hague is trying to organise resistance against Clark – he is on the run in an Earth Alliance ship, and there is an alert out for him across nine systems. The Political Office on Earth assigns all security duties in Earth colonies to the Nightwatch, circumventing Earthforce security entirely. Garibaldi confronts the Nightwatch representatives on Babylon 5, but is relieved of command. Zack Allen is put in charge of Babylon 5 security in his place. Sheridan protests the takeover by Nightwatch to General Smits, but is told in no uncertain terms to 'respect the chain of command'. He realises this is a coded message indicating that the orders for Nightwatch to take over have not been issued by a military authority, but that only military authorities can issue orders to military personnel (of which Nightwatch is primarily formed). Sheridan, Garibaldi, Ivanova and G'Kar 'persuade' Zack to tell the man in charge of Nightwatch on the station that Sheridan is bringing in a shipload of Narn to take over security duties from Nightwatch. Smelling treason, the man in charge arms all his Nightwatch people and assembles them in Bay 8, where he expects the Narn ship to dock. It's a trick: the bay is sealed and Sheridan orders them to lay down their arms, telling them that they are following illegal orders. They disarm and surrender, and Sheridan has them locked up prior to shipping them off station. G'Kar's Narns take on the role of the security force on Babylon 5.

The 'B' Plot: Lady Morella – the late Emperor Turhan's third wife – arrives on Babylon 5 en route to Ragesh 9 for a good-will visit. She is a seer, and Londo has spent months persuading her to come to Babylon 5 so that he can ask her to prophesy the future for him. She prophesies that Londo and Vir will both become Emperor, and that Londo has three chances left to avoid the fire that awaits him.

The 'C' Plot: G'Kar is released from his sentence three weeks early, due to the problems on the station. He tells Ta'Lon that he has had a revelation, and that 'some must be sacrificed so that all may be saved.' He offers the services of the Narn who follow him as replacements for the Nightwatch, but he asks Sheridan to include him in the new and secret alliance which is being formed.

The Arc: Lady Morella tells Londo that he has already wasted two chances to avoid the fire that waits for him at the end of his journey (the same fire Kosh warned the Centauri Emperor about in episode 209 – 'The Coming of Shadows'), and that he has three more. 'You must save the eye that does not see. You must not kill the one who is already dead. And, at the last, you must surrender yourself to your greatest fear, knowing that it will kill you.' His two wasted chances to avoid the fire might have been in episodes 209 (where he deliberately lies about the Emperor's dying words) and 216 (where he ignores the dying wish of his closest friend to stop his actions). 'The eye that does not see' may be a reference to the Eye – the Centauri artefact seen in episode 113 ('Signs and Portents') – although it is worth noting that G'Kar's future self, seen strangling Londo in episode 209 ('The Coming of Shadows'), has only one eye. 'The one who is already dead' might be Captain Sheridan, given the events at the beginning of season four.

Lady Morella sees a flash of a future when an elderly Londo is Emperor of Centauri Prime. Londo has seen this moment too, in episode 209 ('The Coming of Shadows'). She also sees that Vir will be Emperor, and that either Londo or Vir will be dead when the other one succeeds to the throne. We see in episode 317 ('War Without End' Part Two) which way round it will be.

Observations: At one stage, G'Kar says to Garibaldi: 'I might have something for you in a little while, Mr Garibaldi – when the time is right.' That phrase – 'when the time is right' – often crops up in this series.

The part of Lady Morella was written specifically for Majel Barrett.

During the first UK showing of the episode, Channel 4 apparently removed some violence from the fight scene taking place while Sheridan makes his martial-law announcement.

Dialogue to Rewind For: Londo to Lady Morella: 'I believe that I have been touched, that I am meant for something greater – a greater darkness or a greater good I can no longer say.'

Dialogue to Fast Forward Past: General Hague's last message to Captain Sheridan: 'Everything's going to hell, John.' Any time something's going wrong in this series, it's going to hell.

Ships That Pass In The Night: The Earth Alliance ships *Alexander* (commanded by General Hague), *Schwarzkopf* and *Excalibur*. The *Schwarzkopf* previously turned up at Babylon 5 in episode 210 – 'GROPOS'.

Other Worlds: Ragesh 9 is presumably in the same system as Ragesh 3 – the Centauri colony retaken by the Narn in episode 101 ('Midnight on the Firing Line'). We'll be charitable, and assume this is deliberately a second planet and not a blooper.

Culture Shock: Londo's favourite food is spoo (see episode 101 – 'Midnight on the Firing Line' – and 203 – 'The Geometry of Shadows'). Well, he does own shares in a spoo ranch.

Station Keeping: Babylon 5's airlocks are made of a solid beryllium alloy.

I've Seen That Face Before: Majel Barrett, who plays Lady Morella, is the widow of *Star Trek* creator Gene Roddenberry. She has played four major roles in *Star Trek* and its various siblings: the unnamed Number One in the pilot episode 'The Cage' (footage of which was used in the two-part story 'The Menagerie'), the regular character of Nurse Christine Chapel in the original series, the occasional character of Lwaxana Troi in *Star Trek: The Next Generation* and *Star Trek: Deep Space Nine* and the voice of the computer in all incarnations of *Star Trek*.

This is Marshall Teague's third outing as Ta'Lon.

Accidents Will Happen: If we ignore the Ragesh 3/Ragesh 9 ambiguity, nothing.

'Severed Dreams'

Transmission Number: 310
Production Number: 310

Written by: J. Michael Straczynski
Directed by: David Eagle

Major Ed Ryan: Bruce McGill
Captain Sandra Hiroshi: Kim Miyori
David Sheridan: Rance Howard
Bill Trainor: Phil Morris   **Drakhen:** James Parks

Plot: This episode is a perfect example of J. Michael Straczynski's immense screenwriting skill. He balances plot against subplot, makes us think, makes us cry, pulls all the threads together and *still* ensures that the two most powerful moments are those in which characters don't say anything and yet we know exactly what they are thinking.

The 'A' Plot: The Earth Alliance Destroyer *Alexander* – General Hague's flagship for the rebellion against President Clark – arrives at Babylon 5 after a massive space battle. General Hague is dead, and Major Ryan appears to be in charge now. The rebel ship *Churchill*, commanded by Captain Sandra Hiroshi, also appears. Sheridan pulls the plug on all communications with the Earth Alliance except for the ISN newsfeed. Mars declares that it will not implement martial law, and Earthforce attacks it. Orion 7 and Proxima 3 both declare independence from the Earth Alliance in protest. ISN is closed down after reporting this in contravention of Clark's orders. Sheridan, Ivanova, Garibaldi and Franklin unanimously vote to declare independence as well and ally themselves with the rebels. The *Agrippa* and the *Roanoake* both arrive at Babylon 5 with instructions to seize control and place the command staff under arrest. Other ships, including the *Nimrod*, arrive. The battle looks on the verge of being lost when Delenn returns from her trip to the Grey Council with a fleet of Minbari ships. Outgunned and unwilling to start a war, the Earth ships depart.

The 'B' Plot: Delenn visits the Grey Council and forces her way in. She accuses them of having ignored prophecy and her

295

warnings. She walks out and the Grey Council falls apart as the Worker and Religious caste follow her while the Warrior caste remain.

The 'C' Plot: A Minbari Ranger arrives on the station. He has spent some months touring the non-aligned worlds, and has discovered that many of them have been recruited by the Shadows and are declaring war on their neighbours.

The Arc: This episode marks the moment when Babylon 5 becomes an independent state, rather than an extension of Earth. Effectively, much of the series so far has led to the moment of silence when you can see from Sheridan's face that he has made his decision.

Delenn tells the Grey Council that they have ignored prophecy. This prophecy has been referred to before, most notably in episode 201 ('Matters of Honor'). She also reveals that the prophecy foretold the collapse of the Grey Council itself.

Sheridan uses Draal's holographic projector to communicate his intentions to everyone on Babylon 5. He refuses to use Draal in the conflict, because he wants to keep him in reserve.

Observations: During the pre-title sequence, when Major Ryan is eulogising about the captain of the ship he has just destroyed, he says he won't know how to tell their wives. Note the plural form. The wives he is talking about are those of the *Clarkestown*'s captain and of General Hague, who (we later find out) has been killed.

We're told in episode 309 – 'Point of No Return' – that only four ships rebelled along with the *Alexander*, and they have all been destroyed. More must have followed them, including the *Churchill* and the others that Major Ryan refers to.

Babylon 5 loses 30 per cent of its Starfuries – either destroyed or disabled – but it takes on the surviving ships and crew from the *Churchill* (which is destroyed when it rams the *Roanoake*). These new Starfuries are first used in episode 314 – 'Ship of Tears'.

Following his actions in declaring independence, Sheridan refuses to wear his Earthforce uniform.

Actor Jerry Doyle (Garibaldi) broke his arm on set during the filming of the fight with the invading Earthforce personnel.

Dialogue to Rewind For: Sheridan: 'As of this moment, Babylon 5 is seceding from the Earth Alliance. We will remain an independent state until President Clark is removed from office.'

Delenn's warning to the ships loyal to President Clark: 'Only one human captain has ever survived battle with a Minbari fleet. He is behind me: you are in front of me. If you value your lives, be somewhere else.'

Sheridan to Delenn: 'I want you to know that seeing your face at that moment was probably the single finest moment in my life.'

Ships That Pass In The Night: Multiple Earth Alliance Destroyers, including the *Alexander* and the *Churchill* (both rebelling against Earth) and the *Clarkestown*, the *Agrippa*, the *Nimrod* and the *Roanoake* (all supporting President Clark). Alexander the Great was King of Macedonia and conqueror of the Persian Empire in the third century BC. He died in ancient Babylon. Churchill was the British Prime Minister between 1940 and 1945 (the majority of the Second World War), and then again between 1951 and 1955. Marcus Vipsanius Agrippa was a noted Roman general during the reign of Augustus in the first century BC. Nimrod was a great Biblical hunter (Genesis 10: 8–9). Roanoake is the Native American name for the area of North Carolina on which Sir Walter Raleigh founded an ill-fated British colony in 1587.

I've Seen That Face Before: Or rather, I haven't. The character of General William Hague should have arrived on the *Alexander*, but instead we are told that the character is dead. The actor – Robert Foxworth – had a 'scheduling problem' with this episode and the two episodes of *Star Trek: Deep Space Nine* in which he was appearing, and was written out of the script.

Bruce McGill (Major Ryan) previously played the barman who knows more than he's letting on in the final episode of *Quantum Leap*.

Accidents Will Happen: The actor playing Sheridan's father is not the actor who played him in episode 216 – 'Knives'.

Late in the battle, Sheridan attempts to communicate with the *Roanoake*, even though it has already been rammed and destroyed by the *Churchill*.

Questions Raised: How much better can this series get?

How many Minbari ships in a fleet? The answer would appear to be three.

How come Captain Hiroshi defers to Major Ryan when a captain outranks a major?

'Ceremonies of Light and Dark'

Transmission Number: 311
Production Number: 311

Written by: J. Michael Straczynski
Directed by: John Flinn

Lord Refa: William Forward
Boggs: Don Stroud   **Sniper:** Paul Perri
Sparky the Computer: Harlan Ellison
Morden: Ed Wasser   **Lennan:** Kim Strauss

Plot: A lot of American drama series end up doing a siege plot at some stage in their lives, especially the cop shows – and it's unfortunate *Babylon 5* had to do the same. The point about Nightwatch should be that they could be us – we are all capable of being Nazis – but having Nightwatch personnel as amoral as Boggs and as sadistic as Sniper removes the shades of grey and replaces them with a simple good guys/bad guys situation. It's unfortunate.

The 'A' Plot: A small group of Nightwatch personnel hiding on Babylon 5 kidnap Delenn and Lennan, the commander of the Minbari fleet protecting the station. Their intention is to force the Minbari to leave, thus clearing the way for Earthforce ships to take the station. Marcus discovers where the kidnappers are, and Sheridan buys some time by fooling them into thinking he has surrendered. A faked reactor leak forces them out of their hiding place, where

Garibaldi's men take them down. Sniper – a psychotic killer with a pathological hatred of Minbari – throws a knife at Sheridan, but Delenn throws herself in its path and is injured.

The 'B' Plot: (a) Delenn is attempting to remount the rebirth ceremony she tried previously in episode 105 – 'The Parliament of Dreams'. Marcus is terrified of taking part for reasons that he doesn't want to reveal. While Delenn is recuperating in medlab, Sheridan and the rest of the command staff bring a part of the ceremony to her. (b) Lord Refa arrives on the station, and Londo accuses him of fighting wars on so many fronts that the homeworld is left undefended and of conspiring with Morden and his associates. Londo tells Refa he has put poison in Refa's drink, and threatens to activate the poison if Refa does not reduce the number of fronts the Centauri are fighting on and cut his alliance with Morden.

The 'C' Plot: While trying to purge the old passwords from the computer and replace them with new ones, Garibaldi accidentally revives an old artificial-intelligence program with an irritating attitude.

The Arc: Lennier succinctly sums up the story so far when he says, 'Prophecy said one day we would unite with the other half of our soul in a war with the ancient enemy. This we have done.' He's referring to the revelations about Minbari souls transferring to humans as revealed in episode 201 – 'Points of Departure' – and the descriptions of the Shadows given by Delenn in episode 217 – 'In the Shadow of Z'ha'dum'.

The rebirth ceremony involves each of the participants telling someone a secret that they have never told anyone before. Lennier admits to Marcus that he loves Delenn. Sheridan admits to Delenn that he cares for her. Ivanova admits to Delenn that she thinks she loved Talia Winters (referring primarily to episode 219 – 'Divided Loyalties'). Garibaldi admits to Delenn that he has a problem with controlling himself (an ongoing character trait most prevalent in episode 111 – 'Survivors'). Stephen Franklin also admits to Delenn that he has a problem, but doesn't say what it is. He's probably referring to his stimulant addiction (episode

303 – 'A Day in the Strife'). Delenn doesn't admit anything to anyone. Neither does Marcus.

Londo has a recording of Morden admitting he and Refa have been talking (the events shown in the recording come from episode 301 – 'Matters of Honor'). Londo tells Refa that he has severed his own relationship with Morden, as shown in the same episode.

Observations: This episode lies precisely halfway through the planned five-year story arc of *Babylon 5*.

Garibaldi is wearing a sling after the actor who plays him – Jerry Doyle – broke his arm in the previous story.

This is (as far as I can tell) the first story in which we discover that Garibaldi is a Warrant Officer. He calls himself 'Chief Warrant Officer', but (if the current US Navy rank structure is anything to go by) this is a post rather than a rank. The person filling a Chief Warrant Officer post can be a Warrant Officer W-2, W-3 or W-4.

Delenn decides to restage the *nafak'cha* – the rebirth ceremony seen in episode 105 – 'The Parliament of Dreams' (the ceremony lasts all day, and must be held within a certain period of time after the preparations have been made). Part of the ceremony involves everyone telling someone else a secret they have never told anyone (see above). Another part involves everyone giving away something of great value. Sheridan, Garibaldi, Ivanova and Franklin all give away their Earthforce uniforms. Delenn, having somehow anticipated this, gives them replacement uniforms of semi-Minbari design.

Sheridan's security access code is 'Obsidian'; Ivanova's security access code is 'Griffin'; Garibaldi's security access code is 'Peek-A-Boo'. We first discover that Garibaldi's computer access code is 'Peek-A-Boo!' in episode 116 – 'Eyes'.

Three additional 'Sparky the Computer' scenes were filmed but were cut due to time constraints.

The working title for the episode was just 'Ceremonies'.

'I went to Joe early in the second season,' Bill Mumy recalls, 'and suggested that Lennier was deeply in love with

Delenn. Although he would never express that to her, I wanted to play him that way. And he [Joe Straczynski] thought about that, went away for a couple of days, came back and said, 'OK, let's start playing it like that.'

In their infinite wisdom, the UK's Channel 4 cut chunks out of this episode when they first showed it. Marcus's fight in the bar is missing a few seconds, Delenn getting the knife in the back is cut and the scene where Sheridan knocks Sniper around has also been hacked. That's what happens when they show an adult programme at a kids' time.

Koshisms: Kosh is keeping his head well down. Who knows what secrets he might have admitted in the rebirth ceremony.

Dialogue to Rewind for: This episode has more good lines per metre than any other.

Lennier explaining his philosophy to Delenn: 'Opinion does not enter into it. What is, is.'

Delenn's caution to Lennier: 'There is darkness and fire ahead of us. There are no guarantees that any of us will survive it.'

Londo to Refa: 'Is there anyone along our border with whom we are not currently at war?'

Delenn to Londo when she invites him to the rebirth ceremony: 'In the matter of confessions, meditation and the closing of past wounds, Ambassador, you were at the top of my list.'

Marcus being threatening: 'In five minutes I'll be the only person at this table still standing. Five minutes after that I'll be the only person in the *room* still standing.'

Marcus clearing up after his bluff is called: 'Bugger. Now I'll have to wait for someone to wake up.'

Lennier, holding Marcus a few inches above the ground: 'We may sometimes look like you, but we are not you. Never forget that.'

Lennier admitting he loves Delenn: 'I know that Delenn is fated for another, and I have accepted that in my heart.'

The unnamed but psychotic Sniper: 'Always bet on stupidity.'

Sheridan to Delenn: 'I never told you how much I cared

about you – how much you mean to me . . . I can no longer imagine my world without you in it.'

Garibaldi to Delenn: 'No one knows, but I'm afraid all the time of what I might do if I ever let go.'

Ivanova to Delenn: 'I think I loved Talia.'

Franklin to Delenn: 'I think I have a problem . . .'

Literary, Mythological and Historical References: Sniper gets to sing a snatch of the spiritual 'Dry Bones' for no adequately explained reason. Given J. Michael Straczynski's well-documented regard for the 1960s British TV series *The Prisoner*, in whose chaotic last episode this song is sung, we could have counted this as a reference were it not for Straczynski's denials. He has said, 'What happened, actually, was this . . . I'm a big fan of the Red Clay Ramblers, a terrific group that does sort of bluegrass but very offbeat. I was writing that episode, and I was playing with the torture aspect, and had one of their albums on. At just the moment I got to that scene, up came their rendition of "Ezekiel in the Valley of the Dry Bones". The notion was perfect, so I went back to the original version of the song, which is public domain (rather than their variation on it), and used it. Synchronicity.'

I've Seen That Face Before: The series's 'Conceptual Consultant' – respected SF author Harlan Ellison – plays Sparky the Computer.

William Forward returns as Lord Refa.

Don Stroud, who played Boggs, had previously appeared as Caliban in episode 114 – 'TKO'.

Accidents Will Happen: When we see Londo's recording of Morden, the lines spoken by Morden are from conversation in episode 301 – 'Matters of Honor'. Unfortunately, in that episode Morden is sitting down when he says them while in *this* episode the recording has him standing up. Ed Wasser was rehired to film that one line for this story because the staging of the shot in 'Matters of Honor' was unsuitable.

Questions Raised: Lennier leaves the new uniforms in the quarters of Sheridan, Ivanova, Garibaldi and Franklin without their knowing. How did he get in? Isn't this a security breach?

Why don't the captains of the three Minbari ships do anything to rescue their fleet commander or Delenn? We've previously seen Minbari take a very dim view of their people being held captive, but this bunch don't even bother to call Sheridan and ask how things are going. Very odd.

If EarthGov could piggyback a signal on the StellarCom transmission and take control of Babylon 5's computer, why didn't they try it last episode, taking all their weapon systems off line and leaving them defenceless before Clark's ships arrived?

'Sic Transit Vir'

Transmission Number: 312
Production Number: 313

Written by: J. Michael Straczynski
Directed by: Jésus Treviño

Lindisty: Carmen Thomas
Centauri Official: Damien London

Date: 3 July 2260.

Plot: As surreal as they get, with some marvellous moments and numerous chances for Stephen Furst to do his Woody Allen impression as Vir.

The 'A' Plot: Vir's uncle has arranged a marriage for him, and the fortunate lady (a beautiful young Centauri girl named Lindisty) arrives on the station to meet him. The paperwork has already been done, and all that remains are the formalities. Vir is surprised, but is soon taken with her charm and her obvious love for him. A Narn assassin attacks them both, but is killed by Zack Allen. The assumption is that he was after Vir, but it turns out that Lindisty was the target. Her father was an executioner on Narn after the war, and she took an active part in the killings herself. As a result, one of the families that escaped his attentions have declared a *shon-kar* (a Narn blood-oath of vengeance) against her. Another assassin attempts to kill her, but she subdues him. She offers him to Vir to kill, but Vir persuades her to stay her hand.

303

Lindisty returns to Centauri Prime, still caring for Vir, but not understanding his compassion for the Narn.

The 'B' Plot: During his time on Minbar, Vir has been forging transit papers to get Narn from the harsh conditions of the Narn homeworld to the relatively benign environment of Centauri Prime. To do this he has invented a fake Centauri named Abrahamo Lincolni. The Narn are supposed to become slaves when they arrive, but he has also been forging death certificates for them and smuggling them to freedom on other worlds. Londo is appalled when Ivanova tells him, covers the whole thing up and arranges for Vir's recall from Minbar. Ivanova takes over the Abrahamo Lincolni personality, and continues Vir's work.

The 'C' Plot: Sheridan invites Delenn to a tête-à-tête over dinner in his quarters, but his attempts to cook Minbari *flarn* are unsuccessful.

The Arc: Apart from the ongoing Centauri–Narn problems, and the development of the Delenn–Sheridan relationship, this is a relatively quiet episode in arc terms.

Observations: Ivanova has a nightmare in which she walks naked into Command and Control. A nightmare for her, maybe, but a wet dream for many of her fans

The pre-title sequence of this story is probably the most surreal thing ever to occur in the series, with Vir going to his room in the Centauri Emperor's palace and finding it chock-a-block with Narn. Why? What's going on? It's presumably linked to his scheme to smuggle Narn to safety, but is hiding them in the palace really a good idea? Or is it just a nonsensical visual joke?

Londo uses the sword given to him by Urza Jaddo in 'Knives' (episode 216) to kill an insect.

Londo's obsession with the insects infesting his quarters is a thinly disguised cover for his aversion to the spiderlike Shadow craft that he has seen in his dreams.

Londo mentions the alien Vinzini. The name is similar to (but the aliens different from) the Vendrizi who appear in episode 307 – 'Exogenesis'.

This is the second time that Zack Allen has been forced to

gun down a Narn who won't stop when ordered (the first time is episode 212 – 'Acts of Sacrifice'). Is he just unluckier than most?

Nobody in Command and Control is wearing Earthforce uniform. On the other hand, Delenn hasn't had time to run their nice new costumes up yet either, so they're just wearing jumpsuits.

The Narn *shon-kar* blood oath of vengeance is first mentioned in episode 105 – 'The Parliament of Dreams'.

The Minbari version of *flarn* is first mentioned in episode 218 – 'Confessions and Lamentations' – although Antarean *flarn* is mentioned in episode 105 ('The Parliament of Dreams').

Vir mentions in passing that he has recently been hit by G'Kar (episode 306 – 'Dust to Dust') and in the riots (episode 309 – 'Point of No Return').

Londo reveals that the last Centauri Envoy to Minbar also went native – just like Vir. 'Too much exposure to those . . . those damn Minbari can have strange effects,' he says. He previously referred to the last envoy to Minbar in episode 303 – 'A Day in the Strife' – but didn't go into details.

One might ask what happens to the Narn assassin that Lindisty has trussed up in her quarters? Vir refuses to kill him, but we never see him again. Did Lindisty kill him, or did Vir persuade her to let him go? In fact, a line of dialogue was cut from the finished episode in which it was said that the Narn was recovering in medlab.

Dialogue to Rewind For: Londo: 'I do not like insects. I do not like little brown things with eight legs. I do not like *anything* with eight legs . . . well, except for the Vinzini, but only because they are terrible at cards. Something to do with the compound eyes, I think.'

Vir to Lindisty: 'If kisses could kill, that one would have flattened several small towns.'

Culture Shock: Male Centauri have six external genitalia (we saw one of Londo's in episode 121 – 'The Quality of Mercy'). They are graded in terms of intensity. Until meeting Lindisty, Vir never got past number one.

Literary, Mythological and Historical References: Given that the Centauri–Narn conflict parallels in many respects the Nazi–Jewish experience, someone had to do a version of *Schindler's List*. This is it.

Given the possible parallels between Vir's life and that of the Roman Emperor Claudius (as recounted in Robert Graves's *I, Claudius* and *Claudius the God*) in episode 309 – 'Point of No Return' – one might see the same thing operating here. Lindisty's aunt is the Lady Drusella, while Drusilla was a Roman lady close to Claudius. Claudius had an arranged marriage before becoming Emperor, and so does Vir. Suspicious, huh? It's even more suspicious when you realise that Emperor Cartagia is (as we find out in episode 401 – 'The Hour of the Wolf') the spitting image of the Emperor Caligula (Claudius's predecessor).

The title 'Sic Transit Vir' is a Latin phrase that translates as 'thus passes the man' (*vir* being Latin for 'man'). It's an odd title, in that the only thing connected with Vir that dies in this story is his virginity. The phrase itself is derived from '*sic transit gloria mundi*' – 'thus passes the glory of the world' – a form of words spoken during the coronation of a new Pope to signify the transitoriness of earthly glory.

I've Seen That Face Before: Damien London also played a Centauri official – presumably the same one – in episode 121 ('The Quality of Mercy').

Questions Raised: Why did the Narns go after Lindisty rather than her father? Her wedding was arranged by her mother (the Lady Drusella), so one might suspect that her father was already dead, but Vir refers to her parents in the plural.

'A Late Delivery from Avalon'

Transmission Number: 313
Production Number: 312

Written by: J. Michael Straczynski
Directed by: Mike Laurence Vejar

Arthur/David MacIntyre: Michael York
Emmett Farquaha: Michael Kagan
Medlab Tech: James Kiriyama-Lem

Date: It's the fifteenth anniversary of the start of the Earth–Minbari war.

Plot: It's another of those plots where a British icon is used without due care and attention. The symbolic, mythical undertones of Arthur are lost; Michael York gives a one-note performance; and neither of the subsidiary plots is strong enough to save the episode from bathetic banality.

The 'A' Plot: A man claiming to be Arthur, son of Uther Pendragon and King of the Britons, arrives on Babylon 5. He is unsure why he is there, but says that he must be needed. Marcus plays along with him, but Franklin is concerned about his mental health. While 'Arthur' gets involved in a fight in Downbelow and knights G'Kar, Franklin uses his DNA to identify him as David MacIntyre – once gunnery sergeant on board the Earth ship that opened fire on the Minbari, thus starting the Earth–Minbari war. The guilt has obviously driven him into a new personality, so Franklin confronts him with the truth in an effort to cure him. All that happens is that Arthur/MacIntyre retreats into a catatonic fugue. Marcus and Franklin realise that he has arrived on Babylon 5 on the fifteenth anniversary of the day he fired on the Minbari ship in an effort to absolve himself. Playing along with his fantasy, they get Delenn to play the Lady of the Lake and accept Excalibur (symbolic of his guilt) from him. Cured, he leaves Babylon 5 for Narn, where he will help organise the resistance.

The 'B' Plot: Sheridan is worried about the defence of Babylon 5 – he can't rely on the Minbari for ever – so he offers the League of Non-Aligned Worlds a deal. They will be allowed to continue trading there if they contribute to the station's defence. Some agree: others do not.

The 'C' Plot: There's a parcel waiting in the Post Office for Garibaldi containing baloney, mozzarella, anchovies and various other Italian comestibles, but, due to the problems faced by the Post Office in getting the mail to Babylon 5, it'll cost him one hundred credits to get it. Unwilling to pay, he tries to steal it, but is caught. Eventually he pays up, but takes a one-hundred-and-one-credit bribe for not telling anyone that the Post Office should now be paying rental on their offices.

The Arc: It's not an arc story, by any means, but there are three things in it that cast a little more light on the arc.

The first thing is the historical material we discover about the start of the Earth–Minbari war and MacIntyre's presence at the Battle of the Line. This thread has been going since the pilot episode ('The Gathering'), and has been important in two episodes 108 ('And the Sky Full of Stars') and 117 ('Legacies').

The second thing is Marcus's explanation of the symbolism behind the Ranger pin – two figures, one human and one Minbari, representing two halves of the same soul joining together to fight a common enemy (the pin is discussed further in episode 301 – 'Matters of Honor'). The common enemy is, of course, the Shadows. Lennier says much the same thing when he talks about the Minbari prophecy in episode 201 ('Points of Departure'), an episode in which the link between human and Minbari souls is discussed further. This link is explained in episode 318 ('War Without End' Part Two).

The third thing is Marcus's ascribing of characters from Arthurian legend to Babylon 5 personnel. Sheridan, he claims, is Arthur, while Kosh is obviously Merlin. He himself is Lancelot, while Franklin is either Bedevere or Percival. Morden is Mordred, but who, he wonders, is Morgana Le Fay (or, more properly, either Morgana or Morgan Le Fay)? We find out in episode 321 ('Shadow Dancing').

Observations: During the course of this episode, Garibaldi commits attempted armed robbery and blackmail to get what he wants. Does anyone else find this disturbing?

Marcus refers to 'Mr Sebastian' (episode 221 – 'Comes the Inquisitor') and suggests Arthur may indeed be the real Arthur, abducted by the Vorlons and kept in suspended animation as Sebastian was.

Arthur (or, more properly, David MacIntyre) remembers the Battle of the Line, with appropriate flashbacks from episode 108 ('And the Sky Full of Stars').

This episode and the preceding one (312 – 'Sic Transit Vir') were swapped around after filming because something lighter was needed after episode 311 ('Ceremonies of Light and Dark') and because it was felt that an episode with Michael York in would be best shown in the first week of the ratings sweeps.

Ships That Pass In The Night: The Star Liner *Asimov* is the first trade vessel to arrive at Babylon 5 since the split from Earth. The *Asimov* has been there before, of course, in episode 102 ('Soul Hunter') and 110 ('Believers').

The *Prometheus* was the first Earth ship to encounter the Minbari.

David MacIntyre leaves Babylon 5 on board a transport ship that sounds like it's called the *Mukolla*.

Culture Shock: Banta flu is a contagious disease that attacks humans who have eaten alien food which has been mixed in with human food and allowed to 'ferment'.

There is a Brakiri delegation sitting in the League of Non-Aligned Worlds conference room (they don't turn up very often).

Station Keeping: The weapon sensors in the customs area of Babylon 5 are so sensitive they can distinguish a sword from an ordinary piece of metal.

Literary, Mythological and Historical References: Marcus quotes Charles Dickens and the Russian poet and writer Aleksandr Pushkin.

I've Seen That Face Before: Michael York, the British actor who played Arthur/David MacIntyre, is a well-known face in British films of the seventies, although he seemed to vanish from sight during the eighties. His most high-profile role is arguably opposite Liza Minelli in *Cabaret*, although his performances in the more 'mainstream' science fiction films *Logan's Run* and *The Island of Doctor Moreau* have won him acclaim. Oddly, *Logan's Run* was set in 2274 – just fifteen years after this season of *Babylon 5*.

Accidents Will Happen: When Arthur is offered medical help, he tells Franklin, 'I am in no need of a doctor, so take your leeches elsewhere.' Alas, the 'real' Arthur wouldn't have known what a leech was, as they were not indigenous to sixth-century England and, even if David MacIntyre had done enough historical research to know about them, he would have known that as well.

'Ship of Tears'

Transmission Number: 314
Production Number: 314

Written by: J. Michael Straczynski
Directed by: Mike Laurence Vejar

Bester: Walter Koenig   **Carolyn:** Joan McMurtrey
Alison: Diana Morgan

Date: 13 August 2260.

Plot: This episode showcases what J. Michael Straczynski does best – taking a character whom the audience have got used to and turning them enough for us to see their other side. Sometimes it's a dark side, as with Kosh and Sheridan, but sometimes it's a light side, as with G'Kar and (as here) Bester.

The 'A' Plot: Psi Cop Bester arrives on Babylon 5. He tells Sheridan that he wants to fill them in on something, but that if he is given sleepers to suppress his telepathic abilities then he will be unable to help them. Sheridan sends Ivanova in to see him first, as she will be able to detect a telepathic probe. Bester cooperates by not using his telepathic abilities, and tells Sheridan he has become aware that aliens known as Shadows have the ear of President Clark, and that Psi Corps itself has been infiltrated. This worries him – he intends for telepaths to supplant 'mundanes', and for himself to be in charge of them. The machinations of the Shadows are interfering with his long-term plans. He tells Sheridan that a convoy of 'weapons supplies' destined for the Shadows and guarded by their vessels is travelling through hyperspace, and that if the convoy were to be hijacked it would damage the Shadows. The *White Star* intercepts the convoy and destroys or scares off the accompanying Shadow vessels. Taken back to Babylon 5, it is found to contain hundreds of frozen human telepaths with cyberweb implants in their brains. Bester identifies them as 'blips' – telepaths who refused to join Psi Corps or take sleeper drugs. They appear to have been kidnapped from the Psi Corps Re-education Facility on Mars. One of the telepaths is defrosted, and manages to interface with Babylon 5's electrical system before she is sedated. Garibaldi finds a reference in the Book of G'Quan to Narn telepaths helping defeat the Shadows a thousand years ago. It seems that Shadows are afraid of telepaths, and Sheridan theorises that this time around they intend using human telepaths as the central core of their ships in order to counter the threat. Moments after this revelation, news comes in the Shadow vessels are openly attacking Brakiri space.

The 'B' Plot: G'Kar is getting restless. It is some time since Captain Sheridan promised to bring him in on the new alliance, but nothing has happened. Sheridan and Delenn discuss the matter, and Delenn explains the situation with the Shadows to G'Kar. He is unhappy that he was not told earlier that the Centauri had help from the ancient enemy in subjugating the Narn, but he accepts that had the news about the return of the Shadows become widely known then the Shadows would have moved earlier, and the Narn would have been completely wiped out. G'Kar is fully accepted into the War Council.

The 'C' Plot: One of the frozen telepaths is revived, and proves to be Bester's lover. He asks Sheridan to care for her, saying that he will do anything Sheridan wants.

The Arc: The Shadows are terrified of telepaths for some reason – somehow, telepaths can be used as a weapon against them. During the course of the episode, a Shadow mother ship veers wildly away from the *White Star* when it realises

Bester is aboard. A thousand years ago, according to the Book of G'Quan, during the last Great War, the Shadows wiped out all the Narn telepaths they could find. The few surviving Narn telepaths helped G'Quan to defeat the Shadows, but the bloodline was too weak to continue and the Narn telepaths died out (as we discovered as early as the pilot episode – 'The Gathering'). Now, the Shadows are planning to use human telepaths as the central operating system of their vessels – the assumption being that their 'altered' telepaths can somehow counteract the effect of the telepaths they may have to face.

At the end of the episode, the Shadows start openly attacking Brakiri space. What prompted this? Perhaps it was the knowledge that their convoy had been intercepted, and thus their plans were finally exposed.

Observations: Interstellar Network News are back on line, but they're peddling propaganda for President Clark. Their sudden disappearance from the airwaves in episode 310 ('Severed Dreams') is blamed on an attack by saboteurs preparing the way for an alien invasion of Earth.

Bester tells Sheridan that the Shadow convoy is passing through Sector 500. It's in hyperspace, however, implying that there is a direct mapping between points in hyperspace and points in the 'real' universe.

P12 telepaths can locate ships in hyperspace by homing in on the thoughts of their occupants.

We discover in episode 322 ('Z'ha'dum') that the surname of Bester's girlfriend Carolyn is Sanderson.

The alien pilot of the Shadow convoy ship sprays itself with acid rather than be taken alive. This implies that the Shadows don't want their minions to be seen by the enemy.

When one of the Shadow fighters is blown to bits by the *White Star*, the bits wriggle as if they are alive. Which presumably they are.

J. Michael Straczynski has stated that the pilot of the convoy ship was from the same race as the alien surgeons seen in Carolyn's flashback, and that this race is *not* the Streibs seen in episode 211 ('All Alone in the Night').

Jerry Doyle's lines were re-recorded during the War Room scene at the end of the episode to cover some extraneous noise, and because he wandered away from the microphone.

Dialogue to Rewind For: Sheridan to Bester in the *White Star*: 'Try not to drool on the controls.'

Delenn to G'Kar: 'We had the choice between the death of millions and the death of billions.'

Bester, talking to Sheridan about the promise he made to keep his lover safe: 'It's the only promise I ever made that means a damn to me.'

G'kar to Garibaldi: 'Do not thump the Book of G'Quan – it is disrespectful.'

Ships That Pass In The Night: Sheridan starts the episode by checking out the new Starfuries Babylon 5 has inherited from the late, lamented *Churchill*. Unlike previous generations of Starfury, these can operate in a planetary atmosphere (we saw some of them bombing Mars in episode 310 – 'Severed Dreams').

Bester arrives at Babylon 5 in a Black Omega Starfury – part of an elite unit assigned to Psi Corps. The last time we saw Black Omega Starfuries, they were trying to recapture Jason Ironheart in episode 106 ('Mind War').

Station Keeping: We get our first sight of the newly built War Room in this episode.

Other Worlds: According to ISN, Earth has two dozen colonies and deep-range outposts.

Literary, Mythological and Historical References: Bester's first name is Alfred, making explicit the nod towards the science fiction writer Alfred Bester (see episode 106 – 'Mind War'). His first name was revealed to be Alfred in issue 11 of the Babylon 5 comic – 'The Psi Corps and You'.

Bester quotes Edgar Allan Poe's short story 'The Cask of Amontillado' (in which a man is walled up alive by someone who hates him).

I've Seen That Face Before: Walter Koenig returns as Alfred Bester.

Questions Raised: Out of all the telepaths who might have been defrosted, isn't it a huge coincidence that it happens to have been Bester's lover? Still, coincidences do happen – especially in this series.

Was this the first shipment of telepaths to the Shadows, or have there been others?

'Interludes and Examinations'

Transmission Number: 315
Production Number: 315

Written by: J. Michael Straczynski
Directed by: Jésus Treviño

Morden: Ed Wasser   **David Sheridan:** Rance Howard
Dr Lilian Hobbs: Jennifer Balgobin
Brakiri Ambassador: Jonathan Chapman

Date: 23 August 2260.

Plot: There is a palpable sense of the ground shifting beneath our feet in this episode, as *Babylon 5* begins its metamorphosis into season 4. Wow!

The 'A' Plot: It is ten days since the events of the last episode, and the Shadows are attacking openly. Sheridan cannot understand their strategy – they are making hit-and-run attacks on minor powers in the League of Non-Aligned Worlds rather than engaging the major powers. Delenn tells him that this is how they operated during the war a thousand years ago. Sheridan wants to pull the League of Non-Aligned Worlds together into a cohesive fighting force, but some of them want a demonstration that there is some hope of winning. Sheridan asks Kosh to send a Vorlon fleet against the Shadows, just to demonstrate they can be hurt, but Kosh refuses. When Sheridan presses him, Kosh uses force to knock Sheridan to one side. Sheridan refuses to leave, telling Kosh that he will have to kill Sheridan in order to get past him. Kosh reluctantly agrees to do as Sheridan has asked, but warns that there will be a price – he will not be able to help Sheridan on Z'ha'dum. The Vorlon fleet arrives during the next Shadow attack and destroys them utterly. The wavering alien representatives are jubilant, and throw their lot in with Babylon 5. Morden, who is on the station, gets to hear of the Vorlon victory. He breaks into Kosh's quarters, and his Shadow companions engage Kosh in a titanic struggle, during which Kosh projects a mental image of himself as Sheridan's father into Sheridan's mind. Kosh dies and, at the request of the Vorlons, his remains are placed inside his spacecraft, which heads out of Babylon 5 and towards the nearest sun.

The 'B' Plot: Londo is eagerly awaiting the return of his one great love, Adira, to the station. Vir is making the preparations: organising a suite for her, buying underwear, making sure the *jala* is nice and hot and the *bravari* is more than ten years old. Morden accosts Londo in a corridor and accuses him of poisoning Lord Refa's mind against him. Lord Refa has cut all ties with Morden and his associates and the Centauri have pulled back from a number of their border wars. Morden and his associates need the Centauri to continue their campaigns, but Londo refuses to cooperate. So does Vir, when Morden approaches him. Morden discovers that Londo's great love – Adira – is expected on the station, and organises her death. When Londo discovers that she has died by poison he is distraught. Morden implies that Lord Refa has ordered her assassination in retaliation for Londo's poisoning of him. Londo invites Morden to continue their alliance. 'All I want now is revenge,' he says. 'Let the rest of the galaxy burn.'

The 'C' Plot: Dr Franklin is beginning to crack up. He makes a mistake in medlab that would have killed a patient if his medical staff hadn't caught it. Garibaldi tries to help, but is rebuffed. Eventually, shamed by Garibaldi, Franklin runs a blood test on himself and realises that he is addicted to stims. He resigns as Head of Medlab, and goes off to find himself.

The Arc: This story is a major turning point in the arc, what with the long-awaited intervention of the Vorlon fleet against the Shadows, Kosh's subsequent tragic death and Londo's return to the dark side after a long period of vacillation. We find out very little that is new about the arc here, but we can sense the ground beginning to shift beneath our feet. And, of course, we get a hint of what is to come when Kosh tells Sheridan that he won't be there to help on Z'ha'dum.

Observations: This episode takes place two years to the day after episode 113 ('Signs and Portents').

J. Michael Straczynski has said of this episode, ' "Interludes . . ." for me marks a slight transition in the story, from one "shape" to the next up . . . the demarkation between the hero-cycle and the myth-cycle in the arc.'

Adira first appeared in episode 103 ('Born to the Purple').

Londo blackmailed Lord Refa into severing his ties with Morden and pulling back the Centauri forces in episode 311 ('Ceremonies of Light and Dark').

Sheridan's father first appeared in episode 216 ('Knives') and again in episode 310 ('Severed Dreams'), although it is worth reiterating that the figure Sheridan sees in his dream is not his father, but Kosh. Kosh has also appeared as G'Kar's father in episode 306 ('Dust to Dust').

Kosh's comment to Sheridan – 'As long as you're here . . . I'll *always* be here' – echoes his previous statement, 'I have *always* been here,' in episodes 211 ('All Alone in the Night') and 306 ('Dust to Dust').

Kosh's comment to Sheridan – 'You do *not* understand' – is an echo of what he says to Sheridan in episode 213 ('Hunter, Prey').

We see the Shadows again, as in episodes 122 ('Chrysalis') and 217 ('In the Shadow of Z'ha'dum').

Londo has a bad case of flashbacks, first of Adira from episode 103 ('Born to the Purple'), and then of Lord Refa from episode 311 ('Ceremonies of Light and Dark').

The Vorlons knew immediately that Kosh was 'dead'. They ask that everything that was his should be placed in his ship, which then apparently destroys itself and his possessions by plunging towards the nearest star.

Delenn tells Sheridan that Kosh's ship is, in a curious sense, alive.

A scene cut from the transmitted version of the episode for

time reasons had a Ranger following Morden on Babylon 5 and being killed by the Shadows. This may have been the Ranger Garibaldi escorts into medlab when Franklin is having his tantrum.

The background of Brakiri space was taken from an image taken by the Hubble Deep Space Telescope.

Kosh's death was originally intended to happen later in the series. J. Michael Straczynski has said, 'I think, on some level, I was reluctant to do it, because to write this kind of stuff you have to *feel* it yourself, and I think I was avoiding that as much as Kosh was avoiding his fate. I didn't want to go through writing that. So I kept putting it off. I knew it *had* to be done . . . but not yet . . . And that's when, for lack of a better explanation, Kosh stepped up and began to pull me in that direction in the script. It was time. His passing shouldn't be frittered away or minimised: it should happen at the right moment, and this was that moment. I kept trying to dance away in the script, to go back into safer waters . . . but each time was pulled back in this direction, until finally I had to admit that, yes, this was the right time, and the right way, to do this. And Kosh fell.'

Koshisms: Kosh: 'I will not be there to help you when you go to Z'ha'dum.' Sheridan: 'You already said – if I go to Z'ha'dum I will die.' Kosh: 'Yes – now.'

Kosh to Sheridan in the guise of his father: 'I knew what was ahead. I guess . . . I guess I was afraid. When you've lived as long as I have, you kinda get used to it.'

Kosh to Sheridan in the guise of his father: 'As long as you're here, I'll *always* be here.'

Ivanova's Life Lessons: 'When the Vorlon goes to ground, I worry.'

Dialogue to Rewind For: Londo: 'Everyone around me dies, Mr Morden, except the ones that most deserve it.'

Culture Shock: The metal-suited aliens with the insectoid eyes and the proboscis who appeared first in episode 301 – 'Matters of Honor' – are finally given a name. They are called the Gaim in a subtle nod towards writer Neil Gaiman, whose comic character Sandman occasionally wears a helmet that looks very similar.

We finally get a close look at a Brakiri – the race who have been mentioned every so often since episode 111 ('Survivors'). The Brakiri and the Gaim inhabit sectors of space that are very close to each other.

Pak'ma'ra have at least three lungs and two pulmonary systems.

Station Keeping: Everyone who works in medlab and has regular contact with alien races has to have regular blood tests in order to check for infection.

Accidents Will Happen: Medlab has one of those doors that always close after someone has gone through them except when it's dramatically necessary that they don't. In this instance Garibaldi goes into medlab in order to check Franklin's blood tests, and the door remains open for a while so that Franklin can enter without Garibaldi hearing him.

The episode is written as if Franklin has only just realised he is addicted to stims, and yet in episode 311 – 'Ceremonies of Light and Dark' – he admitted to Delenn that he thought he had a problem.

Questions Raised: Adira had already set out for Babylon 5 when Morden found out about her and decided to kill her. Was it just coincidence that he happened to have an agent on her ship who could poison her, or did someone get on board en route? This is further addressed in episode 406 ('Into the Fire').

Why does Morden have to break into Kosh's quarters? Aren't the Shadows able to help?

Where the hell did Dr Lilian Hobbs come from?

'War Without End' Part One

Transmission Number: 316
Production Number: 316

Written by: J. Michael Straczynski
Directed by: Mike Laurence Vejar

Jeffrey Sinclair: Michael O'Hare   **Zathras:** Tim Choate
Rathenn: Time Winters   **Spragg:** Eric Zivot

Date: It's nearly eight days since the Vorlons wiped out the attacking Shadow fleet in episode 315 ('Interludes and Examinations'), making it around 31 August 2260.

Plot: A breathless but immensely plot-heavy episode that moves so fast and ties up so many loose ends that it effectively disguises how dependent it is on coincidence and the right thing happening at the dramatically right time.

The 'A' Plot: On Minbar, Ambassador Jeffrey Sinclair is handed a box which has been sealed in 'the Sanctuary' for over nine hundred years. It contains a letter, addressed to him. After reading its contents, he arranges for a ship to take him to Babylon 5. Meanwhile, a distress call has been received by the station. It's Ivanova's voice saying the station is about to be destroyed, and it's coming from Sector 14 – where Babylon 4 disappeared six years before and appeared briefly two years before. It's also time-stamped eight days in the future. When Ambassador Sinclair arrives on the station, Delenn asks Sheridan, Sinclair, Lennier and Marcus to accompany her to the *White Star*. There she shows them some archive recordings from the last Great War against the Shadows, and explains that during the war, their greatest star base was destroyed, leaving them with no base of operations to fight the Shadows from. A replacement arrived from nowhere – Babylon 4. Without it, they would have lost the war. She also shows them a recording made by the Great Machine on Epsilon 3 when Babylon 4 vanished, six years before. The recording shows Shadow fighters escorting a fusion bomb towards Babylon 4, and the *White Star* attacking them. It would appear that the allies of the Shadows recognised Babylon 4 as the thing that would win the war a thousand years ago, and determined to destroy it before it could be sent back in time. The task facing those people aboard the *White Star* is to stop the allies of the Shadows from destroying Babylon 4 six years ago, move it forward in time to two years ago to allow everyone to evacuate, then move it back a thousand years to act as a base of operations against the Shadows. If they fail then the Shadows might win the war a thousand years ago, or lose it with fewer losses than they actually took, changing history in the future so that Babylon 5 is destroyed by Shadow ships that should have been wiped out a thousand years ago. Zathras – Draal's little helper from Epsilon 3 – arrives in a separate ship and gives them all time stabilisers to stop them being aged to death by the temporal fluctuations around Babylon 4. Together they travel back six years in time and destroy the Shadows' fusion bomb. Unfortunately, the *White Star* is shaken up by the explosion and Sheridan's time stabiliser is damaged. He comes adrift in time. The rest of them attach the *White Star* to Babylon 4, and break into the station. Their mission: to put a beacon near to the centre of the station so that Draal can move it effectively through time.

The 'B' Plot: Sheridan orders Garibaldi to take a Starfury to Sector 14 and investigate what's happening. When Garibaldi gets there he discovers that Sector 14 is in a state of temporal flux caused by a tachyon beam coming directly from Epsilon 3. Garibaldi is ordered back to Babylon 5 by Sheridan, and gets there to discover that Sinclair has been on the station but has left. Shocked, Garibaldi goes to his quarters and discovers that Sinclair has left him a message. On it, Sinclair apologises for not seeing him in person, but explains that, had they met up, Garibaldi would have wanted to go with Sinclair, but that Sinclair wouldn't be coming back.

The 'C' Plot: As a result of his time stabiliser being damaged, Sheridan is flung into the future. He occupies a future version of his body at a time when he is being held prisoner by Emperor Londo Mollari on a Centauri Prime which has been ravaged. Londo sentences him to death.

The Arc: This episode shows us the other side of the events in episode 120 ('Babylon Squared') and gives us a convincing explanation of where the station went and why. It was dragged back one thousand years in time to replace the primary base of operations in the fight against the Shadows, which had been destroyed.

The rodent-like Zathras previously appeared in episode 120 ('Babylon Squared'), but was mentioned in episode 220 ('The Long, Twilight Struggle'). His race seem to be caretakers of a sort, working with Draal.

The Great Machine on Epsilon 3 gets a name check. It was first encountered in episodes 118 and 119 ('A Voice in the Wilderness' Parts One and Two). It has been around for over 500 years (so it wasn't there during the last Shadow war).

Delenn says that the Shadow fighters carrying the bomb to Babylon 4 are crewed by allies of the Shadows – not by the Shadows themselves.

Six years ago, the Shadows were trying to get their fusion bomb next to Babylon 4's fusion reactor to make the explosion look like an accident. They obviously weren't strong enough to make an open attack.

J. Michael Straczynski has said that the sabotage of the first three Babylon stations had nothing at all to do with the Shadows: the sabotage was carried out by other forces opposed to the very notion of the Babylon Project. Babylon 4 was the station that went back in time – that was the only station the Shadows were interested in.

Straczynski has said that Babylon 4 survived the Great War, but was in bad shape. It didn't last very long after that.

Note that it's the *allies* of the Shadows who try to destroy Babylon 4, not the Shadows themselves. At the time Babylon 4 disappeared, the *Icarus* had not yet woken up the Shadows (depending, of course, whether you believe the explanation Delenn gives in episode 217 – 'In the Shadow of Z'ha'dum' – or the one Anna Sheridan gives in episode 322 – 'Z'ha'dum').

When Londo welcomes Sheridan to the future with the words, 'Welcome back from the abyss', he could well be referring to Sheridan's plunge into the abyss on Z'ha'dum in episode 322 ('Z'ha'dum').

Observations: Rathenn, the Minbari who gives the box to Ambassador Sinclair in the opening moments of the episode, first appeared in issue 1 ('In Darkness Find Me') of the *Babylon 5* comic (although he was briefly mentioned in episode 118 – 'A Voice in the Wilderness' Part One). We discovered there that Rathenn was a member of the Grey Council (although he isn't any longer, since Delenn has broken it up). Given his deferential attitude towards Delenn, he is probably a member of the Religious caste.

Both Rathenn and Marcus refer to Sinclair as *Entil'zha*. The Ranger pin is called *isil'zha*, according to Straczynski. Z'ha'dum is where the Shadows live. Note the repeated occurrence of the root syllable *zha*. Interesting . . .

Sinclair has a scar on his face: Straczynski has said that he gained this during Ranger training.

Sinclair and Sheridan have met before, during the Mars riots.

We get to see another of Zathras's race – a being by the name of Spragg.

Rather than go directly to Sector 14 in the *White Star*, Sheridan wants to go and check out Epsilon 3, where the tachyon beam originates. In the original draft of the script, they did, and Draal told them all about Babylon 4 being taken back in time to act as a base during the previous war against the Shadows. Unfortunately, John Schuck was unable to reprise his role as Draal due to work commitments (he was appearing in *Hello Dolly!* on Broadway), and the script had to be rewritten to leave out the Epsilon 3 segment. That's why Delenn comes up with such a clumsy reason why they can't go to Epsilon 3, and why she gets such a massive chunk of expository dialogue in the *White Star* briefing room.

Delenn implies that the Minbari can control time fields, but not highly unstable ones.

We have two flashbacks to scenes from episode 120 ('Babylon Squared').

Garibaldi's attempts to determine the password Sinclair has used to protect his message include 'Peek-A-Boo' – as in episodes 116 ('Eyes') and 311 ('Ceremonies of Light and Dark') – and sock, fasten and zip, all subjects he and Sinclair discussed in episode 120 ('Babylon Squared').

Zathras's one-being ship has rocket motors. *Rocket* motors? Was Draal strapped for cash, or something?

Adam Nimoy was first choice to direct this episode and the next one.

Koshisms: It's said by the 'other' Vorlon about Sinclair, but it's a Koshism by any other definition of the term: 'He is the closed circle. He is returning to the beginning.'

Dialogue to Fast Forward Past: Delenn: 'I wish I had more time, but now time is all we have.'

Garibaldi: 'Eight days from now, we go straight to hell.' Along with all those other things going straight to hell in this series, one presumes.

Other Worlds: We see our first sight on television of Minbar – the homeworld of the Minbari Federation. From what we see of their architecture, it's based heavily on huge crystals. Minbar also has a blue sky. Its capital is called Yedor (we discover this in issue 2 ('Treason') of the *Babylon 5* comic.

Literary, Mythological and Historical References: Londo says to Sheridan at one point: 'What I am doing is what someone should have done a long time ago – putting *you* out of *my* misery.' A very similar line occurs in the James Bond film *Moonraker*, where the villain Drax says to a henchman, 'Put Mr Bond out of my misery.' He also welcomes Sheridan with the words, 'Welcome back from the abyss.' This is, perhaps, a reference to the German philosopher Friedrich Nietzsche, who said, 'And if you gaze for long into an abyss, the abyss gazes also into you.' Previous echoes of this quote occur in episodes 202 ('Revelations') and 306 ('Dust to Dust').

I've Seen That Face Before: Tim Choate reprises his role as Zathras (he previously appeared in episode 120 – 'Babylon Squared').

The voice of the 'new' Vorlon was provided by Ardwright Chamberlain, who also provides the voice for Kosh.

Accidents Will Happen: Garibaldi tells Sheridan that when he was on Babylon 4 he had a flash of the future and saw himself fighting off an attack on Babylon 5. Unfortunately, if you watch episode 120 ('Babylon Squared') it's not Garibaldi who has that flash-forward – it's Sinclair. Now there's nothing to say that Garibaldi didn't have a flash-forward of exactly the same events as Sinclair, but there's no evidence that he did, either.

Considering the amount of space between Babylon 5 and Sector 14, how come Garibaldi's Starfury and the *White Star* manage to pass within a few hundred metres of each other?

There are six Shadow fighters taking the fusion bomb to Babylon 4 – three on escort duty and three actually moving the bomb. One Shadow fighter escort is destroyed by the *White Star*, and the three carrying the bomb are destroyed when it blows up. What happened to the other two fighters? I presume we are meant to assume that the *White Star* destroyed them, but the scenes were dropped for time reasons.

Questions Raised: What exactly is it that hits Sheridan's time stabiliser? Lennier claims in this episode that the shielding on the *White Star* can absorb the energy of any attack, leaving just the physical impact. Well, it isn't just a physical impact that breaks the time stabiliser.

If the Shadows are still asleep on Z'ha'dum, who is piloting the fighters escorting the fusion bomb to Babylon 4?

'War Without End' Part Two

Transmission Number: 317
Production Number: 317

Written by: J. Michael Straczynski
Directed by: Mike Laurence Vejar

Ambassador Sinclair: Michael O'Hare
Zathras: Tim Choate   **Major Krantz:** Kent Broadhurst
B4 First Officer: Bruce Morrow

Plot: The immense amount of plot to get through means there's scant time for any characterisation or nifty dialogue: everything is subservient to moving the series past Sinclair's soul and into new territory. Still, it's exciting to watch.

The 'A' Plot: Ivanova manages to fake a hull breach in order to get the crew of Babylon 4 to evacuate. Sheridan flashes back from the future and goes to help Sinclair fit the beacon to the fusion reactor, but is flung through time again when Major Krantz (Babylon 4's commander) channels more power to the reactor. The power surge pulls the station four years forward through time, causing Sinclair to prematurely age by a number of years – it's because it's his second exposure to the time field, and he'll age more the closer he gets to the time they all came from. A flotilla of seven ships appear from Babylon 5, led by the Sinclair and Garibaldi of two years before. Zathras is captured by Major Krantz's guards, and Delenn manages to stabilise Sheridan during a fleeting appearance by giving him her time stabiliser, so that *she* is now unstuck in time. Delenn appears in front of Major Krantz and the newly arrived Sinclair and Garibaldi, and the captured Zathras gives her a time stabiliser he has repaired. Major Krantz wants to take Zathras with him as they evacuate in Sinclair and Garibaldi's flotilla, but Zathras is caught under a falling beam. They all leave, and Delenn pulls the beam off him. Sinclair tries to warn the departing Garibaldi to watch his back, but Garibaldi's ship is too far away and Garibaldi can't hear him. Once our heroes are back on the *White Star* and the crew of Babylon 4 have been evacuated, the station is moved into its future (Sheridan and Delenn's present) so that the *White Star* can leave. Sinclair reveals he is staying on Babylon 4 and going back in time a thousand years – all the moving in time has prematurely aged him, and if he gets off the station now he will die. Besides, the letter he received back on Minbar was from himself, telling him what was to happen. Reluctantly, his companions leave him and travel back to Babylon 5. Babylon 4, meanwhile, travels back one thousand years in time. While it is doing so, Sinclair enters a chrysalis and emerges as a Minbari. Using the name Valen, he greets the first Minbari to cautiously explore the newly arrived Babylon 4.

The 'B' Plot: Seventeen years in the future, Sheridan is being held captive by Emperor Londo Mollari. He is thrown into a cell, and is joined by the Delenn of that future. She has been interrogated, probably tortured, but she hasn't told 'them' anything. It is obvious from the way she acts towards Sheridan that they are a couple, and she tells him they have a son named David. He tells her that he has been projected into that body from seventeen years before, and she remembers him telling her, long ago, that it had happened. She tells him that they were successful in their fight, but that they paid a terrible price for that success. They are removed from the cell and taken back to Londo. He is drunk, but tells them that only by getting drunk can he escape from his 'keeper' – an alien creature on his neck that controls his actions when he is sober and wants the two of them dead. Usually it is invisible, but when he is drunk it manifests itself as a greyish, tentacled creature with one eye. He tells them that there is a spaceship hidden behind the palace, and that he will let them escape if they promise to help his people. They leave, but in the corridor outside Sheridan is snatched back to his own time. Delenn's last words to him are, 'Do not go to Z'ha'dum!' Meanwhile, in the throne room, G'Kar enters. He is old, and he has lost an eye. Londo knows that his keeper will awake soon and alert the guards, so he asks G'Kar to strangle him before it happens. G'Kar is happy to oblige, but as he does so the keeper wakes up and forces Londo to retaliate. They strangle each other, and the lonely figure of Vir enters the throne room to look down at their bodies . . .

The 'C' Plot: Delenn flashes an unknown distance into the future, into her body in a Babylon 5 bedroom. Sheridan is asleep in the bed, Delenn is watching him. The door suddenly opens and a woman's voice says, 'Hello?'

The Arc: Sinclair's warning to Garibaldi to watch his back is a reference to the events of episode 122 ('Chrysalis'), where Garibaldi gets shot in the back by his aide.

The story arc concerning the missing twenty-four hours of Sinclair's life is finally tied up in this episode. The arc started in the pilot episode ('The Gathering') and was hinted at in various first-season episodes before it was explained in episode 201 ('Points of Departure') that the Minbari believed Sinclair to have a Minbari soul. In this episode we find out *why* he has a Minbari soul, and why Minbari souls are being reborn in human bodies. It's because, a thousand years ago, Sinclair became a Minbari. That is when the connection between the Minbari and the human race began, and this, presumably, is where it ends now that Sinclair has gone back in time.

Observations: Zathras is 110 years old, but is that human years or Zathras years? He is the oldest living caretaker of the Great Machine on Epsilon 3.

Marcus says that Sinclair always told him that a half-truth is the worst kind of lie. This is obviously some kind of Minbari saying, as Delenn quotes it in episode 318 ('A Voice in the Wilderness' Part One). Of course, Delenn tells Sheridan half-truths all the time.

Michael O'Hare's voice-over at the beginning of the episode, 'Previously on *Babylon 5 . . .*' was taken from episode 319 ('A Voice in the Wilderness' Part Two).

Ivanova's Life Lessons: 'Doesn't anything come under warranty any more?'

Dialogue to Rewind For: Delenn to Sheridan: 'I look in your eyes now and I see the innocence that went away so many years ago.'

Londo to G'Kar: 'We have unfinished business between us, G'Kar. Let us make an end of it.'

Dialogue to Fast Forward Past: Major Krantz, trying to be macho: 'We can't afford a brownout if we've got hostiles aboard.'

The entire discussion between Marcus and Ivanova about Valen is a clumsy set-up for the revelation at the end of the episode. There's no reason for them to talk about it otherwise.

I've Seen That Face Before: Bruce Morrow, who plays the Babylon 4 No. 2, is a New York disc jockey.

Accidents Will Happen: When Major Krantz's guards see Delenn appear in Sheridan's spacesuit, they say, 'Major – it's back.' However, as far as we know, they've never seen 'it' before.

The spacesuit(s) worn by Sinclair, Sheridan and Delenn at various times during the episode was/were not the same spacesuit as was in episode 120 ('Babylon Squared'). That costume was not available for filming, and had to be recreated from scratch.

In episode 120 ('Babylon Squared'), Major Krantz tells Sinclair that Zathras appeared out of nowhere in a conference room. Constraints on the running time of the script meant that J. Michael Straczynski couldn't get the right characters in the right place for that to happen, and so in this episode Zathras was discovered elsewhere.

At the end of episode 120 ('Babylon Squared'), an aged Sinclair is talking to someone whom we assume to be Delenn by her voice. All we see of her is her arm as she reaches out and touches his sleeve. She is wearing a red costume. In this episode we see the same scene, but Delenn is wearing a different colour of costume and she doesn't reach out to touch Sinclair's sleeve. 'We couldn't match the clothing properly,' Straczynski has said, 'so we dispensed with it.'

Questions Raised: How come Sheridan kept reappearing in the corner of the Babylon 4 corridor, even though he disappeared from the *White Star*? Why did Zathras know Sheridan was going to reappear there the second time after he'd seen him appear the first time? Why did Delenn get into Sheridan's spacesuit when he reappeared?

'Walkabout'

Transmission Number: 318
Production Number: 318

Written by: J. Michael Straczynski
Directed by: Kevin G. Cremin

Lyta Alexander: Patricia Tallman   **Cailyn:** Erica Gimpel
Dr Lilian Hobbs: Jennifer Balgobin   **Na'Kal:** Robin Sachs
Minbari Captain: Michael McKenzie

Plot: This episode polarises views more strongly than most. The 'A' Plot is fine – classic *Babylon 5*, if such a thing exists – but acceptance of the 'B' plot depends strongly on whether one likes the idea of *Babylon 5* as a musical.

The 'A' Plot: Sheridan wants to test out the theory that

telepaths can be used as a weapon against the Shadows. To do this he recruits the only telepath available – Lyta Alexander. They take the *White Star* and hang around in hyperspace near to where previous attacks had taken place, waiting for the next Shadow attack. They are accompanied by a Minbari ship with three Minbari telepaths, held in reserve in case Lyta isn't strong enough. They had hoped to have the Narn Heavy Cruiser *Ja'Dok* with them as well but her Captain – Na'Kal – refused to expose it to danger. When the Shadows attack in their target area, they emerge from hyperspace. Lyta, spurred by the sudden realisation that the Shadows killed Kosh, holds the Shadow ship at bay while the *White Star*'s weapons destroy it, but the stress takes its toll, and she is too weak to fight the four Shadow ships that arrive in response to a distress call sent by the destroyed ship. Back on Babylon 5, Garibaldi gets annoyed at G'Kar's apparent reluctance to exert his authority, and insists that G'Kar gets the League of Non-Aligned Worlds and the Narn Heavy Cruiser *Ja'Dok* to support the *White Star*'s attack on the Shadows. The Minbari ship emerges from hyperspace, but the three Minbari telepaths can hold only three of the four Shadow ships at bay. All looks lost until the *Ja'Dok* arrives along with a fleet of other ships from the League of Non-Aligned Worlds. Defeated, the Shadows retreat.

The 'B' Plot: Franklin has gone walkabout in order to find himself – he has left his quarters and is travelling in a straight line through Babylon 5, hoping to rediscover who he is when he isn't a doctor. Garibaldi, worried about him, intercepts him and tries to persuade him to come back, but Franklin keeps on walking. In a bar he meets Cailyn, a singer with whom he spends the night. He suspects, from what she says, that Cailyn is a metazine addict. While he is asleep she steals his credit chip and buys a fresh supply of the drug. She collapses before she can take any of it, and Franklin gets her to medlab. Dr Hobbs tells him that Cailyn is suffering from terminal neuroparalysis, and that she will probably not live for more than six or seven months. When he talks to Cailyn, she tells him that the metazine is the only way to stop the pain. He gives instructions that the medlab staff are to give her whatever she needs, and he keeps on walking.

The 'C' Plot: The new Vorlon Ambassador – Kosh – arrives at the station and is concerned about the previous Kosh's death. He obviously suspects that some part of Kosh is still alive inside someone else, but cannot discover who it is. Lyta Alexander tells him that she wasn't present when Kosh died, and she doesn't know who was. When Sheridan speaks to her in Kosh's voice, Lyta begins to suspect that he may be a receptacle for some part of the Vorlon. She tells the new Ambassador that someone on the station retains a part of Kosh, but she doesn't tell him who.

The Arc: Lyta Alexander indicates that there was a closer relationship between her and Kosh than people thought when she tells Dr Hobbs, 'I am his . . . I was his aide.' She later tells the new ambassador (whom, for the sake of convenience, we will call Kosh), 'He wasn't with me when I left – not even a piece of him.'

Lyta Alexander gives an interesting description of the Vorlons when she tells Sheridan, 'Despite their strength, the Vorlons are a delicate people. They do not react well to change, and they're not very forgiving of mistakes. It's been a long time since one of them has died.'

The new Kosh sees an impression of a human figure and two Shadows on the walls of the old Kosh's quarters. It seems as if he is seeing a residual impression of Morden and his 'associates', burned into the fabric of the station by the violence of Kosh's death.

The realisation by our heroes that telepaths can be used as a weapon against the Shadows came in episode 314 ('Ship of Tears').

It appears as if it takes one telepath to hold one Shadow ship at bay while weapons are brought to bear, and that a P5 telepath is the minimum requirement.

Observations: Only around ten Narn ships escaped the Centauri attacks and the takeover of their homeworld.

There is a brief flashback in this episode to Morden watching Kosh die in episode 315 ('Interludes and Examinations').

Cailyn was originally diagnosed as having terminal neuro-logical paralysis by Dr Kyle – the head of medlab in the pilot episode ('The Gathering').

The Shadows are attacking a Drazi ship when the *White Star* emerges from hyperspace.

Ivanova refers to the two previous occasions upon which they have destroyed Shadow ships – episodes 301 ('Matters of Honor') and 308 ('Messages From Earth').

For the first time in the series, the end title music has been replaced with something else – in this case, a middle-of-the-road torch song.

The Narn Captain Na'Kal first appeared in episode 222 ('The Fall of Night').

It's ironic that Franklin's walkabout leads him directly back to medlab. Is life trying to tell him something?

This episode was originally intended to have been shown before 'War Without End' Part One. However, this would have meant the separation of the two parts by a block of repeats in the US.

Koshisms: The new ambassador tells Sheridan: 'We are all Kosh.'

Dialogue to Rewind For: Garibaldi: 'Why is everything around here a long story? Why isn't anything ever a short story – a paragraph?'

Lyta's stark description of what the Shadows did to Kosh: 'They killed him – they tore him apart.'

Dialogue to Fast Forward Past: Cailyn to Franklin: 'I saw you watching me up there, and it was like two lasers shining out in the night.'

Cailyn to Franklin: 'Singing's the only thing that's ever meant a damn to me. It lets me know I'm alive.' Compare this to Bester's 'It's the only promise I ever made that means a damn to me,' in episode 314 ('Ship of Tears').

Ships That Pass In The Night: The Narn Heavy Cruiser *Ja'Dok* returns to Babylon 5. It last appeared in episode 222 ('The Fall of Night').

Literary, Mythological and Historical References: The confrontation between Garibaldi and G'Kar over the rights of a leader parallels in some respects William Shakespeare's *The Life of King Henry the Fifth* Act IV, Scene 1.

I've Seen That Face Before: Erica Gimpel, who plays Cailyn, may be best known in the UK for her performance as Coco Hernandez in the 1984 TV series *Fame*. More recently, she has appeared in the 1994 film *Smoke*.

Accidents Will Happen: During his pre-title-sequence spacewalk, Sheridan's spacesuit is hanging limp and baggy. The pressure of the air inside should be ballooning it out against the vacuum.

In the pilot episode ('The Gathering'), it takes Kosh's ship two hours to decelerate after leaving the jumpgate. In this episode, it takes a ship of the same type only a few minutes to decelerate.

The implication from the pre-title sequence – where the Vorlon ship diverts its course to take a look at Sheridan – is that it recognises that some portion of him is Vorlon. It flashes a message in the Vorlon language across the side of the ship so he can see it. And yet later, when the new ambassador is talking to Lyta, he doesn't know that Sheridan has some part of Kosh inside him. Did the ship not tell him? Or did the message on its side just say, 'Which way to the docking bay, mate?'

There's a mismatched pair of shots when Cailyn and Franklin are in bed together. When we're looking over her shoulder at Franklin, she's holding a tumbler up by her face. When we're looking over his shoulder at her, she's holding the tumbler down by her side.

Cailyn really shouldn't have said that her songs could make people laugh. It's the equivalent of a wooden actor saying, 'We must act, quickly.'

Perhaps the most obvious mistake in the entirety of the series: Patricia Tallman's name is misspelt on the opening credits (she's listed as Patrica Tallman).

Questions Raised: What does that Vorlon message say?

'Grey 17 Is Missing'

Transmission Number: 319
Production Number: 319

Written by: J. Michael Straczynski
Directed by: John Flinn

Neroon: John Vickery   **Jeremiah:** Robert Englund
Rathenn: Time Winters

Plot: And so it begins . . . this episode betrays a complete failure in funding, imagination and time. Words don't exist to describe how much of a betrayal this story is: the 'A' plot would have looked bad as an episode of *Battlestar Galactica*, and the zarg wanders on in a cloud of dry ice like a reject from *The Outer Limits*. *Babylon 5* should be above this sort of thing, it really should. There, rant over and done with. We now return you to the rest of the book.

The 'A' Plot: A maintenance worker disappears in Grey Sector. Investigating, Garibaldi discovers that an entire level of Grey Sector has been sealed off and the signs for the levels above changed to disguise its absence. He forces an elevator to stop 'between' levels, and discovers the missing Grey 17, but is tranquillised by a dart fired from a ventriloquist's dummy. When he wakes up, he discovers that Grey 17 is occupied by a group of humans who believe, as the Minbari do, that the universe itself is conscious in a way humans can never truly understand. It is engaged in a search for meaning, so it breaks itself apart, investing its own consciousness in every form of life. Life forms are the universe trying to understand itself. These philosophical investigators have sealed themselves away from everyone else so that they might better understand the universe, and thus become perfect. The ultimate perfection for them is to be killed by the zarg – a perfect predator that stalks Grey 17 and prevents anyone from leaving. Garibaldi realises that the zarg killed the maintenance worker, and so he kills it using a steam pipe and the bullets from an old revolver he was playing with earlier on. He leaves Grey 17 and . . . er . . . that's it.

The 'B' Plot: Delenn is chosen as the new Ranger One, and

is to be invested in a ceremony on Babylon 5. She is warned by Neroon – her replacement on the now broken Grey Council and a high-ranking member of the Warrior caste – that she is amassing too much power. There are some who believe that she intends using that power to take over Minbar, or worse. Neroon tells her he will kill her if she takes the title of Ranger One – a title that by custom should go to a member of the Warrior caste. Delenn tells Lennier about this and makes him promise he will not tell Sheridan. Instead he tells Marcus, who challenges Neroon to ritual combat. The two are well matched, but Neroon defeats Marcus and is about to kill him when he realises that Marcus and the other Rangers would willingly die for Delenn but would not be prepared to die for him were he Ranger One. With his beliefs challenged he spares Marcus's life and agrees to Delenn's new title.

The 'C' Plot: Sheridan is recruiting telepaths for the war against the Shadows, but can't find enough. Remembering Dr Franklin's underground railroad for escaping telepaths, he asks Ivanova to investigate it. She finds Franklin in a seedy bar, going through the withdrawal symptoms of stim addiction. He tells her where his computer files are located, but only after she promises that nobody will come after him again.

The Arc: Delenn is made Ranger One, and Babylon 5 is made the new home of the Rangers.

There were Rangers during the last Great War, a thousand years ago. Presumably, Valen set them up.

Sheridan is signing up all the telepaths he can find in the war against the Shadows, and investigates the possibility of using those telepaths whom Franklin helped to safety with his underground telepath railroad.

Observations: The box of Sinclair's possessions we see contains a photograph, his Earth Alliance insignia, a Ranger pin and the medal he was awarded for being at the Battle of the Line (we saw this medal originally in the pilot episode – 'The Gathering').

Garibaldi makes a reference to Grey Sector as being like the Centauri Triangle (an analogue, one presumes, of the Bermuda Triangle). Why doesn't he refer to the well-known

'Babylon Triangle', as Grey Sector was called in episode 216 ('Knives').

Delenn's mother has joined the Sisters of Valeria – a religious group. Her father died ten years ago.

The people in Grey 17 share a view of the universe that is followed by the Minbari. Delenn describes this philosophy in episode 304 ('Passing Through Gethsemane').

During his first conversation with Delenn, Neroon accuses the Religious caste of building warships – a task the Warrior caste should be undertaking. The line refers to the fleet of *White Star*-class ships which we see in episode 320 ('And The Rock Cried Out, No Hiding Place').

The zarg costume looks remarkably like the Ikarran costume used in episode 104 ('Infection') with a new head and hands.

For the first UK showing, Channel 4 cut a few seconds during the Marcus/Neroon fight scene in which Neroon deliberately breaks Marcus's ribs.

Dialogue to Rewind For: Lennier to Delenn when she refuses to believe that Neroon will kill her: 'He said he would use any and all means necessary. I respectfully suggest that he intends to go far beyond harsh language.'

Garibaldi to the maintenance supervisor, when she says that her worker must have disappeared into thin air: 'Thin air – why is it always thin air? Never fat air, chubby air, mostly-fit-but-could-stand-to-lose-a-few-pounds air?'

Marcus to Neroon: 'The next time you want a revelation, could you possibly find a way that isn't quite so uncomfortable?'

Culture Shock: The Minbari *den'sha* is a fight to the death. Remember, of course, that no Minbari has killed another Minbari for a thousand years.

Station Keeping: Grey Sector is supposed to have thirty levels, but one of them has been sealed up by its occupants and the signs on the rest of the levels changed to hide the fact.

Literary, Mythological and Historical References: The Book of Jeremiah is one of the books of the Old Testament, and the name Jeremiah is sometimes used to refer to a doleful prophet. The Book of Jeremiah is only two books ahead of the Book of Ezekiel in the Bible, and Ezekiel was the name of the person Jeremiah sent for when Garibaldi faked his stomach cramps. I suspect that none of it actually means anything, but you might as well know it anyway.

The sheer pointlessness of Garibaldi getting shot by a gun in the eye of a ventriloquist's dummy shows up all the more how similar it is to a scene in the James Bond movie *Live and Let Die*.

Anton Chekhov, writing about the structure of drama, once said, 'If you hang a gun on the wall in the first act, by the third act you must use it.' The fact that the bullets from Garibaldi's gun, as seen in the opening moments of the episode, turn out to be the only way to kill the zarg at the end is a suspiciously perfect example of this quotation.

I've Seen That Face Before: John Vickery recreates his role as Shai Alyt Neroon, the Minbari warrior we saw in episodes 117 ('Legacies') and 211 ('All Alone in the Night').

Time Winters reprises his role as Rathenn (we first encountered the character in issue one of the *Babylon 5* comic – 'In Darkness Find Me' – and then again in episode 316 – 'War Without End' Part I).

Robert Englund, who plays Jeremiah, may be better known as that seminal (and I use the word advisedly) horror icon Freddie Kruger in the Wes Craven film *A Nightmare on Elm Street* and its sequels and spin-offs. He also appeared in the TV movies and series *V* as a decent alien.

Accidents Will Happen: The inhabitants of Grey 17 must have cleared up after the disappeared maintenance worker, to the extent of putting all the loose wires back and putting the lid back on the hole he was working in. How did they get past the zarg to do this? Or did the zarg do it himself?

The zarg. Oh dear. And those bullets would have just exploded in the pipe. Even if, by some chance, they hadn't, the one closest to the steam (i.e. the one at the back) would have fired first, causing an explosion anyway.

Questions Raised: If the inhabitants of Grey 17 wanted to seal themselves away from the rest of the station so that they might better understand the universe, why go to the trouble of sealing off an entire level of the station – something that was bound to be noticed eventually? Why not just . . . leave?

Did the inhabitants of Grey 17 look like philosophers and seekers after truth to you? Or did they just look like thugs?

How *did* Garibaldi get out when everything had been sealed?

How did the people in Grey 17 smuggle a zarg onto the station?

Why did the people in Grey 17 go to the trouble of firing tranquilliser darts into Garibaldi through the eye of a ventriloquist's dummy? Who *was* the voice of the dummy, and why did they bother? Why not just kill him?

What does Garibaldi do about the people in Grey 17?

Why does the most dangerous predator in the universe move sooooo slowly?

Why does the most dangerous predator in the universe scream so that its prey knows it's coming?

Why do the Minbari have a special name for a formal fight to the death if no Minbari has killed another Minbari for a thousand years?

'And The Rock Cried Out, No Hiding Place'

Transmission Number: 320
Production Number: 320

Written by: J. Michael Straczynski
Directed by: David Eagle

Rabbi Leo Myers: Erick Avari
Reverend Will Dexter: Mel Winkler
Brother Theo: Louis Turenne
Lord Refa: William Forward
Minister Virini: Francois Giroday
Drigo: Paul Keith   **G'Dan:** Wayne Alexander

Date: 7–10 December 2260.

Plot: There's a distinct feeling in this episode of the writer rummaging around in his toolbox and discovering a style he hadn't used in the series before. The rather surreal ending, with Refa being chased in slow motion while a gospel song is being sung on the soundtrack, is reminiscent of the last episode of *The Prisoner* without actually having anything in common with it.

The 'A' Plot: Centauri Minister Virini is paying a visit to Babylon 5, accompanied by Lord Refa. Refa is trying to poison Virini's mind against Londo, and Londo is doing the same to Refa. Both of their Houses are vying for power back on Centauri Prime. Londo tells Vir that he has conceived a plot to rid himself of G'Kar and impress the Emperor: he will lure G'Kar to the Narn homeworld with news of Na'Toth's survival, and capture him there. Vir will take a false message to G'Kar telling him that Na'Toth is being held captive beneath the former Kha'Ri building. When he gets the message, G'Kar persuades Garibaldi to smuggle him to Narn. Vir, meanwhile, is kidnapped by Lord Refa and forced by a Centauri telepath to reveal what Londo is plotting. Londo rescues Vir and reveals that the entire thing has been set up for Refa's benefit, and G'Kar is in on it. On the Narn homeworld, Refa's troops intercept G'Kar and his people as they enter the Kha'Ri building through secret tunnels. Alas, Refa's men are in the pay of Londo, and they leave Refa alone with the Narn. G'Kar shows Refa a message from Londo, in which Londo tells him how much he wants Refa dead in revenge for the death of Adira Tyree and Prime Minister Malachi. He shows G'Kar documents proving Refa was responsible for the mass bombing of the Narn homeworld with asteroids, and that he set up death camps for the survivors in which five or six million Narn died. As further incentive, Londo has already arranged for the release of 2,000 Narn and for the release of another 2,000 when Refa is dead. He points out that he could have killed Refa anywhere, but he wanted to destroy Refa's House and all opposition to House Mollari as well. Documents will be planted on Refa's body proving that he was collaborating with the Narn resistance.

The 'B' Plot: While Sheridan is worrying about the seemingly random nature of recent Shadow attacks, a group of religious leaders from Earth is visiting the station. They are also connected to the resistance movement against President Clark, and have been collecting messages – open and covert – for the station. One of the religious leaders – the Baptist preacher Reverend Will Dexter – suggests that Sheridan share his thoughts and worries with Delenn, who loves him. Sheridan rejects the suggestion that Delenn loves him, but does talk to her about the Shadow attacks. Together they determine that the Shadows are herding refugee groups into a particular sector of space, ready to wipe them out in one catastrophic attack.

The 'C' Plot: Delenn takes Sheridan out in the *White Star* and shows him their latest weapon against the Shadows – an entire fleet of ships of the *White Star* class, crewed by Rangers.

The Arc: Pretty much a holding episode, this one, but we do discover that the Shadows are planning a major act of psychological warfare by leaving a safe sector to attract refugee groups and then attacking that sector, causing massive loss of life and general dismay. Sheridan makes a Freudian slip when he tells Delenn that it's what he would do – if, of course, he were the enemy. Given the dark side we've seen him display in episodes 217 ('In the Shadow of Z'ha'dum') and, to a certain extent, in 319 ('Walkabout'), this is further evidence of his military pragmatism as compared with Delenn's idealism.

In episode 309 ('Point of No Return'), the Centauri seer Lady Morella gives Londo a prophetic vision of his future. He has three chances to avoid the fire that awaits him, she says. One of these chances is that he must not kill the one who is already dead. Lord Refa is, in a sense, already dead, as Londo has him poisoned in episode 311 ('Ceremonies of Light and Dark'), and yet Londo has him killed in this episode. Is this one chance gone already?

Observations: The events of this episode take place over four days (we go through captions 'Z minus 14 days', 'Z minus 13 days' and, right at the end of the episode, 'Z minus 10 days'). This takes us from 7 December to 10 December.

Londo makes reference to Vir's exploits in saving Narn lives (episode 312 – 'Sic Transit Vir').

G'Kar makes reference to the Rangers smuggling messages from the Narn homeworld to Babylon 5 (episode 221 – 'Comes the Inquisitor').

Londo tells Lord Refa that he is having him killed in revenge for his having had Adira Tyree (episode 315 – 'Interludes and Examinations') and Prime Minister Malachi (episode 209 – 'The Coming of Shadows') killed. Refa, of course, is blameless over Adira's death – she was poisoned on the instructions of Morden.

We discover in this episode that the name of the Centauri Prime Minister (as seen in episode 209 – 'The Coming of Shadows') is Malachi.

The fleet of *White Star*-class ships has been built by the Minbari Religious caste. Neroon referred to this in the previous episode (319 – 'Grey 17 is Missing').

After the precedent set by episode 318 ('Walkabout'), the end title music has been replaced with something else – in this case, the gospel/spiritual song that gives the episode its title. That song, by the way, takes its theme from the Bible, specifically Revelation 6: 15–17: 'And the kings of the earth, and the great men, and the rich men, and the chief captains, and the mighty men, and every bondsman, and every free man, hid themselves in the dens and in the rocks of the mountains; and said to the mountains and rocks, Fall on us, and hide us from the face of him that sitteth on the throne, and from the wrath of the Lamb: For the great day of his wrath is come; and who shall be able to stand?'

Ships That Pass In The Night: Well, the fleet of ships that Sheridan just inherited.

Other Worlds: We get our first close-up sight of the Narn homeworld in this episode – a bleak, dry, red, dusty planet (although what it looked like before the Centauri attack is anyone's guess).

I've Seen That Face Before: William Forward returns as Lord Refa, of course, and Louis Turenne makes a welcome reappearance as Brother Theo.

The man playing G'Kar's Narn contact on the Narn homeworld – G'Dan – is Wayne Alexander. He also played Jack the Ripper in episode 221 ('Comes the Inquisitor').

Accidents Will Happen: When he and Delenn are in the War Room, plotting out the sites of the Shadow attacks, Sheridan tells an operator to 'Move the tactical display inward'. Alas, it stays where it is, but he reacts as if it *had* zoomed inward. You just can't get the staff these days . . .

When G'Kar is playing Londo's message to Lord Refa in the catacombs beneath the Kha'Ri building, he's holding the projector in his hand. At times his hand moves around quite alarmingly, and yet Londo's image moves only when Londo deliberately walks around.

'Shadow Dancing'

Transmission Number: 321
Production Number: 321

Written by: J. Michael Straczynski
Directed by: Kim Freidman

Barbara Cooper: Shirley Prestia
James Cooper: Doug Cox
Anna Sheridan: Melissa Gilbert
Brakiri Ambassador: Jonathan Chapman
Drazi Ambassador: Mark Hendrickson

Date: 15–18 December 2260.

Plot: This is the best end-of-season episode the series has had so far – tense, exciting, edge-of-the-seat stuff. What a pity there's still one more episode to go.

The 'A' Plot: Sheridan and Delenn suspect that the Shadows are planning to massacre the refugees massing in

Sector 83, and plan to attack them as they arrive. To this end Delenn pleads with the League of Non-Aligned Worlds for all the ships they can spare, while Sheridan arranges for Ivanova and Marcus to take the *White Star* and act as scouts, warning the fleet that's assembling in hyperspace the moment the Shadow ships arrive. Once there, Ivanova and Marcus are discovered by a Shadow scout ship that turns tail and runs. They jam its transmissions, but it manages to disable the *White Star* just as the Shadow fleet arrives. Marcus and Ivanova send a transmission to Sheridan's fleet in hyperspace. The fleet arrives, and during the mother of all battles many Shadow ships are destroyed, although Sheridan's fleet loses two ships for every Shadow ship destroyed. Eventually the Shadows withdraw. Back on Babylon 5, the War Council wonder why the station has been left unscathed. They don't have to wait long: a Shadow ship dispatches Anna – Sheridan's wife – to the station to see him.

The 'B' Plot: Franklin is still on walkabout in the Downbelow area of Babylon 5. Trying to break up a fight, he is stabbed and left to die by his attackers and the drug dealer whose life he was trying to save. After losing a lot of blood he starts to hallucinate – and has a conversation with himself in which he is forced to confront the fact that he has run away from all the difficult decisions and confrontations in his life. Provoked by his hallucinatory alter ego, he realises that he wants to live, and so drags himself to the nearest concourse and calls for help. Security guards find him and get him to medlab, where his life is saved.

The 'C' Plot: Delenn tells Sheridan that she will spend the night with him if they survive the battle with the Shadows. It is a Minbari custom that, when two people become close, the female spends three nights watching over the male to see what he looks like when he is asleep and relaxed. After the battle she stays in his quarters while he sleeps, but they're interrupted by a visitor – Sheridan's supposedly dead wife, Anna.

The Arc: The Shadow War hots up, with the biggest engagement to date and a major victory for what we assume are the good guys, unassisted by the Vorlons.

Sheridan's wife, Anna, appears at the end of the episode, and the implication is that she is working for, or with, the Shadows. We first heard in episode 202 ('Revelations') that she was presumed dead after her ship blew up while on an archaeological expedition to alien ruins on a distant planet: we were later told in episode 217 ('In the Shadow of Z'ha'dum') that she and her co-workers accidentally woke an evil alien race known as the Shadows, and that one of the crew – Morden – was still alive. The revelation that Sheridan's wife was also still alive and apparently working for the Shadows was hardly unexpected.

We finally get at least a partial explanation for Sheridan's hallucinatory (and probably Kosh-inspired) dream in episode 211 ('All Alone in the Night'). He dreamt of Ivanova asking him if he knew who she was – symbolic, he now realises, of her later admission that she was a latent telepath. He also dreamt of himself in Psi Corps uniform – symbolic of his now working with Bester. The unexplained elements of the dream are (a) Garibaldi telling him that the man in between was searching for him, and (b) Ivanova dressed for a funeral telling him that he is 'the hand'. Delenn points out that he has two hands, equal and opposite, and Sheridan begins to wonder whether he has an opposite number on the Shadow side – the man in between.

Observations: The events of this episode take place over four days (we go through captions 'Z minus 6 days', 'Z minus 4 days' and, right at the end of the episode, 'Z minus 2 days'). This takes us from 15 December to the midnight of 18 December, based on the date given for the previous episode.

The refugees have been arriving in Sector 83 for around two months, and the number of new arrivals is beginning to tail off. The Shadows first started attacking openly on 13 August 2260 (episode 314 – 'Ship of Tears'). It's now after 7 December 2260, implying that the refugee traffic didn't get moving for two months or so.

Franklin mentions his father being a soldier (as in episode 210 – 'GROPOS').

Sheridan gives Ivanova and Marcus an ancient Egyptian

blessing before they leave. It's the same one he gives to Zeta Wing before they go looking for the *Cortez* in episode 204 ('A Distant Star').

The guest stars listed at the beginning of the episode are a bit odd. Melissa Gilbert is listed only as Anna in order to preserve the surprise that she's playing Sheridan's wife. Shirley Prestia is listed only as Barbara, even though the character's full name is Barbara Cooper. This is presumably so that Melissa Gilbert's credit as Anna doesn't look odd, but the real question is: why does Shirley Prestia get a credit at all? She's in the episode for a minute or so, and plays no part in the events. All her character does is pull her daughter away from Franklin in Downbelow. Is she listed for contractual reasons, or because they wanted a name alongside Melissa Gilbert to make her importance less obvious?

Ships That Pass In The Night: Sheridan and Delenn are aboard a Minbari ship that sounds like the *Dragato*. Another Minbari Cruiser is called the *Emfeeli*. We also see a Shadow scout for the first time, and what may be a Shadow shuttle (it's the one that takes Anna Sheridan to Babylon 5).

Culture Shock: It is a Minbari custom that, when two people become close, the female spends three nights watching over the male to see what he looks like when he is asleep and relaxed, when all his masks are down and his real face is revealed. This begs the question, do Minbari males get to see the real faces of their brides-to-be, or is it a Minbari assumption that females don't hide their true faces?

Minbari have a type of blood described as 'R negative'.

I've Seen That Face Before: Melissa Gilbert, who plays Anna Sheridan, is actually Bruce Boxleitner's wife. She spent a long time working on the American TV series *Little House on the Prairie* and its various TV movie sequels.

Accidents Will Happen: The actress playing Sheridan's wife, Anna, is not the actress who played her in episode 202 ('Revelations').

Questions Raised: Who is the man in between?

'Z'ha'dum'

Transmission Number: 322
Production Number: 322

Written by: J. Michael Straczynski
Directed by: Adam Nimoy

Justin: Jeff Corey **Morden:** Ed Wasser
Anna Sheridan: Melissa Gilbert

Date: 19 December until around 25 December 2260.

Plot: This episode is a huge con trick. By the time it ends we think we know a lot more about the Shadows and the background to the Great War, but in fact we know nothing that we didn't know before the episode started. It has to be said, however, that we get one better than a cliffhanger ending – we get Sheridan flinging himself off a cliff.

The 'A' Plot: Sheridan's wife, Anna, has turned up unexpectedly on Babylon 5. She does not deny that she is working with the Shadows, but implies that Sheridan has been misinformed about their intentions. She extends an invitation to him – if he goes to Z'ha'dum, she will tell him what the Great War is *really* all about. She does tell him that the rest of the crew of the *Icarus* were killed in an accident, and that the Shadows have technology that can help humanity leap ahead by tens of thousands of years. Dr Franklin's tests indicate that she is fully human, except that there is some scarring on the back of her neck. Franklin later determines that some form of implant has been removed from her brainstem, similar to the implants the Shadows use to interface humans with their organic vessels. He tells Sheridan, who realises he is being lured into a trap. He leaves the station with Anna and heads toward Z'ha'dum in the *White Star*, but what Anna doesn't know is that he has two high-yield nuclear weapons with him, loaded by Garibaldi. On Z'ha'dum, Sheridan is introduced to the apparently human Justin, who tells him that the Vorlons and the Shadows are both trying to help lesser races develop, but that they have different methods. The Vorlons prefer to use rules and prohibitions to help races improve themselves, whereas the Shadows believe that only by conflict do races become stronger. Justin claims that the Vorlons allied some of the lesser races against them and defeated them a thousand years ago. Justin extends an invitation to Sheridan to join them – he is a nexus, and whatever decision he makes will influence others. They can't kill him (they say) because if he dies then someone else will take his place – they know this through bitter experience. Sheridan reveals his knowledge that Anna was part of a Shadow ship and tells Justin that the real Anna is dead – the one that currently exists has a different personality. Justin admits that Anna didn't agree with what they were doing, and was used as the core of a Shadow ship. When they realised who she was they pulled her out again, but her personality had died. Sheridan rejects the offer. When a Shadow creature enters the room, Sheridan shoots at it with a concealed weapon. He escapes the resulting mêlée and makes it to a balcony overlooking a long drop into the bowels of the planet. He communicates with the *White Star*, arms the nuclear devices and gets the ship to plunge towards his position. Confronted by Anna and a whole group of Shadows, Sheridan is advised by the spirit of Kosh to jump into the chasm. He does so just before the *White Star* hits the surface and explodes, wiping out the Shadow city.

The 'B' Plot: After Sheridan leaves Babylon 5, Shadow ships emerge from hyperspace and surround the station. Ivanova scrambles all Starfuries and gets them to hold position between the station and the Shadow ships – which are not attacking. Garibaldi goes out with the Starfuries. After Sheridan's act of supreme sacrifice on Z'ha'dum, the Shadow ships all withdraw, re-enter hyperspace again without opening fire. One Starfury is missing, however – Garibaldi's.

The 'C' Plot: (a) G'Kar has managed to get hold of several nuclear weapons with an estimated power of 500 to 600 megatons. The intention is to use them as mines against the Shadow ships, but Captain Sheridan steals two of them for use in a direct assault on the Shadows' home planet, Z'ha'dum. (b) Londo has been given the post of adviser to Emperor Cartagia, but he realises that the promotion is a means of reining him in. An 'associate' of Morden warns him to leave the station in a hurry.

The Arc: Anna tells Sheridan that, when the Shadow ship was discovered on Mars in 2253 (as we discovered in issues 5 to 8 of the *Babylon 5* comic series, 'Shadows Past and Present' and episode 308 – 'Messages From Earth') EarthGov placed a homing beacon on board. Dr Chang's trip to Z'ha'dum on the *Icarus* was partly to follow the signal from the beacon and discover what was on the planet. This doesn't agree with Delenn's story in episode 217 ('In the Shadow of Z'ha'dum') where she tells Sheridan that the crew of the *Icarus woke* the Shadows on Z'ha'dum. In Anna's story, the Shadows were already awake when they arrived (otherwise who was flying the second Shadow ship?).

Justin's take on the Great War is not that different from Delenn's in episode 217 ('In the Shadow of Z'ha'dum). He tells Sheridan that the Vorlons and the Shadows are both older races who developed millions of years ago, alongside other races who have since moved elsewhere. The Shadows and the Vorlons are, he says, both trying to help lesser races develop, but using different methods. The Vorlons are prescriptive (as we saw in episode 109 – 'Deathwalker'), preferring to guide races from behind the scenes and forbid them from doing things that are too dangerous. Justin also claims that the Vorlons have been manipulating races on the genetic level, programming in a sympathetic and submissive response to the general Vorlon form (as we saw in episode 222 – 'The Fall of Night') and also creating telepaths as a weapon against the Shadows themselves. By contrast the Shadows believe that only by conflict do races become stronger. The Shadows prefer to pit races against one another to ensure that the survivors are more powerful, and every so often they will 'kick over all the anthills' to force the lesser races to evolve and develop. Justin claims that the Vorlons, angered with the Shadows' attitude, allied some of the lesser races against them and defeated them a thousand years ago. There's no indication that Justin is lying, and there's no indication that Delenn is lying either. The only point of contention is the one raised in the previous paragraph: Delenn claims that the crew of the *Icarus* woke the Shadows, whereas Anna claims that the Shadows were already awake when they arrived.

Observations: The episode contains flashbacks to episode 202 ('Revelations'), 217 ('In the Shadow of Z'ha'dum') and 317 ('War Without End' Part Two). Well, it would if the excerpt from episode 202 ('Revelations') hadn't been reshot especially for this episode with Melissa Gilbert instead of Beth Toussaint playing Anna Sheridan. J. Michael Straczynski has said that he may replace the footage of Beth Toussaint in episode 202 with a specially filmed insert of Melissa Gilbert for future transmissions.

We discover in this episode that the surname of Bester's lover Carolyn (from episode 314 – 'Ship of Tears') is Sanderson.

Interplanetary Expeditions, who organised the scientific expedition to Z'ha'dum, have been mentioned before, in episodes 104 ('Infection') and 215 ('And Now For A Word').

Koshisms: 'If you go to Z'ha'dum, you will die.'

'Jump – jump now!' (probably the most unambiguous thing Kosh has ever said).

Dialogue to Rewind For: G'Kar's voiceover at the end of the episode: 'It was the end of the Earth year 2260. The war had come to a pause, suddenly and unexpectedly. All around us it was as if the universe were holding its breath, waiting.

'All of life can be broken down into moments of transition and moments of revelation. This had the feeling of both. G'Quan wrote: "There is a darkness greater than the one we fight. It is the darkness of the soul that has lost its way. The war we fight is not against powers and principalities: it is against chaos and despair. Greater than the death of flesh is the death of hope, the death of dreams. Against this peril we can never surrender."

'The future is all around us, waiting in moments of transition to be born in moments of revelation. No one knows the shape of that future, or where it will take us. We know only that it is always born in pain.'

Dialogue to Fast Forward Past: Justin: 'Who decides that the work day is from nine to five rather than eleven to four? Who decides that the hem lines will be below the knee this year and short again next year? Who draws up the borders, controls the currency, handles all the decisions that happen transparently around us? . . . I'm with them – same group, different department.' (The answer to Justin's rhetorical question, by the way, is Sheridan – or people like him. What is Justin trying to say?)

Other Worlds: Z'ha'dum – for the first time that's not a black-and-white flashback. It's a red, old and scoured world whose inhabitants have all moved underground (for security reasons) but still manage to have huge glass domes linking them to the planet's surface.

Literary, Mythological and Historical References: 'Humans have a saying – "what's past is prologue",' Delenn says. She's quoting Shakespeare's last play, *The Tempest* (the play in which a character speaks of 'certain fathoms in the earth', a concept familiar to Captain Sheridan, one feels).

Justin's claims about the Shadows' motives echo theories of (amongst others) Carl Jung (see the essay on the connections between Jung and *Babylon 5* earlier in this book).

I've Seen That Face Before: Jeff Corey, the actor cast as Justin, is an old familiar face in American 'B' movies, especially Westerns. Your best chance of seeing him is as the sheriff in the 1969 *Butch Cassidy and the Sundance Kid* and also in its 1979 'prequel' *Butch and Sundance: The Early Days*.

Questions Raised: Why does Sheridan accept that Anna can't explain everything to him on the station? Why does Anna try such a clichéd old trick and expect it to work?

When the Shadow ships appear around Babylon 5, Ivanova says that she can't communicate with Draal because the Shadows are jamming them. Is Draal asleep? Has he popped down to the shops for a pint of milk? Is he not actually aware of what's happening? He's claimed before that he's been watching and listening to what goes on. Perhaps he's just sulking.

Who is Justin? Is he the man in between?

Season 4:
'No Retreat, No Surrender'

'It was the year of fire; the year of destruction; the year we took back what was ours.

'It was the year of rebirth; the year of great sadness; the year of pain and a year of joy.

'It was a new age; it was the end of history; it was the year everything changed.

'The year is 2261; the place – Babylon 5.'

> – Lennier, Zack Allen, G'Kar, Lyta
> Alexander, Vir Cotto, Marcus Cole,
> Ambassador Delenn, Londo Mollari,
> Dr Stephen Franklin, Commander Susan
> Ivanova, Security Chief Michael Garibaldi,
> Captain John Sheridan.

Regular and Semi-Regular Cast:

Captain John Sheridan: Bruce Boxleitner
Commander Susan Ivanova: Claudia Christian
Security Chief Michael Garibaldi: Jerry Doyle
Ambassador Delenn: Mira Furlan
Londo Mollari: Peter Jurasik   **G'Kar:** Andreas Katsulas
Dr Stephen Franklin: Richard Biggs
Vir Cotto: Stephen Furst   **Lennier:** Bill Mumy
Marcus Cole: Jason Carter   **Zack Allen:** Jeff Conaway
Lyta Alexander: Patricia Tallman

Observations: In order to avoid the problem of having to choose a particular character to read the opening narration – and thus admit by default that they survive long enough to have some kind of historical perspective on events – J. Michael Straczynski had originally toyed with the idea of changing the narrator every few episodes. In the end, he chose to have everyone narrate a part of a line, thus having what must be the first opening of a TV series to be narrated by twelve separate actors.

The title sequence and title music were changed again for season four, reflecting a more upbeat, triumphant feel for the series.

Cast changes were fairly restrained, this time around. As was expected, Andrea Thompson did not return as the telepath Talia Winters. In her place, Patricia Tallman returns as Lyta Alexander, and gets promoted into the title sequence.

In an unexpected turn of events, Foundation Imaging lost the contract to provide computer-generated special effects for the series. Rumours abound as to why that happened, and the true story is unlikely ever to be made public, but the replacement effects provided by Ultimate Effects are indistinguishable from their predecessors'.

The umbrella title for season four was not released until J. Michael Straczynski started work on the last six episodes of the season, because it wasn't until then that he knew whether the arc would have to be compressed into four seasons or Warner Brothers would allow it to extend to its full length of five seasons. That decision would influence which of two titles was given to the season.

'The Hour of the Wolf'

Transmission Number: 401
Production Number: 401

Written by: J. Michael Straczynski
Directed by: David S. Eagle

Morden: Ed Wasser
Emperor Cartagia: Wortham Krimmer
Centauri Minister: Damien London
Lorien: Wayne Alexander
Drazi Ambassador: Mark Hendrickson
Brakiri Ambassador: Rick Ryan

Plot: Intense isn't a strong enough word. Nothing actually happens in this episode, but it's still immensely watchable.

And by this time we would all sit entranced while Andreas Katsulas read out the Los Angeles telephone directory.

The 'A' Plot: It's seven days since Sheridan's disappearance, and the League of Non-Aligned Worlds are pulling back the majority of their ships from Babylon 5, either because they think the war is over or because they want to protect their homeworlds. Ivanova is walking around in a daze, unable to sleep. Delenn demands that Ambassador Kosh help them look for evidence of what happened to Captain Sheridan, but Kosh refuses. Lyta Alexander, discomfited by Kosh's refusal, offers her own help. If the *White Star* can take her to Z'ha'dum, she might be able to detect whether Sheridan is alive. A trip is quickly arranged, and the *White Star* drops out of hyperspace near Z'ha'dum. While Lennier sends messages on all frequencies calling for Sheridan to respond, Lyta Alexander attempts to shield them from the Shadows while simultaneously attempting to 'feel' Sheridan's presence. Both attempts fail and the Shadows detect their presence. Their minds are affected by the Shadows' powers, but Lennier has programmed the *White Star*'s computer to return them to hyperspace if he appears to be affected by anything, and when it does so the spell is broken. Back on Babylon 5, Ivanova accepts that Sheridan is dead, and starts planning to continue where he left off.

The 'B' Plot: Londo returns to Centauri Prime to take up his post as Adviser on Planetary Security. He discovers pretty quickly that the Emperor is barking mad, and has allowed the Shadows to use a small island on Centauri Prime as a base of operations. As a badly radiation-scarred Morden tells him, 'The incident at Z'ha'dum has forced us to look for outside support sooner than we had intended.' Londo confides his worries to a Centauri minister, but the minister warns him to keep quite about the Emperor's mental state. It is rumoured that Cartagia has secretly beheaded those people who have criticised his actions, and talks to their heads. Londo calls Vir on Babylon 5 and tells him to return to Centauri Prime as soon as possible, where they will conspire against the Emperor together.

The 'C' Plot: (a) G'Kar decides to go in search of the

vanished Mr Garibaldi. (b) On Z'ha'dum, Sheridan is eking out an existence when he meets a mysterious alien named Lorien.

The Arc: The Great War has paused for a while. The Shadows are regrouping and reconsidering their tactics after what is effectively their capital city has been destroyed by Captain Sheridan and two large atomic bombs (not to mention a medium-sized spacecraft).

Londo's dream of multiple Shadow ships crossing the sky of Centauri Prime comes appallingly true in this episode. He first had the dream in episode 209 ('The Coming of Shadows') and remembered it again in episode 301 ('Matters of Honor'). It had been speculated then by some fans that the Shadows invaded Centauri Prime at some stage in the future. Not many people had expected them to have appeared by invitation.

We learn in this episode that the Shadows wish to set up a base on Centauri Prime, on the small island of Selene. It was back in episode 301 ('Matters of Honor') that G'Kar said, 'They came to our world over a thousand of your years ago – long before we went to the stars ourselves. They set up a base on one of our southern continents. They took little interest in us. G'Quan believed they were engaged in a war far outside our own world.' History repeats itself – Emperor Cartagia is well aware that the Shadows spread their ships around 'like seeds' a thousand years before.

It becomes clear in this episode that Lyta Alexander is able to carry Vorlons around inside her mind, allowing them to reach places and observe things without themselves being observed. We first suspected this in episode 304 ('Passing Through Gethsemane'). The experience is more draining and more painful with the new Kosh, to the point where she asks him whether everything is OK. His answer – 'Yes' – could be construed as being said in a tone of voice indicating that he has a much darker motivation than the original Kosh.

When the occupants of the *White Star* are broadcasting to Sheridan on Z'ha'dum, they are spotted by the Shadows. An image of a Shadow head with glowing eyes forms against the star field – as it does in episode 305 ('Voices of Authority'). The Shadows appear to be able to influence human minds, as their minions do in issues 5 to 8 of the *Babylon 5* comic (the four-part comic series 'Shadows Past and Present'). The Shadows also talk to Ivanova and Delenn in the voices of their fathers, a trick Kosh uses on G'Kar in episode 306 ('Dust to Dust') and on Sheridan in episode 315 ('Interludes and Examinations').

At the end of the episode, Ivanova says she will need help to continue with Sheridan's work, and says she knows where to go to get it. She's referring either to Draal on Epsilon 3 or to the First Ones near Sigma 957.

Observations: It's supposed to be seven days since Sheridan vanished off to Z'ha'dum, which would make it 27 December 2260, but the opening narration tells us that the year is 2261.

The Hour of the Wolf is, allegedly, the hour between three and four in the morning when all worries are magnified and 'all you can hear is the sound of your own heart'.

Lorien is not named during the episode, but his name appears in the credits.

Koshisms: On Sheridan: 'He has opened an unexpected door. We do now what must be done now. His purpose has been fulfilled.'

'No one returns from Z'ha'dum' (but he's lying, and Delenn knows he is).

'Respect is irrelevant.'

Dialogue to Rewind For: Lennier: 'Initiating "Getting the hell out of here" manoeuvre.'

Londo to Vir: 'I need a friend, Vir, and I need a patriot, and you are both.'

Ships That Pass In The Night: The *White Star* again, despite its having been destroyed in episode 322 ('Z'ha'dum'). We'll be charitable, and assume they just renamed one of the fleet they built.

Literary, Mythological and Historical References: There is a distinct parallel with Robert Graves's books *I, Claudius* and *Claudius the God* (or with Graves's historical source – the Roman historian Suetonius) in *Babylon 5*. Claudius was a tongue-tied youth whom everyone looked down on but who was destined to become Emperor of Rome, while Vir is a tongue-tied youth whom everyone looked down on but who is destined to become Emperor of the Centauri republic. Caligula was a lunatic youth who became Emperor before Claudius and whose behaviour became so increasingly insane that he had to be assassinated, whereas Cartagia is a lunatic youth who has become Emperor before Vir, and whose behaviour is becoming so increasingly insane that he will have to be assassinated. And that leaves the obvious question – what role is Londo fulfilling?

I've Seen That Face Before: Wayne Alexander, the actor playing the stately Lorien, previously appeared as Sebastian in episode 221 ('Comes the Inquisitor') and as the Narn G'Dan in episode 320 ('And the Rock Cried Out, No Hiding Place').

Damien London turns in another performance of barely suppressed hysteria as the Centauri Minister. He previously appeared in episodes 121 ('The Quality of Mercy') and 312 ('Sic Transit Vir').

Accidents Will Happen: During the 'Previously, on *Babylon 5* . . .' section before the episode opens, we see again the shot of Sheridan throwing himself into the abyss from episode 322 ('Z'ha'dum'). It appears he says 'Goodbye' as he jumps, whereas in episode 322, he doesn't. What has happened is that the audio track from an earlier shot, of Sheridan's farewell message to Delenn, has been allowed to run on over his jumping. Clumsy, but understandable.

Questions Raised: Why do the Shadows sometimes choose inhabited planets and sometimes uninhabited planets upon which to base their ships? Sometimes the planets are uninhabited (Mars and Io are examples) but sometimes there is an indigenous race (as in the case of the Narn homeworld and Centauri Prime). Do they sometimes need new recruits for their ships?'

'Whatever Happened to Mr Garibaldi?'

Transmission Number: 402
Production Number: 402

Written by: J. Michael Straczynski
Directed by: Kevin James Dobson

Lorien: Wayne Alexander
Isaac: Lenny Citrano **Harry:** Anthony DeLongis
Emperor Cartagia: Wortham Krimmer
Centauri Minister: Damien London
Centauri: Rick Scarry

Date: The episode starts on 3 January 2261.

Plot: This episode moves slowly but unstoppably, like an avalanche. Quite breathtaking.

  The 'A' Plot: G'Kar is following the trail of Mr Garibaldi, and has discovered that what appears to be a fragment of his Starfury has been sold by a scrap dealer on a storm-racked planet. He questions the dealer in a seedy bar to discover how he came by the fragment, but provokes a fight instead. He is rescued by Marcus Cole, who has followed him to the planet. They leave the bar in a hurry, but the owner reports G'Kar's presence to a Centauri friend of his. Marcus forces the scrap dealer to admit that he was told about the derelict Starfury by a contact in Interplanetary Expeditions named Montaigne. While Marcus returns to Babylon 5 to trace Montaigne, G'Kar prepares to leave for the area of space in which the Starfury was found drifting. He is kidnapped by the Centauri instead and shipped as a captive to Centauri Prime, where the Emperor gives him to Londo Mollari as a gift. Londo offers G'Kar a deal: he will save him from death – if not actually from torture – if G'Kar will help him kill the Emperor. G'Kar agrees, on one condition – that Londo arrange for Centauri forces to be withdrawn from the Narn homeworld.

  The 'B' Plot: Captain Sheridan is still on Z'ha'dum with the enigmatic Lorien, but is beginning to realise that something is wrong. He hasn't eaten for nine days but he isn't hungry; he's been walking in a straight line but he's ended up back where he started; and, most puzzling of all, he doesn't appear to have a pulse. Lorien tells Sheridan that he is trapped between life and death, and needs to let go of life if he is to escape. If he has something to live for, he will survive. Lorien also admits that he is, effectively, the first of the First Ones – the oldest being in the entire galaxy. Sheridan, trusting him, relinquishes his grip on life and relives his fall into the chasm . . .

The 'C' Plot: (a) Delenn has not eaten anything since Sheridan disappeared, but Franklin persuades her to set aside her grief by showing her an extract from Sheridan's diary in which he admits how much he loves her. Revitalised, Delenn calls the Rangers together and tells them that they are to mount a last-ditch attack on Z'ha'dum. (b) Mr Garibaldi is being held in a cell by unknown captors. They keep asking him what he remembers about the ship that captured him, and he keeps replying that he doesn't remember. He starts smashing the cell up, and they tranquillise him. A man in an opaque face mask and wearing a Psi Corps badge enters the cell and stares down at Mr Garibaldi's body.

The Arc: Sheridan dreams of being held in the grip of a glowing, hazy creature of light, who asks him, 'Who are you? What do you want?' The creature, he later discovers, is a representation of Lorien – the first of the First Ones. It's interesting to note that 'Who are you?' is the question Sebastian was so set on having answered in episode 221 ('Comes the Inquisitor') whilst 'What do you want?' is the question Morden was asking in episode 112 ('Signs and Portents').

Lorien disapproves of the conflict going on in the galaxy at large – 'It is a terrible thing when your children fight,' he says.

'I must watch,' Londo says to G'Kar, 'and you must endure, until the time is right.' It's that phrase again – 'when the time is right'.

Observations: Delenn tells Franklin that she once said to Sheridan she would see him again, 'where no shadows fall'. She did this in episode 218 ('Confessions and Lamentations').

This is the first episode of *Babylon 5* (except for the pilot episode) in which Ivanova does not appear. A scene filmed for this episode with her asking Delenn if she can borrow a *White Star* ship was moved to the next episode.

Interplanetary Expeditions have been mentioned before, in episodes 104 ('Infection'), 215 ('And Now For a Word') and 322 ('Z'ha'dum').

Sheridan's log entry is dated 14 May 2260. This would put it somewhere between episode 311 ('Ceremonies of Light and Dark') and 312 ('Sic Transit Vir').

The scene with Delenn reaching out to touch the screen with Sheridan's image on it is a parallel with the scene in episode 202 ('Revelations') in which Sheridan reaches out to touch a screen with Anna's image on it.

There are flashbacks in this episode to episodes 321 ('Shadow Dancing') and 322 ('Z'ha'dum').

Dialogue to Rewind For: Lorien to Sheridan: 'You are quite, quite dead.'

G'Kar to Marcus: 'I've never had a friend before who wasn't a Narn.' Marcus to G'Kar: 'I've never had a friend before who *was* a Narn.'

Sheridan to Lorien: 'You're one of the First Ones!' Lorien to Sheridan: 'No, not *one* of the First Ones . . . I *am* the First One.'

Lorien to Sheridan: 'Do you know you have a Vorlon inside you?'

Other Worlds: Zathran 7.

Culture Shock: Minbari can fast for up to fourteen days, and do so as part of their grieving ritual.

I've Seen That Face Before: Wayne Alexander returns as Lorien, and Damien London returns as the wonderful Minister.

Accidents Will Happen: At the beginning of the episode, Stephen Franklin says that it's been fourteen days since Captain Sheridan was presumed killed at Z'ha'dum and nine days since Mr Garibaldi disappeared while on patrol. This is a script mistake: Garibaldi disappeared on the same day

Sheridan is supposed to have died. The script should have said it has been fourteen days since Captain Sheridan left for Z'ha'dum.

I may be seeing things, but there is a long shot of a ship entering the Babylon 5 docking bay in which the ship appears to vanish before it gets in.

Questions Raised: Whatever happened to Mr Garibaldi?

'The Summoning'

Transmission Number: 403
Production Number: 403

Written by: J. Michael Straczynski
Directed by: John McPherson

Emperor Cartagia: Wortham Krimmer
Lorien: Wayne Alexander
Ambassador Lethke: Jonathan Chapman
Verano: Eric Zivot

Date: 17 January 2261.

Plot: A great deal happens in this episode – to the point where there are three 'B' plots and nothing as trivial as a 'C' plot – and it's all deeply affecting. This season just keeps hitting you in the gut.

The 'A' Plot: It is Delenn's intention to amass a fleet to attack Z'ha'dum, but the Vorlons refuse to help her. When Lyta Alexander tries to find out their plans, the new Kosh lets her have access to his mind, and the sheer shock renders her powerless. Many of the League of Non-Aligned Worlds aren't happy about Delenn's plans, and they hold an open rally to protest her actions. The rally looks set to degenerate into a brawl when Captain Sheridan appears, having returned to Babylon 5 on board a mysterious spacecraft with Lorien. His presence galvanises the crowd, and he manages to swing them behind Delenn's plan.

The 'B' Plot: (a) Ivanova and Marcus set out in one of the *White Star* ships to search for the First Ones. The intention is to find some more First Ones, apart from those at Sigma 957. What they find instead is a Vorlon fleet hidden in hyperspace – thousands of ships, including some three or four miles across. The fleet is attacking Shadow bases, eliminating entire planets which have any contact with the Shadows, irrespective of how many innocent inhabitants might also be on the planets in question. (b) Zack Allen has got a lead on the whereabouts of Mr Garibaldi: the man who salvaged Garibaldi's Starfury has filed a flight plan for his freighter, and Zack intends going after him and questioning him. He leads a mixed fleet of shuttles and Starfuries to intercept the freighter, but when they suggest it prepare for boarding, it ejects a lifepod and blows itself up. The lifepod contains Mr Garibaldi, but there are indications (unnoticed by his rescuers) that he may be under some form of control. He is taken back to Babylon 5, where he claims not to remember what happened to him. It seems clear that he is lying. (c) Emperor Cartagia is torturing G'Kar, but is annoyed at the fact that G'Kar will not cry out. No pain that he or his 'pain technicians' can inflict will make G'Kar scream, but he keeps on trying and promises Londo he will either get his scream or G'Kar will die. When Londo pleads with G'Kar to scream, otherwise he will be killed and Londo's plan to assassinate the Emperor will founder, G'Kar resists. To scream, he points out, would be to submit to a conqueror, and he would not be a Narn if he did that. Finally, less than a second before Cartagia kills him, he screams – not to save his life but to save his race.

The Arc: 'We must play along,' Londo tells Vir, 'until the time is right.' It's that line again.

So – the Vorlons reveal their true colours. During the first half of season one they were presented as very powerful and domineering, it was only during seasons two and three that Kosh lightened up and we were encouraged to think of them as, in some sense, angelic. Now the wheel has come full circle, and we see again the same Vorlons that were prepared to destroy Babylon 5 to prevent anyone finding out what one of them looked like. They're on the warpath, encouraged by the sudden catastrophe to befall the Shadows to launch a strike against all their bases. And the other races in the galaxy are caught in the middle: anyone who has ever sheltered or aided the Shadows – including Earth and Centauri Prime – is on their list.

The episode makes the strong point that the original Kosh was not a typical Vorlon – he had come to have feelings for the lesser races around him. The distinction between Kosh as we knew him and the new ambassador ('We are all Kosh') is still not completely clear. Are they all the same Kosh? And what about the original Kosh's second name – Naranek? How does that fit into the equation?

Observations: Ivanova says that the last time she looked up and saw sky was six years ago. That immediately invalidates the third *Babylon 5* book (*Blood Oath*) in which she spends some time on the Narn homeworld.

There are brief flashbacks in this episode to episodes 322 ('Z'ha'dum') and 402 ('Whatever Happened to Mr Garibaldi?').

The scene early on with Ivanova asking Delenn if she can borrow a *White Star* ship was actually filmed for episode 402 ('Whatever Happened to Mr Garibaldi?') but was shifted to this episode for time reasons during the editing of episode 402.

Koshisms: To Lyta Alexander when she asks for a little respect to be shown her: 'Respect? From whom?'

To Lyta Alexander when she tries to scan him: 'Would you know my thoughts? Would you?'

Ivanova's Life Lessons: Her attempt at speaking Minbari – 'Engines at full . . . high power, hatrack ratcatcher, to port weapons . . . brickbat lingerie.'

Dialogue to Rewind For: Marcus, on board the *White Star*, telling Ivanova where they are headed next – 'Sector 87 by 20 by 42. At least a dozen ships have reported seeing something rather godlike in the area, and since neither you nor I were there it must be one of the First Ones.'

Lyta Alexander, on the Vorlons: 'I don't think they care about what happens to us any more.'

Drazi, to Sheridan: 'I'm sorry, we thought you were dead.'
Sheridan: 'I was – I'm better now.'

Ships That Pass In The Night: Lorien's beautiful ship, which seems to have some echo in the sculpture of Thailand.

Other Worlds: The planet Arkada 7 is destroyed by the Vorlon fleet. It had over four million inhabitants.

Culture Shock: When the open rally against Delenn is going on, there are two aliens on the platform, making speeches to the crowd. One of them is a Drazi, the other is a Hyach. The Hyach have been around for some time in *Babylon 5*, but this is the first time I've been able to indicate one unambiguously and say, 'There, that's a Hyach.'

Literary, Mythological and Historical References: At the beginning of the episode, G'Kar is wearing a crown of thorns. Although a fairly common punishment, it may be a reflection of the biblical tradition that Jesus also wore a crown of thorns when he was being martyred. The biblical parallels don't end there – G'Kar is to be whipped 40 times, a probable nod toward Deuteronomy 25: 1–3, which states: 'When men have a dispute, they are to take it to court and the judges will decide the case, acquitting the innocent and condemning the guilty. If the guilty man deserves to be beaten, the judge shall make him lie down and have him flogged in his presence with the number of lashes his crime deserves, but he must not give him more than forty lashes. If he is flogged more than that, your brother will be degraded in your eyes.'

Just after Marcus tells Ivanova he's a virgin, he says he's picking something up on the ship's scanners. 'A unicorn?' Ivanova quips. This refers to the mythological basis of unicorns, which suggests they are attracted to virgins.

I've Seen That Face Before: Wayne Alexander and Wortham Krimmer, of course. Eric Zivot, who plays Verano, previously played Spragg – a member of Zathras's race – in episode 316 ('War Without End' Part I).

Questions Raised: How did Sheridan and Lorien leave Z'ha'dum without the Shadows realising? Why did they leave? Does that ship belong to Lorien? And, most importantly, how did that tall, thin ship get through the short, wide docking bay entrance of Babylon 5 without turning sideways?

'Falling Toward Apotheosis'

Transmission Number: 404
Production Number: 404

Written by: J. Michael Straczynski
Directed by: David J. Eagle

Emperor Cartagia: Wortham Krimmer
Lorien: Wayne Alexander **Morden:** Ed Wasser

Plot: Given that we have come to know and love all these characters (with the possible exception of Emperor Cartagia), it's gut-wrenching to see what happens to them in this season. The final shot of this episode is probably the single most disturbing moment in this entire series, and all we see is a door closing. Gulp.

The 'A' Plot: Given what is happening with the Vorlon fleet, Captain Sheridan wants to get rid of the new Vorlon Ambassador. He orders Garibaldi and some of his security guards to try to force the Ambassador to leave, knowing that they will fail and thus lull the Ambassador into a false sense of security. They do indeed fail – the Ambassador is far too powerful and protected to be bothered by their PPG fire. Lyta Alexander tells the Ambassador that there is a part of Kosh inside one of the people on the station, and that she will lead the Ambassador to him so that Kosh can be retrieved. The Ambassador, as expected, finds this intolerable, and is lured into a trap – at Sheridan's request Lyta has lured the Ambassador into a position in a cargo bay where massive electrical charges can be passed through him. What with the electrical discharges and the PPG fire from Garibaldi's guards, his encounter suit cracks to reveal the true Vorlon form – a creature like a jellyfish made of light. At the same time, the Vorlon ship in Bay 13 begins to break free, and Ivanova clears it to leave before it rips the station apart. The part of Kosh that was within Sheridan leaves him, along with some of Sheridan's life force and some of Lorien as well, and confronts the Ambassador. Intertwined and fighting, they pass through the hull of the station and explode along with the departing ship. Sheridan has been injured in the struggle, and Lorien replenishes his life force. Sheridan has to admit to Delenn that being recalled from death on Z'ha'dum has its price – he will live for only another twenty years. In a moment of tenderness and honesty between them, Sheridan proposes to Delenn.

The 'B' Plot: With the Vorlons attacking colonies and planets who have had contact, however unwitting, with the Shadows, Londo is worried that Centauri Prime is in the firing line. After all, there are over 100 Shadow ships based there. Neither the Emperor nor Morden is worried, however: Morden doesn't believe the Vorlens will dare attack Centauri Prime, while the Emperor is convinced they will but sees it as a pyre to celebrate his imminent apotheosis. Londo suggests that the Emperor travel to the Narn homeworld to put G'Kar on trial in order to ensure that the Emperor will be remembered by someone after the Centauri have all been immolated. The Emperor agrees.

The 'C' Plot: Garibaldi is worried about Lorien – he doesn't know who he is, what he wants or why he is following Sheridan around. He's also getting worried that Sheridan is keeping things from him. As if that wasn't enough, Garibaldi is *also* getting worried that people keep asking what happened to him when he was lost during the Shadow attack.

The Arc: A pretty stationary story in arc terms, but there are some features of interest. The Vorlon Ambassador dies in a fight with the remains of Kosh, of course. Also, Emperor Cartagia makes passing reference to Centauri Prime ending 'in fire' ('Let it all burn, Mollari. Let it all end in fire'), which is exactly what Kosh told Emperor Turhan would happen in episode 209 ('The Coming of Shadows'). And, of course, we have G'Kar's blinding by Emperor Cartagia – a moment prefigured in episodes 209 ('The Coming of Shadows') and

317 ('War Without End' Part Two) when we see G'Kar seventeen years in the future, minus an eye.

Observations: It's a three-day trip from Centauri Prime to the Narn homeworld.

Doctor Franklin suggests using the nearby planet Epsilon 3 as a refugee camp for those people fleeing the depredations of the Vorlons. Let's hope he has a lot of face masks – it has got a poisonous atmosphere for oxygen breathers.

Franklin tests Garibaldi for Shadow implants in the back of his neck (as seen in episodes 314 – 'Ship of Tears' and 322 – 'Z'ha'dum'). There aren't any – which doesn't mean he's not under *someone*'s influence, of course.

This isn't the same Garibaldi who went away. In episode 318 ('Walkabout') he gets really irritated with G'Kar over the apparent reluctance of the Narn captain Na'Kal to risk his life when ordered to. He even has a little speech about how sometimes you have to trust your leader when he orders you into an apparently hopeless situation – you have to trust that he knows best. Well, Garibaldi ain't trusting his boss in this episode – he is very reluctant to go into the Vorlon Ambassador's quarters to confront him.

The head closest to Londo on the Emperor's table is actually a cast of Andreas Katsulas's head.

Koshisms: 'A human imprisons one of us? Intolerable.'

Other Worlds: We're positively inundated with planets in this episode, many of them being names you couldn't possibly pronounce but which more or less work when they are shown on screen. Dura 7, Tizino Prime and Ventari 3 are believed to have fallen to the Vorlons, while 7 Lukantha, D'Grn IV, the Drazi Fendamir Research Colony, Kazomi VII, Lesser Krindar and Greater Krindar, L'Gn'Daort, Mokafa Station, Nacambad Colony, Oqmrritkz and Velatastat are at risk.

Literary, Mythological and Historical References: 'Right now, our greatest enemy is fear,' Ivanova says. This echoes several past writers and speakers, including American President Franklin D. Roosevelt ('Let me assert my firm belief that the only thing we have to fear is fear itself') and writer Henry

David Thoreau ('Nothing is so much to be feared as fear').

Emperor Cartagia has had the head of Minister Dugari removed because said Minister was always coughing. The Roman Emperor Caligula did a similar thing to Tiberius Gemellus, as reported in Robert Graves's novel *I, Claudius*. The Roman historian Suetonius reported, however, that Caligula had Gemellus killed because his breath smelt of an antidote to poison and this was an insult to Caligula's hospitality, although Suetonius claims that Gemellus's breath actually smelt of medicine taken for a persistent cough. The parallels between Cartagia and Caligula also point up the fact that Vir's career is paralleling that of the stuttering Claudius – the unlikeliest emperor of them all.

I've Seen That Face Before: Wortham Krimmer (as the Emperor Cartagia) and Wayne Alexander (as Lorien) and a remarkably short appearance by Ed Wasser as Morden.

Questions Raised: 'The Vorlons have gone mad,' says Morden. By 'gone mad' he means they are attacking people with disproportionate force for an aim far above the comprehension of most species. So what does that make the Shadows?

'The Long Night'

Transmission Number: 405
Production Number: 405

Written by: J. Michael Straczynski
Directed by: John Lafia

Ericsson: Brian Cranston
Emperor Cartagia: Wortham Krimmer
Centauri No.1: Carl Reggiardo
Centauri No. 2: Mark Bramhall
Drazi Ambassador: Ron Campbell   **G'Lorn:** Kim Strauss

Plot: It's compulsive viewing: an episode that ranges effort-lessly between long, deeply touching personal conversations concerning guilt and big strategy sessions concerning the fate of the galaxy.

The 'A' Plot: Cartagia has gone to the Narn Homeworld, accompanied by Londo. There he intends putting G'Kar through a show trial and then executing him. Londo's conspiracy to kill Cartagia has widened to include other Centauri officials, and the signal for the attempt to begin is when G'Kar distracts Cartagia's personal guard by snapping his (deliberately weakened) chains and runs amok. Londo will then take the Emperor aside and stab him between his hearts with a syringe containing an undetectable neurotoxin. The plan starts to go wrong when Cartagia has G'Kar's chains replaced, thinking they look weak, but G'Kar's righteous anger gives him the strength to snap them anyway. Cartagia manages to unwittingly knock the syringe from Londo's hand, but Vir picks it up and stabs Cartagia, killing him. Londo is named Prime Minister, and recommends that the Centauri leave the Narn well alone from now on. They leave for Centauri Prime, with three days left to get rid of the Shadows there.

The 'B' Plot: Sheridan is almost ready to strike against the Vorlons, but a report from a ship passing through sector 900 – on the edge of Vorlon space – indicates that the Shadows are using a new weapon, something equivalent to the Vorlon planet-killer. *White Star 14*, which is in the area, reports back that the weapon fires millions of missiles into a planetary crust. When the missiles detonate, they split the crust open and turn the planet inside out. Sheridan orders Ericsson, the captain of *White Star 14*, to sacrifice himself and his ship in order to get false information to the Shadows, luring them to Corianas 6 – the next planet on the Vorlon's list. Sheridan knows that the Shadows and the Vorlons are dancing around each other, avoiding direct confrontation, and he intends putting them face to face.

The 'C' Plot: Following the Centauri withdrawal, G'Kar realises that his people wish to take their revenge, and start the entire cycle over again.

The Arc: Emperor Cartagia finally gets his comeuppance in this episode, but any man who dresses like a Morris dancer deserves everything that happens to him. Unexpectedly, it is Vir who kills him, rather than Londo.

367

Observations: There is a reference to Lord Refa having Prime Minister Malachi killed (an event shown in episode 209 – 'The Coming of Shadows'). There is also a reference to Londo having Lord Refa killed (as shown in episode 320 – 'And the Rock Cried Out, No Hiding Place').

Centauri have at least two hearts.

Corillium is a very hard metal.

The original intention, up until the episode was being written, was for Londo to have killed the Emperor, but J. Michael Straczynski changed things at the last moment when he realised Vir would be the perfect, and the most unexpected, assassin.

A scene filmed for this episode involving Ivanova and Lorien talking was moved to the following episode (406 – 'Into The Fire') instead.

Dialogue to Rewind For: G'Kar – 'I did not fight to remove one dictator just to become another myself!'

Dialogue to Fast Forward Past: Captain 'Call Me Subtle' Sheridan's way of telling Ericsson that he won't be coming back. 'You're not a married man, are you, Ericsson?'

Ships That Pass In The Night: *White Star 14.*

Other Worlds: Coriana 6 (in sector 70 by 12 by 5) has over 6 billion inhabitants.

Dorac 7 has a small Shadow base on it.

Literary, Historical and Mythological References: 'My eye offended him,' G'Kar says, explaining why Cartagia had his eye plucked out. This is a reference to the Bible, the Gospel of St. Matthew, C.18 v9: 'If thine eye offend thee, pluck it out, and cast it from thee: it is better for thee to enter into life with one eye, rather than having two eyes to be cast into hell fire.'

Sheridan reveals that, when he took command of Babylon 5, he found a poem left on his desk. The poem was Tennyson's *Ulysses*, indicating that the person who left it was Ambassador Sinclair (see the pilot episode, 'The Gathering').

'Into The Fire'

Transmission Number: 406
Production Number: 406

Written by: J. Michael Straczynski
Directed by: Kevin James Dobson

Lorien: Wayne Alexander   **Durano:** Julian Barnes
Centauri Minister: Damien London   **Morden:** Ed Wasser

Plot: And so, it . . . ends. The war is over; the Vorlons, the Shadows, the rest of the First Ones and Lorien himself have all left. We're on our own now. And what an exit they get . . .

The 'A' Plot: Sheridan draws the line at Coriana 6 – placing his ships in the way of the Vorlon fleet and attracting the Shadow fleet to the same point. He calls in reinforcements from the First Ones to hold the two fleets at bay and attempts to communicate with both sides. It works: the Vorlons take Sheridan's mind elsewhere to reason with him, and the Shadows do the same with Delenn. Lorien, unbeknownst to both the Vorlons and the Shadows, transmits images of the negotiations to everyone else in the fleet. Sheridan and Delenn are offered the chance to choose between the Vorlons and the Shadows, but they both refuse to make that choice. Both of them point out that there is a third option – not to join in the game that the two sides are playing. Sheridan asks both sides to leave the younger races in peace, pointing out that neither side knows who they are or what they want any more. Lorien throws his weight behind Sheridan and, after some discussion, both the Shadows and the Vorlons agree to leave the galaxy, passing beyond the Rim to whatever lies beyond. Lorien agrees to go with them. The war is over, and the younger races are on their own . . .

The 'B' Plot: Londo and Vir have 24 hours to get rid of every trace of Shadow influence on Centauri Prime before the Vorlon fleet arrives. Londo offers Morden the chance to withdraw the Shadow ships from the island of Selene, and when Morden refuses Londo has Morden's 'associates' killed and blows up the island. He then kills Morden in order to eradicate what he thinks of as the last remaining Shadow influence on the planet, but he has forgotten one last source of contamination. He, too, has been touched by Shadows. The Vorlons arrive, and Londo orders Vir to kill him. The Vorlons are about to fire when they are recalled to provide reinforcements at Coriana 6. Centauri Prime is safe – for the moment.

The 'C' Plot: Ivanova and Lorien contact the six remaining First Ones and convince them to join with them against the Vorlons and the Shadows.

The Arc: After Londo has Morden killed, he places Morden's head on a pike in the garden and tells Vir to go outside. Vir gazes up into Morden's dead eyes and remembers the conversation he had with Morden in episode 217 ('In the Shadow of Z'ha'dum'): 'I'd like to live long enough to be there when they cut off your head and stick it on a pike as a warning to the next ten generations that some favours come with too high a price. I want to look up into your lifeless eyes and wave – like this.' We even get a flashback to that very speech.

In episode 309 ('Point of No Return') Lady Morella prophesies that Londo has three chances to avoid the fire that lies before him. One of them is: 'And, at the last, you must surrender yourself to your greatest fear, knowing that it will kill you.' In this episode, Londo begs Vir to kill him, rather than let the Vorlons destroy his world. Is this what Lady Morella was referring to?

Captain Sheridan turns upon the Shadows and the Vorlons the two questions they have been asking all along: 'Who are you?' and 'What do you want?' Unsurprisingly, neither race can answer the questions themselves.

To cap the episode, Captain Sheridan defines the three ages of mankind (as set up in the opening narration for the pilot episode – 'The Gathering' – and the first season). The First Age is when the races of the galaxy are too primitive to make decisions about their own fate; the Second Age is when they are manipulated from outside by more powerful forces; the Third Age is when they are able to stand on their own and make decisions about their own fate.

Observations: There is a discussion of Adira, the dancer Londo fell in love with in episode 103 ('Born to the Purple')

370

and who was killed by Morden's associates in episode 315 ('Interludes and Examinations'). We still don't know how Morden's agents got on to the Centauri liner to poison her.

Sheridan's ploy with the mined asteroids is very similar to the stunt he pulled in order to destroy the *Black Star* during the Earth–Minbari war.

The Vorlon saying 'Understanding is a three-edged sword' gets another airing in this episode. It was previously said in episode 109 ('Deathwalker').

The voice of the Shadow spokesman is provided by Ed Wasser (Morden).

A scene filmed for the previous episode (405 – 'The Long Night') involving Ivanova and Lorien talking was moved to this episode instead.

Koshisms: To Sheridan – 'You thought we could not touch you. You were wrong.'

'You do *not* understand.'

Dialogue to Rewind For: Londo, on the damage after Morden's associates have been killed – 'I will have to have that painted over, I suppose.'

Sheridan, blowing up some nuclear mines to get the attention of the Vorlon and Shadow fleets – 'Good morning gentlemen, this is your wake-up call.'

Lyta Alexander, when the Vorlon and Shadow fleets turn and head toward Sheridan's rag-tag fleet – 'Captain – they're pissed.'

Sheridan to the Vorlons and the Shadows – 'Who are *you*; what do *you* want.'

Marcus – 'Did we just win?' Ivanova – 'Don't jinx it.'

Sheridan – 'It's a new age, Delenn – a Third Age . . . We began in chaos, too primitive to make our own decisions. Then we were manipulated from outside by forces who thought they knew what was best for us. And now, now we're finally standing on our own.'

Dialogue to Fast Forward Past: Londo talking about Morden having poisoned Adira – 'He played me – he played me like a puppet!' (You play violins, but you don't

371

play puppets – you manipulate them.)

Ships That Pass In The Night: *White Star 9*. The *Stra'kath* – a Drazi warship.

Culture Shock: There are over two dozen races taking part in Sheridan's crusade. (How many can *you* name?)

Lorien and his race were born immortal. Lorien believes that subsequent races were given lifespans because the sentient universe realised that, for there to be change and growth, lives had to be limited.

Questions Raised: Where do we go from here?

'Epiphanies'

Transmission Number: 407
Production Number: 407

Written by: J. Michael Straczynski
Directed by: John Flinn

Bester: Walter Koenig   **Centauri Minister:** Damien London
Psi Corps Official: Victor Iunidin
Earth Alliance Pilot: Robert Patteri
News Anchor: Lauren Sanchez

Plot: A new start; a new direction.

The 'A' Plot: President Clark, worried at the sudden loss of his Shadow allies, is becoming increasingly concerned over the threat posed to him by Babylon 5. He sets in motion a four-pronged attack, with Psi Corps, Earthforce, Nightwatch and the Ministry of Peace each advancing a piece of the plan, but none of them knowing what the others are doing. Following an ISN announcement that Babylon 5 is now off-limits to all humans following reports of possible terrorist activity emanating from it, Psi Cop Bester is ordered to attack a squadron of Earthforce Starfuries with his own Black Omega Starfuries and then leave evidence making it look like Babylon 5 was responsible. Bester travels to Babylon 5 and offers to help Sheridan fight Clark's plans if Sheridan will take him to Z'ha'dum. Ivanova travels to the jumpgate in Sector 49 with Alpha

Squadron, where they help the Earthforce Starfuries there to destroy the attacking Black Omega forces. President Clark is wrong-footed, but Bester has his own plans afoot, and may have been involved in sending a coded message to Garibaldi which has caused him to resign as Head of Babylon 5 Security.

The 'B' Plot: Bester wants to ransack Z'ha'dum in an attempt to discover if the Shadows left behind any technology that could be used to remove the organic components from his lover, Carolyn – held in cryogenic suspension on Babylon 5. Sheridan, Delenn and Lyta Alexander accompany him there, and find a fleet of the Shadows' Dark Servants leaving, having (probably) stripped the planet. Sheridan suspects a trap, and turns tail. Moments later, the planet explodes. They return to Babylon 5, where Sheridan accuses Lyta of having deliberately triggered the explosion telepathically. She admits it, giving as her possible reasons (a) the fact that she might be still operating under unconscious Vorlon instructions, (b) that she doesn't think Shadow technology should fall into anyone else's hands, or (c) that she hates Bester and will thwart whatever he wants to do.

The 'C' Plot: The Centarum vote to delay deciding upon a new Emperor. In the interim, they elect the ubiquitous Minister as Regent, and Londo returns to Babylon 5. The Regent wakes up during the night and discovers that an alien parasite has been attached to his neck – probably by Dark Servants of the now departed Shadows.

The Arc: The Shadows are gone, but their Dark Servants remain. They are undoubtedly the beings responsible for placing an organic 'controller' on the new Centauri Regent's neck. We saw that Londo had one of these in his future in episode 317 ('War Without End' Part Two). Does this mean that the future we saw then will now no longer happen in quite the way we thought and that the Regent has taken Londo's place, or will Londo also get a 'controller' at some later date?

After some twenty episodes in which Earth had remained quiet, President Clark makes his long-awaited next move against Babylon 5. He's using Bester, amongst others, not realising that Bester had come to an arrangement with Sheridan in episode 314 ('Ship of Tears') – the same episode in which we found out about his lover, Carolyn, and what the Shadows had done to her.

Lyta Alexander has come out of her time with the Vorlons with some hidden extras. As well as the methane gills we saw in episode 304 ('Passing Through Gethsemane') she also appears to have enhanced telepathic abilities – she can block Bester's telepathy and can send messages over many light years. What else did they do to her?

Bester knows something about Lyta's past: something she doesn't want anyone else to know about.

Observations: We get a flashback to Mr Garibaldi's experiences in episode 402 ('Whatever Happened to Mr Garibaldi?').

Zack Allen has a problematic past, and Garibaldi was the only person who would hire him.

Some material was obviously snipped out during Delenn and Sheridan's conversation aboard the *White Star*: after Delenn says '. . . the picture always ends with your head imploding!', their postures and relative positions suddenly change.

Dialogue to Rewind For: The new Regent, admiring the curtains in the Throne Room – 'I'm thinking . . . pastels.'

Other Worlds: Disneyplanet. (But does it have twin moons that rise above its horizon like huge ears?)

Station Keeping: The jumpgate in Sector 49 is the last stopover point for vessels heading from Earth to Babylon 5.

Literary References: Ivanova's quip that 'Reports of our disloyalty have been greatly exaggerated' refers to Mark Twain's famous put-down: 'The report of my death was an exaggeration.'

I've Seen That Face Before: Walter Koenig returns as Bester.

Questions Raised: What did the Vorlons do to Lyta's telepathic abilities?

What does Bester know about Lyta's past?

What is Bester's 'ace in the hole', and does it have anything to do with the coded message received by Mr Garibaldi?

The Future

As I write these words, in the middle of February 1997, the future of *Babylon 5* is uncertain. On the one hand there have been indications that the show might not make it to a fifth season; on the other hand there has been talk of a spin-off series and two TV movies. Depending who you talk to at Warner Brothers, the show could go either way. Even J. Michael Straczynski doesn't know (or, if he does, he's not admitting anything).

By the time you read this we might know a lot more, but all we actually know for sure at the moment are the titles of the next nine episodes. They are:

408   'The Illusion of Truth'
409   'Atonement'
410   'Racing Mars'
411   'Lines of Communication'
412   'Conflicts of Interests'
413   'Rumors, Bargains and Lies'
414   'Moments of Transition'
415   'No Retreat; No Surrender'
416   'The Exercise of Vital Powers'

As to what happens after that, there are four obvious possibilities. Firstly, the ideal one – the series is renewed for a fifth season and the arc culminates in episode 522 (currently entitled either 'Farewell' or 'Sleeping in Light'). Secondly, one we could live with – the decision is made to finish the arc in the fourth season in case the show isn't renewed, but it is and season five comprises an extension of the arc and/or stand-alone stories. Thirdly, one we could still live with but wouldn't be happy about – the decision is made to finish the arc in the fourth season in case the show isn't renewed, and it isn't. Fourthly, the disaster scenario – the fourth season is written with the assumption that the arc will run to five seasons, but the show isn't renewed and the show ends prematurely.

There has to come a point of no return (to coin a phrase) during the writing of season 4 at which a decision is made either to complete the arc within that season or not. J. Michael Straczynski has already said that he has deliberately been pulling some elements of the arc forward into season 4 and laying other elements back into season 5 to give himself room for manoeuvre, but there is only so much that can be done before a solid decision must be taken. That decision must be taken soon. The filming of season 4 continues, relentless.

Ironically, while the debate over the future of the series continues, its future in spin-off projects seems assured. Firstly, Warner Brothers have asked J. Michael Straczynski for a treatment on a sequel. The working title for this putative new series is *The Babylon Project: Crusade* and it would probably involve the Rangers. Secondly, TNT have asked for two *Babylon 5* TV movies to be made. These would be shown alongside the series proper when TNT start 'stripping it' (i.e. showing it daily) on American TV in 1998. The first TV movie (working title *In the Beginning* but now retitled *Last of the Fallen*) will be a prequel to the series, set during the Earth–Minbari War (similar to the concept Straczynski originally had for the first *Babylon 5* novel). The second, entitled *Guardians*, will probably be set during the series itself and expand upon plot threads seen there (in a similar sense, possibly, to the comic arc which he wrote but then withdrew from DC). Both movies would be made after filming on season 4 has finished and (hopefully) before season 5 filming starts.

We can only hope . . .

BOOKS AND
COMICS

The Books

Observations: An early possibility which was discussed for the *Babylon 5* novels was to take the most heavily arc-related episodes from a particular season, stitch them (or parts of them) together into a novelised form, and publish them so that the major part of that season's arc was together in one novel. Practicalities intervened, and this interesting approach was dropped.

Later J. Michael Straczynski said, 'I suggested a structure rather like *The Winds of War*, set during the Earth–Minbari War, in that we have all of our characters in different places, seeing the story and the war from their perspectives, and how their paths intersect during that time in odd or unlikely ways. Dell [Books] didn't think that was the way to go, that unless it was set in the present, people would feel disappointed.'

After the approach to the *Babylon 5* novels had been finally agreed between Dell and Straczynski, Kevin J. Anderson was approached by Dell to write the first one. As well as being a writer of SF novels and short stories, both alone and with Doug Beason, Anderson had also hit the big time with a set of *Star Wars* novels under the umbrella title *The Jedi Academy Trilogy*. 'I was initially approached to write the first *B5* novel for Dell Books,' he says, 'based mainly on my success as a *Star Wars* writer, and because I love the show *B5*. They intended to launch their series of novels as a very "high-end" publishing programme, with bestselling big-name authors and major promotion. However, thanks to legal entanglements between the television studio (as I understand it) and the publisher, they ate up most of the time available for an author to write the book. Along the way, they downsized their ambitious plans quite extravagantly, with the result that the amount of money they actually offered and the amount of time they allowed me to write it was literally *half* what they had originally told me. Just at that time, too, I had been offered the opportunity to write a brand-new hardcover *Star Wars* novel *(Darksaber)*, and I chose instead to devote my time and energy to that. John Vornholt picked up the ball and produced the first *B5* novel in record time.'

John Vornholt was also a fan of the series. 'I saw the pilot for *B5* at Loscon [an American SF convention] before it aired on TV,' he says, 'and I've been watching it from the beginning. It's still one of the few programs I never miss. I was hired to write two of the first three *B5* novels, even before I submitted any ideas. They had approached other writers, but I was the first one who said yes to the money they were offering. I submitted two ideas to begin with, one called *El Diablo*, which JMS turned down, and the idea which became *Voices*. I thought *Voices* would be my second book, but it turned out to be my first. I don't recall much about *El Diablo*, except that all the different races were competing to capture a valuable asteroid.'

Voices

Written by: John Vornholt

Date: The book is supposedly set a few weeks after the Mars rebellion, which occurred in the last few months of 2258, but Sheridan is Captain of Babylon 5, which puts it in 2259. Given that it's definitely set before episode 203 ('A Day in the Strife'), because Ivanova is still a Lieutenant Commander, all that can be said is that the events of the book take place sometime in the first few months of 2259.

Plot: Exclamation marks! Everywhere! And not just in dialogue! This book is completely misaimed, assuming that the fans of *Babylon 5* are kids who will be happy with a relatively unsophisticated runaround plot with cursory characterisation and scant description of the scenery as it passes. Not an auspicious start.

The 'A' Plot: A planned conference of high-level telepaths on Mars is disrupted by a bomb. The conference is shifted to Babylon 5, but during the initial meetings a second bomb goes off, badly injuring Psi Cop Bester. Analysis indicates that the bomb was carried into the meeting room by Talia Winters. She is arrested by Garibaldi, more to prevent Psi Corps getting their hands on her than for any other reason, but she escapes from the station with the assistance of Ambassador Kosh. Garibaldi suspects a commercial telepath named Emily Crane of planting the bomb – Crane asked Talia to carry a data crystal into the meeting for her – and sets off for Earth to interview her (the conference having broken up and the delegates returned to their planets of origin). Garibaldi is accompanied by Harriman Gray, a military telepath acting as assistant to Bester. Gray has a list of the staff from the bombed hotel on Mars, and Garibaldi recognises Emily Crane's face as a recent addition to the staff. She admits nothing when they question her in Boston, but Garibaldi notices a document referring to Senate Bill 22991 on her desk. A friend of Gray's reveals that Bill 22991 is a secret bill to privatise Psi Corps and thus nullify its power. Garibaldi is captured by Emily Crane and her companions, who intend keeping him prisoner for twenty-four hours until the bill is enacted, but is rescued by Harriman Gray and Bester. Crane and her companions are killed, and although Bester now knows who was responsible for the bombings he refuses to help Talia Winters, on the basis that he doesn't want to admit that Psi Corps was wrong. Garibaldi and Gray head for Mars to confront Arthur Maltin, head of the Mix – the largest group of commercial telepaths and the man hoping to take control of Psi Corps. They meet Talia Winters on Mars, along with her reprobate uncle Ted. Just as they, and Bester, catch up with Malten he is killed by the Free Mars movement, who are angry at him for pretending to be a Martian terrorist. Bester crushes the bill, and Garibaldi blackmails him into clearing Talia's name.

The 'B' Plot: Escaping from the false charge of murder, Talia appeals to Ambassador Kosh for help. He arranges for her to be smuggled out of Babylon 5 hidden in a self-contained cargo container in a methane breathers' ship. She is accompanied by Deuce, a petty criminal who may or may not be implicated in the bombing of the telepaths' conference. They are jettisoned over Earth and land in an American wilderness, where they are picked up by contacts of Deuce's – Caucasians known as Bilagaani who are living the lifestyle of American Indians. She travels from there to Mars to find her uncle – a Free Mars activist who, she believes, is the only person who can help her evade the authorities. She meets up with him, Garibaldi and Harriman Gray on Mars, where her name is cleared.

The Arc: Ambassador Kosh hires Talia Winters for a business transaction. When she turns up, the only person there is Kosh. He tells her that he wants her to scan his invisible companion Isabel. She refuses, but he is insistent. When she blocks out everyone else in the room, she fleetingly picks up the thoughts of someone else – someone she can't see. Kosh leaves, satisfied, and after considerable thought Talia decides that Isabel is the nascent telekinetic ability given to her by Jason Ironheart in episode 106 ('Mind War').

Observations: There are references to Colonel Ari Ben Zayn (episode 116 – 'Eyes') and the death of the Psi Cop Kelsey (episode 106 – 'Mind War'). Garibaldi remembers a favour Talia Winters did for him that was connected with Mars – almost certainly the events of episode 118 ('A Voice in the Wilderness' Part One).

Bester gets his buttocks blown off in this story. Is this gratuitous detail, or what?

'*Voices* was the fastest novel I ever wrote,' Vornholt says, 'eighty thousand words in twenty-five days. It was insane.'

Koshisms: Kosh is at his most enigmatic in this book. 'Anger is a blue sea.' 'The wings fly at midnight.' 'Apple pie and hush puppies.' 'Gone, like the pickled herring.'

Prose to Flick Past: Page 149 – 'The first rays of sunlight brought the slate-colored clouds to life, and they looked like the underbellies of a herd of buffaloes, slowly stampeding across the sky.'

Ships That Pass In The Night: Transport *Freya*. Given its antecendents (see **Literary, Mythological and Historical References** below) it's probably a sister ship to the earth Liner *Loki* that turned up in episode 305 ('Voices of Authority'). The *Glenn* also turns up, as does transport *Bradley*.

Other Worlds: Betelgeuse 6.

Culture Shock: An Antarean turns up on the station. Briefly.

Literary, Mythological and Historical References: Transport *Freya* is named for the Norse goddess (sometimes known as Frigga), wife to Odin and mother of Thor. Clarke Spaceport (orbiting Earth) is probably a reference to the famed SF author Arthur C. Clarke.

I've Seen That Face Before: This book has more guest appearances than any of the later ones, with the Psi Cop Bester (first appearance in episode 106 – 'Mind War'), the military telepath Harriman Gray (first appearance in episode 116 – 'Eyes') and the petty criminal Deuce (first appearance in episode 115 – 'Grail').

Author John Vornholt is best known for the various original *Star Trek* novels he has written, although he has also written one fantasy novel and several children's books.

Accidents Will Happen: There's a reference to Babylon 5's rarely seen third-in-command, Major Atumbe, except that here he's referred to as Major Atambe.

The temperature on Mars is described as being between 200 degrees Celsius and 300 degrees Celsius. This can't be the Mars that *we*'re familiar with, where recorded temperatures don't go above 0 degrees Celsius and have, in fact, gone down as far as minus 100 degrees Celsius. *Voices*, John Vornholt is the first to admit, 'could have benefited from a few more days of research.'

Questions Raised: Is 'Invisible Isabel' – the secret part of Talia Winters that Kosh put her in touch with – really her nascent telekinetic ability? Or is it actually her submerged secondary personality, the one that wakes up and takes control in episode 219 ('Divided Loyalties')?

Why does Kosh help Deuce to escape from Babylon 5? For that matter, why does he help Talia escape?

What exactly is the source of the blinding headache that makes Talia leave the conference room just before the explosion rips through it? Did someone else induce it to get her to leave, thus saving her life, or was it her submerged secondary personality saving its own life?

Accusations

Written by: Lois Tilton

Date: J. D. Ortega is killed on 18 April 2259, and the action of the story continues for several days, if not weeks, afterwards. We're told that the story is set between episodes 209 ('The Coming of Shadows') and 211 ('All Alone in the Night').

Plot: *Accusations* is reasonably well written and involving, but ultimately too confusing. There's too much play on the power politics of industrial concerns whose representatives we never see, and the ill-explained economics of the Earth Alliance. When a writer puts a thought like 'A lot of things weren't clear cut' in the mind of one of her major characters, it's almost an admission of defeat. When added to the fact that every character apart from those we know from the series is two-dimensional, there's a definite feeling of incompleteness about the book.

The 'A' Plot: J. D. Ortega, Ivanova's old Starfury instructor, arrives on Babylon 5 and sends her a message asking to meet. He fails to turn up for the meeting, and when Ivanova investigates she discovers that he is wanted on charges of suspected terrorism and conspiracy. While Ivanova is out on a mission, Ortega's body is discovered. He has been poisoned. A note discovered near his body has one partial word on it: 'hardwir'. Three Earthforce investigators are dispatched to the station: Commander Wallace, Lieutenant Khatib and Lieutenant Miyoshi. They tell Sheridan that Ortega was in possession of information which they are seeking to recover. They immediately sequestrate Garibaldi's files, intimidate witnesses and have Ivanova removed from command, given her previous association with a suspected terrorist. Another dead body is discovered – Fengshi Yang, a criminal resident on Mars. Investigating Yang's murder, which is nominally unconnected with Ortega's murder, Garibaldi discovers that he was probably killed by the newly arrived Lieutenant Khatib – who has himself been murdered. Sheridan has Wallace recalled to Earth for mishandling the investigation (and for possible conspiracy in it), and Ivanova has Talia Winters scan her mind to determine the meaning of the fragmentary clue 'hardwir'. She realises it means Ortega has hardwired the information in the displays of her Starfury, and she retrieves it. The information is the atomic composition of a new artificial element which will render morbidium superfluous to Earthforce requirements, hence the activity on the part of both Earthforce and the companies that mine morbidium on Mars to recover it.

The 'B' Plot: Raiders are attacking Earth ships near Babylon 5: receiving an emergency distress beacon, Ivanova leads a group of Starfuries to help the *Cassini*, a transport ship, but discovers that it has been gutted by the time they arrive. Ivanova recognises a pattern in the attacks, and submits a report to Earthforce suggesting that the only transports being attacked are those whose journeys start on Mars and which are carrying morbidium ingots (morbidium being an element used in the manufacture of PPG weapons). During a Raider attack on the ship *Cyrus Mac*, she captures a Raider. During questioning, he admits that a Martian company – AreTech – are selling the Raiders the routes of their own ships, then claiming the insurance money when the ships are attacked.

The Arc: As with all the books, with the exception of *The Shadow Within*, there's precious little connection with the arc. The only slight hint here is the nicely played relationship between Ivanova and Talia, which has grown to the point where Ivanova asks Talia to scan her mind despite her well-documented hatred of telepaths.

Observations: There are passing mentions of the previous problems with Raiders (occurring intermittently through most of the first half of season 1, but primarily in episodes 101 – 'Midnight on the Firing Line' and 113 – 'Signs and Portents'), the dockers' strike (as in episode 112 – 'By Any Means Necessary'), Garibaldi's old girlfriend Lise Hampton (she turned up in episodes 119 – 'A Voice in the Wilderness' Part Two and 120 – 'Babylon Squared'), and the Mars Rebellion (which occurred in episodes 118 and 119 – 'A Voice in the Wilderness' Parts One and Two).

One point of interest about this book is that a character named Admiral Wilson turns up. This is the first and last time in the entirety of *Babylon 5* that someone of this rank has appeared – above the rank of captain, everyone in Earthforce seems to be from the Army/Air Force rank structure (colonels and generals).

Ortega is poisoned with chloro-quasi-dianimidine.

Ships That Pass In The Night: Transport *Gonfalon* is a Centauri ship (a gonfalon is a banner hung from a crossbar). Transport ship *Cassini* (see **Literary, Mythological and Historical References** below). The *Asimov* (which turned up in episodes 102 – 'Soul Hunter', 110 – 'Believers' and 313 – 'A Late Delivery from Avalon'). The *Duster* (an ore-carrier). The Earth Transport *Cyrus Mac*. The heavy hauler *Kobold* (a kobold being a pixie of familiar spirit in German mythology). The Earth Liner *Heinlein* (see **Literary, Mythological and Historical References** below). The Earth Supply Transport *Redstone 4*.

Literary, Mythological and Historical References: Transport ship *Cassini* is named for Giovanni Domenico Cassini, the French/Italian astronomer who discovered the moons of Saturn and the division in Saturn's rings.

The Earth Liner *Heinlein* is named for the famed SF writer Robert A. Heinlein, who (aptly, given the plot of this book) wrote a novel or two about Mars. The *Heinlein* is probably owned by the company who run the *Asimov* and the *Pournelle*.

I've Seen That Face Before: There are minor appearances by Ms Connelly – the Dockers Guild representative who turns up in episode 112 ('By Any Means Necessary') and Ombuds Wellington (who appeared in episodes 115 – 'Grail' and 121 – 'The Quality of Mercy').

Accidents Will Happen: The cover painting is reversed – look at the artist's signature in the bottom left-hand corner and compare it with the other books. The interesting thing is, Ivanova's dress uniform jacket is actually correct (the left-hand collar covering the right-hand collar) implying that either the artist was provided with a reverse photograph of

Ivanova or decided to reverse her image for artistic reasons. The cover itself could have been reversed by accident, or to improve the effect of the book jacket on the shelves.

The Ombuds are referred to on four separate occasions as the Ombunds.

Blood Oath

Written by: John Vornholt

Date: Sheridan is Captain of Babylon 5, which puts it in 2259. Ivanova is now a full Commander, so it's set after episode 203 ('A Day in the Strife'), and internal evidence puts it before episode 209 ('The Coming of Shadows'). All that can be said, therefore, is that the events of the book take place sometime in the first few months of 2259.

Plot: It all hangs together, and there are fewer exclamation marks, but it depends too much on one of the television episodes to stand up at all well as a novel. Added to that, G'Kar's ploy of blowing his own ship up to avoid an assassination attempt is also used in issue nine of the *Babylon 5* comic, 'Duet For Human and Narn in C Sharp'.

The 'A' Plot: G'Kar receives a data crystal from Mi'Ra, daughter of Du'Rog. G'Kar ruined Du'Rog's family name during his scramble for a position in the Third Circle, and Du'Rog had paid for two assassination attempts against G'Kar's life. The attempts failed and Du'Rog is now dead, but Mi'Ra has sworn a blood oath against G'Kar. It's now the sole focus of her life that she kills him. G'Kar fakes his own death in a spaceship accident and travels to Narn to kill her first, but Na'Toth, Garibaldi and Ivanova are travelling on the same ship to attend his memorial service. Also with them is Al Vernon, a human who has lived on Narn and claims to be able to help them. They all discover that G'Kar is still alive, and travel with him to the Narn city in which Mi'Ra lives. G'Kar goes to see his wife, and she persuades him to settle things with Du'Rog's remaining family. They send money to his widow – Ka'Het – and then go to talk to her, but Mi'Ra has them ambushed. After an extended chase through Narn catacombs they are captured. Mi'Ra is about to kill G'Kar when Al Vernon offers her a deal – he has information that will clear her father's name and will give it to her if she calls off the blood oath. She does, and Vernon admits that he was given the information by Londo Mollari. Back on Babylon 5, Londo tells G'Kar that he would rather have G'Kar alive and owing him his life than dead in some family squabble.

Observations: Katassium is a substance poisonous to Narns but temporarily disabling to humans.

Na'Toth makes reference to the blood oath she swore in episode 109 ('Deathwalker').

'For *Blood Oath* I had two months,' Vorholt says, remembering the amount of time he had to write *Voices*, 'which is still pretty fast. JMS didn't tell me much. My books were supposed to take place during the second season, but they were written during the first season – so JMS told me about Captain Sheridan before he told the masses about the new commander. I asked him for information on the Narn homeworld for *Blood Oath*, but he told me to make it up. I thought that was very cavalier of him, until I realised he was going to destroy the planet in a war.'

Ships That Pass In The Night: The *K'sha Na'vras* is a Narn cruiser. The *Hala'Tar* is another Narn ship. The *Borelian* is a Centauri transport.

Other Worlds: Betelgeuse Four (but there's a Betelgeuse 6 in Vornholt's previous book – *Voices* – so the consistency is a little suspect). Antareus.

Culture Shock: The best data crystals are grown on Minbar.
D'Bok is an ancient Narn goddess of the harvest.
Narn foodstuff includes sislop cakes, lukrol and mitlop.

Literary, Mythological and Historical References: There are two separate mentions of Mark Twain's work (especially his famous quip, 'The report of my death was an exaggeration.').

Accidents Will Happen: Al Vernon doesn't so much quote Mark Twain as misquote him. Vernon uses the commonly believed version – 'Reports of my death have been greatly exaggerated' – whereas Twain actually wrote, 'The report of my death was an exaggeration.'

At one point, Ivanova thinks that every day for two years she and Garibaldi had relied on each other, suffered through countless crises and a traumatic change in command. Well, episode 101 ('Midnight on the Firing Line') took place in early 2258, and Ivanova is relatively new on the station. She certainly hasn't been there six months, as she wasn't present during the events of the pilot episode ('The Gathering'). So, she arrived in the last half of 2257. This book is set in the first few months of 2259. That makes it eighteen months rather than two years. Picky? Sure, but if you can't trust an Earthforce officer to get it right, who can you trust?

Clark's Law

Written by: Jim Mortimore

Date: The plot takes place on and around 12 December 2259.

Plot: All *Babylon 5* books should have been like this. *Clark's Law* shows evidence of deep thought concerning the implications of the plot and serious commitment to writing the best book possible under the circumstances – not traits for which the other five will be remembered.

The 'A' Plot: A delegation from a humanoid alien race known as the Tuchanq arrive on Babylon 5. Their world had been under Narn control for many years until they rose up against their oppressors, and they are hoping that the Earth Alliance will help them rebuild it after the years of exploitation and pollution. The Tuchanq conception of identity is tied up with their Song of Being – a philosophical concept that has to do with a continued stream of consciousness. The Tuchanq do not sleep, and if their Song of Being is interrupted then (they believe) they will go insane unless they obtain a new Song from another being. During their arrival on the station there is a fight with a group of Narn, during which Ivanova has to stun both parties. Those Tuchanq whose Songs of Being have been broken have to be ceremonially brought to the point of death by their comrades and then revived as new-born Tuchanq with new Songs of Being, but one – D'arc – escapes from medlab before this can happen. The other Tuchanq consider her to be mad – and so does she. The only way to regain her sanity to is obtain another Song, and she does this by attacking a human businessman in one of the station's cargo airlocks. Dying, the businessman manages to destroy the controls which operate the airlock, causing a massive pressure leak. By the time security and medical teams get to them, the businessman is dead and D'arc is brain-damaged. At her trial – the first under President Clark's new sentencing rules – D'arc is convicted of murder and sentenced to death, despite evidence that the brain damage (and, perhaps, the loss of her Song of Being) has caused the destruction of her original personality and its replacement by another one. Spontaneous protests erupt across the station as pro-life groups fight with Home Guard sympathisers. Captain Sheridan is forced by circumstance to go through with a public execution, but unbeknownst to everyone except Mr Garibaldi and the Tuchanq he substitutes the body of the dead businessman, suitably disguised by a changeling net, for a sedated D'arc. As far as the public are concerned the execution has been carried out. The riots subside, and the Tuchanq leave. Put off by the complexities of human justice, they ask the Centauri for help. The Centauri take effective control of the Tuchanq's homeworld, leaving them little better off than when the Narn were there.

The 'B' Plot: Londo Mollari pays a group of Home Guard sympathisers to disguise themselves as Tuchanq using changeling nets and assassinate G'Kar. His plan is that public sympathy will swing against the Tuchanq and the Centauri will be the only government left who will offer them aid. G'Kar is only wounded and the identity of the assassins discovered, although only G'Kar suspects Londo's involvement. G'Kar stabs Londo in his quarters, but the Centauri manages to call for Vir's help. G'Kar flees and Vir gets Londo to medlab, hiding G'Kar's ceremonial dagger first out of a sense of obligation. Londo will die unless the alien life-giving machine belonging to Dr Franklin is used on him, but nobody on the station is willing to give up any of their life force to save a man they hate and/or fear. Londo's life is eventually saved by the mysterious Mr Morden, who somehow manages to transfer a large amount of life force to Londo without apparently affecting himself.

The 'C' Plot: The widow of the murdered businessman arrives on Babylon 5 to pick up his body, but is frustrated to discover that it is being held by Dr Franklin pending the trial of the alien accused of his murder. During the trial process, she discovers that she doesn't want D'arc executed in punishment. When the trial is over, her husband's body has disappeared – used by Sheridan as a substitute for D'arc's body in the execution.

The Arc: There is a lot of play on the word 'shadows', and a neat reminder that the Narn and the Centauri are as bad as each other. Of all the books, with the exception of *The Shadow Within*, this one acknowledges the arc the most, although it's not part of it.

Observations: Former Earth Alliance President Luis Santiago had been President since at least 2249. Before that came President Jarrold.

G'Kar remembers his father, who was killed by the Centauri. His father's death was originally described in episode 215 ('And Now For a Word'), and we later saw it in episode 306 ('Dust to Dust').

Clark's Law was written in seven weeks (twice as long as John Vornholt was given for *Voices*). The only major change made between manuscript and publication was that Mortimore had originally described the Narn as being unable to see the colour blue, and thus D'arc paints herself blue to avoid being seen by them in the prologue. This was changed at the insistence of J. Michael Straczynski.

Koshisms: 'Fear is a mirror.' 'Obligation is a hangman's noose.' To Sheridan: 'You are the light, yet the hope of darkness.' To Sheridan: 'You are touched by shadows.'

Ships That Pass In The Night: DSEV (Deep Space Exploration Vessel?) *Amundsen*, named after Norwegian explorer Roald Amundsen, the first man to reach the South Pole, was the first vessel to encounter the Minbari, and the one that opened fire on them (but see **Accidents Will Happen** below). Jumpgate layer *Eratosthenes* (named for the Greek geographer and mathematician whose map of the ancient world was the first known to contain lines of longitude and latitude.).

Other Worlds: Tuchanq is a former Narn colony whose ecology has been wrecked. Anara VII has two rings and fifteen moons.

Culture Shock: This book has more alien races per square metre than any other. We get the Tuchanq, of course – a humanoid race with sensory organs shaped like a mane of spines instead of eyes. Sometimes they are biped, sometimes quadruped, and they never sleep. Then we get the Ylinn (reptilian and squat), the Thrantallil (who breathe liquid metal hydrogen), the Cauralline (reptiles with six eyes), the Throxtil (big things with five legs and five arms) and the Bremmaer (who are furry), not to mention the Xoth, the Cthulhin, the Morellians, the Deneth, the Ynaborian Sinining and the Froon. A Baltan freighter also turns up at the station, and we discover that N'grath is a Trakallan (a race inhabiting a planet orbiting the star Beta Lyrae). The Sh'lassa get a name check (they were referred to, you will recall, in episode 210 – 'GROPOS').

Centauri have livers and spleens.

Station Keeping: There are around 700 security guards working on Babylon 5.

Literary, Mythological and Historical References: The alien race known as the Cthulhin are a reference to H. P. Lovecraft's Cthulhu – an elder god who sleeps beneath the sunken city of Ry'leh. Lovecraft's 'Cthulhu Mythos', as his cycle of stories has become known, are the model for the First Ones mentioned in episodes 217 ('In the Shadow of Z'ha'dum'), 301 ('Matters of Honor') and 305 ('Voices From Earth').

A ship mentioned in the background – the *D'Alembert* – is a reference to E. E. 'Doc' Smith and Stephen Goldin's 'Family D'Alembert' series of ten SF novels (of which only part of the first book was written by Smith).

The Song of Being/Song of the Land aspect of the

Tuchanq's belief system is derived from Bruce Chatwin's travelogue *The Songlines* – a book concerning (amongst other things) the beliefs of the Australian Aborigines.

I've Seen That Face Before: A character named Ronnie, who works in Communications and knows all about computer-generated images, is probably a reference to Visual Effects Supervisor Ron Thorton.

Author Jim Mortimore is a British writer who is already responsible for four original novels based on the TV SF series *Doctor Who* (one of them in collaboration with me) and three novelisations of the crime thriller series *Cracker*.

Accidents Will Happen: On page 94, Jeffrey Sinclair turns into Geoffrey Sinclair.

The Centauri Emperor in the year 2259 is named Narleen Jarn in this book. In fact, episode 209 ('The Coming of Shadows') names him as Emperor Cartagia (and this book was written after that episode was transmitted).

G'Kar's wife's name is J'Ntiel in this book: it's Da'Kal in the book before it (*Blood Oath*).

In this book the *Amundsen* is the first Earth vessel to encounter the Minbari, and the ship that starts the war, but in episode 313 (transmitted later) it's the *Prometheus*.

Questions Raised: Given that he was using a changeling net, why did Sheridan have to use the businessman's body as a substitute for D'arc's? Why not just use a dummy, or a sack filled with wet sand?

The Touch Of Your Shadow, The Whisper Of Your Name

Written by: Neal Barrett Jnr

Date: The events of the book take place in early 2260, somewhere between episodes 222 ('The Fall of Night') and 303 ('A Day in the Strife').

Plot: Probably the third best of the books, this is a well written and absorbing tale with decent characterisation and some nice lines. It's marred only by the fact that a lot happens but nothing actually matters. A mysterious space phenomenon that looks like a gigantic glowing green space worm, 9,200,000 miles long and 522,000 miles wide, is approaching the station. Sensors can't detect it, probes don't register it, but everyone on Babylon 5 starts having nightmares about death and destruction. Riots and fights break out. A group of Narn kidnap Londo Mollari and a group of Centauri kidnap G'Kar. Refugees flee. A travelling evangelist con artist attempts to blow up the station. The phenomenon gets closer . . . and closer . . . then passes through the station and disappears. The nightmares stop.

Observations: The book contains references to Talia Winters being a spy (episode 219 – 'Divided Loyalties'), Garibaldi disguising himself in a raincoat and hat (episode 213 – 'Hunter, Prey') and Garibaldi having built a Kawasaki Ninja ZX-11 motorcycle (episode 116 – 'Eyes').

Ships That Pass In The Night: The *Simak* and the freighter *Pegasus*.

Other Worlds: The planets Cotswold and Trivorian.

Culture Shock: The inhabitants of the planet Cotswold are amphibians (just like the people who live in the Cotswolds in England, of course).
  Trivorians have three eyes, and their tears are corrosive.

Station Keeping: Babylon 5's Bay 8 is supposedly haunted by the ghost of a dead Starfury pilot.

Literary, Mythological and Historical References: The space ship *Simak* is named for the classic SF writer Clifford D. Simak.

I've Seen That Face Before: Neil Barrett Jnr has been writing science fiction since 1960 and has garnered a considerable reputation for savagely dissecting the American dream. He has written nearly forty novels, along with a number of short stories.

Accidents Will Happen: The homeworld of the Minbari is referred to as Minbari, not (as it should be) Minbar.

Betrayals

Written by: S. M. Stirling

Date: The book is set during the Narn–Centauri war, which means that it's set between episodes 209 ('The Coming of Shadows') and 220 ('The Long, Twilight Struggle').

Plot: It's complex, both in plot terms and in emotional terms, but there's really nothing at risk. The T'llin are too nice to kill anyone, and Ivanova's tormentor accidentally kills himself before she can get to him. Who cares?

The 'A' Plot: A peace conference between the Narn and the Centauri will be taking place on Babylon 5, although both sides are treating it merely as an opportunity to pause for breath. During the build-up to the conference, both Garibaldi and G'Kar become aware that there is a significant build-up of T'llin on the station. The T'llin homeworld was conquered by the Narn some years before, and they and their planet were treated in much the same way as the Centauri had previously treated the Narn and the Narn homeworld. G'Kar is worried that the T'llin will attempt to publicise their plight, thus making the Narn look less sympathetic in the eyes of any potential allies, but all the T'llin want is to be recognised by one or another alien government. Although everyone they approach is sympathetic, nobody will actually help them. They attack Na'Toth twice but, when Garibaldi tries to find them, they vanish. As the peace conference is about to start, the T'llin take over the docking bay through which the Narn and Centauri delegations are arriving, and seal off the area. They use the threat of violence to force the two delegations to sit down together and talk, but their real aim is to show the delegations that, were the situations reversed, the Centauri and the Narn would have killed all the hostages. Instead the T'llin surrender, having made their point.

The 'B' Plot: Ivanova is having problems with a member of her staff named Larkin. His inefficiency and lack of attention are nearly causing serious accidents as ships attempting to dock find themselves on collision courses. Larkin reacts badly to Ivanova's criticism, and starts faking recordings of her dead brother accepting bribes. He leaves these recordings outside her quarters in an attempt to unnerve her. Garibaldi and Ivanova realise quickly that Larkin is their main suspect. Frightened, he tries to escape but ends up dying in an airlock accident.

The 'C' Plot: A con artist named Semana McBride attempts to sell G'Kar the Centauri artefact known as the Eye of the Republic. It's actually a fake – a shape-shifting alien she carries around with her – but when Londo Mollari hears of its presence he starts bidding for it too. Na'Toth manages to sabotage G'Kar's negotiations, and Londo ends up paying one million credits for a cake.

The 'D' Plot: One of Garibaldi's security guards, Midori Kobayashi, invites Delenn and Lennier to a Japanese tea ceremony. She explains that the Minbari fleet would have devastated her home planet during the war if the Minbari had not surrendered first, and she wishes to express her gratitude. Kobayashi later dies saving the lives of Sheridan and various ambassadors and dignitaries, including Delenn.

The 'E' Plot: President Clark's niece arrives on the station. She wants to become a journalist and uses her position of influence to get into places where the accredited journalists are not allowed – such as the hostage situation caused by the T'llin.

The Arc: The Narn and the Centauri are still at war. That's it.

Observations: G'Kar's personal spacecraft cost 800,000 credits (it must have been the replacement for the one he sabotaged in the third book, *Blood Oath*).

The Centauri Eye of the Republic which Semana McBride so convincingly fakes previously turned up in episode 113 ('Signs and Portents').

After writing over 100,000 words of this book, I'm starting to see things where they don't really exist. Those T'llin names, for instance. One of them – Miczyn – could well be derived from the name of the series' creator, J. *M*ichael Stra*czyn*ski. Or not. Another of them Segrea, is an anagram of 'grease'. A third, Halestrac, is an anagram of 'the sarlac' – the creature Jabba the Hutt tries to feed Han Solo and Luke Skywalker to in the film *Return of the Jedi*. Jeez, I need a holiday.

Ships That Pass In The Night: Drazi ship *Eimen*. Earth ship *Destiny*, Centauri ship *Voira*, Earthforce ship *Kropotkin* (destroyed during the Earth–Minbari war), Earth freighter *Orion's Belt*.

Other Worlds: T'll – the home of the T'llin, a dry, desert world that has been taken over by the Narn. Nippon – a planet colonised primarily by humans of Japanese descent.

Culture Shock: The T'llin are a humanoid race with sharp features, nictitating membranes on their eyes and a blue, scaled skin. They are well adapted to life on a desert world, and are able to voluntarily enter a state of hibernation in which their vital signs slow down so much they appear to be dead.

Literary, Mythological and Historical References: Garibaldi, looking up at the inside of Babylon 5 at the beginning of the book, compares it to Pellucidar. Pellucidar is the world within a hollow Earth created by Edgar Rice Burroughs in *At the Earth's Core* and its six sequels.

The Earthforce ship *Kropotkin* is probably named for Prince Peter Alexeivich Kropotkin, a Russian anarchist during the late nineteenth and early twentieth centuries.

I've Seen That Face Before: G'Kar's wife, Da'Kal, is one of the Narn delegation at the peace conference. She previously turned up in the third book (*Blood Oath*).

S(tephen) M(ichael) Stirling is a Canadian writer with a growing reputation for hard-edged militaristic science fiction. As well as writing numerous books on his own, he has collaborated with Jerry Pournelle (who has a spacecraft named after him in episode 206 – 'A Spider in the Web'), and David Drake. He has written both original material and work set within universes created by others (including Larry Niven's *Man-Kzin Wars* series and Jerry Pournelle's *CoDominion* sequence).

Accidents Will Happen: The T'llin have four fingers on their hands on page 24 and only three fingers on their hands on page 50. Or perhaps some of them are missing some fingers.

The changeable third-in-command on the station, Major Atumbe, becomes Major Atembe.

Captain Sheridan remembers on page 86 that he has met the T'llin leaders, but he doesn't actually meet them until page 129.

The Pak'ma'ra Ambassador becomes the Pakmoran Ambassador.

President Clark is described as being a fairly good-looking man. I think not.

Questions Raised: Over one hundred T'llin managed to get on board Babylon 5 without any record of their arrival. Why, if that was possible, did the Prime Olorasin and the Prime Phina have to smuggle themselves on board disguised as part of a statue?

The Editor Speaks

Jeanne Cavelos, author of the seventh *Babylon 5* book, *The Shadow Within*, who started the books at Dell, and has also edited the line as a freelancer, says: 'In the beginning, the authors had very little to go on. They only have the episodes to go by; they do not have inside information. A few of them had a couple of questions answered by JMS by e-mail. The authors also had a bible to consult, but it was written at the time of the pilot and had limited, dated information. All of the books have been written in about three to eight weeks, and have been edited by me in three days. Any changes have to be done quickly, usually over the phone. That's why you may catch errors or inconsistencies. Recently, JMS has become more involved in choosing the authors for the books and in the books series in general – he wrote an open letter to potential authors suggesting possible backstories. I think this is helping to improve the books and make them more of a reflection of what is important and distinctive about *B5*.'

The Comics

Observations: Back in 1994, J. Michael Straczynski was saying of the proposed comic series, 'As a comics reader, what makes me crazy are books published as media tie-ins that are *only* that, just tie-ins, throwaways, unchallenging, and restricted by the same rules that limit a TV show. In a comic, you don't *have* the same limitations of budget, and location, and casts. So why lumber a comic with those restrictions? The editor and I both feel the same way . . . that the stories should be challenging, and inventive, and sometimes controversial and should try and *surpass* the series.'

John Ordover (editor of Pocket Books' *Star Trek* line), Peter David (writer of episodes 207 – 'Soul Mates' – and 214 – 'There All the Honor Lies') and Bill Mumy (the actor who plays Lennier) were all interested in writing scripts for the *Babylon 5* comic.

Issues 12 to 15 of the *Babylon 5* comic were scripted by J. Michael Straczynski, but will not now be used. 'I had written a four-issue mini-series to kick off the next batch of comics,' he explained. 'It came back, and I found it had been completely – and not very well – rewritten by the editor. I said, "This can't stay, this is all wrong, it could change the meaning of sentences entirely," and she said, "Well, no, it's going through that way." And I said, "You don't understand. In my position I have approval over all licensing and merchandising." When a book comes through, I tend to go through it and revise it . . . When a mask comes in for costume approval, I find some poor stooge in the office to pull the mask on and see how it looks. And so I can always change it back the way I want to at that point, because I have creative control over it. And she said, "No, no, no, our policy is, outside writers can't have editorial control over the books. When you're writing the book, you aren't functioning as the creator any more. You're a writer. If you *don't* write the book, you have creative control because you're not the writer." "So, if I write it I can't control it, because then I'm just the writer, and if I don't

write it I can't control it, because then I'm *not* the writer?"
"Yes." *"No."* '

Straczynski's four-issue mini-arc would have used Marcus
Cole as its primary character, and would have involved events
on all the major alien homeworlds apart from the Vorlon one.

The contract for the comic series still extends to issue 24.
DC apparently intend publishing them as one-off issues and
mini-series of a few issues at a time.

'In Darkness Find Me'

Issue Titles: Issue One: 'In Darkness Find Me'
Issue Two: 'Treason'   Issue Three: 'In Harm's Way'
Issue Four: 'The Price of Peace'

Written by: J. Michael Straczynski (Issue One)
Mark Moretti, based on a premise by J. Michael Straczynski
(Issues Two to Four)

Drawn by: Michael Netzer
(Penciller – Issues One, Two & Four)
Rob Leigh (Inker – Issues One, Two & Four)
Carlos Garzon (Artist – Issue Three)

Date: The action of issue 1 begins on 6 January 2259 and
lasts for several days (if not weeks). It's obviously set after
the events of episode 202 ('Revelations') as Garibaldi is
conscious and not walking with a stick.

Plot: The plot is needlessly complicated and derivative, but
readable on a page-by-page basis. The likenesses in issues 1,
2 and 4 are pretty bad, but issue 3 manages to capture Sinclair
and Delenn very well.

The 'A' Plot: Commander Sinclair is recalled to Earth and
told by President Clark that the Minbari have asked for him to
be assigned to Minbar as the Earth Ambassador. He is also
told that Minbari souls are being reborn into human beings,
leading to a gradual reduction in the Minbari population. En
route to Minbar they pick up a passenger, and Sinclair's
escort – a Minbari named Racine – tells him that a ceremony
is to be carried out on Minbar to install a new leader for the

Grey Council. On Minbar a long-range sniper's rifle is found in Sinclair's belongings, along with a map of the route the new Minbari leader would be taking. Sinclair is arrested for conspiracy to assassinate the Minbari leader. Alyt Neroon is chosen to head the prosecution. The trial leads to Sinclair's conviction but, in accordance with ancient Minbari law, he offers his life to prevent war. Impressed, the new Minbari leader and Head of the Grey Council pardons him.

The 'B' Plot: Babylon 5 received a distress call from Starliner *Chiyoda-Ku*. Zeta wing is sent out, and discover the ship drifting in space. The ship is towed back to the station, where it is discovered that twenty-four people on board are dead and one is alive – just. Those who are dead were either asphyxiated or shot. Dexter Hall – the survivor – is taken to medlab but an attempt is made on his life by an armed assassin. Hall disables the assassin with a burst of mental energy and flees to Talia Winters's quarters, where he passes out. Talia tells Ivanova that Hall is a Psi Cop who had infiltrated a Home Guard group on the *Chiyoda-Ku*. Earthforce Internal Affairs investigator Colonel Rabock is sent to Babylon 5 to question Dexter Hall. The assassin (whose name, we discover, is Jason Colby) twice attempts to assassinate Talia Winters, but is distracted at the last minute. Senator Hidoshi tries to convince Captain Sheridan that Dexter Hall is actually a rogue P12 telepath codenamed Cypher, but neither Sheridan nor Garibaldi believes it. Talia Winters probes Hall's mind before he dies, and finds that he had discovered a Home Guard plot to assassinate the new Minbari leader. Hall had been discovered, but had managed to kill all the Home Guard members on the *Chiyoda-Ku*. Colonel Rabock arrives, but Sheridan doesn't realise that it's actually an imposter named Thomas Webster who is actually working for Home Guard. Webster contacts his own superior, who tells him that the plan was not to kill the Minbari leader – that would have started a war – but to alert the Minbari to the plot, thus provoking them to sever all diplomatic ties. Webster is told to kill Jason Colby, who has become a liability, but Colby has been intercepting the message and takes Webster hostage. They get to Webster's ship and leave Babylon 5, but

Webster reveals himself to be the rogue Psi Cop named Cypher and attempts to disarm Colby. Colby fires his PPG, and the ship blows up – taking with it any evidence that might have cleared Sinclair. We discover in the closing panel that Webster's superior is a high-ranking member of Psi Corps.

The Arc: Ambassador Sinclair flashes back to his actions in ramming a Minbari battle cruiser during the Battle of the Line (effectively the flashback we saw in episode 108 – 'And the Sky Full of Stars' – complete with much of the same dialogue). He is also made to remember exactly what happened when the Minbari kidnapped him (some of which was seen in the same episode).

During Sinclair's remembrance of what happened aboard the Minbari battle cruiser, he recalls Delenn saying, 'It is true. There is no mistake – he has a Minbari soul.' Rathenn then goes on to tell him the same story Lennier tells Sheridan in episode 201 ('Matters of Honor') – that the souls of dead Minbari are not being reborn in Minbari bodies, but are somehow migrating to human bodies and being reborn there, in whole or in part.

Rathenn tells Sinclair that the Minbari wiped all knowledge of his capture and torture from his mind with the agreement of the Earth government. President Clark's reaction suggests this is correct.

The connection between Home Guard, the 'rogue' Psi Cop Cypher, his Psi Corps superior and the plot to sever ties between the Minbari and the Earth Alliance is all part and parcel of the ongoing plot arc that has encompassed the assassination of President Santiago (episode 122 – 'Chrysalis') and, ultimately, Babylon 5 seceding from Earth (episode 310 – 'Severed Dreams').

Observations: Sinclair refers to Garibaldi's injuries (as sustained in episode 122 – 'Chrysalis').

Rathenn makes a passing reference to the Soul Hunters (episode 102 – 'Soul Hunter').

There appears to be no overall title for this four-issue story, although it is generally referred to by the title of the first episode ('In Darkness Find Me').

Captain Sheridan refers in passing to the events of episode 109 ('Deathwalker').

Colonel Rabock's shuttle lands in Bay 13. As Kosh is present on the station, his ship must be berthed somewhere else (it's in Bay 13 in episodes 213 – 'Hunter, Prey' – and 404 – 'Falling Toward Apotheosis').

Issue 1 of the comic also contained a one-page overview of season one of *Babylon 5* as well as a one-page article on designing and building Starfuries. Issue 2 contained a two-page article on make-up with special emphasis on the Minbari. Issue 3 contains a two-page article on design in *Babylon 5* written by the series' Production Designer (John Iacovelli), Art Director (Roland Rosenkrantz) and Propmaster (Marc-Louis Walters). The article pays special attention to the weapons on the series, and has a sketch of an Earthforce grenade launcher (never seen in the series). Issue 4 contained a two-page article on customs in the series, written by *Babylon 5*'s Costume Designer Anne Bruice.

The entire four-issue comic run was republished as a complete graphic novel in the UK by Titan Books. The subsidiary articles were not republished.

Ships That Pass In The Night: Minbari Flyer *Zhalan* (but see **Accidents Will Happen** below). Starliner *Chiyoda-Ku*. Minbari Cruiser *Solaris*. Shuttle *Vortex*.

Culture Shock: The capital city of Minbar is Yedor. The seat of government is known as the Palatium.

Station Keeping: Babylon 5 has at least 94 docking bays.

Literary, Mythological and Historical References: Sinclair takes a poem by Alfred, Lord Tennyson with him to Minbar, hoping to read it to the Grey Council. The poem in question is *Ulysses*. It has been referred to before in the series, in the pilot episode ('The Gathering') and episode 105 ('The Parliament of Dreams').

The Minbari Cruiser is called *Solaris*. This is also the title of an influential science fiction novel by the Polish author Stanislaw Lem (later filmed by the Russian director Andrei Tarkovsky in 1971).

I've Seen That Face Before: This story marks the first chronological and actual appearance of the Minbari Grey Council member Rathenn. He also appeared in episodes 316 ('War Without End' Part One) and 319 ('Grey 17 is Missing').

Senator Hidoshi puts in a brief appearance (he previously appeared in episodes 109, 112 and 119 – 'Deathwalker', 'By Any Means Necessary' and 'A Voice in the Wilderness' Part Two).

Alyt Neroon is on Minbar, prosecuting Sinclair during his trial. This is Neroon's second chronological appearance: we first saw him in episode 117 ('Legacies') and then again in 211 ('All Alone in the Night') and 319 ('Grey 17 is Missing').

Mark Moretti was writer and artist for the Valiant Comics title *Ninjak*.

Carlos Garzon is a talented and experienced artist who has drawn strips for, amongst others, Marvel's *Spiderman* and *Doom Patrol* and D.C.'s *Star Trek: The Next Generation*.

Accidents Will Happen: Earthdome looks nothing like the way it does in episode 301 ('Matters of Honor').

Nobody really looks like any of the characters they're meant to be, but President Clark looks *completely* unlike the one we've seen on television.

During Sinclair's forced remembrance of the Battle of the Line and his torture aboard a Minbari battle cruiser, there are two discrepancies with his flashback in episode 108 ('And the Sky Full of Stars'). Firstly, the dialogue between Sinclair and the other pilots during the battle is different. In episode 108, Sinclair says, 'If I'm going out, I'm taking you bastards with me,' then says to his computer, 'Target main cruiser. Set for full-velocity ram.' In this issue of the comic, he says, 'If I'm dying I'm taking you demons with me,' then says to his computer, 'Target lead Minbari cruiser. Set for full-velocity ram.' The word 'demons' was substituted for 'bastards' after the pages had been pencilled and inked but before they were printed, and without J. Michael Straczynski's knowledge. Secondly, the Minbari Grey Council comprises nine members in episode 108 but only eight members in this issue of the comic (maybe one of them popped out to the toilet).

During Sinclair's forced remembrance he overhears the Minbari talking amongst themselves. Surely they would have been talking in Minbari and he didn't understand the language at that point as far as we know.

When Rathenn explains the Minbari soul problem to Sinclair, he explains that, 'gradually, over nearly six thousand years, the soul-well grew smaller.' This conflicts with Lennier's explanation in episode 201 ('Matters of Honor'), in which the figure is given as one thousand years. The events of episode 317 ('War Without End' Part Two) confirm that it is one thousand years rather than six thousand years.

Delenn's Flyer is referred to as the *Zhalan*. In episode 211 ('All Alone in the Night') it was called the *Zhalen* (this spelling was confirmed by J. Michael Straczynski in a posting to GEnie).

Keffer cannot tell whether there are any bodies in the *Chiyoda-Ku* until he manoeuvres his Starfury so he can see in through the windows. This contradicts episode 218 ('Confessions and Lamentations') where the sensors on a Starfury could distinguish between live Markab and dead Markab on a spacecraft. Keffer also says there are no life-support signs, but one of the passengers is later discovered to be alive.

Jason Colby disguises himself in what he says is a Babylon 5 security uniform to kill Dexter Hall. Unfortunately, the uniform he puts on is a blue Earthforce uniform. Babylon 5 security uniforms are grey – Babylon 5 security is funded by Earth but is not part of Earthforce.

Kozorr – the Minbari who arrests Sinclair – accuses him of treason, but Sinclair is a human. How can a human commit treason against another race?

Neroon is referred to as Alit Neroon. The correct spelling (confirmed by J. Michael Straczynski in a posting to GEnie) is Alyt.

The new Minbari leader and Head of the Grey Council stays on Minbar after his coronation, and yet we are told in episode 120 ('Babylon Squared') that the Leader of the Grey Council lives their life aboard a War Cruiser kept far away from Minbar.

At one point Captain Sheridan tells Senator Hidoshi, 'I'm

an Earthforce Commander with a station to run.' No he's not, he's an Earthforce Captain with a station to run.

'Shadows Past and Present'

Issue Titles: Issue Five: 'With Friends Like These . . .'
Issue Six: 'Against the Odds'
Issue Seven: 'Survival the Hard Way'
Issue Eight: 'Silent Enemies'

Written by: Tim DeHaas,
based on a premise by J. Michael Straczynski

Drawn by: John Ridgway

Date: The 'contemporary' events in the story take place after episode 122 ('Chrysalis') but before episode 209 ('The Coming of Shadows'). If we assume the various issues of the comic are sequential, then this story takes place before the events of issues 9 and 10, placing it before episode 204 ('A Distant Star').

Plot: This story is very important to the *Babylon 5* universe, tying in directly with the arc, and Tim DeHaas's script is fully up to the task. John Ridgway's artwork is as variable as usual, alas: his likenesses are usually OK when based on photographs but go completely to hell when they're not. And he can't draw Morden at all.

The 'A' Plot: Monitoring diplomatic transmissions between Londo Mollari and Centauri Prime, Garibaldi becomes convinced that there is a connection between Londo and the destruction of a Narn outpost in Quadrant 37. He hears Londo arrange to meet Lord Refa at a particular location, and arranges to follow Londo in a shuttle. The mysterious Mr Morden realises Garibaldi is on to Londo, and arranges for Londo and Refa to change their plans. Garibaldi leaves the station with Warren Keffer, who won't let Garibaldi go without him. While waiting in orbit around an unknown planet for Londo and Refa to arrive, they are attacked by a Shadow fighter. Their shuttle is damaged and crashes on the planet. They begin to walk to a nearby Centauri settlement. Behind them the Shadow fighter lands and eliminates all traces of the crash site. Six humanoid figures start tracking them. When they catch up, the figures arrange an ambush – camouflaging themselves – and attempt to mentally influence Keffer into killing Garibaldi. Keffer accidentally shoots one of the aliens, forcing it to revert to its own form, then he and Garibaldi shoot the rest. They are picked up by a Centauri patrol and, after Londo Mollari has identified them, returned to Babylon 5, where Garibaldi explains to Sheridan what has happened. Sheridan believes him, but can do nothing.

The 'B' Plot: Garibaldi tells Keffer about a time, six years before, when he was a burnt-out drunkard working as a shuttle pilot on Mars. A certain Lieutenant Commander Sinclair came to hire him as a pilot, accompanied by two junior Earthforce lieutenants named Foster and Sanchez. Sinclair wanted to fly over the surface of Mars to look for something, but he wouldn't tell Garibaldi what. After a few days of fruitless searching, their shuttle suddenly loses power and they crash. Foster is killed by the impact, and Sanchez's leg is broken. Garibaldi and Sinclair head off across the Martian surface to get help. They discover an alien ship using an energy beam to dig another alien ship out of the ground. A ground vehicle approaches and they hijack it, knocking the two human occupants out and taking their spacesuits. The suits have no communications capability, leading Sinclair and Garibaldi to realise that they are dealing with telepaths. Sinclair tells Garibaldi that he is investigating suspected covert human/alien activities, and that two previous investigation missions failed to return. They attempt to drive away in their ground vehicle, but are mistaken for the original crew and directed towards the excavation site. They are led into a vast building inside which is a transparent dome. Inside the dome is what appears to be a semi-organic alien machine into which naked human bodies are sliding on a conveyor belt. Garibaldi attracts too much attention and has to be rescued by Sinclair. They drive away, leaving a grenade to distract their pursuers. Using the ground transport, they return for Sanchez and call for help from Earthforce. By the time a team gets to the site, there is no trace of any alien ships or of the telepaths' installation. Everything has been cleared up – except for one thing. Garibaldi discovers a Psi Corps badge where the building was.

The Arc: The creatures pursuing Garibaldi and Keffer across the Centauri planet are creatures working for the Shadows, rather than Shadows themselves (similar to the 'Dark Soldier' in episode 205 – 'The Long Dark'). They are hairless, naked, a reddish brown in colour, and have lumpy craniums, four fingers, pointed ears, sharp teeth and green, slitted eyes. They can also disguise themselves – not by becoming invisible, like the Shadows, but by blending into their surroundings like chameleons – and they can influence people's minds by implanting urges and emotions. Oh yes – they also have inbuilt self-destruct mechanisms that blow them up if they are killed so as to destroy any evidence.

The events Garibaldi and Sinclair see on Mars are the flip side to the story Dr Mary Kirkish recounts in episode 308 ('Messages From Earth'). It was Dr Kirkish's team that found the alien ship buried beneath the Martian surface. They were instructed to keep their distance from it, and observed as a second alien ship arrived and dug it out with an energy beam. The direct involvement of Psi Corps is something we didn't know before, but we discovered in episode 314 ('Ship of Tears') that human telepaths were being used as components in Shadow ships, so it all fits together.

One of the last panels in issue 8 of the comic is a flashback to the events on Mars. It's confusing – the rest of the flashback has been Garibaldi's story, whereas this panel is from a different, omniscient point of view. It shows Talia Winters in a white smock being apparently prepared for some kind of surgery or procedure. The clear implication is that this ties in with the events of episode 219 ('Divided Loyalties'), in which we discovered that Psi Corps had implanted a secondary personality beneath Talia's original personality – one that could spy for them. Is that what the installation on Mars was for – to implant secondary personalities into telepaths? If so, what did the Shadows have to do with it? Or was Talia being prepared as a potential pilot for a Shadow ship? Only time will tell.

Observations: In issue 5, G'Kar refers to the Narn vessel that was destroyed in episode 202 ('Revelations') and the Centauri attack on the Narn outpost in Quadrant 37 in episode 122 ('Signs and Portents'). In issue 6, Garibaldi refers to how he caused a friend's death on Io – an event he talks about in more depth in episode 111 ('Survivors'). In issue 7 we get a montage flashback of what happened to him on Io.

Issue 7 of the comic contains an interview with J. Michael Straczynski and Claudia Christian (Ivanova) transcribed from an on-line interview.

The entire four-issue comic run was republished as a complete graphic novel in the UK by Titan Books. The interview was not republished.

Dialogue to Flick Back For: Morden to Londo Mollari: 'Your star is rising, Ambassador. Let me and my associates handle its ascension.'

Station Keeping: Garibaldi makes random checks on diplomatic gold-channel transmissions to check for evidence of illegal activity.

I've Seen That Face Before: Writer Tim DeHaas has also written for television – his most visible credit being on the *Star Trek: Voyager* episode 'Phage'.

John Ridgway is a British artist. He worked for some time on the UK comic strip version of *Doctor Who* in *The Doctor Who Magazine*, and also on the *Swamp Thing* spin-off *Hellblazer*.

Accidents Will Happen: The area of Mars in which Garibaldi and Sinclair see the Shadow ship digging its colleague from the ground is completely unlike the area of Mars in which the same events take place in episode 308 ('Messages From Earth').

Questions Raised: Garibaldi makes random checks on diplomatic gold-channel transmissions to check for evidence of illegal activity. Isn't this in itself an illegal activity? Shouldn't diplomatic transmissions be inviolate from prying eyes?

What exactly does Garibaldi intend doing when Londo and Refa meet? They'll be turning up in spaceships – he's in another spaceship. Is he just going to sit there and watch their spaceships dock? How will that help him get to know what they're doing?

Garibaldi is mistaken for a telepath, and plays along by reading the body language of the other telepaths around him. Don't they suspect anything when they don't get a reply? Don't any of them attempt to scan him?

'Laser – Mirror – Starweb'

Issue Titles:
Issue Nine: 'Duet for Human and Narn in C Sharp'
Issue Ten: 'Coda for Human and Narn in B Flat'

Written by: David Gerrold

Drawn by: Rebecca Guay (Penciller)
Rick Bryan (Inker)

Date: The events of the story take place between episodes 203 ('The Geometry of Shadows') and 204 ('Distant Star').

Plot: Nobody would be able to get away with a plot this weak on any other comic title – it's only the fact that this is *Babylon 5* that saves it.

The 'A' Plot: Ambassador G'Kar attempts to flee the station for an unexplained reason. If his ship launches it will disrupt the approach of a Narn transport, so Garibaldi tries to stop him. G'Kar sprays Garibaldi with a paralyser spray and slings him into what Garibaldi believes to be his ship, but Garibaldi fires a netlike starweb at G'Kar, pinioning him. G'Kar reveals that they are not in his ship but are in the central axis tube that runs the entire length of Babylon 5. He has sent out his ship on automatic to create a false trail while he hides on the station from a Narn assassin named Greegil D'Farkin. Greegil wants to kill G'Kar because G'Kar would not sleep with Greegil's wife – a terrible insult under Narn law. An H-100 cleaning robot detects the two of them in the cleaning tube and attempts to eradicate them – they flee along the entire five-mile length of the tube and escape from the far end, where Sheridan, Greegil and a security team are waiting for them. Sheridan distracts Greegil while Garibaldi's security staff detain and disarm him.

The 'B' Plot: Captain Sheridan leaves the station in a shuttle in an attempt to catch up to G'Kar's ship, which he believes has Garibaldi on board. He is accompanied by Greegil D'Farkin, a Narn who claims to have important information about G'Kar. They find G'Kar's ship, but it is empty. Their arrival sets off a timed bomb which blows G'Kar's ship up. They return to Babylon 5, where Greegil attempts to kill the recently discovered G'Kar but is stopped by Sheridan and Garibaldi.

Observations: The plot of these two issues was taken from a script proposal that David Gerrold pitched to J. Michael Straczynski for the first season of the series.

Dialogue to Flick Back For: G'Kar: 'I did not cheat. I expanded the context of the game.'

Ships That Pass In The Night: Narn Starcruiser *D'Vordo*.

Culture Shock: Narn can hibernate for six days at a time. *Phroomis* is a Narn delicacy traditionally made from the skin of someone who has betrayed the eater, dried and pickled, served with bloodberry and leech sauce.

Station Keeping: Some areas of Babylon 5 are cleaned by robots.

I've Seen That Face Before: Rebecca Guay has previously worked on Vertigo Comics' *Black Orchid* title, as well as Acclaim Comics' *Magic: The Gathering*.

Accidents Will Happen: The overall title for the two issues is given as 'Laser – Mirror – Starweb!' in Issue 9, and 'Laser – Mirror – Starweb' (without the exclamation mark) in Issue 10.

'The Psi Corps and You'

Issue Title: Issue Eleven: 'The Psi Corps and You'

Written by: Tim DeHaas

Drawn by: John Ridgway

Plot: This one-off issue of the *Babylon 5* comic doesn't have a plot as such. Like the fake Psi Corps advert in episode 215 ('And Now For a Word') it's an exercise in postmodernist propaganda. Its overall form is a comic for young people on Babylon 5, telling them how wonderful Psi Corps is and what they should do if they suspect they might be a telepath. Three exemplary stories are told in its pages, but because they are nominally told by Psi Corps itself they might not be true. Story 1 is about William Karges, one of the first telepaths to occur in the human population, about the year 2150. Karges had hidden his telepathy and become head of the President's personal security staff. He read the mind of a potential assassin and saved the President's life, but his secret was revealed in the process. The President set up Psi Corps to 'help telepaths function in society'. Story 2 concerns Lieutenant Andrew Denmark, a pilot during the Battle of the Line. He too was telepathic, and used his powers to keep morale up in his squadron for long enough to enable Sinclair to make his suicide attack on the Minbari War Cruiser. The third story involves little Alfie Bester, a child whose friends encourage him to join Psi Corps when they realise he is a telepath.

The Arc: Psi Corps are creepy people who rewrite history to suit themselves, but we knew that already.

Observations: Earthforce security guard uniforms haven't changed much in a hundred years: the ones on page 7 of this issue are the same as the ones on page 7 of issue 1.

The comic contains a 'How to Find Out if You're a Telepath' questionnaire at the back. The letters page also contains a note that this would be the last issue of the comic for a while, although it would probably return in a different form.

Accidents Will Happen: The Markab drawn on page 2 definitely isn't a Markab. The Drazi on the same page isn't a Drazi either. Perhaps John Ridgway didn't have any photo references.

Afterword

And so it begins . . . the series that was meant to last for five years and then come to its natural conclusion looks likely to spin off into an infinite progression of sequels and TV movies due to pressure from the TV networks. The series that would resist the siren call of marketing imperatives has spawned two sets of trading cards, a computer screensaver, a role-playing game, two soundtrack albums and some plastic spaceship models. The series whose media tie-ins would be classy material written by the top people in the field and tied directly to the story arc has only provided us with some badly written books and some badly drawn comics.

Nobody mention the word 'franchise'.

None of that matters. What matters is that the *idea* of *Babylon 5* lives on in us. It's what we always wanted an SF series to be and never thought one could be – intelligent, involving, dramatic, serious in places and funny in others and, above all else, with spaceships so good they look as if they were actually filmed on location. It made us laugh, cry and think. It provided some of us – cynical as we are – with a series to be obsessive about for the first time since we were teenagers.

What matters is that, for a few years at least, *Babylon 5 was* a dream given form . . .

INDEX

Babylon 5 episode titles are in quotation marks. '*' indicates working or unused episode title. Titles of other shows or books etc are in italics. Recurring characters, as per the list on page 55 onwards, are not indexed. Entries for the main alien species/worlds, ie Minbari, Centauri, Narn, Vorlons, Shadows, are restricted to references that give specific information on that species/world.

419

427